Adrian Mole

and the Weapons of Mass Destruction

'Adrian Mole has progressed from being a minority enthusiasm to something like a national figurehead . . . Sue Townsend has done more than write a comic series descended from *Just William*. She has held a mirror up to the nation and made us happy to laugh at what we see in it' *Sunday Telegraph*

'Enormously funny' *Sunday Telegraph*

'A very, very funny book' *Sunday Times*

'A classic. The Adrian Mole diaries are thoroughly subversive. [He is] a true hero for our time' Richard Ingrams

'Funny, moving and a poke in the eye for adult morality' *Sunday Express*

'Written with great verve, and showing an uncanny understanding of the young. Sue Townsend holds the balance between innocence and precocity and the result is both hilarious and salutary' *Daily Telegraph*

'Life's no fun for an adolescent intellectual. For the reader it is a hoot' *New Statesman*

'The new book takes up the diary where the last left off, and is quite as classic' *Financial Times*

'The funniest, most bitter-sweet book you're likely to read this year' *Daily Mirror*

'I not only wept, I howled and hooted and had to get up and walk around the room and wipe my eyes so that I could go on reading' Tom Sharpe

'Marvellous, touching and screamingly funny . . . set to become as much a cult book as *The Catcher in the Rye*' Jilly Cooper

'[Adrian Mole is] one of the great comic creations' *Daily Mirror*

'The author's accuracy and comic timing left me wincing with pleasure' *New Statesman*

'Wonderfully funny and sharp as knives' *Sunday Times*

'Mole still makes me laugh and laugh' *Daily Express*

Praise for The Queen and I

'Laugh-out-loud funny' *Sunday Telegraph*

'No other author could imagine this so graphically, demolish the institution so wittily and yet leave the family with its human dignity intact' *The Times*

'Absorbing, entertaining . . . the funniest thing in print since Adrian Mole' Ruth Rendell, *Daily Telegraph*

'Kept me rolling about until the last page' *Daily Mail*

Praise for Public Confessions of a Middle-aged Woman Aged 55¾

'I want to be this funny. I want to be as funny, witty, sceptical and as unrepentantly cynical as Susan Lilian Townsend' *The Journal*

'Proof, once more, that Townsend is one of the funniest writers around' *The Times*

'Anyone who loved *The Secret Diary of Adrian Mole* will enjoy this collection of witty and sharply observed jottings from the inimitable Sue Townsend. Great stuff from a master of British satire, observation – and prose' *OK!*

'Sue Townsend is eloquent, wise and above all full of fun . . . whether she's happy, nostalgic or just plain angry, her wit and honesty make her an unmissable read' *Sainsbury's Magazine*

'It's as if Townsend has caught our idiosyncrasies on candid camera and is showing a rerun of all the silly clips' *Time Out*

'What a fantastic advertisement for middle age – it can't be bad if it's this funny' *Heat*

'Townsend has such a witty way with words that it makes her consistently amusing . . . a welcome addition to any bookshelf' *Hello!*

'Townsend is every woman's favourite Everywoman' *Good Housekeeping*

Praise for Number Ten

'Hilarious. Sue Townsend's laughter is infectious' *Sunday Telegraph*

'A wickedly entertaining and passionate swipe at New Labour' *The Times*

'There is a gem on nearly every page. Nothing escapes Townsend's withering pen. Satirical, witty, observant . . . a clever book' *Observer*

'Poignant, hilarious, heart-rending, devastating' *New Statesman*

'A delight. Genuinely funny . . . compassion shines through the unashamed ironic social commentary' *Guardian*

'She has unrivalled claim to be this country's foremost practising comic novelist' *Mail on Sunday*

'As ever with Townsend, her brilliance lies in her simplicity . . . It's a great comic novel, this tale of two Britains, and should be on the bedside tables of Downing Street' *Independent*

'Townsend is one of our finest living comic writers . . . This is a wickedly entertaining and passionate swipe at New Labour' *The Times*

'No Townsend novel can fail to entertain . . . fans will find a smile on every page' *Sunday Times*

'Brilliant satire. Very contemporary, a bit controversial and loads of fun' *Daily Mirror*

By the Same Author

Adrian Mole
and the Weapons of Mass Destruction

Sue Townsend

MICHAEL JOSEPH
an imprint of
PENGUIN BOOKS

MICHAEL JOSEPH

Published by the Penguin Group

Penguin Books Ltd, 80 Strand, London WC2R ORL, England

Penguin Group (USA) Inc., 375 Hudson Street, New York, New York 10014, USA

Penguin Books Australia Ltd, 250 Camberwell Road, Camberwell, Victoria 3124, Australia

Penguin Books Canada Ltd, 10 Alcorn Avenue, Toronto, Ontario, Canada M4V 3B2

Penguin Books India (P) Ltd, 11 Community Centre, Panchsheel Park, New Delhi – 110 017, India

Penguin Group (NZ), cnr Airborne and Rosedale Roads, Albany, Auckland 1310, New Zealand

Penguin Books (South Africa) (Pty) Ltd, 24 Sturdee Avenue, Rosebank 2196, South Africa

Penguin Books Ltd, Registered Offices: 80 Strand, London WC2R ORL, England

www.penguin.com

First published 2004

1

Set in 12.25/15 pt Minion
Typeset by Rowland Phototypesetting Ltd, Bury St Edmunds, Suffolk
Printed in Great Britain by Clays Ltd, St Ives plc

A CIP catalogue record for this book is available from the British Library

Hardback ISBN 0–718–14689–1
Trade paperback ISBN 0–718–14690–5

This book is dedicated to the memory of
John James Alan Ball,
Maureen Pamela Broadway
and Giles Gordon.

And to the Lovely Girls,
Finley Townsend,
Issabelle Carter,
Jessica Stafford
and Mala Townsend,
with all my love.

Acknowledgements

I would like to thank my husband, Colin Broadway, for the practical and loving support he gave me throughout the writing of this book.

2002

Private and Confidential   Wisteria Walk
The Right Honourable   Ashby de la Zouch
   Tony Blair, MP, QC   Leicestershire
10 Downing Street
Whitehall   September 29th 2002
London sw1A

Dear Mr Blair

You may remember me – we met at a Norwegian Leather
Industry reception at the House of Commons in 1999. Pandora
Braithwaite, now the Junior Minister for Brownfield Regener-
ation, introduced us, and we had a brief conversation about
the BBC during which I opined that the Corporation's attitude
towards provincial scriptwriters was disgraceful. Unfortunately, you were called away to attend to some urgent matter
on the far side of the room.

I am writing to thank you for warning me about the imminent threat to Cyprus posed by Saddam Hussein's Weapons of
Mass Destruction.

I had booked a week's holiday at the Athena Apartments,
Paphos, Cyprus, for the first week of November for me
and my eldest son at a total cost of £571 plus airport tax.
My personal travel adviser, Johnny Bond, of Latesun Ltd,
demanded a deposit of £57.10, which I paid to him on
September 23rd. Imagine my alarm when I turned on the
television the next day and heard you telling the House of

Commons that Saddam Hussein could attack Cyprus with his Weapons of Mass Destruction within forty-five minutes!

I immediately rang Johnny Bond and cancelled the holiday. (With only forty-five minutes' warning, I could not risk being on the beach and out of earshot of a possible Foreign Office announcement.)

My problem is this, Mr Blair. Latesun Ltd are refusing to refund my deposit unless I furnish them with proof:

   a) that Saddam Hussein has a stockpile of Weapons of Mass Destruction,

   b) that he can deploy them within forty-five minutes, and

   c) that they can reach Cyprus.

Johnny Bond, who was, according to his colleagues, 'away from his desk' yesterday (I suspect that he was on the Stop the War march), has dared to question the truth of your statement to the House!

Would it be possible to send a handwritten note confirming the threat to Cyprus so that I can pass it on to Johnny Bond and therefore retrieve my deposit? I can ill afford to lose £57.10.

I remain, sir,

Adrian Mole

PS I wonder if you would ask your wife, Cherie, if she would agree to be the guest speaker at the Leicestershire and Rutland Creative Writing Group's Literary Dinner on December 23rd this year. Will Self has turned us down – rather curtly, in fact. We don't pay a fee or expenses but I think she would find us a lively and stimulating group.

Anyway, Mr Blair, keep up the good work.

Saturday October 5th 2002

I viewed a loft apartment at the Old Battery Factory, Rat Wharf, today. Mark B'astard, the estate agent, told me that Canalside properties are being snapped up by the 'Buy to Let' crowd. It is in a great location, five minutes' walk along the towpath from the bookshop where I work. The loft has one huge room and a bathroom with glass-brick walls.

When Mark B'astard went for a pee I could see his blurry outline, so if I buy the apartment I will ask my mother to run me up some curtains.

I stepped out on to the tensile-steel and mesh balcony and looked at the view. The canal lay below me, sparkling in the autumn sunshine. A flock of swans glided past, a grey bird flew by and a narrowboat came into sight under a bridge. When it passed my balcony, a bearded man with a grey straggly ponytail waved and said, 'Lovely afternoon.' I could see his wife in the bottom of the boat, washing up. She saw me but did not wave.

Mark B'astard had tactfully withdrawn while I soaked up the atmosphere of the place. But now he rejoined me and pointed out several original features: the genuine acid burns in the floorboards, the hooks where the blackout curtains were hung in the war.

I asked him what the scaffold-clad building next door was being turned into.

'A hotel, I think,' he said.

He went on to tell me that Eric Shift, the scrap-metal multi-millionaire who would own the freehold of my property, had bought up the whole of Rat Wharf and was hoping to transform it into Leicester's equivalent of the Left Bank in Paris.

I confessed to Mark that I had always wanted to dabble in watercolours.

He nodded and said, 'That's nice,' but I got the impression that he didn't know what I was talking about.

Mark looked around longingly at the stark white wall space and said, 'This is the sort of place I'd like to live in, but I've got three kids under five and the wife wants a garden.'

I commiserated with him and told him that, until very recently, I was the full-time father of two boys, but that the British Army was looking after Glenn, the seventeen-year-old, and the nine-year-old, William, had gone to live with his mother in Nigeria.

B'astard looked at me enviously and said, 'You're young to have your kids off your hands.'

I told him I was thirty-four and a half and that it was time I put myself first for a change.

After B'astard pointed out the integral granite cheese-board in the kitchen worktop, I agreed to buy the apartment.

Before we left I went out on the balcony for one last look. The sun was setting behind the distant multi-storey car park. A fox walked along the opposite towpath with a Tesco's carrier bag in its mouth. A brown creature (a water vole, I think) slipped into the canal and swam out of sight. The swans floated majestically by. The biggest swan looked me straight in the eye, as if to say, 'Welcome to your new home, Adrian.'

10 p.m.
I went into the kitchen, turned the volume down on the radio and informed my parents that I would be moving out of their spare room and into a loft apartment in the Old Battery Factory on Rat Wharf in Leicester at the earliest opportunity.

My mother could not hide her delight at this news.

My father sneered, 'The Old Battery Factory? Your grandad worked there once, but he had to leave after a rat bite turned septic. We thought he'd have to have his leg off.'

My mother said, 'Rat Wharf? Isn't that where the rough sleepers' hostel is opening next year?'

I said, 'You've been misinformed. The whole area is being transformed into Leicester's cultural quarter.'

When I asked my mother if she would run me up some curtains for the glass-brick lavatory, she said sarcastically, 'Sorry, but I think you're confusing me with somebody who keeps a needle and thread in the house.'

At 7 o'clock my father turned the sound up on the radio and we listened to the news. Britain's military chiefs were demanding to know what their role would be if Britain goes to war with Iraq. Share prices had fallen again.

My father banged his head on the table and said, 'I'll kill that bastard financial adviser who talked me into putting my pension into Equitable Life.'

When the *Archers* theme tune played, my parents reached for their cigarettes, lit up and sat listening to the agricultural soap opera with their mouths slightly open.

They are doing things together in yet another attempt to save their marriage.

My mother and father are elderly baby-boomers of fifty-nine and sixty-two respectively. I keep waiting for them to give in to old age and take up the uniform that other old people adopt. I would like to see them wearing beige car coats, polyester slacks and, in my mother's case, a grey cauliflower perm, but neither of them will give in. They are still squeezing themselves into stonewashed jeans and black leather fitted jackets.

My father thinks that by growing his grey hair long he will be mistaken for somebody who used to be in the music business. The poor fool is deceiving himself. He will always look like a retired storage-heater salesman.

He is forced to wear a baseball cap at all times now because he has lost most of the hair on top of his head, causing a youthful folly to be revealed: on his stag night, after he had drunk ten pints of Everards Bitter, he agreed to have his head shaved and 'I am a nutter' tattooed in green ink on his scalp.

Fortunately the stag night was held a week before the wedding, but it explains why, in my parents' only wedding photograph, my father looks like the convict Abel Magwitch from *Great Expectations*.

My father has had his other tattoos removed on the NHS, but they will not fund the green ink one. For that he would have to go to Harley Street for laser treatment and pay over £1,000. My mother has been urging him to take out a bank loan, but my father says that it's easier and cheaper to wear a cap. My mother says that she can't bear reading 'I am a nutter' when my father has his back turned to her in bed, which is most of the time apparently.

11 p.m.
Had a bath using my mother's quince and apricot aroma-therapy oil. The stuff floated on top of the water, looking like the oil slick that killed most of the wildlife in Nova Scotia. It took a quarter of an hour under the shower before I was able to wash the gunk off my body.

Used two mirrors to measure bald spot. It is now the size of a Trebor Extra Strong Mint.

Checked emails. There was one from my sister, Rosie, telling me that she is thinking of leaving Hull University; she is disenchanted with nano-biology. She said that Simon, her boyfriend, needed her full-time help to overcome his crack habit. She asked me not to tell our parents of her dilemma as they were both totally 'prejudiced' about crack addicts.

There were the usual spam deals from firms offering to stretch my penis.

Sunday October 6th
New Moon

My mother moped around the house in her dressing gown all day. At 3 o'clock in the afternoon I asked her if she was going to brush her hair and get dressed. She said, 'Why should I? Your dad wouldn't notice if I walked around naked with a rose between my teeth.'

My father sat all day next to the stereo, playing and replaying his Roy Orbison records.

Their marriage is obviously a dead parrot. It is like living in a Bergman film. Perhaps I should tell them that their precious daughter is unlikely to win a Nobel Prize as she is shunning the laboratory and embracing drug rehabilitation. That would liven them up a bit and get them talking to each other. Ha ha ha.

Spent the afternoon writing letters. As I was about to leave the house to walk to the post box, my mother said, 'You are the only person I know who uses snail mail.'

I replied, 'You are the only person I know who still believes that smoking is good for your lungs.'

She said, 'Who are you writing to?'

I didn't want to tell her that I was writing to Jordan and David Beckham, so I hurried out of the house before she could see the names and addresses on the envelopes.

Jordan
c/o *Daily Star*
Express Newspaper Group
10 Lower Thames Street
London EC3

Wisteria Walk
Ashby de la Zouch
Leicestershire

October 6th 2002

Dear Jordan

I am writing a book about celebrity and how it ruins people's lives. I know what I am talking about. I was a celebrity in the 1990s and had my own show on cable TV called *Offally Good!* Then the fame machine spat me out, as it will spit you out one day.

I would like to arrange an interview on a mutually convenient date. You would have to come here to Leicester because I work full-time. Sunday afternoons are good for me.

By the way, I was talking with my father about your breasts recently. We both agreed that they are very intimidating. My father said a man could fall into that cleavage and not be found for days.

My friend Parvez described them as being like Weapons of Mass Destruction, and my chiropractor predicted that you would suffer from lower-back problems in the future due to the weight you were carrying on your ribcage.

It is rumoured that you are contemplating having even bigger implants inserted. I beg you to reconsider. Please contact me at the above address. I'm afraid I cannot offer a fee or expenses, but you will of course receive a free copy of the book (working title: *Celebrity and Madness*).

I remain, madam,

Your most humble and obedient servant,

A. A. Mole

David Beckham   Wisteria Walk
c/o Manchester United Football Club   Ashby de la Zouch
Old Trafford   Leicestershire
Manchester M16

October 6th 2002

Dear David

Please take a few moments to read this letter. I am not an inane football fan requesting a signed photo.

I am writing a book about celebrity and how it ruins people's lives. I know what I am talking about. I was a celebrity in the 1990s and had my own show on cable TV called *Offally Good!*

Then the fame machine spat me out, as it will spit you out one day.

I would like to arrange an interview on a mutually convenient date. You would have to come here to Leicester because I work full-time. A Sunday afternoon would be good for me.

And please don't take offence at what I'm about to say – perhaps you were away when grammar was taught at school – but you do not seem to know the very basics of grammatical sentence construction, i.e. last night on television you said, 'I seen Victoria on a video when she were a Spice Girl an', y'know, I like said to me mate, I fink I've just saw the gel I'm gonna marry.'

The sentence should read: I SAW Victoria on a video when she was a Spice Girl, and I said to my mate, I think I've just SEEN the girl I'm going to marry.

Please contact me at the above address. I'm afraid I cannot offer a fee or expenses, but you will of course receive a free copy of the book (working title: *Celebrity and Madness*).

I remain, sir,

Your most humble and obedient servant,

A. A. Mole

Monday October 7th

Rang my solicitor, David Barwell, on the way to work. His secretary, Angela, said, 'Mr Barwell is busy having an asthma attack due to the new carpet that has been fitted over the weekend.'

I advised her to expect a correspondence from Mark

B'astard regarding the lease on Unit 4, The Old Battery Factory, Rat Wharf, Grand Union Canal, Leicester.

She said bitterly, 'I shan't bother telling Mr Barwell. It's me that does all the work. All he does is sit behind his desk and fiddle with his inhaler.'

I had to wait ten minutes outside the shop; Mr Carlton-Hayes had trouble finding a parking space. I watched him walk up the High Street. He looked as if he was on his last legs. I don't know how much longer he can carry on with the shop. This is just my luck.

He said, 'Terribly sorry to keep you waiting, my dear.'

I took the keys from him and opened the door. Once inside, he leaned against the recent biographies to catch his breath.

I said to him, 'If we had a few chairs and sofas in here like I suggested, you could sit down and be comfortable.'

He said, 'We're not Habitat, Adrian, my dear, we're booksellers.'

I said, 'Customers expect to be able to sit down in bookshops nowadays, and they also expect a cup of coffee and to be able to visit the lavatory.'

He said, 'A properly brought-up person micturates and defecates and drinks a cup of coffee before they leave their house.'

We had the usual quotient of mad people in during the day. A steam train enthusiast with a ginger beard and sellotaped spectacles asked me if we had a copy of the 1954 Trans-Siberian timetable in Russian. I showed him our Railway section and invited him to search through the mildewed railway ephemera that Mr Carlton-Hayes insists on keeping in stock.

A woman with a crew cut and dangly earrings asked if we were interested in buying a first edition of *The Female Eunuch*. I wouldn't have bought it. It was in very poor condition, missing its dust jacket, and the pages were covered in annotations and exclamation marks in red ink. But Mr Carlton-Hayes intervened and offered the woman £15. Sometimes I feel as though I work in a charity shop rather than Leicester's oldest-established second-hand and antiquarian bookshop.

However, just as we were about to close a young woman came in and asked if we had a copy of *Soft Furnishings for Your Regency Doll's House*. As far as I could make out, she had a passably good figure and a not-bad face. She had the thin wrists and fingers I like in a woman. So I spent some time pretending to search the racks.

I said, 'Are you sure such a title exists?'

She said that she had once owned a copy but had lent it to a fellow doll's house hobbyist who had emigrated to Australia, taking the book with her. I commiserated with her and listed all the books I had loaned over the years and had never seen again. She told me that she had a collection of eighteen doll's houses and that she had made most of the soft furnishings herself, including up-holstering the tiny chairs and hanging the tiny curtains. I mentioned that I would need some curtains making when I moved into my new loft apartment and asked her if she would be interested. She said the longest curtains she had ever made were only six inches in length.

Her hair could do with a colour-wash to brighten it up a bit, but her eyes are a pretty blue behind her glasses.

I told her that I would search the Internet tonight when I got home and asked her to call back tomorrow.

I asked for a name and telephone contact number.

'My name is M. Flowers,' she said. 'I haven't got a mobile, because of the health risk, but you can contact me on my parents' landline.' And she gave me the number.

Mr Carlton-Hayes said, 'She works in Country Organics, the health food shop in the marketplace.'

We went into the back. I counted the takings; Mr Carlton-Hayes sat behind his desk, smoking his pipe and reading a book entitled *Persia: The Birthplace of Civilization*.

I asked him what had happened to Persia.

He said, 'It turned into Iraq, my dear.'

When I got home to Ashby de la Zouch, I hurried to my room, switched my laptop on and typed 'Soft Furnishings for Your Regency Doll's House' into Google. It came up with 281 sites. I clicked on WoodBooks.com and they offered me a title, *Making Period Doll's House Furniture* by Derek and Sheila Rowbottom, but they didn't actually mention Regency, so I tried McMurray's Books, who offered me two which might be suitable, *Soft Furnishings for Your Doll's House* at $14.95 and *Miniature Embroidery for the Georgian Doll's House: Queen Anne, Early and Late Georgian and Regency Styles* at $21.95.

I immediately rang the telephone number given to me by M. Flowers.

A man answered. He boomed, 'Michael Flowers here. To whom am I speaking?'

I said I was Adrian Mole from the bookshop and would like to speak to Ms Flowers.

The man shouted, 'Marigold! Chap from the bookshop.'

So her name is Marigold Flowers. No wonder she didn't give me her full name. She took some time to come to the phone. While I waited I could hear Rolf Harris singing 'Jake the Peg' in the background. When that came to an end, 'Two Little Boys' started up. Was it possible that somebody in Marigold's family had a long-playing record, cassette, CD or video of Rolf Harris singing and was actually *playing* it?

Eventually Marigold said quietly, 'Hello. Sorry I took so long. I was at a tricky stage with the shepherd's pie.'

'Eating it or making it?' I joked.

'Oh, making it,' she said gravely. 'If one doesn't distribute the carrot rings evenly, it throws the whole thing out of kilter.'

I agreed and said that she was obviously a perfectionist, like me. I told her about the titles I had tracked down. She said that she already had a copy of *Soft Furnishings for Your Doll's House*, but she sounded enthusiastic about the *Miniature Embroidery* book and asked me to order a copy for her.

To keep her on the phone, I asked her if dolls went in for loft-type homes. She said that she would get in touch with the National Association of Miniature Enthusiasts, of which she was a member, and that it could be her next project.

When I put the telephone down I felt that old feeling, that mixture of joy and fear, I feel just before I fall in love.

Tuesday October 8th

There was an incredible coincidence last night. My mother defrosted a shepherd's pie she had made some weeks earlier. The carrots were chaotically distributed. Surely this is a sign. I asked my mother what had compelled her to take the shepherd's pie out of the freezer. She said, 'Hunger.'

Wednesday October 9th

A letter from Glenn.

Royal Logistics Corps
Deepcut Barracks
Surrey

Dear Dad

Hope you are well. I am well. I'm sorry I have not wrote to you before. I have been very busy doing my basic training. They keep us going 24/7. It is nothing but shouting and being sarcastic. Some of the lads cry in the dormitories at night. Sometimes I feel like walking out and coming home, Dad. I hope I stick it. Will you come to my passing-out parade on Friday November 1st? I would like Mum and Grandma and Grandad to come. I know William can't come because he is in Africa. I think you was wrong, Dad, to send William to live with his mum. It was you who brought him up. You should have kept him here in England with you. I know Jo Jo is nice, but William can't speak Nigerian and he doesn't like the food. I seen Pandora on the telly the other night. I told some of the lads that she used to be my dad's girlfriend, but nobody believed me because she is posh. They are taking the piss out of me now, Dad, and calling me Baron Bott. That is all the news.

Warmest wishes,
Your son, Glenn

I just remembered, tell Grandma Pauline she has got to wear a hat. It is the law.

Why did he need to add 'your son'? How many other Glenns do I know who are in the army?

I showed my mother Glenn's letter.

She said, 'I'll wear the mink hat I've had in the wardrobe for the last thirty years. There aren't likely to be any anti-fur protesters on an army parade ground, are there?'

Thursday October 10th

A middle-aged fat man came into the shop this morning and asked for a 'clean copy' of *Couples* by John Updike.

I said, quite wittily I thought, a clean copy of *Couples* is an oxymoron surely.

Fatty said irritably, 'Have you got it or not?'

Mr Carlton-Hayes had heard our conversation and was already searching through American Hardback Fiction. When he found *Couples*, he delivered it into Fatty's podgy hands, saying, 'A fascinating social document about the sexual mores of people with rather too much time on their hands, I think.'

Fatty mumbled that he would take it. As he was leaving the shop, I saw him look at me and distinctly heard him mutter, 'Moron.' Though, thinking about it later, he could have said, 'Oxymoron.'

Nigel called in this afternoon after his eye clinic appointment at the Royal Hospital. He is supposed to be my best friend, but it is over six months since I saw him in the flesh.

The last time I spoke to him was on the phone. He had said that he couldn't bear the gay clubs in the provinces, where they huddle together for validation and companionship, instead of like the London clubbing scene, 'the music and the sex'.

I had said that there was more to life than music and sex.

He'd replied, 'That's the difference between us, Moley.'

I was shocked at how much he has changed. He is still handsome, but his face looks a bit ragged around the edges, and it's obviously been a while since he'd seen his hair colourist.

He was still visibly shocked at his recent bad news. He said, 'The consultant examined my eyes and was quiet for a horribly long time, and then he said, "Did you drive yourself here, Mr Hetherington?" I told him that I had driven up from London. He said, "I'm afraid I can't allow you to drive back. Your sight has deteriorated so much that I'm going to put you on the partially sighted register."'

I desperately searched for something positive to say, but could only come up with, 'You've always enjoyed wearing dark glasses, Nigel. Now you can wear them all year round, night and day, without people thinking you're a prat.'

Nigel leaned against the bargain books table, dislodging a pile of unread *Finnegans Wakes*. I would have helped him to a chair had there been one in the shop.

'How can I live without my car, Moley?' Nigel said. 'How am I going to get back to London? And how can I be a media analyst when I can't read the fucking papers?'

I said that if Nigel was partially sighted, it was probably a good job that he wasn't driving down the M1 and negotiating London traffic.

Nigel said, 'I have been making a lot of mistakes at work lately. And it's months since I've been able to read normal print without a magnifying glass.'

I rang Computa Cabs and asked for a taxi to take Nigel to his parents' house. The controller said that most of the taxi drivers were at the mosque, praying for peace, but that he would send one ASAP.

While we waited, I suggested to Nigel that he learns Braille.

He said, 'I've never been good with my hands, Moley.'

I asked Nigel if he could still see colours.

He said, 'I can't see anything much.'

I was very shocked. I had been hoping that Nigel would help me decorate my loft apartment. He used to be good with colours.

I helped him into the cab and told the driver to take

him to 5 Bill Gates Close, The Homestead Estate, near Glenfield.

Nigel said in a bad-tempered way, 'I can still speak, Moley!'

I hope he is not going to become one of those bitter blind people, like Mr Rochester in *Jane Eyre*.

Friday October 11th

I phoned Johnny Bond at Latesun Ltd this morning and we wrangled over the £57.10.

He said sneeringly, 'Has your mate the Prime Minister coughed up any proof yet?'

I replied that Mr Blair was staying with Mr Putin in his hunting lodge, trying to persuade him to join Britain and America to fight Saddam Hussein.

Bond said, 'He'll never get Russia, Germany and France to back his illegal little war.'

Saturday October 12th

Miniature Embroidery for the Georgian Doll's House was delivered by FedEx this morning. Mr Carlton-Hayes was very impressed.

I said, 'If we had a computer in the shop, Mr Carlton-Hayes, we could order books online and double our turnover.'

'But Adrian, dear,' he said, 'we tick along very nicely,

don't we? You and I earn a living wage, we cover our expenses, and we spend our days surrounded by our blessed books. Aren't we content just as we are?'

It was not a rhetorical question. He genuinely wanted to know. I mumbled something about how much I liked the job, but, diary, I long to modernize this place. We haven't even got an electric till.

At lunchtime I walked to the marketplace. Marigold was in Country Organics, prescribing lima beans to a miserable-looking woman with low-level depression. When the woman had gone, clutching her recycled paper bag, I said to Marigold, 'I thought I'd deliver it in person.'

She took the book out of the FedEx envelope and shouted, 'Mummy, it's arrived.'

A tall woman with a face like a pretty pig joined us at the counter. I have never seen anybody so pink. Either she has a dermatological condition or she has had a recent accident with a sun lamp.

I said, 'How do you do, Mrs Flowers?' and held out my hand.

She said, 'I won't shake your hand if you don't mind.'

Marigold looked uncomfortable and said, 'Mummy thinks that hand-shaking is an outmoded practice.'

Mrs Flowers took the book and leafed through it, narrowing her squinty eyes even further. Marigold watched her anxiously, as if awaiting her verdict. I began to feel a little nervous myself. I always feel uncomfortable in the presence of women who are taller than me.

I said, 'I hadn't realized the book was for you, Mrs Flowers.'

She replied, 'It isn't for me, but Marigold is easily taken

advantage of. How much are you going to charge her for this?'

I said that the book cost $21.95 and that the cost of postage and packaging was a further $25.

Mrs Flowers said, 'How much is that in good English money?'

I handed her the invoice.

'£29.75! For a little book with only 168 pages?'

I said, 'But it's been flown from America in three days, Mrs Flowers.'

She threw the book on to the counter and said to Marigold, 'If you want to squander your money, then go ahead, but it makes nonsense of me and Daddy scrimping and saving to try and keep the business going.'

I said to Marigold, 'Perhaps I ought to take it back.'

And she said quietly, 'Perhaps you should. I'm sorry.'

When I got back to the shop, I told Mr Carlton-Hayes that *Miniature Embroidery for the Georgian Doll's House* was unwanted by the customer.

He said, 'Never mind, Adrian. I'm sure there must be somebody else in Leicester who is interested in miniature Georgian-style embroidery.'

Sunday October 13th
Moon's First Quarter

An email from Rosie:

Aidy, have you seen the news about the bombing in Bali? My friend Emma is on her way to Australia via Bali. Can you phone the emergency number for me please – I've got no credits on my mobile. Her name is Emma Lexton and she is twenty.

I emailed her back:

Information is only being given to next of kin. I am sending you £10 by first-class post. Don't give it to Simon. Please ring Mum. She is worried about you.

Monday October 14th

No replies from the Right Honourable Tony Blair, Jordan or Beckham.

Dear Mr Blair
    Perhaps my letter of September 29th has been mislaid or overlooked in the confusion of these turbulent times. I enclose a copy and would appreciate an early reply. My travel company, Latesun Ltd, are still refusing to return my deposit of £57.10.
    I remain, sir,
    Your most humble and obedient servant,
    A. A. Mole

Only four of us turned up for the Leicestershire and Rutland Creative Writing Group meeting tonight. There was me, Gary Milksop, Gladys Fordingbridge and Ken Blunt. We met as usual in Gladys's front room, hemmed in by cat ornaments and photographs of her vast family.

I opened the proceedings by reading from my dramatic monologue, 'Moby-Dick Speaks', wherein we get the whale's point of view on being harpooned.

After a few moments Gladys interrupted me, saying, 'I can't make head nor tail of it. What's going on? Is it supposed to be the fish talking or what?'

Ken Blunt stubbed his cigarette out into a cat ashtray and said, 'Gladys, a whale is not a fish, it's a mammal.'

I continued, but I could tell that I had lost my audience.

At the end, Gary Milksop twittered, 'I liked the bit about Captain Ahab looking like a man who had been born without a soul.'

Gladys read her latest crappy cat poem – something about 'I love my little kitty because she is so pretty . . .' Naturally, because she is eighty-six, this received a round of applause.

Milksop followed with the latest chapter of the Proustian novel he has been writing and rewriting for fifteen years. It took 2,000 words to describe his first memory of eating a HobNob.

Milksop cries if he gets negative criticism.

Ken Blunt said, 'Well done, Gary. I like the bit about the HobNob melting into the tea.'

I informed the group that I had not yet managed to arrange a guest speaker for our dinner on December 23rd, but that I had several irons in the fire.

Ken said he hadn't written anything for this week's meeting because he had been doing double shifts at Walkers Crisps. They are introducing a new line.

Gladys said, 'What flavour will they be?'

Ken said, 'I've signed a confidentiality agreement.'

She said, 'It's hardly *Tinker, Tailor, Soldier, Spy*, is it? It's only a few bleeding crisps.'

I changed the subject by telling them that I was moving into a loft apartment at the Old Battery Factory, Rat Wharf, soon, and that in future meetings could be held there.

Gladys said, 'My husband worked there once. He spilt acid down his front. It only just missed his manhood.'

Gladys was not who I had in mind when I started the group.

Tuesday October 15th

Marigold came in at lunchtime and bought *Miniature Embroidery for the Georgian Doll's House* but asked me not to tell her mother. She said that she would keep the book in the attic, where she kept most of her doll's houses. She said that neither of her parents was capable of climbing the loft ladder.

I said that I would love to see her doll's house collection and was perfectly capable of climbing a loft ladder.

She said that her parents were 'funny' about visitors.

I said, 'Do they never go out?'

She said they went out on Fridays to the Madrigal Society.

I said, 'Well, what a coincidence. Friday is the only night of the week I am free.' I smiled to show her that this was a little joke and to try and put her at her ease.

I am not at all interested in doll's houses. The last I remember seeing belonged to Rosie; it was a plastic, vulgar ranch-house-style thing, inhabited by Barbie and her boyfriend, Ken.

I asked Marigold if she would like to meet up after work for a drink. She said that she wasn't very good with alcohol.

'Coffee then?' I said.

'Coffee?' she said, as though I had suggested fresh pig's blood.

I said that I had heard that red wine was good for the circulatory system.

She said, 'OK, I'll join you in a glass of red wine, but I can't tonight. I'd need to give my parents notice.'

'How about tomorrow?' I said.

'All right,' she said, 'but you will have to give me a lift home. We live in Beeby on the Wold and the last bus leaves Leicester at 6.30.'

For some reason we had been almost whispering. Marigold gives the impression that she is a spy living in enemy territory. Her skin is exquisite. I longed to stroke her face.

When I got home to Ashby de la Zouch my parents informed me that they had decided to sell up. Some fool has offered them £180,000 for their semi, including its hideous carpets and curtains. I pointed out that they would have to pay the same amount for a similar property.

'Aha!' said my father triumphantly. 'We are not buying a similar property. We are going to buy a wreck and do it up.'

I left them poring over the *Leicester Mercury* property

guide, ringing the more dilapidated houses in the worst areas.

Their tired old faces were suffused with enthusiasm. I hadn't got the heart to pour cold water on to their mad plans.

Neither of them would know what a joist was if it sprang up and hit them in the face.

Wednesday October 16th

I dressed carefully in natural organic-type colours this morning. Mr Carlton-Hayes complimented me on my aftershave. I told him that Pandora had bought it for me as a Christmas present four years ago and that I only wore it on very special occasions. Mr Carlton-Hayes told me that he had read in the *Bookseller* that Pandora had written a book called *Out of the Box*; it is due to be published in July 2003.

I asked Mr Carlton-Hayes if he would order a few copies, pointing out that Pandora was a local MP and was constantly on *Newsnight*, smarming up to Jeremy Paxman.

He asked me if Pandora's book was likely to be ghost-written. I said it was highly unlikely – Pandora was a control freak who had once gone berserk when I had changed the station on her car radio.

I met Marigold, as arranged, in the Euro Wine Bar – it used to be Barclays Bank – and we sat where the paying-in queue used to form. I asked for the wine list. The waiter shouted over the salsa music that there was no wine list and that the choice was red or white, in sweet or dry.

Marigold said she would have sweet red because her blood sugar was low. I ordered the dry white.

Conversation was difficult because of the noise. There was a speaker directly over our heads. I looked around at the other customers. They were mostly young and seemed to be lip-reading. Perhaps they were on an outing from the Royal National Institute for Deaf People.

After a while Marigold and I gave up trying to converse and she sat and looked at the dozens of miniature silver things on her charm bracelet.

A hen party – a collection of females dressed as mini-skirted nurses wearing fishnet tights – came in and sat at the next table. One of them took out a clockwork penis, which went round in circles until it broke free and collided against Marigold's leg. I paid our bill and we hurried out into the street.

I asked Marigold if she liked Chinese food.

She said, 'If I'm careful with the monosodium glutamate.'

As we passed the clock tower, I looked around at the crowds of young people gathered there, and realized that, at thirty-four and a half, I was probably the oldest person in the immediate vicinity. Even the policemen in the parked Transit van looked like kids.

Thursday October 17th

It took for ever to get to sleep last night. I lay awake in the dark, thinking about Marigold. She is a fragile, sensitive creature. She needs somebody to give her confidence in herself and free her from her overbearing parents.

I took her to Wong's and ordered Menu C, and we ate prawn crackers, wanton soup, crispy duck with pancakes, lemon honey chicken and sweet and sour pork balls with egg-fried rice.

I asked the waiter, Wayne Wong, whom I have known since our school days, to remove the cutlery and bring us chopsticks, and I also asked Wayne to tell the chef to go easy on the monosodium glutamate.

Marigold seemed to be impressed at my confident, cosmopolitan restaurant manner.

Wayne had seated us at the best table in the house, next to the giant fish tank, where Koi carp costing 500 quid a throw were swimming about.

Marigold said, 'I find them a little intimidating.'

I put my hand on hers and said, 'Don't worry. They can't get out of the tank.'

I asked her if she would like us to move table.

She said, 'No, it's just that they're so big. I prefer small things.'

This is the first time since I became sexually mature that I have worried that a woman will find my genitalia too big. I can't wait for our next meeting tomorrow.

Friday October 18th

Rosie sent a text which said:

M's safe in Woolgoolga.

It wasn't until I was halfway to Leicester that I realized what she was texting about.

I told Mr Carlton-Hayes that I was going to Marigold's house tonight to have a look at her doll's house collection.

He said in tones of astonishment, 'You're going to Michael Flowers's house? Do be careful, my dear, he's a dreadful man.'

I asked him how their paths had crossed.

He said, 'Flowers used to be the vice-chairman of the Literary and Philosophical Society here in town. We had a vehement disagreement about Tolkien. I said that the opening paragraphs of *The Fellowship of the Ring* were enough to make a strong man retch. I'm afraid we came to blows in the car park of the Central Lending Library.'

I said, 'I hope you came off best.'

He said almost dreamily, 'I rather think I did.'

I explained that Michael Flowers and his wife would be out at the time of my visit, at the Madrigal Society.

When he had gone in the back I took a copy of *The Fellowship of the Ring* and read the opening paragraphs. I couldn't see what the fuss had been about. It certainly wasn't worth coming to blows over, though perhaps 'eleventy' was an invented word too far.

I looked through at Mr Carlton-Hayes in his baggy cardigan. It was hard to imagine him brawling in a car park.

Marigold made me park in Main Street, Beeby on the Wold. Then we cut through fields to the Gothic-looking house she has lived in all her life and entered by the back door. She said she didn't want the neighbours to see me entering the house. I looked around. There were no neighbours.

It was freezing cold in the dark interior. Apparently, Michael Flowers doesn't believe in central heating. He believes in wearing layers of wool and keeping busy.

Marigold was obviously very nervous.

I said, 'Perhaps this is not a good idea.'

She said, 'No, I'm a woman of thirty. Why shouldn't I show my doll's houses to a friend?'

We passed through the gloomy hall. There was a stack of library books and cassettes on the hall table, waiting to be returned to the Central Lending Library. One of the cassettes was *Rolf Harris in Concert*.

I said, 'Rolf Harris and madrigals?'

She said, 'My father has eclectic tastes.'

We crept up two flights of stairs like burglars. I went up the loft ladder first, because Marigold was wearing a skirt. Then Marigold went around switching the lights on in the doll's houses. I was enchanted with the first few. The delicacy of the stitching on the soft furnishings was awe-inspiring, and when Marigold demonstrated the flushing toilet I was gobsmacked. I was impressed with the next batch, but quite frankly, diary, by the time I had inspected the eighteenth I was more than a little bored. However, I feigned interest.

I was relieved when we were walking across the fields back to the car. I held her delicate hand. I wanted to ask her to marry me, but I fought the impulse.

When we reached the village we sat in my car and talked about our families. We have both suffered. She said that her greatest fear was that she would never leave home and that she would be trapped in her parents' house for ever. Her elder sisters, Poppy and Daisy, had fled years ago.

At 10 o'clock she said that she had better go home and prepare a late supper for her parents. I stroked her face. Her skin felt as soft as a silk shirt I used to have. She is almost beautiful when she smiles. She has got good-quality teeth.

When I got home I told my mother a little about Marigold.

She said, 'She sounds like a nightmare. Take my advice and keep well away from needy people. They suck you into their own miserable world.'

She should know – she married my father.

Saturday October 19th

At lunchtime today I walked to Country Organics to give Marigold a copy of *What Not to Wear* by Trinny Woodall and Susannah Constantine. I haven't mentioned it before, diary, but Marigold has very little dress sense. Somehow she has not realized that pop socks should not be worn with a mid-calf skirt. Or that lime-green shoes are not a good idea.

When she saw the title, her lower lip trembled and her eyes filled with tears. She was obviously touched.

There was a big bombastic man behind the counter wearing a hairy tree-patterned jumper, obviously hand-knitted by a friend, or an enemy. He was lecturing an elderly couple about GM crops in a booming voice. He said, 'Let's be honest, mark my words, there won't be a single tree growing in this country in fifty years' time. If GM crops are planted, we can say goodbye to our song-birds and butterflies. Do you want that?'

The elderly couple shook their heads.

His completely bald bonce glinted under the fluores-cent lights. His yellow beard was crying out for a trim. It was Michael Flowers. I hated him on sight. I felt like shouting, 'Yes, Flowers, I can't wait until trees, song-birds and butterflies are a thing of the past.' But of course I didn't.

Marigold must have sensed my mood. She did not introduce me to her father. I left the shop with a heavy heart.

Sunday October 20th

Because they are 'between cars', my parents asked me to give them a lift to Harrow Street, in the Grimshaw area of Leicester, to view what my father somewhat grandilo-quently called a property. The photograph on the estate agent's particulars showed a boarded-up terraced house with vegetation growing out of the chimney pot.

I pointed out that Harrow Street was a police no-go area. But they said that after viewing the property they had promised to drop in for a cup of tea with Tania Braithwaite and Pandora, who was visiting her mother on the second anniversary of her father's death. I still go weak at the knees whenever Pandora's name is mentioned, so I was putty in their hands.

5 Harrow Street was a waste of time. My father was too frightened to get out of the car. My mother was brave enough to look through the letter box. She said that a flock of pigeons had broken in and made themselves at home. She made it sound as though the birds were sitting around drinking tea and watching television.

As my mother was getting back into the car, a youth in a top with the hood pulled over his face approached her and said, 'Yo, woman, do you wanna score some draw?'

My mother said, 'Not today, thank you,' as if she was refusing a Betterware catalogue.

She turned to my father in the back and said, 'Do you remember those Saturday nights when we used to smoke dope, George?'

My father said, 'Shush. Not in front of Adrian, Pauline!'

I said, 'When was this? Was I born?'

My mother said, 'It was the 1960s, Adrian. Everybody did it.'

I said, 'Everybody? Grandma Mole? Winston Churchill?'

I was disgusted with them and didn't speak until we got to Tania's house.

Pandora was looking ravishingly beautiful in a cream trouser suit. I will never stop loving her.

A large photograph of Ivan was on the sideboard next to a burning candle and a vase of red flowers. The photograph had been taken when he was still married to Tania. Nobody mentioned the fact that he was on honeymoon with my mother when he drowned. Also nobody mentioned that my father was living with Tania when the tragedy occurred.

When Pandora went into the garden to smoke a cigarette, I followed her and asked her if she would agree to be interviewed for my book, *Celebrity and Madness*.

She threw her treacle-coloured hair back and snapped, 'How dare you call me a celebrity? I'm a serious politician with a crippling workload.'

I said that I had often seen her in the pages of *Hello!* on the arm of various old blokes.

She said that she was powerless to stop the paparazzi. She smoked in silence while I watched her lovely face. Then she sighed deeply. I asked her what was wrong.

She said that she missed her dad and added, 'Has your mother ever talked to you about it?'

I told her that I only knew what had been written in the papers and that my mother had been deeply traumatized into silence by the tragedy.

Pandora said bitterly, 'So traumatized that she seduced

your father away from my mother within a week of my dad's funeral.'

I said, 'It's baby-boomer behaviour, Pandora. That entire generation is morally corrupt.'

I told her about my parents' 1960s drug habit. She laughed and said that a few spliffs on a Saturday night didn't constitute a habit.

I told her about poor blind Nigel and she said she already knew and had put him in touch with the top man at the RNIB.

'For counselling?' I asked.

'No. For fund-raising,' she said. 'Nigel's well connected with the gay mafia. He is a direct route to the pink pound.'

Tania called us in for tea and we spent an uncomfortable hour eating and drinking and reminiscing about Ivan. However, we were all careful to avoid mentioning the circumstances of his watery death.

To break the tension I told Pandora that I had written to Tony Blair, asking him to send some documentation verifying the Weapons of Mass Destruction/Cyprus/forty-five-minute statement.

My mother said, 'The tight git is fretting about losing his holiday deposit.'

Pandora said that she rarely saw Mr Blair nowadays as he was never in the country. I asked her if war with Iraq was inevitable.

She said, 'I've heard a rumour that the MOD is about to call up reservist medical staff.'

My mother said, 'So there'll be even fewer doctors and nurses in the hospitals.'

My mother had obviously been gossiping while I was outside with Pandora, because Tania said, 'I hear you have got a new girlfriend, Adrian.'

Pandora said, 'What's her name?'

I took a deep breath and said, 'Marigold Flowers.'

Pandora laughed, showing a half-masticated Brie and cranberry sandwich, and said, 'Christ, a comedy name. You must bring her to meet me. I'll give her tea at the House.'

I will, diary, but not until Marigold has had a chance to read and study and implement the advice given in the *What Not to Wear* book.

Monday October 21st
Full Moon

My solicitor, David Barwell, phoned to say that he has received the papers from Mark B'astard and my mortgage company and warned me that there was an £8,000 short-fall. He asked me how I intended to cover this.

I said, 'But I had worked out on my calculator that I only needed £3,000 in cash.'

Barwell said, 'Perhaps the batteries were low.'

I said, 'It runs on solar power.'

He said, 'But we haven't enjoyed much sunshine lately, have we, Mr Mole? You've obviously got your sums wrong.' And he asked me again how I intended to find the difference.

I told him that I had £4,000 worth of hard-earned savings in the Alliance and Leicester Building Society and that I hoped to borrow the rest somehow.

He said, 'The law doesn't operate on hope, Mr Mole, it operates on certainties. You will need to bring the full deposit into my office before the end of the week, or the property will be put back on the market.'

He then asked me if I wanted to be put in touch with an independent financial adviser. I told him that it was on the advice of an independent financial adviser that my father had invested his pension in Equitable Life.

Barwell was silent for a long time and then he said, 'Point taken.'

I immediately phoned my bank in Calcutta and explained my predicament to the woman on the end of the line. She said she would send me a bank loan application form.

I asked if it would be posted from Calcutta.

She said, 'No, Watford.'

Tuesday October 22nd

No sign of bank form.

Saw Marigold after work. She was wearing a tartan plastic Alice band.

Wednesday October 23rd

Phoned Calcutta. A bloke said that a bank loan form had been sent to A. Vole at Leicester, North Carolina, USA, on Monday October 21st.

I requested that the form be sent again and gave the correct name and address. I stressed the urgency.

Life of Pi won the Booker Prize last night. My mother asked what it was about. I told her it was about a Hindu Christian Muslim boy who spends a year on a lifeboat in the Pacific with a Bengal tiger.

She said, 'Why didn't the tiger eat the boy?'

I said, 'If the tiger had eaten the boy there would have been no novel.'

She said, 'But it doesn't make sense.'

My father, the esteemed literary critic, joined in, saying, 'A kid wouldn't last five minutes with a hungry tiger.'

I said, 'The story is an allegory.' And I left the kitchen before they could ask me technical questions about the lifeboat.

Thursday October 24th

Took my Hugo Boss suit to the dry-cleaner's and pointed out the white stains on the trousers. I was careful to tell the woman behind the counter that the stains were evaporated milk and had been there since last Christmas.

*

My mother phoned me at work and told me that a letter from Barclays had arrived. I asked her to open it and read what it said over the phone. After an agonizing wait (how long does it take to open an envelope, for Christ's sake?) my mother told me that the communication from Barclays was my Visa statement. However, there was a blank cheque attached to the statement and a letter, saying, 'Dear Mr Mole, The attached cheque can be used where your Barclaycard may not be accepted: e.g. payment of utility bills, local tradesmen, home improvements or school fees. Cash rate applies. Please see conditions on reverse of this statement.'

I asked my mother what the conditions were.

She scanned the back of the statement and said, 'It says something about . . . "for any amount as long as you remain within your credit limit . . ."'

I asked her what the interest would be on the cheque.

She said, 'It's 2 per cent for cash advances.' She went on, 'It says here your credit limit is £10,000. How did you wangle that?'

I told her that Barclaycard had been most obliging to me in the 1990s, when I presented my cable television show, *Offally Good!*

She said, 'But you didn't make any money out of that.'

I said, 'No, but it's credit that counts. Barclaycard have faith in me.'

I asked my mother to do me a huge favour and bring it to the shop, so I could sign the cheque immediately and deliver it to Barwell's office. She reluctantly agreed, but only after I pointed out to her that I was in danger of losing my loft apartment.

She said, 'I need to buy shoes for Glenn's passing-out parade anyway.'

What is it about shoes and women? Why do they need new shoes for every occasion? I have three pairs: a black pair, a brown pair and a pair of flip-flops for when I am on holiday. These are perfectly adequate for my needs.

10 p.m.
Barwell has had his asthma-inducing carpet removed and has replaced it with laminated floorboards.

A Visa cheque for £8,000 made out to David Barwell, Client Account, and signed A. Mole is safely in the system.

Angela got me to sign a lot of legal papers. She asked me if I wanted to read them before I added my signature.

I glanced through them quickly and said, 'It's all mumbo-jumbo to me.'

She said, 'It's all mumbo-jumbo to Mr Barwell.' She looked towards his office and said bitterly, 'He's complaining about the floorboards now. They're too slippery apparently.'

According to Angela, I could be moving into my loft in a week!

Friday October 25th

9.45 p.m., Wisteria Walk
As I was filing my financial papers away into my fireproof cabinet, I read for myself the letter from Barclaycard inviting me to cash their cheque. I was astounded, appalled and horrified to read that the interest rate

charged on my cheque is 21.4 per cent, and not 2 per cent as my mother had erroneously told me on the phone. The 2 per cent is the charge they will make for processing the cheque (£160).

There has been no sun in the last few days so, rather than trust my calculator, I phoned my friend Parvez, who has just passed his accountancy exams.

He said he charged £25 for the first ten minutes of phone advice and thereafter £2 a minute. I hurriedly gave him the figures and asked him how much I would end up paying for my £8,000.

After eleven minutes, during which Parvez asked me a lot of time-consuming and unnecessary questions, he said, 'It's gonna cost you an arm, a leg and a torso. A minimum of £162.34 a month. If you pay the minimum each month, it's going to take thirteen and three-quarter years to pay off and it will cost you £26,680.88 if interest rates don't go up. You've fallen into the compound interest trap, Moley, innit?' He then said, 'I'm taking on new clients at the moment. Do you want to book an appointment?'

I said, 'Couldn't we just go out for a drink together and have a chat?'

He said, 'Accountancy ain't my hobby, Moley.'

I agreed to go and see him at his house and try to make sense of my financial affairs.

Saturday October 26th

Took the car in for a service. I told Les, the mechanic, I occasionally hear a knocking sound coming from the engine.

He said, 'What kind of knocking?'

I said, 'It's as if a tiny trapped human is trying to get my attention.'

Les muttered that it was more likely to be the big end going.

I told Les that I was driving to Deepcut Barracks in Surrey to see my son's passing-out parade on Friday.

He said, 'You 'ope.'

Sunday October 27th

Pandora was right: reservist doctors and nurses are being called up. Britain is now on a war footing.

I phoned Marigold tonight.

Her mother answered and said, 'Netta Flowers speaking.' I asked to speak to Marigold, but Netta said, 'She's in the attic. I daren't disturb her.'

She made Marigold sound like Mr Rochester's mad wife.

I have started packing my few belongings. I won't need a removal lorry. The contents of my life will fit into the back of an estate car, including books and clothes.

Monday October 28th

Rose at 6.30 and caught the bus from Ashby de la Zouch into Leicester. It was quite pleasant sitting at the front, looking at the countryside. I was able to think about my life during the journey. Where did I want to be ten years from now? Did I want the bother of getting married and starting another family? Or should I concentrate on trying to get published?

I dictated a letter into my Philips Professional Pocket Memo 398 to Clare Short.

Dear Clare

Forgive me for addressing you by your Christian name, but you are so friendly and approachable I was sure you wouldn't mind. I wonder if you would agree to come to Leicester and be interviewed for my new book, *Celebrity and Madness*. My thesis is that all celebrities eventually go mad and start to think that they are superhuman.

I cannot pay a fee or expenses, but I'm sure that you are adequately recompensed for your ministerial duties. Sunday afternoons are good for me.

As a famously honest and straightforward person, I hope you won't mind a bit of plain-speaking when directed towards yourself. The scarves you have taken to wearing lately are less successful than you think. In my opinion only French women know how to wear a scarf. Why don't you pick up a copy of French *Vogue* the next time you are in an upmarket newsagent's?

I look forward to hearing from you in the near future.
I remain, madam,
Your most humble and obedient servant,
A. A. Mole

When I was getting off the bus, a woman said to me, 'You're right about them scarves.'

Tuesday October 29th
Moon's Last Quarter

Sharon Bott came into the shop this afternoon. She had been shopping at Evans for clothes to wear at Glenn's passing-out parade. She took the vast garments out of the bags and held them against her. There was a pink jacket that could have graced a hippo, and a pair of wide-legged trousers that an elephant would have found a comfortable fit.

I introduced Sharon to Mr Carlton-Hayes. In doing so, my two worlds collided. Sharon Bott, the mother of my first, illegitimate son, Glenn, represents the venality and weakness of my flesh, whereas Mr Carlton-Hayes personifies my intellectual and cerebral self.

Sharon looked around and said, 'All these books.' She gave a little laugh as if Mr Carlton-Hayes and I frittered away our working day in meaningless and frivolous activity.

I told Sharon that Glenn had invited us to a party on Friday night to celebrate his passing out.

Sharon said, 'That'll be a late drive back for you.'

I said I had no intention of driving back from Surrey in the early hours, due to my poor night vision, and suggested that we stay in a hotel.

Sharon almost swooned with delight. 'A 'otel,' she said. ''ow lovely.' Then her face clouded over. 'But, Aidy, I can't afford to pay for a 'otel. And anyway I'm scared to sleep in a room on my own.'

Before she left, I talked her into buying a pile of Barbara Cartlands that Mr Carlton-Hayes had been anxious to get rid of.

I rang Les and enquired about my car. He said, 'The little 'uman is still in the engine.'

Wednesday October 30th

Another bus ride.

Rang Les this morning. He said that the little 'uman was either dead or had escaped.

I could hear coarse male laughter in the background.

I said, 'Are you telling me my car is mended and available for collection?'

Les said, 'It's out at the moment having a test drive. Why don't you call for it at about 5 o'clock?'

At 3 p.m. Mr Carlton-Hayes and I were rearranging the window display. The theme was the Middle East. I looked up to see my own car being parked in a disabled bay and a young man in mechanic's overalls get out and go into the Foot Locker shop opposite.

I immediately got on the telephone to Les, who said that one of his lads had been tipped off that the new Adidas trainers had arrived in Leicester and that it was first come first served. He said, '' 'ave a heart, Mr Mole. You were young once.'

I said icily that I was only thirty-four.

Les said, 'Sorry. I took you to be a much older gentleman.'

Working with antiquarian books has obviously aged me prematurely.

Picked the car up on the way home from work. Les charged me £339 less the petrol for the Foot Locker expedition. I paid him with my Visa card.

Les said, 'I've given you a complimentary Christmas tree air freshener.'

I could barely open my mouth to say thanks.

Spent the evening trying to book three cheap hotel rooms in the Deepcut area, but the only rooms available were ridiculously expensive. I was forced to book two doubles, one for my parents and one for me and Sharon Bott. I will sleep on the floor if necessary. We are staying at the Lendore Spa Hotel.

I rang Pandora and caught her just as she was about to go into the lobby to vote on the MPs' working hours bill.

She snapped, 'What do you want?'

I said that if she bumped into Tony Blair, I would be grateful if she could remind him that he hadn't yet answered my letters.

She said, 'Look, I've got to go.'

I asked her if she was supporting the new hours bill or was against it.

'Against it, of course,' she said. 'It's only the mummies and daddies who want to tuck their kiddies up in bed who want the hours changed.' She added harshly, 'All women MPs should have their bloody wombs removed before making their maiden speech.'

Friday November 1st
All Saints' Day

Glenn's passing-out day.

Saturday November 2nd

Rose at dawn yesterday, showered, made tea, took tea into parents. There was a bottle of wine and two glasses on my father's bedside table. The television was still on from the night before. It took a long time to wake them.

I was worried that they had both, in an amazing co-incidence, fallen into a simultaneous coma. I urged them to hurry, to get themselves ready for departure at 8.30, as I had to pick my suit up from the dry-cleaner's, then drive to the opposite side of town to pick Sharon up.

As I was closing their door, I heard my father say, 'Bags I sit in the passenger seat, next to Adrian.'

*

When we drew up outside Sharon's house, her new partner, a youth of twenty-seven, Ryan, came to the front door and stared at my car and its occupants. He was holding Sharon's latest baby in his arms.

Sharon appeared in the doorway, carrying a large suitcase, a cigarette, a handbag, a black velvet hat, an umbrella, a vanity case and a pair of gloves.

'Christ', said my father, 'she looks like a contestant from *Crackerjack*.'

I got out of the car and opened the boot.

Ryan joined me at the back of the car. 'What time will you be bringing her back tomorrow?' he said.

I replied that it depended on weather conditions and the volume of traffic on the motorways.

'I need her back for 12.30,' he said. 'I've got a gig at Cooper House.'

He made it sound as though he was Fat Boy Slim playing at Stringfellows, whereas in fact I knew that he earned £8 a fortnight for playing a few Vera Lynn records at Cooper House, the old people's home.

It took longer than I had hoped to get to Deepcut Barracks, due to the many cigarette stops demanded by my passengers. I was forced to change into my suit, shirt and tie in the back of the car in the car park at the barracks.

When I stepped out, my mother gave a little scream and said, 'What's that white stuff on your trousers?'

She spat on a handkerchief and tried to remove the stains, but they had been baked on by the dry-cleaning fluid.

I spent most of the day, when I remembered, with my

hands flat against my thighs, like a man who was about to bend down and pat the head of a small child.

An extremely tall and cultured man, General Frobisher-Nairn, in a dress uniform with many medals, told the seated crowd of relations and friends on the parade ground that we should be proud of our sons and daughters who were about to serve their Queen and country.

Then the young soldiers marched up and down to the sounds of the regimental band. We couldn't see Glenn at first, then Sharon spotted him and burst into tears. I put my arm around her.

My father filmed the ceremony on his mini video camera.

I was quite proud when, during the inspection, General Frobisher-Nairn spoke to Glenn for a full minute.

When Glenn joined us in Tela Hall, where we were served afternoon tea, I asked him what the general had said.

Glenn said, 'He asked me where I was from. I told him, "Leicester, sir." He said, "Leicester? Isn't that where they make Walkers Crisps?" I said, "Yes, sir." He said, "Do you like crisps, Bott?" I said, "Yes, sir." "And which flavour do you prefer, Bott?" I said, "Cheese and onion, sir." Then he said, "Splendid, Bott." And I said, "Thank you, sir."'

I didn't say anything to Glenn, but quite frankly, diary, I was disappointed at the banality of their exchange. Especially at a time when there is talk of war in the air.

We didn't stay long at the party, which was held in the back room of a pub. My parents made fools of themselves, dancing to 'Let's Twist Again', and I think Glenn was relieved when we announced that we were going back to the Lendore Spa Hotel.

Before we left he said, 'I'd like to have my photo took with my mum and dad.'

One of his mates, a timid-looking soldier called Robbie, took our photograph. Glenn stood in the middle and Sharon and I put our arms around his shoulders. Glenn looked ecstatic.

I felt a pang of sadness that Glenn grew up without a mum and dad who lived together in the same house and loved each other. He is catching a plane early in the morning from Gatwick to Tenerife for a week's leave with a crowd of his soldier mates.

I gave him fifty quid, though I could ill afford it.

The Lendore is owned by a couple called Len and Doreen Legg. As nobody else in our party had a valid credit card, it was mine that Len Legg took a print of.

My father asked if the bar was still open. Len Legg sighed and rolled his eyes, then took a huge bunch of keys from his pocket and unlocked the grille over the bar.

'Thank you, mine host,' said my father, and asked if there was a bottle of cold champagne.

'Not cold,' said Len. 'But I could put it in the freezer for half an hour.'

My father said, 'No, don't bother. In half an hour I'll have worked out that I'm paying a 300 per cent mark-up, and I'll have gone off the idea. It's now or never with champagne.'

*

After we had been served our drinks, Doreen Legg came
to the door of the bar and said in a whiny voice, 'I thought
you were coming to bed, Len.'

Len said, 'You can see how I'm placed, Dore.'

Doreen Legg looked at us accusingly and said, 'He's
been up since 5.30.'

My mother said, 'As residents of this hotel, under EU
law, we are entitled to drink in this bar for twenty-four
hours should we wish to do so.'

I asked Doreen Legg if they did bar food.

Doreen said, 'Not after 10.30.'

Sharon shifted nervously on the banquette next to me.
It was 11.15 and she has to eat at two-hourly intervals.

My father volunteered to go out and search the area
for food.

Doreen Legg told us that everything was shut, but that
we would find the minibar well stocked with chocolate
and nuts.

My mother spoke in a loud voice about the hotels she
had stayed in abroad, how welcoming the staff were, how
good the food was.

Len Legg stood behind the bar, listening and cleaning
his nails with a chewed-down match.

When we were going up in the juddering lift I reminded
my parents that the contents of the minibar were not
complimentary.

I had been hoping that the room I was to share with
Sharon would have twin beds, but it was not to be. A
large pink candlewick-covered bed dominated the room.

Sharon walked around the small room like a tourist. She was enraptured by the trouser press and thrilled by the television on a bracket on the wall. She admired the fullness of the dirty net curtains, opened every drawer and cupboard, and, when she found the Gideon's Bible, said, 'Somebody's left their book behind.'

She found the minibar inside the sliding wardrobe. I hadn't got the heart to stop her from ripping open a tin of mixed nuts. I checked the minibar price list.

'My God,' I said, 'they're £8.50.'

I went into the bathroom and changed into my pyjamas.

When I came out Sharon was eating a Nestlé's Crunchy Nut. She flicked a piece of stray chocolate from the corner of her lips into her mouth with her tongue and said, 'Aidy, no offence, but I don't dog around no more, so don't expect nowt tonight.' Then she went into the bathroom and emerged five minutes later wearing what looked like biblical robes and got into bed. She said sleepily, 'That's the best bathroom I've ever seen, an' don't you think it's nice of them to put all them little soaps and bottles of stuff in there for the guests?'

I lay awake for a while and wondered what Marigold would say if she could see me and Sharon lying side by side. Would she understand or was she the jealous type?

As Sharon and I entered the breakfast room I could hear my mother's voice. She was having a toast row with Doreen Legg. It was a monologue I had heard many times before.

'I ordered a full English breakfast with toast. You brought my breakfast, but my toast arrived fifteen minutes later. And when it arrived it was cold and uncooked. The so-called toast you brought to me had not in actual fact been toasted. It had perhaps spent thirty seconds in a toaster. I do not think it was unreasonable of me to ask you to take the so-called toast back to the kitchen and retoast it.'

Doreen Legg said, 'Nobody else has complained, madam,' and looked around the breakfast room, where other guests were sheepishly chewing at their uncooked toast.

My father said obsequiously, 'I don't mind raw toast. But my wife's very fussy about hers.'

My mother said, 'George, this isn't toast.' She waggled a piece of the limp white bread in his face.

I thought it was time to intervene. I said, 'Mrs Legg, we are paying £95 each for our rooms. Is it impossible to get a few slices of white bread, browned on both sides, without all this melodrama?'

I led Sharon to the breakfast buffet and explained that she could help herself to the cereals, fruit juice and the bowl of fermenting fruit salad.

I must say that I was very proud of Sharon. She must have broken some kind of record, and she still managed a full English with fried bread and extra toast.

When we went back to our room to pack our bags, I emptied the complimentary toiletries into Sharon's suitcase and included the spare toilet roll and a white flannel.

In the daylight the room looked grubby and I could see that the carpet bore the stains of multi-occupation.

A jackknifed lorry delayed us on the M25. We were caught in a tailback for two and a half hours and my father was forced to urinate into an empty Diet Coke bottle.

Sharon rang Ryan using my mobile to tell him that she would be late. She told him excitedly about the hotel, but he cut her off. She fell into a sad silence for the rest of the way home.

Just before she got out of the car I said, 'It might be best not to mention to Ryan that we shared a room, or a bed. He may not understand.'

Sharon said, 'It's OK, Aidy. Ryan and me promised to tell the truth to each other, 24/7.'

I carried her suitcase up the path. Ryan was glowering out of the front-room window. The baby was screaming in his arms. I begged Sharon to lie and to tell Ryan that she slept in a single bed in a single room.

As I finish writing this entry I feel a growing sense of unease.

Sunday November 3rd

Since Cherie Blair has chosen to ignore my invitation to speak at the Leicestershire and Rutland Creative Writing Group on December 23rd, I have written to Ruth Rendell.

Dear Ms Rendell

As one writer to another, where do you get your ideas from? Do you write by hand or use a word processor? How long does it take to write one of your novels? Do you write from personal experience or are your characters and plots totally fictional?

Let me cut to the chase.

I am the membership secretary of the Leicestershire and Rutland Creative Writing Group. We have been badly let down recently by Cherie Blair. She has failed to respond to an invitation to be the main speaker at our Christmas dinner to be held on December 23rd this year (venue to be arranged).

I realize it is short notice, but could you do the honours?

We cannot afford to pay a fee or expenses, but I think you will find us a lively crowd.

I hope you will reply in the affirmative. However, should Mrs Blair decide to accept our invitation after all, I hope you will understand if I have to disappoint you at the last minute. She is, after all, the highest lady in the land.

I remain, madam,

Your most humble and obedient servant,

A. A. Mole

Monday November 4th
New Moon

It was a quiet morning in the shop. Mr Carlton-Hayes was in the back, smoking his pipe and reading *Tony Benn's Diaries*, which were published last week.

I was cataloguing the *Rupert* annuals when Sharon's

partner, Ryan, burst in to the shop and gave me a mouthful of foul abuse, claiming I had 'knobbed' Sharon during our stay at the Lendore Spa Hotel.

I told him, truthfully, as you will attest, diary, that Sharon and I had remained in a state of grace all night.

I will do anything to avoid physical violence, but when somebody thumps me on the shoulder, I thump them back. After a little untidy skirmishing, Mr Carlton-Hayes came from out of the back and, in a loud, authoritative voice, ordered Ryan to leave the shop.

When Ryan said, 'Fuck off, you stupid old bastard, before I shove your pipe up your arse,' Mr Carlton-Hayes handed his pipe to me and hit Ryan hard on the jaw.

Ryan left, saying that he would be back with his brother.

When he'd gone, Mr Carlton-Hayes took his pipe from me and said, 'You seem to have a frightfully dramatic romantic life, Adrian. I do envy you.'

Tuesday November 5th

I rang Marigold last night and asked her if she would like to accompany me to a Fire Service organized bonfire party, all proceeds to go to their strike fund. Marigold said that she was afraid of fireworks and would be barricading herself inside their house, together with the family pets. Her frailty both excites and irritates me.

My parents have found a couple of pigsties on the outskirts of Mangold Parva. They both stand on an eighth of an acre of unprepossessing land, half a mile along a farm track. There is planning permission for conversion to two dwellings. However, they have no water, gas, electricity or main drainage.

They showed me a photograph, and my mother pointed excitedly to where they intended to fit French doors. I advised them against it, but madness has taken them over. They are suffering from *folie à deux*, like Myra Hindley and Ian Brady.

They are going to live in a tent and do the conversion themselves.

'A tent?' I queried.

My mother said, 'We bought it from Millets today. It's got three bedrooms, a kitchen area and a patio with bad-weather sheeting for the odd rainy day.'

'Don't forget the integral groundsheet,' said my father.

I said, 'But a winter in a tent in Mangold Parva will kill you.'

My father said, 'You're forgetting one thing, lad, me and your mother are baby boomers. We were born in the 1940s. We grew up without central heating, tissue paper, vitamins, hot water on tap. We walked four miles to school and four miles back in short trousers through the snow. It will take more than a few draughts to kill us off.'

I asked them what they were doing with their furniture. They said they were getting rid of it all. My mother asked me if I would like to take some of the best pieces to my new loft apartment. I almost laughed in her face.

Wednesday November 6th

I rang David Barwell and asked if a completion date had been set. Angela said she had given Mr Barwell the papers but he had reacted badly to the glue used to stick down the laminated floorboards and was away from the office.

Mr Carlton-Hayes had his little Roberts portable tuned to Five Live at 12 o'clock for Prime Minister's Question Time. We heard Mr Blair telling Parliament that he had just spoken on the telephone to President Bush, who told him that there would be a UN resolution announced at 3.30 saying that it was all right to go to war with Iraq.

Mr Carlton-Hayes asked me what my opinion of Tony Blair was. I said I admired him and supported him and trusted him implicitly.

Rang Marigold and asked if we could meet after work. She sounded tired and said that she hadn't slept well due to 'the horrendous noise' of the fireworks last night. She said it was time that we, as a civilized country, banned all fireworks.

I didn't tell her that last night I wrote her name in the dark with a sparkler.

Thursday November 7th

Rang solicitors. Angela said the place was in chaos. The laminated floorboards were being ripped up. I stressed that I needed to be given a completion date.

Went to Parvez's house. He has set up business in his spare bedroom. He has bought a home office from IKEA, and a black leather swivel chair, but one wall is still covered in Postman Pat wallpaper.

I was surprised to see him wearing traditional Muslim dress. He said that he had started going to the mosque again.

I told him that his new goatee beard suited him and made his face look thinner.

He sat me down and interrogated me about my financial position. I told him that my monthly income is £1,083.33.

He then ran through a comprehensive expenditure questionnaire and tapped the answers into his laptop. It included how much I spent on newspapers each week (£8), how much my car cost to run (£100 a month), takeaway beverages (an astonishing £15 at two cappuccinos a day, five days a week), broadband Internet connection (£35 a month). I was aghast. By the time we had finished, I discovered my outgoings exceed my income by almost £5,000 a year.

When the form had been filled in, Parvez said disapprovingly, 'Don't you remember when we did *David Copperfield* at school, Moley?'

I said that it was one of my favourite books.

He said, 'Remember Mr Micawber? "Annual income twenty pounds, annual expenditure nineteen nineteen six, result happiness. Annual income twenty pounds, annual expenditure twenty pounds ought and six, result misery" – Citizens' Advice Bureau, debt counselling, bankruptcy and homelessness.'

We stared at Parvez's laptop, where the stark truth was written out in numbers.

I said, 'What can I do?'

Parvez said, 'You can't move into that loft apartment, Moley. You don't earn a loft apartment salary.'

I told Parvez that it was too late, that I had signed the papers and that the money had been transferred.

Parvez said, 'Do you want me to give you some financial advice, Moley?'

I said, 'No, I can't afford it.' And went home.

Friday November 8th

A triumph for Mr Blair! After many weeks of trying to convince foreign leaders that Saddam Hussein's Weapons of Mass Destruction were a serious threat to the world, resolution 1441 was passed unanimously. Even Syria voted with the fourteen other countries.

My mother tried to stir my father from his early-morning torpor by discussing this with him.

My father said, '1441, wasn't that the name of the perfume my mum used to wear?'

My mother sighed and looked sad. She said, 'No, George, that was 4711.'

When he had gone out of the kitchen, she said, 'I wish I was married to somebody like Roy Hattersley, somebody who was interested in politics.'

She lit her first cigarette of the day and we watched the news on the kitchen television. Mr Blair was very impressive. He looked sternly into the camera and said directly to Saddam Hussein, 'Disarm or face force.' His voice trembled with emotion.

My mother said, 'He looks as though he's about to burst into tears.' She shouted at the screen, 'Butch up, Tony.'

4 p.m.
Marigold came in to the shop this morning. She couldn't stay long because she was on her way to the Karma Health Centre to have an Indian head massage. She has suffered from migraines all her life. I was astonished to hear that having her head rubbed for half an hour was going to cost £25. I advised her to buy a packet of Nurofen Extra instead and told her that they always work for me. Migraines are the only thing we have in common.

She asked me if I would like to accompany her to a concert the Madrigal Society is giving in Leicester Cathedral. She said her father was singing a solo. He is a counter-tenor.

5.30 p.m.
Mr Carlton-Hayes has gone home. I am sitting here waiting for Marigold. I don't know where this relationship is going. I can't think of a more horrible way to

spend a Friday night than sitting in a cold cathedral listening to Michael Flowers singing in a woman's voice.

Midnight

Marigold and I walked to the cathedral arm in arm. She was wearing a red beret and a khaki trouser suit. I didn't say anything, but she looked like a paratrooper on leave. Perhaps she is subconsciously preparing herself for war.

You would have thought that Michael Flowers would have changed his clothes for the occasion, but, oh no, he has worn the tree sweater for twenty consecutive days to my knowledge. When I mentioned this to Marigold, she said that detergents are a major pollutant of our rivers and waterways.

Michael Flowers started the concert by giving what he said would be a short address about the history of the madrigal, but he droned on for twenty-five minutes, seemingly oblivious to the fidgeting and boredom of his audience. Eventually the terrible singing started.

Netta Flowers loomed over the other choristers. She was also vocally dominant. Her deep contralto seemed to make the pew Marigold and I were sitting in reverberate.

Afterwards, when we were mingling in the vestry, convention forced me to congratulate Mr and Mrs Flowers on their performances.

Mr Flowers said, 'Are you two young people going to a rock and roll club later?'

I almost laughed out loud. He smells of damp wool.

*

Later, in Wong's, I asked Marigold if she had ever considered leaving home. She pushed a clump of bean sprouts around her bowl with a chopstick and said that she had expected to be married by now.

Saturday November 9th

Marigold rang early this morning to say that her parents had told her that I was an admirable young man. She sounded very happy. I didn't have the heart to tell her that I had been awake half the night wondering how I could end the relationship.

Sunday November 10th

Watched the old blokes and old women marching past the Cenotaph. Some of them looked like they were on their last legs; others didn't have legs and were pushed past in wheelchairs. My father asked me why I was sniffing. I said I was allergic to poppies.

He said, 'Your grandad Arthur was in the Second World War.'

I asked him where my grandad had fought.

My father said, 'He wouldn't talk about the war, but if he saw it on telly or heard "Lili Marleen", he'd cry like a baby. Your grandma Mole would send him out to the backyard with a clean handkerchief, until he'd recovered himself. She was a hard woman.'

*

My mother has made some change of address cards on her Apple Mac. Their new address is going to be The Piggeries, The Bottom Field, Lower Lane, Mangold Parva, Leicestershire.

I said, 'Aren't you being a little premature?'

She said, 'No, we bought the pigsties at an auction yesterday afternoon.'

Nobody ever tells me anything in this house. I'll be glad to see the back of it.

I rang Nigel at his parents' house. He has been living in their granny annexe since putting his London flat up for sale. His sight has deteriorated even more. I asked him if he wanted to go and see *The Lord of the Rings* with me.

He said, 'No, it all takes place in Middle Earth in half-darkness, and anyway elves and gnomes are seriously naff.'

I asked Nigel if his hearing had improved since he had gone blind.

He said, 'Yes, I can now hear a page being turned in Hay-on-fucking-Wye, aren't I a lucky boy?'

Monday November 11th
Moon's Last Quarter

Mr Carlton-Hayes and I seemed to be the only people in the High Street who observed the one-minute silence at 11 o'clock, apart from a few pensioners and a black bus driver who got out of his cab and stood with his head bowed.

*

Rang Barwell. Angela said the papers were ready for signing. To make conversation, I asked her what floor covering Mr Barwell would be having on his office floor next.

She said that Barwell had an appointment at 4 p.m. to talk to his allergy consultant.

I asked Mr Carlton-Hayes if I could nip out for an hour. He told me to take as long as I needed.

It should have been a happy occasion, but as I signed the documents which committed me to paying £723.48 a month, I could not help remembering Parvez's warning, 'Citizens' Advice Bureau, debt counselling, bankruptcy, homelessness and misery'.

Barwell was wheezing and coughing throughout the little paperwork ceremony. I suggested that the air in his office was rather stale and offered to open the window.

He wheezed, 'The window doesn't open. I have to keep the pollen out.'

I pointed out to him that his windows were made of ultraviolet polyvinyl chloride and advised him to replace them with a traditional wooden frame. I told him in detail about the Radio Four documentary I had heard the night before about Sick Building Syndrome. He appeared interested at first, but then seemed to lose concentration and kept looking at his watch.

I pick the keys up for Rat Wharf on Friday.

Tuesday November 12th

Last night at the Leicestershire and Rutland Creative Writing Group meeting, Ken Blunt asked me if I had fixed a speaker for our Christmas dinner on December 23rd and if I had found a suitable venue. I told him that neither Mrs Blair nor Ruth Rendell had replied as yet.

Gary Milksop said that he had applied for the position of Creative Writing for Disadvantaged Adults Facilitator at the Life-Long Learning Centre.

I said, 'But, Gary, you are not qualified to teach creative writing.'

He said that he had a BA in Education and had almost finished writing his novel.

He said it was a part-time position and was worth £10,000 a year. He showed me the advertisement. It said at the bottom, 'Preference will be given to a published writer.'

I pointed out to Milksop as kindly as I could that he had not yet earned a single penny from his writing and reminded him that he had decorated the chimney breast of his bed-sitting room with publishers' rejection letters.

Gladys read us her latest cat poem:

> 'Poor Blackie's up in heaven,
> God took her life away,
> He said, you'll go to Devon,
> And have a holiday.

Once there, you'll find your pussy friends,
Their ghosts do walk the prom,
Here are Ginger, Ming and Fluff,
Marmalade and Tom.'

She told us that Blackie had been run over by a lorry last Thursday.

Ken Blunt said that Gladys's poem was a failure because it was not truthful. He said that she had obviously chosen Devon because it rhymed with heaven, and that the idea that dead cats prowled the promenades of Devon was totally absurd.

'This poem is untruthful
This poem is absurd,
This poem is a contrivance
To rhyme with Douglas Hurd.'

I pointed out to Ken Blunt that 'a contrivance' didn't scan properly.

Gary Milksop said that Gladys should collect her cat poems together and send them to a publisher.

Ken Blunt said, 'What for, cat litter?'

Gladys said that we were mocking Blackie's death and that we should leave. I was glad to get out of there. I was covered from head to toe in cat hair.

Ken Blunt asked me and Gary if we fancied a drink. We went to the Red Cow near the university. It was full of students singing along to Rolf Harris songs. Gary Milksop told me that Rolf Harris is a cult figure in student circles. How come I didn't know this?

We discussed the future of the Leicestershire and Rutland Creative Writing Group and came to the reluctant conclusion that Gladys was holding us back. Her cat poems now dominate the meetings. Ken said expulsion is the only answer.

I was deputed to tell Gladys Fordingbridge that she is no longer a member of the Leicestershire and Rutland Creative Writing Group.

I asked Ken what he was working on at the moment; he said, 'Nowt.'

Marigold rang and left a message on my mobile to say that she was '. . . concerned that you haven't been in touch. Are you poorly?' I didn't want to speak to her so I scribbled a note:

Dear Marigold

Forgive me for my silence. You have been on my mind constantly. My breathing still quickens when I think about your delicate wrists and the way your glasses slip down your nose.

If you had had a mobile I would have been in regular text contact. This is a v. busy week for me. I move into Rat Wharf on Friday and I will no doubt be engaged in settling in for some time afterwards. But I will contact you when I have some free time.

Yours, with very best wishes,
Adrian

PS I expect your father is annoyed with Geoff Hoon for agreeing to let President Bush install Star Wars missiles on

England's fair and pleasant land. Myself, I think it is a price we have to pay for freedom.

Wednesday November 13th

I reminded my parents that the fire fighters go on strike at 6 p.m. today. I begged them not to smoke in bed and also not to leave cigarettes smouldering in ashtrays while they cut their toenails etc. It would be a disaster if this house burnt down before I move to Rat Wharf and they move to what they now call the Piggeries.

Thursday November 14th

Mr Carlton-Hayes has given me three days off to move. I cannot bear to drag the old cheap pine bed I have been sleeping in since childhood to my new cutting-edge loft apartment. It would be like putting an antimacassar on a Terence Conran sofa. I need to buy a futon, new bed linen, simple but stylish kitchen equipment, a table and two chairs for my balcony, bookcases, a television and curtains for my glass lavatory. The problem is I have no money at all.

When I explained my predicament to my mother, she looked up from her book, *The Beginners' Guide to Renovating Property*, and said, 'Nobody uses money any more. Money as such doesn't exist. Everybody I know lives on credit. Get yourself a store card.'

*

I have found a small firm to help me with my move tomorrow, Two Gals 'n' a Van.

I spent a confusing and demoralizing afternoon on the phone, listening to Vivaldi and various robots. It appears that the gas at Rat Wharf is supplied by Severn Trent Water, the electricity by the gas board, my water by a French company with a name I can't pronounce. The cable company ntl is in charge of my phone. They are connecting me to over 200 television channels tomorrow at 2 o'clock.

The two girls of Two Gals 'n' a Van are not girls. They are strong-looking middle-aged women called Sian and Helen. They came round to assess how many journeys the van would have to make between Ashby de la Zouch and Leicester tomorrow.

The answer was one.

They gave me some cardboard boxes and left me upstairs, packing my books. My mother had invited them downstairs to have a cup of tea.

Soon afterwards my father came up to join me. I could hear female laughter coming from the kitchen. I asked my father what the women downstairs were talking about.

He said, 'Just women's silly slobber – the price of cabbage, was Princess Diana murdered, will Hans Blix find any Weapons of Mass Destruction, cats, the change of bloody life, *Sex and the City*, and how men are not needed any more.' He lowered his voice. 'Helen is trying to get pregnant. Sian has been doing the business with a turkey baster and a bottle of sperm that's been donated by their gay-boy friend.' He shook his head sadly. 'Where did we go wrong, Adrian? We let them go to work, we let them be bloody vicars, they drive cars, there's one who's a captain in the navy, we bought them machines to make it easier to do their housework, but they still hate us, and they'd rather have sex with a kitchen tool than with a man.'

My father kicked at my boxes and said, 'You've not got much to show for thirty-four years of life, have you?'

When he'd gone, I lay down on my childhood bed and wept for about one minute and thirty seconds.

Friday November 15th

Sian and Helen moved me into Rat Wharf this morning. My address is now a prestigious one: Unit 4, The Old Battery Factory, Rat Wharf, Grand Union Canal, Leicester. It is entirely to my taste – very spare, very masculine and very hard-textured.

While the 'gals' carried the heavy boxes of books upstairs, I opened my sliding door and stood on the mesh balcony, gripping the steel rail which overlooks the canal. A gang of swans immediately swam up and began hissing aggressively. The biggest one, who for some reason reminded me of Sir John Gielgud, the great classical actor, was particularly vicious. An old-fashioned tramp, with string round his trousers, was staggering past the dye works on the opposite bank, swigging from a can of Kestrel.

From my vantage point above the water I could clearly

see several supermarket trolleys, milk crates and what must have been hundreds of Kestrel lager cans lying on the bed of the canal. The water had a curious phosphorous-looking mien to it, and a noxious smell that was certainly not there when I viewed the property in October. I would have liked to have stood on the balcony longer, but quite honestly, diary, the malevolent stare of Gielgud, the biggest swan, drove me inside.

I asked Sian what she thought of my loft apartment.

She said, 'It'll be nice when you've got some colour on the walls and a few bits and pieces to make it cosy.'

I said that I didn't do cosy and explained that I intended to live an uncluttered life, a bit like Mahatma Gandhi.

Helen pointed to a box that contained my clothes and said, 'So what's in there, loincloths?'

I pointed out that it was Tarzan who wore a loincloth, Gandhi had worn a dhoti, which was quite a different thing.

Before they left, Helen told me that when they were taking the boxes out of the van in the car park, they had seen a 'stroppy flock of swans'. She warned me to take care, adding, 'A swan can break a man's arm, you know.'

I paid them £80, money I could ill afford. I was glad to see them go. I wanted to walk around my beautiful space and listen to my footsteps on my genuine wooden floor.

I unpacked my books and stacked them on the floor in alphabetical order while I waited for ntl to call. The swans kept up a constant racket outside. Occasionally Gielgud would fly past my balcony window. I had forgotten that swans could fly. I had the eerie feeling that he was spying on me and mocking me because I had so few possessions.

At 4 o'clock I telephoned ntl to ask why their engineer had failed to turn up as promised. A woman said she would ring me on my mobile when she had made contact with their 'field operative'.

Marigold rang to ask how I was enjoying my first after-noon in my new apartment. I told her about the swans and she said, 'Be careful, Adrian. A swan can break a man's arm, you know.'

I, rather irritably perhaps, informed her that I had known this fact since I was four years old.

She thanked me for my letter and said with a little laugh, 'There's a certain ambiguity about it. Read one way it sounds like you're giving me the brush-off, read another way it sounds the same.' She gave another little laugh. 'You're not giving me the brush-off, are you, Adrian?'

Why didn't I tell her the truth, diary? Why didn't I tell her that after spending time with her the world seems a darker place, one devoid of joy and hope? She is coming round tomorrow after work.

At 5.30 my telephone rang and an ntl person informed me that the field operative had attempted to call but had been beaten back by swans in the car park, then added, 'A swan can break a man's arm, you know.'

I have arranged to be in the car park to escort the ntl engineer to my apartment at 10 o'clock in the morning.

Having no bed yet, I made a platform of books, which I lay on in a sleeping bag. But it was an uncomfortable night: *Frankenstein* dug into my breastbone and kept me awake.

Saturday November 16th

I am still without ntl. The engineer refused to get out of his van because Gielgud and the other swans were walking around the car park, looking as though they owned the place. Before he drove away he said, 'A swan can break a man's arm, y'know.'

I met the owner of Unit 2 on the stairs. He is a professor of golf course management at De Montfort University. His name is Frank Green. He said the swans were a bloody nuisance and that he was thinking of selling his apartment and moving to a land-locked location.

I went to Debenhams and confessed to a kindly woman behind the counter in the furniture department that I had no money. She agreed with my mother that a store card would solve my problems and pointed out to me that should I activate the card today, I would get a 10 per cent discount on everything I bought. Within a quarter of an hour and after lying about my salary and showing my passport and Visa card, I was given £10,000 worth of credit.

I should have had somebody with me, somebody sensible. Did I really need a white towelling bathrobe? Was a white sofa with non-detachable covers a wise choice? And did I really need a home entertainment centre with a cinema screen and Dolby Surround Sound?

I had never slept on a futon before, but I was too shy to test it in the shop. I bought it anyway. I also bought bookshelves and an aluminium bistro table and matching chairs for the balcony, a Dualit toaster and a cafetiere (the last two items are loft living must-haves).

I phoned Sian and Helen and asked if they were free to collect these items from the store's delivery bay. They arranged to meet me at 4 o'clock.

In the intervening hour I bought a hexagonal-shaped black dinner service, a wine rack and a bottle of extra-extra virgin olive oil which Debenhams import from an olive grove owned by a close friend of Gore Vidal's.

When Sian and Helen eventually turned up, I was sitting among my new purchases like a latter-day Howard Hughes, a victim of consumerism.

Sian said, 'I thought you were strapped for cash.'

I told her about the store card and Helen asked how much interest I would be paying. When I told her 29 per cent, she said, 'Leave the stuff here, cancel the card, get in the van and I'll put my foot down.'

But, diary, I couldn't do it. What is the point of living in a loft if you can't pad around the wooden floors in your white towelling bathrobe, sit on your white sofa while waiting for the coffee to brew in your cafetiere, then take the pot to the galvanized table on the balcony and eat a croissant from your hexagonal-shaped black plate?

*

Marigold managed to walk swan shit all over my gleaming floorboards. She offered to clean them with a mop and bucket, and when I irritably informed her that I had not yet bought such mundane articles, she said, 'Life is not only composed of white sofas and extra-extra-virgin olive oil, you know, Adrian.'

She gave me a house-warming present – a collection of hanging feathers, which she called a 'dream catcher'. Its purpose, apparently, is to catch my dreams and make them come true. I didn't tell Marigold that I have a recurring dream whereby Pandora Braithwaite falls to her knees and begs me to make love to her.

We sat out for a while on the balcony, drinking coffee. Marigold was wearing a rainbow version of the sweater her father had been wearing for the last month, but after a short time she shivered and said, 'I catch cold very easily. I'd like to go in now.'

When she asked if she could use my toilet, I felt honour bound to tell her that her outline would be seen through the glass bricks, so she said she would wait until she got home. I hoped it wouldn't be too long.

She watched me unpack my home entertainment centre and was horrified by the amount of packaging materials that came out of the boxes. When she started banging on about the evils of polystyrene, I found myself defending it. I said it was a beautiful, practical and light material. We were soon having a heated discussion about the earth's resources. This somehow led into the letter I had sent her on November 12th, which she quoted back to me word for word.

She said, 'Sooner or later all of my boyfriends write a similar letter.'

She picked at a piece of polystyrene, crumbling it between her fingers. Annoyingly, a slight draught blew it across the floor. I should have told her there and then that I no longer wanted to go out with her. After all, it was the first day of my new life. But courage failed me and I heard myself accepting an invitation to have Sunday tea with her parents at the house in Beeby on the Wold.

Rosie rang and begged me to send her £200 minimum. She said that Simon's dealer was threatening to break Simon's legs. I told her the truth, that I was in debt to the tune of thousands of pounds.

I asked her if she had started writing her dissertation yet.

She said, 'Go and shag yourself.'

I took that to mean no.

I advised her to get Simon out of her life.

She said, 'I can't, he needs me. None of our friends will talk to him. He spent last night in a police cell because he stole an NSPCC charity collection box from the uni bar.'

Sunday November 17th

I slept uneasily on my new futon. I'm not used to sleeping so close to the floor. I woke at 5 a.m. and worried for an hour about having tea with the Flowers family. I then read half a chapter of John Major's autobiography. It never fails to get me back to sleep.

I was next woken by the sound of my father's voice shouting, 'Get back, you bastards, get back.'

And my mother screeching, 'George, George, don't antagonize them. They can break a man's arm, y'know.'

I put on my white bathrobe, went to the balcony and looked down. The swans had surrounded my parents on the towpath. My father held a copy of the *News of the World* in front of him as though it was a rapier and he was the Count of Monte Cristo. As I watched, the swans retreated and regrouped in the middle of the canal. Once again Gielgud stared at me. I swear to God that there was a sneer on his beak. What has he got against me?

The soles of my parents' shoes were covered in swan shit, so I made them take them off at the door.

They walked around in silence and then my father said, '190,000 for this. It's just one big room with a glass bog!'

My mother said, 'It'll be all right when you've got some carpet down.'

They lit up cigarettes, but I informed them that the loft was a no-smoking area and ushered them out on to the balcony. A stiff breeze was ruffling the swans' feathers.

My mother gave me a postcard of a lunar landscape. I was puzzled until I turned it over. It was from Glenn in Tenerife.

Dear Dad

Me and the lads are having a great time. It is dead hot and I have gone brown. I had a phone call from Mum. She told me that you and Ryan was fighting in the shop. I hope you done him over good, Dad. Don't worry about me missing the holiday we was going to have. I will be going to Cyprus with the army soon. Ha ha ha.

Best wishes,

Your son, Glenn

I made the coffee and took it out to the balcony and heard my father say, 'You see that humped-back bridge in the distance, Pauline? It was under that bridge that I lost my cherry with Jean Arbuthnot. I was seventeen and it felt like I'd won the pools that night.'

'Did you wear a condom?' she asked.

'A condom?' he said. 'Nobody wore a condom in the 1950s.'

'It's a wonder she didn't get pregnant then,' said my mother censoriously.

'We did it standing up, Pauline,' he explained, as if talking to a moron. 'You can't get pregnant if you do it standing up, not the first time.'

When they'd finished smoking they looked around for an ashtray, then, not finding one, flicked the ends into the canal.

My mother helped me to assemble and wire up the entertainment centre while my father read the *News of the World*, occasionally complaining about the sexual immorality of today's youth.

When he got up to go to the toilet I gave him the usual warning about his outline being visible, but he said, 'I've got nothing that your mother and you haven't seen before.'

However, I still chose to turn my head away, but couldn't fail to hear the thunderous sound of his urination. He urinates, defecates, coughs, sneezes and belches louder than any man I have ever known. How my mother sticks it, I don't know.

When the entertainment centre was operational and the speakers were in place, I sorted out my *Phantom of the Opera* CD. The volume setting had inadvertently been turned to full and Sarah Brightman's opening shrieks nearly knocked us off our feet. I hurried to turn it down, but even with the volume on low the floor reverberated and the bricks of the glass lavatory shook. Professor Green in the apartment below banged on my floor. Somebody else in the apartment above banged on my ceiling. I became uncomfortably aware of my neighbours.

My mother told me that she had rung Rosie yesterday.

'How did she sound?' I said.

My mother's face broke into a big smile and she said, 'Oh, fantastic. She's doing incredibly well. She's almost finished her dissertation and she's going out with a lovely boy called Simon. She needed £200 to buy a new printer for her computer so that she can print her dissertation out.'

How little our parents know about us. Do my children lie to me?

*

Just before they left, my father told me that he had placed a bet with Ladbrokes that Hans Blix, the United Nations chief weapons inspector, wouldn't find any Weapons of Mass Destruction after his return to Iraq tomorrow.

My mother scoffed, 'A fool and his money are soon parted.' Then she said, 'Tony Blair obviously knows something we don't know. He sees secret documents, George. He reads all the intelligence reports. He's in touch with MI5, MI6, the CIA, the FBI, Mossad and Rupert Murdoch.'

My father said, 'We lied to Adrian about the tooth fairy, Pauline. He was eleven before he found out that it was me who put a quid under his pillow rather than bleeding Tinkerbell.'

My mother said, 'And your point is?'

My father shouted, 'My point is, people we trust lie to us. Just think of Jeffrey Archer.'

My father was a great Archer fan and felt betrayed when it was revealed that Archer had lied at his first trial.

When I arrived outside Chez Flowers in Beeby on the Wold, Marigold came running out to meet me.

She said nervously, 'Just a few pointers. Don't mention that you live in a loft or that your father used to sell electric storage heaters, that your parents smoke, that you have a son in the army or that you were once an offal chef in Soho. And please, please don't mention Mexico.'

I said that I had never been to Mexico, I knew no Mexicans and I did not speak Mexican, so it was highly unlikely that I would 'bring up Mexico'. I protested to her that these conversational prohibitions meant that I could well remain mute throughout my visit.

Marigold said, 'Stick to talking about books and how marvellous *I* am.'

I entered the house with a heavy heart and with Marigold hanging on my arm.

I had bought Netta a bunch of flowers from the BP garage. When I gave them to her she said, 'How perfectly lovely, a forecourt bouquet. I'm sure I can revive them if I plunge them into water immediately. Please excuse me.'

She hurried off with the bouquet as though she was rushing them into intensive care to hook them up to a heart and lung machine.

Michael Flowers was in his study. He pretended to be too engrossed in a big leather-bound book to notice when Marigold knocked on the half-open door and walked in, with me following behind. The tree sweater was looking the worse for wear. He pushed his spectacles on to the top of his head and rose to his feet.

'You bearded me in my lair, young sir,' he said. 'I was just looking up the derivation of the word "mole". It seems, Adrian, that a mole is a burrowing animal with hairy forearms, a blemish or spot, a fleshy growth in the uterus, a measurement in physics, a harbour protected by a breakwater, or a spy who has infiltrated an organiz-ation and over a long period of time has become a trusted member of it. Which of these are you?'

Through the study window I could see Netta throwing

half of the flowers I had just bought her on to a large compost heap at the bottom of the garden.

Marigold saved the day. She said, 'I think Adrian is more of the spy. He's terribly secretive.'

I said, 'On the contrary, Marigold, my life is an open book.'

Michael Flowers said, 'Yes, books. Marigold tells me you work for that dreadful old libertarian Hugh Carlton-Hayes.'

I thought of Mr Carlton-Hayes's kind face, his cardigans and his soft white hair, and felt honour bound to defend him. I said, 'Mr Carlton-Hayes is the most decent man I know.'

Flowers said, 'I'll let you keep your illusions for now, Adrian.'

A sulky girl with extraordinarily long hair wearing a T-shirt which said 'Bitch' banged in and snarled, 'I've been ordered to tell you that tea is apparently ready.'

It was Poppy, Marigold's middle sister, who had returned home temporarily to recover from an unhappy love affair with a fellow maths teacher.

I was led into the sitting room and made to sit down and introduced to the cats, Saffron and Fleur.

Poppy had the longest hair I have ever seen. Apparently she has been growing it since she was twelve. She fiddled with it, pulled it over her shoulders, pushed it back, sat on it, twirled it on top of her head and let it fall. I knew I was expected to comment on the length of her hair and that she had built her whole personality around this hirsute feature, but I could not bring myself to mention it.

Marigold said, 'It takes Poppy four and a half hours to dry her hair.'

Apart from a slight inclination of the head, I could not respond.

I was given the choice of having apple and blackberry, nettle, peppermint or basil and borage tea.

Netta said encouragingly, 'We grow and dry our own herbs. There are no additives and preservatives. Everything is quite pure.'

I was handed a plate of stodgy brown lumps. These turned out to be scones made by Netta using stone-ground flour that was posted to her from a windmill in Somerset.

Michael Flowers said, 'We try to eat much as they did in the Middle Ages, before our food became adulterated.'

I was very hungry and would have given anything for a Mr Kipling Iced Fancy. However, I took a scone and nibbled at it from time to time. It tasted as if it had been baked in AD 1307 over a fire made of twigs and dried cow dung.

The talk eventually centred around the absent Daisy, Marigold's eldest sister, who had sent a letter to her parents the week before, denouncing them and blaming them for her miserable childhood.

Michael Flowers said, 'Poor Daisy, she was always rather a strange child.'

Netta, Marigold and Poppy started to slag off Daisy, who was in public relations in London.

The more they slagged her off, the more I liked the sound of her. Apparently she was ruining her health and her feet by teetering from premieres to book launches while wearing skimpy clothes and five-inch heels.

Michael Flowers shook his head. 'Such a shallow life,' he said. Then my interrogation began. 'We know so little about you, Adrian. Tell me about your family.'

I said that my mother's parents, the Sugdens, had been potato farmers in Norfolk.

Flowers said, 'Yes, there is something of the Fens about you.'

I said that my father's family were unskilled factory workers in Leicester.

Flowers said, 'That's nothing to be ashamed of.'

I said that I wasn't in the least ashamed.

Flowers said, 'We can trace our ancestors back to the Magna Carta. How far back does your family go?'

I don't know what made me say it, diary. As soon as the words were out of my mouth I regretted them, particularly when I saw the distress on Marigold's face. My excuse was that I was goaded beyond endurance. I wanted to see Michael Flowers discomforted.

I said, 'The Sugdens were yeomen farmers and were mentioned in the Domesday Book, and the Moles were believed to be Mexican refugees who fled religious persecution, and came to England on the return journey of the *Mayflower*.'

Flowers tugged at his beard and muttered, 'Mexicans.' Then he left the room, saying, 'I have wood to chop.'

Marigold walked me to the car in silence.

Just before I drove away she said, 'That was terribly cruel of you. The *Mayflower* made no return journey.'

She put her frail hands underneath her glasses and wiped her eyes.

I apologized and once more heard myself making a date to see her again.

As I drove through the gently undulating Leicestershire countryside, I thought about Mr Carlton-Hayes. I know nothing about his private life. He occasionally refers to his partner, Leslie. I have no idea if Leslie is a man or a woman.

It was dark when I drove into the car park at Rat Wharf, but I could see the white shape of Gielgud watching me from behind a clump of reeds as I got out of my car and ran to the entrance of the Old Battery Factory. He seems to take an unhealthy interest in my comings and goings.

Monday November 18th

Walked to work along the towpath. No sign of swans, but saw an alarming number of rats. At one time I felt like the Pied Piper of Hamelin.

Tuesday November 19th

When we were reorganizing the Travel section I asked Mr Carlton-Hayes if he had any children. He said he had a son, Marius, who was in a secure mental hospital and a daughter, Claudia, who worked in Ethiopia, distributing food for UNICEF. He said, 'Leslie and I are awfully proud of them,' then added quietly, 'both of them'. I still don't know if Leslie is the mother of his children or a male soul mate.

Parvez paid me an unexpected visit tonight. When I opened the door he was panting and sweating, having been chased by 'a bloody great white thing' across the car park.

I told him that it was almost certainly Gielgud the swan.

Parvez said, 'A.S.C.B.A.M.A.Y.K.'

He looked around my apartment and admired my new furniture, then he asked me awkward accountant-type questions. Eventually I cracked and admitted I'd got a store card. He clapped a hand to his head dramatically and said, 'Where is it?'

I took it out of my wallet and handed it to him. He searched in his pocket, found a small Swiss Army knife, prised out the mini scissors and cut my card in half. He said, 'You'll thank me for this one day.'

I didn't tell him that there was only £89 left to spend on it and that I owed Debenhams £9,911.

Parvez asked me if I was going to the Neil Armstrong Comprehensive reunion on Saturday night.

I said that wild horses would not drag me to such an occasion, and that the thought of seeing such dullards as Brain-box Henderson and the rest of my classmates filled me with horror.

*

I need every penny I can get, so I wrote to Latesun Ltd, threatening legal action unless they sent me a cheque for £57.10 immediately. I said that Britain was preparing to invade Iraq on the grounds that Saddam Hussein had Weapons of Mass Destruction. What more proof did head office need?

Wednesday November 20th
Full Moon

After work I took Marigold to Wong's for a meal. She was wearing what looked like a giant romper suit in a pink fleece fabric.

Wayne Wong asked me if I was going to the Neil Armstrong reunion.

I said that I had other things planned and Marigold smiled and squeezed my hand.

Wayne added, 'Pandora's coming up from London especially. She's giving a long-service medal to Miss Fossington-Gore, who's retiring at the end of term. Barry Kent's coming an' all. He's bought a minibus for the school.'

Marigold said, 'You don't mean *the* Barry Kent, the novelist and poet, do you?'

Wayne said, 'Adrian was in Barry's gang at school.'

'Only for a week,' I said.

'Oh, I love his stuff,' breathed Marigold. 'I can recite his poems off by heart. Do you think you could get him to sign my copies of his books?'

I mumbled something about if I ran into him.

'Why don't we go on Saturday?' said Marigold.

I did not like her use of the word 'we'. I did not want to parade Marigold in front of my friends, especially Pandora.

I said that I would be working on my *Celebrity and Madness* book on Saturday night. But this was a lie. Nothing on earth would keep me from seeing Pandora, even if I have to share her with my ageing school mates.

I drove Marigold home. She kept her head turned away and looked out of the car window, though there was nothing to see. Every now and again she sniffed and blew her nose. At one point I asked her if she was crying.

She said, 'I haven't met any of your friends. Are you ashamed of me?'

I said, 'You've met Wayne Wong.'

She said, 'That's only because you like Chinese food and he gives you a 10 per cent discount.' She went on, 'When am I going to meet your parents?'

I said, 'It wouldn't be good for you, Marigold. They both chain-smoke.'

She said, 'I could have a puff of my inhaler before being introduced.'

I was careful not to make a definite arrangement to see her again.

Thursday November 21st

I was woken this morning by the sound of scaffolding poles being thrown into a lorry. The building next door is due to open soon. As I walked past on my way to work, a sign was being erected above the door on what looked like a restaurant on the ground floor, the Casablanca.

I asked one of the scaffolders when it was due to open.

He said, 'Two months ago.'

I find the cynicism of the British workman utterly depressing.

Friday November 22nd

I sent a text to Brain-box Henderson, who is arranging the Neil Armstrong reunion, saying that I would be coming on Saturday night, and confirming that I would be prepared to pay £10 towards the buffet and the retirement gift for Miss Fossington-Gore.

Glenn rang to say that he had been posted to a secret location and was due to start his desert training.

When I asked him if he was in England, he said, 'Yes. But I can't say no more.'

He told me that Ryan was still threatening to beat me up.

I said sarcastically, 'Thanks for telling me, Glenn.'

He replied, 'That's OK, Dad. I thought you ought to know.' He put the phone down after saying, 'Goodnight, God bless.'

For curiosity I dialled 1471 and a robot gave me a number, which I dialled. After a few rings a voice said, 'Aldershot Barracks.' So much for security!

*

It was a busy day in the shop. Some people have already started their Christmas shopping. I sold a copy of *A Christmas Carol* for £25 and Mr Carlton-Hayes bought a copy of *Scoop* for £30 from an old man who was selling his Waugh collection to pay his gas bill.

I asked Mr Carlton-Hayes about Michael Flowers's aversion to Mexico. He laughed his gentle laugh and said that Flowers's first wife, Conchita, had been Mexican, but she had failed to settle in Leicestershire and had eventually run back to Mexico City with a pork butcher from Melton Mowbray.

Saturday November 23rd

I didn't know what to wear to the reunion. I rang Nigel for advice. He said, 'Wear what you feel comfortable in, Moley.'

It wasn't the moment to tell him that I never feel comfortable in any of my clothes. It isn't a question of fit or texture; it is a question of style. Who am I? And what do I want to say about myself?

I asked Nigel what he was wearing and he said, 'Paul Smith.'

I think Nigel is on to something. I ought to find a designer who matches my personality and stick to the one brand.

After a lot of dithering, I wore my Next navy suit, a white shirt and a red silk tie. I cut my fringe with the nail scissors and splashed myself liberally with Boss aftershave.

*

I picked Nigel up on the way. There was a frustrating wait while he stumbled around the granny annexe, 'looking' for his keys, coat and the white stick he has taken to using since he almost fell, Mr Magoo-like, into a workman's trench. I made no attempt to help him, as I have often heard blind people on the radio going on about how much they resent other people doing things for them.

After long minutes of fruitless searching, Nigel said, 'For Christ's sake, Moley, give me a hand.'

In the car I told Nigel that it was time he got himself organized and that he must learn to put things in the same place so that he knows where to find them each time. I asked him how he was coping financially now that he apparently had no income.

He said that he was living on disability allowance. To cheer him up, I made a joke. I said, 'So, it's goodbye to Paul Smith of Covent Garden and hello to George at Asda, is it?'

Nigel didn't even smile. He seems to have lost his sense of humour along with his sight.

I got him out of the car and escorted him across the car park and up to the school assembly hall. He kept dragging his feet and falling over his stick, and once he snapped, 'For Christ's sake, slow down. You're dragging me along as if I'm a bag of rubbish.'

We were greeted at the door of the assembly hall by an old bald bloke wearing nerd glasses and a Norman Wisdom-type suit. It was Brain-box Henderson, who is an old fogey at thirty-five.

We paid our £10 and Henderson gave us raffle tickets in return. The first prize was a tour of the House of Commons and tea on the terrace with Pandora. Second prize was a first edition signed copy of *Aden Vole* by Barry Kent. Third prize was a giant teddy bear donated by Elizabeth Sally Stafford (née Broadway), who was now running her own interior design company.

Some of my former school mates had changed out of all recognition. Claire Neilson, who once had tangled blonde curls and luscious lips, was now a tense, twitchy woman who kept looking at her watch and wondering aloud if the children were in bed.

Craig Thomas waved from behind the double decks of his mobile disco, Funk Down Sounds. He was wearing a baseball cap, back to front. He was the only one dancing to Michael Jackson's 'Billy Jean'.

Barbara Bowyer and Victoria Louise Thomson were standing at the makeshift bar, slagging off the absent Pandora, saying that she had done nothing for women since she'd been in office.

When they saw me and Nigel, they screamed, 'Aidy! Nige!' And ran to embrace us. I asked Victoria Louise what she did for a living and she said, 'I marry increasingly older men, darling.'

She is currently divorcing number three and planning to marry number four. Later on that night I heard her saying, 'I can't remember the last time I peeled a vegetable. I think it must have been 1995.'

Barbara Bowyer was easily the most beautiful woman in the room. She used to be the ward sister in the Coronary

Care Unit at the Royal Hospital, but she's now training to be a heating engineer.

She said, 'It's still pipes, pumps and valves, but double the money.'

I said jokingly, 'You can drain my pipe any time you like,' but I don't think she could have heard me, because she turned away and speared a chipolata with a toothpick.

A group of elderly people were sitting at a corner table. Claire said, 'Just look at that lot. How come that collection of clapped-out geriatrics used to put the fear of God in us?'

The old people were our teachers: Miss Fossington-Gore (Geography), Mr Jones (PE), Miss Elf (Drama), Mr Dock (English). Sitting with them was the current headmaster, Roger Patience, who once predicted that Glenn 'would never make anything of himself'.

Mr Dock was looking longingly towards the bar, so I beckoned him over and bought him half a pint. He was delighted to learn that I was working for Mr Carlton-Hayes.

'I remember you, Mole,' he said. 'You were the only lad I ever taught who cried when Lenny murdered the girl in *Of Mice and Men*.'

Nigel said waspishly, 'Moley cries at the drop of a hat. I caught him blubbering over a dead hamster in *Animal Hospital* one afternoon.'

When Mr Dock returned to his table, I joined him and talked to the teachers.

Mr Jones said that he did not remember me. I told

him that I was nearly always ill on PE days. He said, 'But there were so many.'

I said, 'It was my dog that ran off with the football in the last five minutes of the final of the inter-counties schools match between Leicestershire and Bedfordshire.'

'Ah, yes, I do remember you now,' said Jones. 'You once brought a note to me purporting to be from your mother, "Adrian has got diarrhoea through holes in his shoes."'

Oh, how the table of old educators laughed.

Mr Dock said, 'Did he spell diarrhoea correctly?'

Jones said, 'How would I know? I taught PE.'

By 9.30 the room had filled up a bit, the sandwiches on the buffet table had started to curl slightly at the sides and a few people were dancing to Boy George singing 'Do You Really Want to Hurt Me?'

Nigel seemed to be the centre of attention. He was surrounded by sympathetic women offering to come to his annexe to clean and do his washing and ironing.

There was a hooting from the car park and Brain-box Henderson shouted over the music, 'Come and see the new minibus.'

Kent was behind the wheel of a white minibus with his shaved head and leather jacket, from which hung heavy silver chains. A seven-foot-tall minder wearing a dark overcoat got out of the passenger seat and said to the small crowd, 'Keep away from Mr Kent, please. He don't like being touched. And no photos. He don't want no publicity.'

Roger Patience was summoned and an awkward little

ceremony took place, during which Barry Kent handed over the keys and logbook.

The two men made startlingly hypocritical speeches.

Kent said that his days at Neil Armstrong Comprehensive had been the happiest of his life.

Patience said that Barry Kent had 'by all accounts been a challenging but brilliant young man who had brought honour to the school'. Then he got behind the wheel of the minibus and started the engine.

Brain-box Henderson put his large head through the driver's open window and said, 'Mr Patience, have you passed the local authority minibus driving test?'

Patience admitted that he had not and took his foot off the accelerator.

Pandora rang me on my mobile to tell me that she was just coming up to Junction 21 and would be with us soon. She said, 'Is there any food left? I'm fucking famished.'

I told her that the buffet had curled up and died and offered to take her out for a meal after she had performed her duties. She made a noncommittal sound and rang off.

I joined Wayne Wong, Parvez and Victoria Louise, who were smoking by the bike sheds in the playground. We had a good laugh about Brain-box Henderson's shrunken suit, Miss Fossington-Gore's beard and moustache, and Craig Thomas's pathetic disco.

Pandora's silver Saab turned into the car park, scattering gravel. I hurried over to open the driver's door. She sat in the car for a while, brushing her hair and applying lipstick.

I told her that she looked tired.

She said, 'Gee, thanks.'

She joined the smokers by the bike sheds, saying, 'I need a fag before I go inside and face the grizzly Fossington-Gore.'

Brain-box Henderson hurried over and advised Pandora to keep her tribute to Miss Fossington-Gore short as they were running late and the caretaker wanted to have the hall cleared by 11.

Pandora said, 'No probs.' She stubbed her Benson's out on a bike rack and we went inside.

'Sexual Healing' had drawn people on to the dance floor. There was an excited murmur when Pandora made her entrance, and Roger Patience broke off from fawning over Barry Kent to go forward and greet Pandora, and to formally welcome her back to the school.

Brain-box Henderson hurried to the mobile disco and asked Craig Thomas to turn Marvin Gaye off. He then tapped on the side of a wine glass with a fork and silence fell.

Brain-box then led Pandora, Roger Patience and Miss Fossington-Gore on to the stage, where there was a Formica table on which stood a large gift-wrapped box.

There was a lot of clapping and whistling, and Barry Kent made a yee-haw sound, like a cowboy riding a bucking bronco at a rodeo.

Roger Patience went on about Pandora, telling the audience that she spoke five languages fluently, including

Russian and Mandarin (as if we didn't know!), that she got a double first at Oxford, that she was the Labour member for Ashby de la Zouch and that she was a junior minister in the Department of the Environment. He said these were all great achievements, but he was sure that Pandora's greatest triumphs were yet to come – that the *Daily Telegraph* had hinted recently that Pandora could well be Britain's first woman Labour prime minister – 'So, Gordon Brown watch out!'

There was polite laughter. Then Pandora, looking magnificent in a tailored Lauren Bacall jacket and what looked like men's trousers, addressed us. She started, 'Let me make it absolutely clear that without the guidance and inspirational teaching of Miss Fossington-Gore I would not be here today – at least, not in my capacity as Member of Parliament and Junior Minister. It was Miss Fossington-Gore who said, on hearing of my ambition to be a catwalk model for the House of Balenciaga, "Oh, I'm sure we can do a little better than that, dear."'

Miss Fossington-Gore bowed her head modestly.

Pandora blabbed on mostly about herself and her achievements for another five minutes. Then she handed the gift-wrapped box to Miss Fossington-Gore and said, 'I'm sure this will look lovely on your mantelpiece. May the hours and minutes it records of your retirement be precious.'

Miss Fossington-Gore took a small handkerchief from under the cuff of her cardigan suit and said, 'The class of '83 was quite remarkable. Not only did it have Pandora Braithwaite, it also had Barry Kent. And let us not forget Adrian Mole, whose TV series, *Offally Good!*, I quite enjoyed. I would, before I open my present, like to say a few words about Nigel.' She gestured towards Nigel, who was sitting down with his white stick held in front of him like those old blokes in Greek cafés. 'Nigel has been terrifically brave since suffering severe sight impairment.'

I looked across at Nigel and saw him swearing under his breath. There was a huge round of applause and stamping and cheering for Nigel's bravery.

Then Miss Fossington-Gore, who is a vegan and who lives alone in a one-bedroom flat, painstakingly opened her present and found a George Foreman family-size grill. However, good breeding and a lifetime of repressing her true feelings saved the day, and she gave a gracious little speech thanking the assembled company for their kindness and generosity.

When told what the present was, Nigel gave a bitter laugh and said, 'Will it fit her mantelpiece?'

Barry Kent was invited on to the stage to draw the raffle. He turned a simple task into something akin to lighting the Olympic flame. Claire Neilson, who had gone home to check on her children, won the giant teddy bear. By a cruel irony, the second prize was won by Nigel, and the first prize was won, to Pandora's considerable disgust, by Brain-box Henderson.

Kent then left for East Midlands Airport, saying that he had to meet a publisher in Amsterdam in the morning.

I am amazed, diary, at how much I still dislike Barry Kent and how much I long for his downfall.

*

When the caretaker came in jangling his keys, Craig put on 'Every Breath You Take' and announced that it was to be the last record. I asked Pandora if she would like to dance and amazingly she agreed.

She is slightly taller than me in high heels, but I have reached the age where it no longer matters quite as much as it once did.

I sang along with Sting, 'I'll be watching you', until Pandora asked me to stop. But for once she didn't try to lead and allowed me to shuffle her around the dance floor.

I am, of course, still madly in love with her. She has spoiled me for any other female. She is a ten-out-of-ten woman, whereas Marigold is, tragically, two and a half, or perhaps three on a good day.

I asked Pandora if she would like to join a group of intimates for dinner at the Imperial Dragon, explaining that Wayne Wong would give us a 10 per cent discount.

She said, 'You're still penny-pinching then?'

I replied, 'On the contrary, I've just forked almost 10,000 quid out to furnish my new canalside loft at Rat Wharf.'

However, for the second time that night she surprised me and agreed to come to dinner.

Pandora, Nigel, Parvez, Barbara, Victoria Louise and I shared an Emperor's Banquet. We sat at a large round table. I sat in between Nigel and Pandora. I asked the waiter, Wayne's brother, Keith Wong, to take Nigel's chopsticks away and bring a fork and spoon, explaining that this would make life easier for Nigel as he was almost blind.

To my astonishment, Nigel had a mini temper tantrum and demanded that Keith return his chopsticks.

Nigel said, 'Keep your nose out, Mole,' and turned his back to me and talked to Parvez about his finances.

Parvez said, 'You're not as badly off as Adrian. He's saddled himself with a pile of debts.'

I said, 'Parvez, don't accountants take a vow of silence, or a Hippocratic oath or something? My finances are not a suitable subject for dinner-table conversation.'

Barbara Bowyer asked Pandora what Tony and Cherie were 'really like'.

Pandora said, 'I'm keeping my trap shut about the Blairs. Adrian keeps a diary, you know.'

Nigel said, 'You'd better not write anything about me.'

I said, 'Don't flatter yourself, Nigel.' And I said to Pandora, 'Your secrets are safe with me. My diary is not for publication.'

Pandora said, 'That's what that creepy butler Paul Burrell said. I hear he's toting Diana's secrets around.'

'And anyway,' said Nigel, 'who would be interested in publishing the diary of a provincial nonentity?'

I took a prawn cracker from the lazy Susan in the middle of the table and bit into it to disguise how much his remark had hurt me.

At 11.45 p.m. my mobile rang. It was Marigold, asking me how the writing was going. Unfortunately, at that moment Keith Wong was serving the next course, shouting, 'OK, you got yuck sung, you got seaweed, you got prawn toasts, you got wantons, and you got vegetable spring rolls.'

Marigold said, 'Where are you?'

I thought about lying and saying it was the television in the background, but Marigold knew that ntl had not yet connected my television, so I was forced to tell the truth.

Pandora laughed at a joke Parvez made.

Marigold said, 'Who are you with?'

Pandora said suggestively, 'Can I help you to a spring roll, Aidy, darling?'

Marigold said, 'Who is that?'

I left the table and walked over to the fish tank. A large carp swam to the glass. It looked disconcertingly like Marigold without her glasses. I gained courage and said to the fish, 'Look, Marigold, this is not working for me. Perhaps we shouldn't see each other again.'

She said in a flat voice, 'You're with another woman, aren't you?'

I said I was with three women and two men.

Marigold sobbed, 'Three couples.'

I said, 'Please, don't cry.'

She said, 'I've spent all evening working on a loft apartment doll's house. It was going to be your Christmas present.'

I didn't know how to break off the conversation. It seemed heartless to point out to Marigold that my food was getting cold. I had to let her ramble on about her disastrous track record with men. The carp in the tank continued to stare mournfully at me. I could see my reflection in the glass. I looked a bit mournful myself.

Eventually Marigold rang off, saying in that spooky flat voice, 'There's no point in living without you.'

The fish swam to the bottom of the tank and lay there without moving. I went back to the table. Keith Wong was putting down a dish of duck and pineapple, but when I pronged a bit with a chopstick it tasted like sawdust in my mouth.

I drank four tiny cups of sake and told my dinner companions about Marigold. The general consensus was that Marigold had to go.

Wayne Wong said, 'No offence, Aidy, but you can do a lot better. She ain't exactly a laugh a minute, is she?'

Pandora said, 'She sounds like one of those snivelling whiny types that give women a bad name.'

Nigel said, 'But any woman who fell for Adrian would have to be half off her rocker.'

Then Pandora said, 'You forget, Nigel, that I was once in love with Adrian myself.' She took my hand and held it. 'We were both fourteen. We were going to live in a farmhouse and have lots of children. Adrian was going to be an ice-cream man during the day and I was going to milk cows and bake bread and wait for him to come home.'

Suddenly we were both weeping. 'It's that fucking rice wine,' said Pandora. 'It always does this to me.'

Nigel broke the party up by saying he had to get up early in the morning, because a woman from the RNIB was coming to interview him to vet his suitability for a guide dog.

Parvez, being a Muslim, was the only one sober enough to drive, so the rest of us left our cars parked outside the restaurant and we squeezed into Parvez's people carrier and I invited everybody back to Rat Wharf for a nightcap.

Gielgud was waiting for me in the car park, but I scared him off with a Star Wars light sabre belonging to Ali, Parvez's youngest son, which had been left in the car.

I switched the lamps on and made coffee and warned everybody about the glass lavatory. People went out on to the balcony and Pandora said how beautiful the swans looked in the moonlight. I hoped that, for once, Gielgud wouldn't spoil the party.

Sunday November 24th

Parvez took everyone home except Pandora. We stayed up talking until it was almost light. She told me about the terrible workload she had, of how she could never get on top of the paperwork, of how the press monitored her every statement. She was almost certainly under constant surveillance. She knew for sure that her phones were tapped, and said that it was a relief to be able to talk openly and freely with an old and trusted friend.

I said, 'We should have moved into that farmhouse, Pandora.'

She laughed and said, 'It's a real shame that we were not sexually compatible.'

I pointed out to her that her theory had never been tested. However, I made no move in that direction and neither did she.

*

At 5 a.m. I rang for a taxi, and when I heard it blaring its horn in the car park I escorted her to its door.

Just as I was preparing myself to sleep on the futon, my phone rang and left a text message from Pandora. It said:

Thanks, Aidy. I do love you, Pan.

My mobile rang again at 7.30 a.m. It was Marigold, telling me that she had written me a letter explaining to me why she had done what she had done. She put the phone down. I immediately rang back. The phone rang and rang. Eventually Michael Flowers picked the phone up and bellowed, 'Who is this?'

I told him it was me and he said, 'It's 7.35 on a Sunday morning. This is terribly inconsiderate of you. I realize you're besotted with Marigold, but you must try and restrain your passion. Come to lunch. I've got something to show you.'

I heard myself asking, 'What time?'

It was a gruesome meal, not only badly cooked and gracelessly served, but a meatless, flavourless repast served with cloudy home-made beer poured from an earthenware jug.

A smoky log fire burned half-heartedly in the grate in the dining room. Through the window, a row of forlorn frozen brassicas could be seen in the garden. A robin perched on the handle of a deserted spade, unaware that it had become a living cliché.

Marigold's eyes were swollen with crying. Every now

and again throughout the meal, she pressed pads of cotton wool impregnated with witch hazel to puffy eyes.

Netta Flowers tried to enlist my help in stewarding a 'Stop the War March' she was organizing in Beeby on the Wold.

I said, 'I doubt if you will need stewards. I can't imagine that there will be tens of thousands thronging the village green.'

She said that she had received messages of support from Little Snetton, Frisby on the Wreake, Long Lampton, Shepshed, Melton Mowbray, Short under Curtly and Burrow twixt Soar.

I interrupted her recitation of these centres of civil disobedience and said that I fully supported Mr Blair's stand against Saddam Hussein and his Weapons of Mass Destruction.

I asked Marigold for her opinions about a possible war in Iraq. She looked down at her plate of badly cooked root vegetables and said, 'I think war is wrong. Why can't people be nice to each other?'

Perhaps she is an idiot savant.

After lunch was over I offered to wash up. To my considerable annoyance, Netta Flowers said, 'That would be super. And you'll find clean tea towels drying on the Aga.'

So I was obviously expected to wash and dry.

Marigold said that I would find her in the attic after I'd finished.

The Flowers family make their own washing-up liquid out of lemon and glycerine and keep it in a screw-top jar next to the sink. When it came to washing the burnt roasting pans, I went into the sitting room and asked if there was a Brillo Pad in the house. You would have thought from the consternation and shock this caused to Mr and Mrs Flowers that I had asked then to hold down a baby seal while I clubbed it to death.

Finally, when the last battered tin and chipped crockery had been put away, Michael Flowers led me to his study and invited me to 'peruse his library shelves and give a quick valuation'.

I told him that Mr Carlton-Hayes did the valuations and explained that I was still a novice in the antiquarian and second-hand book trade.

He said, 'Give me a ball-park figure, a guesstimate.'

I said that it would take many hours of work and that I would need reference books etc.

He plucked a book off a shelf and said, 'This, for instance.'

It was *Tales of an Empty Cabin* by Grey Owl. It was in a slip case, a little scuffed and stained but sound. I took the book out and opened it. It was the Lovat Dickson 1936 edition and was signed 'Grey Owl.'

I examined the book more carefully and said to Flowers, 'The cloth boards are a little scuffed. The spine is faded. The top gilt edge is nice, but the fore and lower edges are a bit foxed, and it's a shame that the ribbon bookmark has lost its colour.'

'So, how much?' said Flowers impatiently.

I looked at the sepia illustrations and at the colour plate of Grey Owl's strong face in his Indian headdress, and I wanted the book for myself. I knew that the book that I was holding in my hand was worth at least £250.

I was barely able to control my voice. I asked as casually as I could, 'Do you have any more books by Grey Owl?'

Flowers said that he had collected them at one time, but when he saw the film starring Pierce Brosnan and he found out that Grey Owl was a fraud and was really an Englishman called Archie Belaney, he no longer wanted the fraudster's books in his house.

I told Flowers that the book might fetch £50 and offered to take it off his hands. Flowers seemed pleased enough and hunted along the shelves for his remaining Grey Owls.

The other books he had were *Men of the Last Frontier*, *Pilgrims of the Wild* and *Sajo and Her Beaver People*. They were all first editions and signed by the author. All three were in fair condition. My mouth watered. I told Michael Flowers that the books would probably fetch £200.

Flowers said, 'That will go towards the council tax for the bloody shop.'

As I write this now I feel ashamed of myself. I have always wanted to be an honest person. When faced with a moral dilemma of any kind, I have asked myself what George Orwell would do. But it is Michael Flowers's fault. He brings out the worst in me.

I joined Marigold in the attic. She was laying strips of varnished wood on to the floor of a loft apartment doll's house. On her work bench was a tiny white sofa and a futon bed, and on a mini balcony sitting on a little metal chair was me, Adrian Mole, wearing a white bathrobe and glasses; and on the other chair was Marigold, wearing her khaki trouser suit and red beret outfit. The two dolls were holding hands.

I noticed with alarm that on the cloth middle finger of each doll's hand was a matching gold-coloured band.

Marigold said, 'I've got something to tell you. Please sit down.'

I sat on a paint-spattered old chair.

Marigold did a lot of face twitching and hair twirling. She threw her head back and gazed into the eaves, she examined her nails, she sighed, then she said in a small voice, 'I have decided to offer myself to you. Sexually, I mean. You have been a perfect gentleman so far, but I feel that our relationship has now entered a different phase. It may surprise you, darling, that I am relatively sexually inexperienced, but I now feel that I am ready to put my heart, my soul, my body into your care.'

I felt my genitals wither as she spoke. I had to get away. I told her that I was unworthy of her, that I was vastly sexually experienced, and that I had had many lovers, not only in this country but abroad as well. I said that I was not the quite boring man she thought I was, that I was an unpleasant devious person who would break her heart one day. But this seemed to excite her and she lunged at me, then fell on my lap and kissed my neck.

As you know, diary, my neck is my Achilles' heel. One thing led to another and, within the space of a minute, I was fumbling with her bra strap.

She said huskily, 'Slide the board into the hatch.'

It was some time before I realized that this was not sexual linguistics, but that she literally wanted me to secure our privacy by sliding the cover over the open hatch to the attic.

In doing so my ardour cooled a little, but the sight of her pretty breasts and rosy nipples revived me, and it wasn't long before we were engaging in sexual intercourse on a pile of old fur coats that had been thrown into a dark corner of the attic.

As soon as I had come to my senses and after telling her she was beautiful etc., etc., etc., I asked her if she was on the pill.

She said that she didn't believe in putting chemicals into her body.

As I write this, diary, I wish that I had not put anything into her body.

As I was climbing down the loft ladder I got a text message:

Where are you, Aidy? I'm at Rat Wharf. Love Pandora.

I almost certainly exceeded the speed limit in my rush to get to Rat Wharf, but I was too late. Pandora sent me another text to say that she was on the motorway going back to London.

Monday November 25th

Mr Carlton-Hayes valued the four Grey Owls at £725. I told him that the books belonged to Michael Flowers and that I had estimated their total value at £200.

Mr Carlton-Hayes said, 'And was the dreadful Michael Flowers happy [pronounced heppy] with that [pronounced thet]?'

I said, 'He seemed pitifully grateful. I think he's on his way to Carey Street.'

Mr Carlton-Hayes was delighted at my literary reference.

He phoned a private collector of Canadian frontier history and gently reminded the boff of the rarity of finding four signed Grey Owl first editions. The boff said he had sold his collection to pay for his daughter's college fees. Mr Carlton-Hayes commiserated with him and phoned a bloke who collects fraudsters' signed first editions, Josh Pullman in Brighton, who immediately offered £1,000 for the set.

Apparently Mr Pullman's Jeffrey Archer collection is second to none. I went out to Brucciani's and bought two takeaway cappuccinos and two of their split cream buns to celebrate the sale, and also to mark a significant anniversary. It is a year since I started work at Carlton-Hayes Antiquarian and Second hand Books. I admire my employer more than any person I have ever met. He is up there with Nelson Mandela and Tony Blair. He can even eat a split cream bun with dignity.

On my way to the post office to post Mr Pullman his books, I took a cheque for £200 to Michael Flowers.

Marigold was behind the counter. Her eyes were still puffy. There was nobody in the shop. Marigold said that her parents were at the bank, having an emergency meeting with the business accounts manager.

She came from behind the counter and kissed my neck. But this time it left me cold and I was relieved when she said, 'Have you heard the latest news? The Madrigal Society is amalgamating with some members of the cathedral choir and they are calling themselves the Leicester Mummers.'

I said no, I had not heard this earth-shattering news. I continued, 'Have you phoned the *Guardian* and asked them to hold the front page? Does the editor of the *Today Programme* know? Have you phoned CNN?'

Marigold said, 'Adrian, sarcasm is the lowest form of wit.'

I said that I was not being sarcastic, I was being satirical.

She said that she had joined the Mummers and would be rehearsing or performing most evenings before Christmas. She invited me to join the group, but her invitation was only half-hearted.

I said, 'Surprisingly, Marigold, I do not wish to dress up as a yokel in a smock and mask and perform in deeply unfunny medieval plays on cold village greens to a scornful or indifferent public. There are some traditions which should be allowed to die – madrigals, mummery and Morris dancing.'

Marigold said, 'I told Mummy and Daddy last night that we had become lovers. They are very happy for us. Mummy gave me a box of organic condoms. The latex is made in Malaysia under fair trade conditions. Daddy said that you can sleep in my bed on Saturdays and Thursdays.'

An old bloke came in and asked for a packet of sunflower seeds. While she was serving him, I took the opportunity to leave the shop without making a date to see her again.

Tuesday November 26th

I received a redirected letter this morning from Ms Ruth Rendell, regretting that she could not join the Leicestershire and Rutland Creative Writing Group on December 23rd as she would be in Australia.

This reminded me that I have got to tackle the Gladys Fordingbridge problem. I will do it tomorrow.

I have also decided to ask Mr Carlton-Hayes for a rise. My mortgage and store card payments are due next week. My wages, after tax and National Insurance, are £ 1,083.33 a month, and I have a horrible feeling that my mortgage, Visa and store card payments are in excess of £900. Perhaps I should sit down and work out my monthly outgoings. I can't afford to hire Parvez, not at £125 an hour.

Wednesday November 27th
Moon's Last Quarter

I telephoned Gladys and arranged to go round at 7.30, so when Marigold rang I was able to tell her, truthfully, that I was visiting an old lady and would not be able to see her after mummery rehearsals.

Gladys has found a publisher for her cat poems. A community worker at the old people's club she attends on Monday afternoons has convinced her that her poetry 'is really, really good'. She has said that Gladys's 'voice must be heard'. She is to be published by Grey Panther Community Press.

She read me her latest poem:

> 'Naughty paws
> Lives indoors
> Doesn't stray
> From the litter tray
> He loves his Whiskas
> But will never throw a discus
> No athlete he
> He stays near me
> I love my paws
> He stays indoors.'

She wanted my advice on what to call her book. I suggested *Poems about Cats*, but Gladys said that was too plain and she wanted something a bit fancy.

I said cruelly, 'Then call it *Contemplations on our Feline Friends*,' and Gladys said, 'That's champion. Thank you, Mr Mole.'

I lied and told Gladys that, according to the rules of the Leicestershire and Rutland Creative Writing Group, she would have to leave because, once published, she would have to renounce her amateur status.

She seemed quite proud of this and even asked if she could dedicate the book to me.

I said that I would be delighted, but I did not feel proud of myself as I wished her luck with the book and left her house for the last time.

Thursday November 28th

Spent an uncomfortable night in Marigold's single bed, which she has had since she was a small girl. It is the shape of Cinderella's coach.

Marigold said, 'It was hand-made by a crafts person and painted by a disabled retiree.'

In the morning I woke to find parallel lines running down one side of my face, having been pressed against a carved pumpkin all night.

The sex was fair to middling and lasted about seven minutes.

Friday November 29th

Had sex with Marigold on futon at Rat Wharf. We both had to keep our vests on as the underfloor heating didn't seem to be working.

Saturday November 30th

Considering there are only three Saturdays left before Christmas, business was very slow. The shop was full of browsers at times, but hardly anybody bought anything.

On the way back from the post office I was handed a flyer by a dopey-looking youth in a woolly hat. It said:

Randy Applestein,
America's Mr Motivator,
is holding a seminar in the Garden Room
at the Great Eastern Hotel in Leicester on
Sunday December 8th.

Treble your turnover,
Achieve your Life Goals,
Look good – feel good.

Power breakfast and lunch included.
Money-back guarantee.

I asked the dopey youth in the bobble hat if he had attended a seminar himself. He said that he had.

I gave the leaflet back to him and said, 'The seminar obviously didn't work for you. I hope you got your money back.'

My parents came into the shop. They were looking for building manuals. My father looked uncomfortable. The proximity of so many books makes him nervous. Since leaving school, he has only finished one book, *Jonathan Livingstone Seagull*.

He said, 'Aidy, have you got anything on pigsty conversion?'

I pretended to look along the shelves, and then said with a heavy irony which was lost on him, 'No, we don't seem to have anything in at the moment. There's been quite a rush on pigsty conversion manuals.'

He looked pleased to hear this, and said, 'Yeah, John Prescott has opened up the can of worms that used to tie up greenfield development. He's beckoned me and your mother inside.'

I said, 'Inside what, the can of worms?'

He said, 'No, the greenfield with the pigsties in it. Me and your mum are surfing the crest of a new trend.'

I laughed in his face. My father is ill equipped to spot a trend: he was the last man in Leicester to give up flared trousers.

My mother collected a hefty pile of manuals on bricklaying, joinery, electrical wiring and plumbing, and stacked them on the counter.

Mr Carlton-Hayes tied them together with brown string and made a loop for ease of carrying.

My mother said to him, 'You could do with a few chairs in here, Mr Carlton-Hayes.'

To my amazement, he said, 'Yes, I was thinking of bringing some from home.'

My mother said, 'And the smell of coffee is always attractive in a bookshop.'

He said, 'Do you think so, Mrs Mole?'

'Oh, yes,' she said. 'If you give your customers a free cup of coffee, they feel obliged to buy something.'

I said mockingly, 'And how about a mince pie and a slice of Yule log, and a chocolate Santa for the children?'

Mr Carlton-Hayes said, 'That's rather a charming idea.'

I had a horrible vision of a badly behaved kid smearing chocolate over some of our precious books.

Once started, my mother could not stop. 'You could unblock that fireplace,' she said, pointing to the boarded-up chimney breast. 'A Christmas tree in the window with fairy lights would be welcoming.' She half closed her eyes and seemed to sway a little, lost in a reverie of refurbishment.

Mr Carlton-Hayes was like a benign snake, hypnotized by its charmer. He was caught up in my mother's vision of Christmas past. And to my astonishment he allowed my father to pull away the sheet of plywood that was blocking the fireplace. A dusty and sooty fire grate was revealed, a leftover from when Mr Arthur Carlton-Hayes founded the shop in 1929.

My mother continued to interfere and rang a chimney sweep and arranged to have the chimney swept on Tuesday morning.

Then, while I served a late surge of customers, she and Mr Carlton-Hayes began to plan to convert the shop. I wondered to myself who would cart the logs, brew the coffee, buy the mince pies and wash everything up afterwards.

My mother suggested to Mr Carlton-Hayes that we go and eat somewhere *en famille*. He said that he would like to join us but that he would have to phone Leslie first. I told her about my 10 per cent discount at the Imperial Dragon.

Wayne Wong told my mother that Pandora had spent last Saturday night at Rat Wharf, and then said, 'I'm glad you've finished with that weirdo, Marigold.'

I informed him coldly that I had not yet finished with Marigold and that I would be seeing her later that night. He said that he was sorry to hear it. My mother was agog, of course.

She said, 'Why don't you phone her and ask her to join us?'

I explained that she was at mummery practice at the cathedral. I watched my mother's face carefully. She managed to keep it straight, and Mr Carlton-Hayes appeared to be engrossed in the menu, though I did notice that his eyebrow twitched when I said the word 'mummery'.

My father always gets overexcited in restaurants and tonight was no exception. He kept getting up and going to look at the fish in the aquarium and tapping on the glass.

My mother had to keep saying, 'George, don't do that.' She sounded like a recording of Joyce Grenfell.

Mr Carlton-Hayes was an artist with the chopstick. Even Wayne complimented him. Mr C-H murmured that he had spent some time in Indo-China, but seemed reluctant to go into detail.

Even before the main course came, my mother was advising Wayne on how to do a makeover on the restaurant, saying that he should get rid of the old-fashioned dragon motif and clad the walls with animal-skin prints.

Over a Christmas Banquet Special at £12.99 a head, I was interrogated by my mother about my long-term aims in life. Did I intend to marry again? Was my dream still to be a full-time professional writer? Or did I see my future in selling antiquarian and second-hand books?

I said that I was happy in my job and hoped that I would be working for Mr Carlton-Hayes for many years to come.

He looked a bit sad and said, 'Our little shop is losing rather a lot of money each week. It's been kept afloat in recent years by income from investments, but the stock exchange has not been kind to me recently.'

I said, 'Mr Carlton-Hayes, perhaps we ought to call in a business consultant.'

He said, 'But don't they cost a fearful amount of money?'

My father said, 'You have to spend brass to make brass.'

He sounded like a cruel mill owner who was about to shackle a small child mill worker to a spinning jenny.

Using the paper tablecloth, I wrote out a simple business plan for the shop. There were four bullet points:

- Open a section selling a selection of new titles
- Start a readers' club
- Buy a coffee machine
- Introduce chairs

Had sex with Marigold in coach bed, as ordered by Mr Michael Flowers.

Sunday December 1st

Somebody moved into one of the apartments this morning. When I went to get the papers there was a removal van parked in the car park. The swans were on the opposite bank, menacing a fisherman.

Barry Kent was in the *Sunday Times*. It was a feature called 'How I Spend My Money'. He told the interviewer, Topaz Scroggins, that he gives his huge income mostly to charity, but he apparently begged Topaz not to reveal this in the paper. Topaz wrote, 'I hope he will not feel betrayed, but I felt that the readers of this newspaper should know that Barry Kent, despite his gritty, uncompromising image, is a true humanitarian who wears his genius lightly.'

Monday December 2nd

I got a House of Commons Christmas card from Pandora, an obscene picture of a snowman with the carrot in the wrong place from Aunty Susan and a letter from Glenn.

Dear Dad

I think the war might be kicking off. We done some desert training today. Me and Sergeant Brighouse went to the builder's merchants and ordered ten tons of sand for the same-day delivery. Sergeant Brighouse told me that if he had ordered the sand through army supplies it would have took three months to come. Anyway, the sand came in the afternoon. We emptied the bags on the assault course and Sergeant Brighouse made me and the lads stand behind the heap, then he started the generator up and sand blew in our eyes. He was shouting, 'You're in the fucking desert now, you O-level reject bastards.'

Then he made us take our boots off and fill them with sand. Then we had to put them back on and run round the assault course until we was knackered. Then he shouted, 'Right, that's your fucking desert training done.'

Me and my best mate, Robbie Stainforth, have met two girls on the Internet. They are from Bristol and we are driving to see them on Sunday. Their photos are OK. I hope they are not fifty-year-olds with no teeth. I think you would like Robbie, Dad. He reads a lot of books and knows a lot about everything. When he seen me reading the *Sun* he set fire to it for a laugh.

  All the best, Dad

  Your son, Glenn

PS We might not get any leave this Christmas, but we can have parcels.

  Enclosed was a photograph of Glenn and Robbie Stainforth. They were in their khaki uniforms, holding a little trophy of a man with a fat belly throwing a dart. Robbie had a shy smile. I had forgotten that soldiers can wear glasses. On the back of the photograph Glenn had written, 'Me and Robbie was the finalists in the regimental pairs darts match, and we won. I was bought eleven pints by the lads. Dad, I have never felt so bad.'

I watched Rowan Williams being sworn in as Archbishop of Canterbury. He reminds me a little of Michael Flowers. I longed to take my nail scissors to his beard, and I suspect his wife cuts his hair. And I know Jesus wore sandals, but this is the twenty-first century. He is reputed to have a great brain and a powerful intellect. He certainly likes the sound of his own voice. He makes Donald Sinden sound like David Beckham. However, I wish him well. Being in charge of the Church of England must be as hard as Iain Duncan Smith trying to persuade Tories to vote Conservative.

*

Reply to Glenn's letter.

Dear Glenn

I don't know why Sergeant Brighouse made you do desert training, because you certainly won't be going to Iraq. If Saddam refuses to give up his Weapons of Mass Destruction there is bound to be a long-drawn-out period of negotiation. The diplomats will sort everything out. And anyway, you are too young. You are still only seventeen and are not old enough to fight. So rest assured, son, the nearest thing to danger you will experience this year will be meeting up with a girl you found on the Internet.

Have a good time, but remember to drive carefully on the M4. Keep well back from lorries. They are constantly jackknifing or shedding their loads, and white minibuses are notoriously accident-prone. Steer clear of them. A thousand people die on Britain's roads every year, and countless thousands are injured or permanently disabled.

Please don't drink eleven pints again. You are putting a terrible strain on your system, not to mention your bladder.

Make sure you have a condom with you. Bear in mind that over half of Britain's women have a sexually transmittable disease: 30 per cent have chlamydia, for instance, 20 per cent have genital warts and an unknown quantity have syphilis, which causes your nose to rot away and eventually fall off.

But have a good time in Bristol, son, and congratulations to you and Robbie on your darts triumph.

Love Dad

Tuesday December 3rd

Don't ask me why, but I had expected the chimney sweep to be a bow-legged little man covered in soot, wearing a flat cap and carrying circular brushes over one shoulder. However, the 'sweep' was wearing a suit, collar and tie, was perfectly groomed and had immaculately clean fingernails. He attached a bag over the opening of the fireplace and turned on a vacuum machine. It was all over in ten minutes.

I said, 'I don't suppose you officiate at many weddings nowadays, do you?'

He said that his grandfather used to hang about outside the church, dressed in traditional chimney sweep clothes, but had stopped doing it after an unfortunate incident with a bag of soot and a crinoline-styled white wedding dress.

I suggested to him that he should think about describing himself as a chimney sucker rather than a chimney sweep. But he seemed unwilling to take this on board.

The fireplace is very pretty. There are old-fashioned, tulip-patterned red tiles surrounding the grate.

I went to the BP garage at the bottom of the High Street and lugged back two mesh bags of logs. I went out again for matches and firelighters. When I got back I found Mr Carlton-Hayes tearing up strips of the *Guardian* and twisting them into spills for the fire. Don't ask me why, diary, but it was quite an emotional moment when Mr Carlton-Hayes touched the first firelighter with a *Guardian* spill. The little fire roared away and the logs began to spit and crack in the grate. Mr Carlton-Hayes had to stamp on some of the flying embers. Mindful of the recent announcement by the striking fire fighters' leader, Andy Gilchrist, that he intends to topple New Labour, I left the shop yet again and ran across the road to Debenhams and bought a fireguard.

Later we cleared a space around the fire by moving some bookshelves. We then amalgamated British Politics with American History, which made space for two armchairs.

The fire was an instant success. A teenage boy who came in looking for an aircraft book for his dad's Christmas present said it was the most realistic fire he had ever seen. When I told him the log fire was not a gas facsimile, he said the fire was cool.

Mr Carlton-Hayes joined us and said that it was a shame 'one couldn't buy coal these days'.

The youth said, 'Coal, what's that?'

Mr Carlton-Hayes patiently explained to the boy that once upon a time men descended into the bowels of the earth via a cage on a pit head pulley. Once there, they crawled on their hands and knees through dark tunnels until they reached what was called the coal face, whereupon they hacked at the coal with pickaxes. Coal was the fossilized remains of trees. Large lumps of coal were thrown on to a conveyor belt and taken to the surface of the mine, where it was broken into small pieces, put into hundredweight sacks and delivered by lorry to every household in the land, where it was burnt in fireplaces and kitchen ranges, supplying heat for comfort and for cooking.

The boy listened with something akin to wonder, reminding me of the famous oil painting of the old sailor mending his nets and telling two young boys about his maritime adventures.

The youth said, 'So have I got this right? You used to, like, chuck these lumps of black shiny stuff on to the fire and set them alight?'

I told the youth that in my boyhood coal had been superseded by electric storage heaters, which consisted of a pile of electrically heated bricks inside a metal box.

The boy's eyes widened further.

'My father used to sell them,' I added. 'Before he was made redundant, like the miners.'

Mr Carlton-Hayes said, 'The miners were not made redundant, Adrian, their jobs were stolen from them by Mrs Thatcher.'

The youth said, 'We haven't done Thatcher yet. We're still on the First World War.'

I managed to flog him *The Observer's Book of Aircraft* for his dad.

Wednesday December 4th
New Moon

3 a.m.
Unable to sleep tonight due to money worries. Will my car have to go?

Thursday December 5th

Received an invitation for a New Year's Eve party from Tania Braithwaite. It is fancy dress. I can't afford to hire an elaborate costume: I may go as Osama bin Laden. All I will need are a few sheets, an old bathrobe, a pair of sandals and a false beard.

Friday December 6th

According to the *Daily Mail*, Cherie Blair is dabbling in the occult and cannot decide whether to have tea or coffee in the morning without consulting a medium in Dorking called Sylvia. Mrs Blair surrounds herself with gurus and mystics. It seems you cannot move in No. 10 before tripping over crystals and astrological charts.

Marigold said, 'It's good to know that someone of the New Age is married to the most powerful person in Britain.'

Saturday December 7th

We are getting through four bags of logs a day at a cost of £3 a bag.

I was slightly nervous all day while I was at work. I had given my parents a spare key to my apartment and ntl were calling at 11.30 to connect me to over 200 television channels, at a cost of £66 a month. I will find the money somehow. A man of my intellect cannot afford to ignore global culture.

I got home from work to find my mother on the balcony, feeding the swans with croissants she had taken from my freezer. When I objected that (a) I do not want to encourage the long-necked bullies to congregate below my balcony, and (b) the frozen croissants were for my personal consumption – I eat two every morning before going to work – she said swans are strange creatures with special powers, you have to be nice to them or they'll turn against you and make your life a misery.

I could see that the ntl engineer had turned up as promised. My father was watching Formula One racing live from Adelaide. I asked him to turn the volume down. He dithered over the five remote controls that are needed to operate the home entertainment centre, but only succeeded in turning the volume up to a torturous level that made my heart beat faster and my ears vibrate. It sounded as though Michael Schumacher was in my living room, revving his engine.

I tried to turn the television off at the front of the set, but there was no obvious button or switch. The noise became intolerable.

My mother screamed, 'Where's the operating manual?'

Before I could find the relevant page, there was an angry banging on my door. I opened it to find a tall, gaunt-looking young woman with long blonde hair parted in the middle. She looked like the type of woman my mother would have described as 'living on her nerves'.

She shouted, 'Turn it down.' Her voice sounded tight in her larynx. Her hands were clenched. I could imagine that under the white tracksuit she was wearing, her buttocks were also clenched.

I shouted above the screaming of the Formula One cars that I couldn't work the remotes. The young woman pushed in, picked up one of the five remote controls and pressed a button. Silence fell.

She said, 'Sorry, but I cannot bear noise. I live above you.'

I introduced myself and my parents. She shook our hands and said that she was Mia Fox. I apologized for disturbing her and said that I was normally a considerate neighbour. She said that she would have to go back upstairs because she had left something on the stove.

My father asked me if he could watch the Miss World Competition. He said, 'We've only got terrestrial and the BBC are refusing to show it.'

I have watched the Miss World Competition with my father since I was a small boy. In those halcyon days I knew no better. My father would spend an hour before the competition started on drawing up two identical charts, one for him and one for me.

My father taught me to give points for face, bust, legs, bum and niceness. We would enter the marks for each contestant. It was one of the few activities that I ever shared with him. I was a great disappointment to him when I was a boy. I did not like football, cricket or fishing, but he was proud of my skill in predicting who would wear the crown and sash and weep tears of joy on being pronounced Miss World.

I heard from the radio next to my futon on the BBC World Service that Miss Turkey won. Apparently they are going mad in Istanbul.

Iraq has presented the United Nations with 12,000 pages of documentation about their weapons programmes. So it looks as though war has been averted, thank God.

Sunday December 8th

Marigold rang me at 8.30 this morning and begged me to come to Beeby on the Wold for lunch. She said something terrible had happened.

I said, 'Why can't you tell me over the phone?'

She said that she couldn't possibly talk about it over the phone and started to cry.

I wanted to shout, 'I don't care what catastrophe has happened to you. I would sooner eat my own arm than drive fifteen miles and spend five or six hours with your gruesome family, being patronized and used as a domestic drudge.'

But I didn't. I agreed to be there on time for the humanist prayer that Michael Flowers intoned at the head of the table instead of saying grace.

I stopped at an off-licence and bought a bottle of French rosé as I had read in the *Sunday Times* that it was newly fashionable if served chilled.

Marigold ran out of the house to greet me as I parked.

She didn't look like a woman who'd had a recent terrible experience. However, she did look terrible. She was wearing harem pants, a plaid shirt and the tartan headband. Her hair needed washing and her spectacles were smeared.

I could not resist taking them off and cleaning them with my handkerchief.

She said, 'So you do love me?'

I made a noncommittal grunting noise and said, 'So what has happened?'

She said, 'Mummy and Daddy might be getting a divorce. They've called the family together to talk about it. Daisy has come up from London and Poppy is here.' She was pulling me towards the front door.

I said, 'But the family won't want me there. I'll leave you all in peace to talk it over among yourselves.'

Marigold said, 'Please don't go. I need your support. But please don't be offended by anything Daisy might say. She's half Mexican, you know.'

The front door opened and Michael Flowers bellowed, 'Come in, come in, my boy. The food is on the table!'

Daisy Flowers sat next to me in the dining room. Her perfume was overpowering. She looked as though she had stepped out of the pages of *TV Quick*. Her black hair was piled on top of her head and skewered together by what looked like a thin bone. She had dark olive skin and her breasts wobbled like the jellies my grandma used to serve up for Sunday tea. I didn't know where to put my eyes. Her legs were hidden under the table. She was almost, but not quite, as beautiful as Pandora Braithwaite.

She said, 'Hello, Adrian. I know everything there is to know about you. Marigold is never off the phone to me.'

Her voice was deep. I asked her if she had a cold. She laughed and threw her head back, exposing her lovely throat. I wanted to sink my teeth into her neck.

Poppy sat opposite. She had tamed her hair into two immensely long, fat plaits. She looked disturbingly like a middle-aged Heidi. She said disapprovingly, 'Daisy has been smoking since she was thirteen years old, that's why she sounds like a mating walrus.'

Netta Flowers came in with a gravyboat full of what I presumed to be vegetarian gravy and set it down. My rosé wine was the most colourful thing on the table.

Michael Flowers got to his feet, paused dramatically and then announced, 'This could be the last meal we eat together as a complete family unit. Netta and I are no longer sexually compatible. My darling wife informed me last night that she is about to embark on a sexual adventure with Roger Middleton.'

Netta looked around at her daughters for their reaction. Poppy and Marigold looked down at the tablecloth.

Daisy reached for the rosé, took a corkscrew from out of her bag and said, 'Roger Middleton? The seriously weird lavender supplier with the nose?' She pulled the cork and slopped the rosé into my glass before filling her own.

Poppy said, 'Roger Middleton is half your age, Mummy.'

Netta smiled and adjusted the ruched neckline of her gypsy blouse.

Flowers said, 'For what we are about to receive, may Mother Nature make us truly grateful.'

Bowls of food were passed around and various brown baked things were put on to plates.

I thought about the magnificent roast dinners that my grandmother used to make for me, of how she would cut the fat off the beef and hand it to me as a special treat.

When everyone had food on their plates, Michael Flowers said, 'I would like to open the debate. The question is, should Mummy and I have an open marriage during which Mummy and Roger Middleton have it off and I cast myself into the uncertainties of the singles circuit? Or should we divorce, sell the house and shop, and go our separate ways?'

When nobody said anything, he said, looking at me, 'C'mon, family, what do you think, eh?'

I grew more alarmed with every minute that passed. For some inexplicable reason, he was treating me as though I were a member of his family.

Marigold half sobbed and said, 'But, Daddy, I want you and Mummy to live in this house for ever.'

Netta said, 'Oh, Mazzie darling, you're being a teensy-weensy bit selfish. You'll be getting married yourself and leaving us one day, won't you? Perhaps one day soon?'

The Flowers family looked at me *en masse*. I felt a bit like sobbing myself.

Marigold said, 'Nobody will ever marry me, will they? I'm far too plain and dull.'

She waited for a response.

Netta said, 'Remember what your therapist told you, Mazzie. You must learn to love yourself first.'

Poppy said, 'She should have spent the money on having her hair done.'

Daisy added, 'Or buying a few decent clothes.'

Marigold buried her head in my shoulder. I felt obliged to put my arm around her.

Daisy said to me, *sotto voce*, 'If I were you, I'd run while there's still time.'

Michael and Netta Flowers both got to their feet and said, 'Hug time,' and enveloped Marigold in their parental embrace.

Daisy turned her head away and put her index finger down her throat.

I don't know how I got through the rest of the meal. Netta and Michael Flowers talked openly and frankly about their psycho-sexual problem in toe-curling detail. At one point we were forced to listen as Netta recounted how she had pleasured Michael during a Bob Dylan concert on the Isle of Wight.

Eventually Poppy stood up and said to her parents, 'I can't listen to any more of this filth. You have both put me off sex for life. I hated the way you both walked around the house naked and wouldn't allow us to have locks on any door.'

The meal ended in tears and recriminations. Michael Flowers said over the heads of the sobbing women, 'It's so good that a family can talk openly and frankly about these things, isn't it, Adrian?'

I said, 'But nothing has been decided. Is Netta going to sleep with Roger Middleton or not?'

Netta said, 'I will decide by visiting a rowan tree at

midnight. If an owl hoots after I have sung my rowan song, I will sleep with Roger in an open marriage. If the owl is silent I will divorce Daddy and take him to court, for half the value of this house and half the value of the shop.'

Then, to my horror, she sang the rowan song:

> 'O rowan tree, O rowan tree,
> Hey nonny no, how sad I be,
> There is a man that I do love,
> He be my dear, my turtle dove,
> If I do lie with him abed
> And he do kiss my bonny head,
> Will he stay or will he go?
> Hey nonny, nonny, nonny, no.'

When she had finished singing, Daisy, quite cruelly I thought, gave an owl impression.

I started to clear the table, but Michael Flowers said, 'No, let the women take care of the washing-up. I'd like to see you in my study.'

I would sooner have climbed into the bear pit at Whipsnade Zoo naked and covered in honey than gone into Flowers's study, but I went anyway, because anything, anything, was better than staying in a room with three weeping women.

Flowers sat behind his desk and put a hand over his eyes. I didn't know whether to remain standing or sit down on the battered leather and mahogany chair in front of the desk.

He said, 'Adrian, I think I am a good man. I have certainly tried to better the lives of humankind. I walked in a wet duffel coat to Aldermaston every Easter weekend for ten years. I donated and erected tents for the women at Greenham Common. I sent a fruit basket to Nelson Mandela at Robben Island. I delivered 100 vegetarian samosas to the picket line at a Nottingham coal field and I attempted to bring a little culture to the working men's clubs by singing Schubert, but bingo put paid to that. I'm bitterly disappointed with the English working classes, Adrian. They've chosen consumerism over art, materialism over culture and celebrity-worship over robust spirituality.

'I have asked for so very little for myself. My needs are few: sufficient daily quantities of vegetables and fruit, good bread, a jug of home-brewed ale, books of course. But most of all, Adrian, most of all I have had the love of my family. I have been blessed with two extraordinary wives and three daughters, two of them loving.'

He raised his head and banged his fist on his desk, causing the ink bottles and nibbed pens he uses to jump. 'I have only one regret.' He looked me in the face and locked on to my eyes. I was unable to tear my gaze away from his. 'I desperately wanted a son. And, Adrian, I think I've found him. You and I have so much in common. I too despise sport and low culture. And I, like you, adore Marigold. I honestly feel, Adrian, that you are the son I never had. Please say that I can lean on you in the dark days to come.'

He held his hand out. What could I do, diary, but take

it? My audience in his study lasted fourteen minutes, yet I did not speak one word.

Monday December 9th

A scandal has broken out concerning Mrs Blair, the prime minister's barrister wife. She has allowed a convicted fraudster called Peter Foster to negotiate on her behalf to buy two riverside apartments in Bristol, costing in total over half a million pounds.

Foster is wanted by the Australian police for selling false slimming pills. On September 1st he was told by immigration officials at Luton Airport that he would be deported within two days on the grounds that he was 'not conducive to the public good'. Mr Foster is the lover of Cherie Blair's guru and aromatherapist, Carole Caplin.

I wonder why she didn't use an estate agent. I know that in opinion polls they are less respected than politicians and journalists, but surely even an estate agent is more trustworthy than a convicted fraudster.

The Leicestershire and Rutland Creative Writing Group met in the snug at the Red Cow. Only Ken Blunt turned up. Gary Milksop left a message on my mobile to say that he was stuck on the M6, where a lorry had shed its load of frozen turkeys, but he said, 'I'll see you on the 23rd. I'll be bringing my partner and a couple of friends. Please text details of venue, time and dress code.'

Ken read to me a vicious piece of polemic called 'Bush's Poodle'.

> 'Bitch America is on heat
> She straddles the globe
> Defecating hamburgers, apple pie and Coke
> Tony, the toy poodle, minces at the rear
> Sniffing the bitch's arse and trying to mount.'

A couple of old blokes who were sitting in the snug looked up in alarm. Ken has got a loud voice.

After I'd read him a few pages of my *Celebrity and Madness* book, Ken said, 'I'm not surprised you've not found a publisher. It's bloody crap. Who wants to read about a load of fake-tanned tosspots?' He then said, 'And this dinner on the 23rd, have you booked a venue?'

I told him that I had.

He then said, 'So who's the guest speaker?'

I told him that it would be a pleasant surprise.

He said almost menacingly, 'I hope so. My wife is a keen autograph hunter.'

As soon as I got home to Rat Wharf I sent a text message to Pandora:

Keep the evening of 23 12 2002 free. U R guest speaker at VIP dinner in Leicester.

Tuesday December 10th

According to Asif, the garage log bloke, the photo-
copiers at the United Nations cannot cope with copy-
ing the 12,000-page document listing Iraq's weapons
programme.

Syria wants to know why America, Britain, France,
Russia and China will see the document first.

Asif said, 'America needs time to use the Tippex and
blank out all the bad bits, what it's done in the past, like
selling weapons to Saddam, innit?'

I said, 'As if, Asif.'

Mr Carlton-Hayes arranged for two armchairs to be
delivered today. They are Edwardian and are covered in
worn brown velvet.

I sat by the fire in one and checked his stock list. I was
asleep within minutes.

When I woke, Marigold was sitting in the opposite
chair. She said that she would be at mumming rehearsals
each night this week. She asked me if I would join the
group and play Joseph opposite her Mary.

I told Marigold that I was an official agnostic and
couldn't possibly take part in any religious enactment
whatsoever.

Marigold said, 'Mummery simply means mime. It isn't
necessarily religious. It has its roots in paganism. Mummy
and Daddy were founder members of the New Secular
Society.'

I threw another log on the fire and said, 'I cannot tolerate mime, Marigold.'

Marigold said, 'You are a very intolerant person.'

I told her that a combination of mime and madrigals was my idea of hell.

Marigold said, 'My idea of hell is a life without you.' Then she said, 'You should wear gloves when you're handling logs. A splinter could lead to septicaemia.' Then she left the shop.

Before her parting remark I had handled logs with a nonchalance bordering on recklessness. But for the rest of the day I handled them as if they were sticks of dynamite.

Wednesday December 11th
Moon's First Quarter

A hundred Hollywood stars signed a petition against a pre-emptive strike on Iraq. I have never heard of any of them apart from Gillian Anderson, the *X-Files* woman.

Pandora rang me at work to say that she won't be in Leicester until the 24th, when she is attending a constituency drinks party. I begged her to change her plans.

She said, 'Gordon and Sarah Brown have invited me for champagne and mince pies at Downing Street. He wants to talk to me about my political future. Is your "VIP" dinner more important than that?'

I had to admit that it wasn't.

Thursday December 12th

An email from William asking me to go to Nigeria for Christmas. As if! As I write, I am completely penniless, there is no petrol in the car and my fridge freezer contains two croissants and a wizened lemon.

Direct debits have snatched my wages from my account.

Friday December 13th

My credit card bill arrived. I was gobsmacked to see how much Barclays were charging me per month for the money I had borrowed for my deposit on Rat Wharf.

My solicitor, Dave Barwell, has sent me a Christmas card of a robin wearing a Santa Claus hat. Inside was a bill for £569.48 for 'professional services'.

I ate the croissants and squeezed the lemon juice into a mug of hot water. I felt like a monk in a monastic order.

I was glad when lunchtime came and Mr Carlton-Hayes offered me one of his cheese sandwiches.

Saturday December 14th

Barclaycard are a truly magnificent organization. I received a letter from them today which said, 'As a valued Barclaycard customer we are delighted to advise you that your credit limit has been increased to £12,000. Your new credit limit is available to use straight away and will show on your statement.'

Perhaps there is a God. Barclaycard have given me £2,000 to spend immediately.

Sunday December 15th

My fridge freezer is packed with food. The car's petrol tank is full. However, so are all the car parks within two miles of the city centre, so I walked along the towpath to Water Meadow Park, the out-of-town shopping centre. I kept a wary eye out for the swans. A cruel east wind was blowing around the squat buildings.

Next, Marks & Spencer, WH Smith and DFS looked as though they had been dropped on to the former water meadows from outer space, and the shoppers streaming into their front entrances looked to me to be similarly alien.

Cars were queuing to get into the car parks and also to get out of the car parks. The main approach roads were clogged with shoppers. A police motorcyclist was trying to unjam the traffic. A police helicopter hovered overhead and car horns were blaring. It sounded more like Rome than the East Midlands. When I passed a makeshift garden hut/Santa's grotto that had been erected in the north car park and saw a queue of shivering children waiting their turn to see the great man, I had a moment of utter desolation and I turned around and walked home.

*

Marigold rang me eleven times tonight. I didn't ring her back. She makes me unhappy.

Monday December 16th

Two teenage girls wearing miniskirts, crop tops and thin cotton jackets came into the shop this morning and made immediately for the fire. The sight of them filled me with irritation. If they were so cold, why didn't they wear more clothes?

Since they showed no interest in the books, I tried out a bit of sales patter. I asked them if they had done their Christmas shopping yet. They said they hadn't.

I told them that books make very good Christmas presents, and one of them said, 'Yeah, my mum sometimes reads a book when there's nowt on the telly.'

I asked her what her mother's interests were.

She said, 'I don't think my mum is interested in owt really.'

After a few more probing questions, I ascertained that the girl's mother was called Pat, that she was forty-three, that she worked part-time in a light-bulb factory, that she was the mother of three children, that she drank cocktails when she went out on Saturday nights with her husband, that she was an Elvis fan and grew her own tomatoes.

After a few minutes I brought the girl a selection of suitable books: *One Hundred Cocktails to Make at Home*, *Elvis – a Life in Pictures* and *Vegetables on Your Window Sill*. None of them was more than £3.

She said she would take the cocktail book and asked if I could gift-wrap it. Young people today are so spoilt.

Before they left the shop, I asked the girls why they were wearing skimpy clothes on such a cold day.

They giggled, and after the shop door was closed I heard one girl say to the other, 'What an old perv!'

I wanted to run after them and explain that I wasn't a dirty old man, but, feeling that this would have made matters worse, I stayed inside the shop.

Tuesday December 17th

Marigold came into the shop at lunchtime and said that she was unable to eat or sleep. She said, 'If I had known that falling in love with you was going to make me so miserable, I would have frozen my heart against you.'

She asked Mr Carlton-Hayes if he would display a poster advertising the mummers' various performances.

He was too kind to refuse, though the poster was badly designed. The group of mummers looked more like characters from *The Night of the Living Dead*.

She asked if I would be there when the mummers make their debut outside the Ball and Wicket at Thrussington Parva on Thursday night. I couldn't think of a suitable excuse, so I said yes.

After she'd gone, Mr Carlton-Hayes said, 'Forgive me if I'm speaking out of turn, Adrian, but that young lady seems to have you wrapped around her little finger.'

Diary, I should have fallen on his neck and confessed that I needed to talk to him about my Marigold dilemma, but pride would not allow me to be open and honest with him. Because the truth is, diary, I never want to see Marigold or her horrible family again, though I exclude Daisy from the above statement. I would like to see a lot more of Daisy. In fact I would like to see the whole of Daisy, every inch of her, inside and out.

Wednesday December 18th

Dreamed that Ken Blunt and Marigold had gone into Habitat with my Visa card and bought a king-size bed.

Thursday December 19th
Full Moon

Mr Carlton-Hayes was very kind to me today. He said, 'Adrian, my dear, you don't have to go to this mummery-fummery thing tonight, you know. Simply tell the young lady that you do not care for her and wish to be free of any obligations.'

I wish I had taken his advice. I drove to the Ball and Wicket at Thrussington Parva and had half a lager shandy in the bar.

The landlord, a surly fat man, told me that the mummers were in an upstairs room getting changed into their masks and costumes.

A group of Morris men and Morris women in civilian clothes came into the bar. They looked almost normal, though there was rather a lot of facial hair. They were joined by a group of folk musicians carrying strange-looking instruments that later turned out to be medieval. Among them was Poppy. Her hair was tied at the back with a holly-printed ribbon, but it still cascaded over her bum.

The surly landlord laboured behind the bar, pulling pints of real ale. He went to the bottom of the stairs and shouted, 'Noreen, Noreen, I'm down 'ere on my own!'

I bought Poppy a drink and we sat in the corner. I asked her why she was not taking part.

She said, 'Medievalism is not my thing. The clothes were terrible. I prefer the Romans.'

I said, 'But the Romans were invaders.' She pulled a hank of hair over her shoulder and stroked it as though it were an animal, and said, 'The Romans were a civilizing force. They had hot baths and amazing hair products.'

I asked her how often Daisy came to Beeby on the Wold.

She tossed her hair back and said, 'Often enough to cause a row.'

At 8 o'clock a bearded man wearing a smock and gaiters came into the bar and announced in a stentorian voice, 'My lords, my ladies, gentle folk of the parish and those that toil by thy hands, please be of knowledge that the mummers be about to enact the story of how Jesus be born.'

It was drizzling outside and I had not brought an umbrella. My mother had borrowed it and failed to bring it back.

The street lights were on and several of the mummers held old-fashioned lanterns aloft, but it was still hard to see what was going on, even though the moon hung above Thrussington Parva like a globular ceiling light.

It was a peripatetic performance. We trooped around the village. Marigold/pagan Mary gave birth to Jesus outside the former post office. I think it was a mistake for her to have worn her glasses over the top of her mask; it made her look like Jeff Goldblum in *The Fly*.

The three kings presented their gifts outside Mrs Briggs's Internet tea room. The madrigals were sung in that peculiar sort of English that only singers use. It was impossible to understand the words.

Afterwards in the pub I told Marigold that she was 'very brave'. She took this as a compliment.

Friday December 20th

Woke up and had a panic attack about the arrangements for the writers' group Christmas dinner. I texted:

Pandora, cancel Brown, VIP dinner more important. U O me a favr. Adrian. X.

Saturday December 21st

We were busy all day in the shop. There was a run on Marilyn Monroe memorabilia and snooker auto-biographies. We almost sold out of Dickens, and all six copies of Barry Kent's second anthology, *Making Love with Wendy Cope*, were bought by a man with a baby strapped to his chest.

We didn't close until 7.30.

Mr Carlton-Hayes had brought in a bottle of sherry. For some reason, sherry always reminds me of old women's corsets. But it was very pleasant winding down, sitting by the fire.

Mr Carlton-Hayes told me that he is most appreciative of my help and hoped that I was happy working for him. He said that I sometimes looked *distrait*.

Emboldened by the sherry, I told him that a combination of worries – money, Marigold and the swans – kept me awake at night. He nodded sympathetically but didn't offer any solutions, such as increasing my wages.

As I walked down the High Street towards the towpath, I passed crowds of marauding, drunken teenagers of both sexes. A youth in a vest was being sick in the doorway of Dixons.

The moon lit my way home along the towpath. The swans came to meet me halfway, but didn't get out of the water. Gielgud wasn't there. I hope he is dead.

My apartment was unbearably hot when I got home from work. The thermostat which controls my underfloor heating seems to have a life of its own. I opened the sliding doors and sat on the balcony to cool down.

With a sinking heart I saw Gielgud swim across the canal. I told him to push off, but he stayed there, motionless, trying to stare me out. I stared back, determined not to drop my eyes first. Eventually his wife came to join

him and two pairs of eyes glittered in the darkness, but
it was the cold that drove me back inside.

I could not get rid of the image of Gielgud and his
wife, floating side by side. I wondered how long they had
been together, and why they had been attracted to each
other in the first place. I envied them their relationship.

Suddenly adrenalin surged through my body and pro-
pelled me out of the door and into my car. I drove to
Beeby on the Wold and waited outside the Flowerses'
empty house. It was 11 o'clock before they arrived home.

Marigold's parents went inside the house. A man with
a big nose followed them. Marigold came round and
opened my car door and sat next to me. I asked if the
man with the big nose was Roger Middleton.

She said, 'Yes. They're starting the open marriage thing
tonight.'

I said that I had something to tell her.

She said despairingly, 'Oh, no, not again! Why does
this always happen to me? Why do men satisfy their lust
and then throw me aside like a dirty tea towel?'

I was longing to go home, but I knew I was in for at
least half an hour of tears and self-denigration from
Marigold.

First of all I told her I was not worthy of her, was not
ready to commit, blah, blah, blah, etc., etc., etc. Then I
told her about Plato's allegory – that the first humans
had four legs, four arms and two heads and were perfectly
happy cartwheeling around the earth, but the gods looked
down on them and became jealous and cut each human
in half. The humans now had two arms, two legs and one
head each. They seemed happy enough on the surface,

and they were able to walk and to play, but inside they were in turmoil, and were forever looking for their other half, so that they could feel complete again.

I said, 'Marigold, you will find your other half one day. He is out there now, looking for you.'

She peered through the windscreen as if expecting to see her other half standing by the laurel hedge.

There followed ten minutes of loud crying, five minutes of silent weeping and sniffing, and a couple of minutes of broken-voiced pathos.

I was relieved when she said, 'I'm going to bed. I just want this dreadful day to be over.'

I escorted her to the front door. She let herself in and we stood for a moment in the hall, then I gave her a friendly pat on the shoulder and said, 'Well, goodbye then.'

I drove home with my Abba tapes playing at full volume. I think I must have broken the speed limit several times. It felt as though the car had wings.

Sunday December 22nd

Michael Flowers rang me at 8.30 this morning to tell me that Marigold had been admitted to the Royal Hospital in the early hours with suspected appendicitis. He said that she had been calling for me. He said, 'I phoned that mobile contraption you carry with you, but the bloody thing kept repeating, "It has not been possible to connect your call. Please try again later." She's in a great deal of physical and psychic pain, Adrian. Please go to her. She needs you.'

I went to the balcony and looked out. I could see the lights of the monolithic Royal Hospital in the distance. Gielgud was standing by the driver's door, barring the way to my car. Was he trying to tell me not to go to the hospital? Since meeting the Flowers family I see signs and portents everywhere.

On the way to the hospital I phoned Pandora. She answered at once. I begged her to come to Leicester tomorrow. She laughed.

I asked her if she had Keith Vaz's number. She said she had but refused to give it to me. I asked if she knew any celebrities who would help me out at the last minute.

She said, 'On December 23rd, with one day's notice, for no fee and no expenses, are you mad?' Then she dropped her voice and said, 'Seriously, Aidy, are you mad? The last time I saw you you seemed a bit lonely and sad. And that bloody loft, it's so white and cold.'

I told her that Marigold was in hospital and she said, 'It will turn out to be nothing. She's a bloody diva.'

I pointed out that Pandora had not even met Marigold.

But she said, 'Wayne Wong likens her to Chairman Mao's wife, small but lethal.'

It took for ever to find Marigold. She had been moved from Accident and Emergency to an overnight observation ward. I eventually found her in Surgical 2, in a bay with five other women. The nurse on the desk said, when I enquired about Marigold and gave my name, 'Oh, you're the fiancé.'

I should have contradicted her and asserted my single

status, but she had already turned away and was almost running down the ward.

Marigold was watching the small TV set next to her bed. But when she saw me approaching she closed her eyes and turned her head away and appeared to fall into a deep sleep. I had no wish to 'wake' her, so I sat by her bed and watched the news.

Mr Blair was speaking about the danger to the world if tyrants like Saddam Hussein were not challenged. How anybody could doubt Mr Blair's word is a mystery to me. The man radiates honesty and sincerity.

Eventually Marigold 'woke up' and appeared to be surprised to see me sitting there. She held her little hand out and I took it and squeezed it. I had bought her *Hello!* and a bunch of seedless black grapes from the hospital shop.

She pointed to the notice above her bed which said 'Nil by mouth' and told me that until the doctors had finished their investigations she was not allowed to eat or drink in case she had to have an operation to remove her appendix.

And she rejected *Hello!*, saying that she pitied rich, famous people and couldn't care less about their clothes and houses.

I tried desperately to find a topic of conversation but failed, and we sat in an awkward silence and watched *Scooby-Doo!* on television.

At the end, after the janitor had ripped his face mask off and exposed himself as the evil scientist who threatened to blow up the world, Marigold started to cry and said, 'I'll be in hospital for Christmas, and I so wanted us to spend our first Christmas together, Adrian.'

She had completely blanked our conversation of the night before.

An exhausted-looking African doctor came to examine her abdomen.

I tried to leave, but the doctor said, 'No, stay where you are. You're Miss Flowers's fiancé, are you not?'

Marigold said yes and I could hardly contradict her in the current circumstances.

I watched as the doctor palpated her lower torso. Marigold reacted as though the doctor's fingers were burning rods searing into her flesh.

After she had rebuttoned her pyjama jacket, the doctor said, 'Your pain is a mystery to me. There is no swelling, you have no temperature, your blood pressure is better than mine. I do not think you have appendicitis. Have you suffered an emotional disturbance recently?'

Marigold said, 'I have been in agony all night.'

The doctor looked at me and said, 'I presume you are having normal sexual relations with your fiancée?'

I took offence at this and said, 'Are you asking me if I am a sexual deviant?'

He said, 'No, you have misunderstood me.' And he turned to Marigold and said, 'Is there pain on intercourse?'

She replied, 'No physical pain.'

I sat with her for another hour, until her mother and father turned up.

*

Netta gave Marigold half a dozen cards. One was an invitation to Tania Braithwaite's New Year's Eve fancy dress party.

Marigold looked puzzled until I explained that Tania was my ex-stepmother.

I said, 'Don't feel that you have to go to the party, Marigold.'

Netta said, 'No, you must go, Mazzie. It will be something to look forward to.'

9 p.m.

I have left messages for Keith Vaz, MP, Patricia Hewitt, MP, Jim Marshall, MP, Gary Lineker, Martin Johnson, the Tigers captain, Rosemary Conley, Willie Thorne, the Lord Mayor of Leicester and the manager of Marks & Spencer, asking each of them to speak at the dinner.

I then had a brainwave and rang Wayne Wong and asked him if Engelbert Humperdinck was spending Christmas in Leicester with his family as usual.

Wayne said, 'Mr Humperdinck's people haven't made a booking yet.'

While I was on the line, I asked Wayne to book a table for eight people for 7.30 tomorrow.

Wayne said, 'We're fully booked, Aidy. It's Christmas Eve eve.'

He must have heard the desperation in my voice because, after listening to my pleas, he relented and said with ill grace, 'I'll fit you in somewhere, but you'll have to be out by 9.30.'

Monday December 23rd

Woke this morning with a black cloud of anxiety hanging above me. On the walk to work I phoned Ken Blunt and Gary Milksop and told them about the arrangements for tonight.

Ken Blunt said, 'Did you manage to get a celebrity speaker?'

I told him that a guest would be joining us for dinner at the Imperial Dragon and that we would be going back to my loft apartment for coffee and the after-dinner speech.

The bell on the shop door never stopped ringing as customers trooped in and out. At one time there was a queue for the fire.

My parents came in. They were doing their last-minute Christmas shopping. My mother asked me what I wanted for Christmas. I told her to buy me rope so that I could hang myself.

She said, 'Why are you so mardy-arsed? Unless you tell me otherwise I'm buying you two pairs of Calvin Klein underpants. I hope you are coming to Wisteria Walk for your Christmas dinner. It'll be the last time, as we're moving out the day after Boxing Day.'

I asked my parents what they wanted for Christmas.

My father said, 'A sledgehammer would be useful.'

And my mother said she had run out of Clinique's Deep Comfort Body Butter moisturizing cream.

She told me that my sister and her boyfriend, Simon,

were expected for Christmas Day and warned me to buy presents for them. And she said, 'And Christmas Day will be the first anniversary of the new dog's death, remember.'

My father said, 'He ought to bloody remember. He killed it.'

I said, 'Look, how many times do I have to tell you that I did not give the new dog that turkey bone. It jumped up and stole it from my plate!'

I asked my mother if she knew any celebrities who would be available at short notice for an engagement that evening.

She said that she knew Gary Lineker's cousin's ex-wife, who told amusing anecdotes about Gary when he was a little boy.

I said, 'Unless Gary was reading Dostoevsky at a tender age, I doubt if the woman could keep the creative writing group interested.'

At 5.30 I asked Mr Carlton-Hayes if he would be the guest speaker at the creative writing group dinner.

He said, 'My dear, what a shame. I'm hosting a drinks party for the neighbours this evening. The only person you'll get at this late juncture is somebody who likes the sound of their own voice.'

We said simultaneously, 'Michael Flowers.'

I checked with the mumming poster. Flowers did not have a performance that evening. I rang him immediately. Netta answered and said that her husband was at the hospital, visiting Marigold. She volunteered the information that Marigold would be discharged in the morning.

I rang Surgical 2 and asked to speak urgently to Michael Flowers. The nurse asked me if I was a relation. I said no.

She said, 'Then I'm afraid I can't put you through.'

I was desperate to speak to him, so I said that I was Marigold Flowers's fiancé.

When Michael Flowers came to the phone, I explained to him that I had been badly let down at the last minute by Cherie Blair and had to find a replacement for her by 7.30 tonight. I asked him if he would do the honours.

He said, 'As your future father-in-law, of course I'd be thrilled to help you out of your dilemma.'

He asked me if I had a message for Marigold.

I said, 'Yes, please give her my best wishes.'

Flowers said, 'Come, come, Adrian, you can do better than that, you love-struck swain. No need to be shy with me. Tell the girl you love her.'

What could I do, diary? I was putty in his hands.

I phoned Nigel and asked him to be my partner at the dinner. He said ungraciously, 'Why not? It'll save me cooking.'

I led Nigel into the restaurant, steering him by the front of his shirt. He still banged into chairs and tables on the way, and dropped his white stick twice. His language was unrepeatable. He has developed quite a temper since turning blind.

Wayne had managed to insert an extra table next to the fish tank. The lights inside the tank cast an unpleasant green glow over the table, but I could hardly complain.

Ken Blunt and his wife, Glenda, resembled middle-aged Martians. She is a bit vulgar-looking but friendly enough.

She said, 'I don't mind Ken writing. It is a cheap hobby, not like golf.'

Gary Milksop's eyes lit up when he saw Nigel. Not surprising, because Gary's partner turned out to be a ferret-faced youth with a pencil-thin beard and ears that stuck out like mug handles.

I wish it had been possible to warn Milksop that he stood no chance with Nigel. Nigel likes horny-handed men of toil who order him about and make his life a misery.

Milksop's friends were two serious-looking girls he said he had met at group therapy the previous month. They seemed to think that he was some kind of genius.

Flowers kept us waiting and then made an entrance, shouting, 'I'm expected at the writers' table.' He was wearing a green tweed suit and a large trilby hat.

I said our celebrity guest had arrived.

Ken Blunt turned round and said, 'It's that gobshite from the health food shop in the market.'

Glenda Blunt put her autograph book away in her handbag.

Disappointment settled over the table like heavy snow. It was a most unsatisfactory meal. Wayne Wong kept reminding me that we had to be out by 9.30.

Ken Blunt and Michael Flowers quarrelled about Iraq. Ken is violently anti-American – Glenda told me that he won't allow Coca-Cola in the house – and Michael Flowers claims to be a pacifist (he doesn't know that I know that Mr Carlton-Hayes knocked him out in that car park fight).

At one point I said that, despite his wife's behaviour in letting the writers' group down, I still had complete faith in Mr Blair and that the Weapons of Mass Destruction would soon be found, but that it was like looking for a needle in a haystack the size of France.

Nigel said, 'Or looking for a piece of turkey in this fucking turkey chow mein.'

Gary Milksop said that Iraq was about oil. His acolytes nodded and gazed at him as though he were some kind of political guru.

Nigel stubbornly refused to accept help in locating bits of turkey and continued to drop noodles down his Kenzo shirt front.

The two serious girls talked to each other but seemed reluctant to add anything to the general conversation.

Michael Flowers went into monologue mode – talk about death by anecdote. At the end of the meal he proposed a vote of thanks to me, saying, 'We have Adrian, my future son-in-law, to thank for arranging this delightful occasion.'

Nigel gave a horrible sardonic laugh and called for champagne.

Wayne Wong brought over a magnum bottle of Pomagne and nine glasses and said, 'What are you celebrating?'

Nigel said, 'Adrian's engaged to Marigold Flowers.'

Wayne Wong said, 'No, you're joking me. Not that thin woman who's scared of the fish?'

I said hurriedly, 'Wayne, this is Marigold's father, Michael.'

Wayne briefly shook Flowers's hand, then said to me, 'It's 9.25, so you'll have to drink up quick.'

When our glasses were charged, Nigel began to sing Cliff Richard's winning Eurovision song, 'Congratulations'.

The other diners in the room joined in and Ken Blunt pulled me to my feet to acknowledge the congratulations of the room.

One of the serious girls took a photograph of me and Michael Flowers embracing and shaking hands. She promised to send me a copy via Gary Milksop.

It seems that, against my will, I have become officially engaged to Marigold Flowers.

Gielgud and the other swans were gathered together in a corner of the car park. I pointed them out to Michael Flowers, who said, 'Methinks we should proceed with caution. A swan can break a man's arm, you know.'

We sat in Flowers's Range Rover and waited for the others to arrive.

It was impossible to avoid the swan shit on the stairs and inevitably some of it was trampled on to my floorboards.

I made coffee and gave the usual warning about the glass wall of the lavatory. My warning did not inhibit Michael Flowers, whose urination sounded like the Zambezi in spate.

Nigel and Gary Milksop sat next to each other on the white sofa. The two serious girls sat cross-legged on the floor. Ken Blunt and his wife lolled awkwardly on the futon. I brought the chairs in from the balcony to a chorus of swans hissing. Ferret Face took one chair and Michael Flowers the other. I was quite happy leaning against the kitchen counter. I just wanted the awful night to be over.

Flowers kept us waiting. He assumed the posture of Rodin's *The Thinker* first, then lifted his head and said, 'Before I address you, can we move closer together and form a circle.'

A lot of awkward furniture shifting took place, and Flowers said, 'I want you to hold hands and close your eyes, and feel the atmosphere in this room.'

I closed my eyes and held Ken Blunt's and Ferret Face's hands and felt embarrassment, suspicion and boredom.

Flowers intoned what he said was a Buddhist mantra, which he urged us to join in with.

At the end Ken Blunt pulled his wife to her feet and said, 'We've got to go home now to let the dog out.'

As I saw them down the stairs, Ken said, 'I'd sooner dance barefoot on drawing pins than stay to hear what he's got to say.'

When I went back into the room Flowers was saying, 'I was reading Voltaire at six and Tolstoy at seven.'

Gary Milksop lisped, 'Have you ever written a novel, Mr Flowers?'

Flowers said that in the 1960s he had written 'the definitive English novel'. He had asked his dear friend Philip Larkin to read the manuscript. According to Flowers, Larkin had written back to say, '*Hello to All This* is the novel of the age. Humbler writers such as myself,

Amis et al. should push our pens aside and weep. Mike, my good friend, you are a genius. Every publisher in London will be beating a path to your door.'

Nigel said, 'I know I am just an ignorant gay-boy, but I've never heard of *Hello to All This*.'

Flowers bit his lower lip and turned his head, as though trying to control strong emotions. 'No,' he said, in what I imagine he thought was a hollow-sounding voice. 'My first wife, Conchita, burned my manuscript.'

Gary Milksop, Ferret Face and the two serious girls gasped in horror.

Nigel said, 'And it was the only copy?'

Flowers nodded. 'It was handwritten in purple ink on fine hand-blocked paper.'

Nigel's lip curled. 'And you sent this through the post to Philip Larkin?'

Flowers bridled. 'The postal workers of this country are the finest workers in the land. I trusted them implicitly.'

I said, laying a trap, 'But you still have the Larkin letter?'

'No,' he answered. 'Conchita destroyed everything that was precious to me.'

One of the serious girls broke her silence and said, 'I did my MA on Philip Larkin – 'Philip Larkin, Uber-Nerd' – I read everything there was to read but I don't remember him mentioning Michael Flowers.'

Flowers smiled and sighed. 'You dear sweet girl, poor old Phil's papers were burned.'

'So,' I said, 'there is absolutely no evidence whatsoever that you were a intimate friend of Philip Larkin? Or that you wrote a masterpiece called *Hello to All This*?'

*

I couldn't stand any more and excused myself, saying I needed air. I stood on the balcony for a few minutes until the cold forced me back inside.

When I returned Flowers was saying, 'I did my best to halt the encroaching dictatorship of the motor car. I tried to stop the production of the Ford Cortina. I lay down outside the gates of Dagenham. I had the prescience to see that supplying the proletariat with motor cars would destroy the environment, England and eventually everything we hold dear.'

Nigel said, 'My dad had a Cortina Mark 4. It was duck-egg blue and had leopard-skin seats. Did any of the car workers give up their well-paid jobs because you were sufficiently worried to lie down in the road?'

Flowers said, 'I was deeply disappointed by the workers' response. I'm afraid they lampooned me and several of them took the opportunity to give me what I believe is called now "a good kicking".'

Gary Milksop offered to give Nigel a lift home and ordered Ferret Face to drive the serious girls to the flat they shared.

Flowers stayed talking to me long after the others had gone. He talked mostly about Conchita. He said, 'I went to Mexico after seeing a production of *The Royal Hunt of the Sun* at Loughborough Town Hall. I was a young man searching for an alternative civilization and I thought I had found it in the remnants of Aztec culture. I met Conchita in the courtyard of the La Croix Hotel.'

'Was she a fellow guest?' I asked.

'No, she was sweeping it,' he said. 'We exchanged a

few words. She complimented me on my Spanish and asked me if I needed a guide to see the Mayan ruins of Palenque.

'We were lovers almost immediately. She took me to meet her family. They were dreadfully poor – ten of them living next to a rubbish heap in a shack with an earth floor. Her little brothers were running around in white vests and no pants. I gave her father $50 and brought her to England.' He sighed. 'It was like transplanting an exotic hothouse flower into a sodden English field. She was briefly happy when Daisy was born, but before Daisy was three years old she had deserted us and gone back to Mexico.'

'With a pork butcher from Melton Mowbray,' I prompted.

He winced and said, 'Please,' as if I had pulled the scab off an old wound.

Seconds ticked by and I wondered if it would be rude if I changed into my pyjamas in the bathroom. But he started up again, saying, 'Netta quite literally saved my life at Stonehenge.'

I said, 'Literally? You mean one of the stones was about to fall on you and she –'

He said, 'Perhaps not literally, but she turned my life round, took charge of me and loved me, until very recently.' He paused, and then said, 'I'm finished with women. I'm going to channel my energies into something far more important – the future of this great country.'

When he finally left, I threw myself down on the futon, too exhausted to undress. I composed a letter in my head.

Dear Martin Amis

I have a request. Could you please take a quick look through the whole of your dead father's correspondence, diaries, journals and other written material to see if you can find any reference, however slight, to Philip Larkin's friendship with a Michael Flowers of Beeby on the Wold. In particular a letter from Larkin mentioning a manuscript called *Hello to All This*. I know that your father and Philip Larkin were the best of friends . . .

Tuesday December 24th
Christmas Eve

My father rang me first thing this morning. This is such an unusual occurrence that my immediate thought on hearing his voice was that my mother was either severely incapacitated or dead.

He said, 'You've broken your mother's heart. Why didn't you invite us to your engagement party last night? Are you ashamed of us? I know we smoke and drink a bit and your mother can be opinionated, but –'

I interrupted him by saying, 'Dad, it wasn't an engagement party.'

I then heard my father saying, 'Pauline, he says it wasn't an engagement party.'

I heard my mother's muffled voice from across the room saying something angry and tearful.

My father translated, 'Your mother says that everybody in the Imperial Dragon sang congratulations to you last night, according to our milkman.'

I said to him, 'Tell Mum that the milkman should check his facts before passing on gossip.'

My father took the phone away from his lips and relayed this message to my mother. She shouted something incomprehensible, though I managed to make out the words 'liar' and 'engaged'.

My father started to repeat my mother's response, but I broke in and said, 'Can I hear it from the horse's mouth please?'

My father said, 'The horse is lying on the settee, crying her bloody eyes out.'

I told my father that I didn't know how I had got engaged, it had all been a horrible mistake, and I didn't love Marigold or even like her much. I said that I would ring him and my mother later that night.

When I got to work the shop was already full of customers looking for last-minute presents. Mr Carlton-Hayes was struggling to serve a queue of people.

At 11 this morning Netta Flowers rang to say that Marigold was safely home from the hospital. She said, 'She's anxious to see you, Adrian. Would you like to join us for Christmas tea tomorrow?'

I said, 'I'm sorry, Mrs Flowers, but my family are holding a memorial service for a very beloved pet dog at teatime tomorrow.'

Netta said, 'Marigold's spirits are very low. I have given her an Indian head massage and strewn her room with lavender, but nothing seems to calm her.'

I'm sorry to relate this, diary, but I mouthed silent

obscenities into the phone while writing 'To Mum from Adrian' on a gift tag.

Netta then said, 'Even Daisy can't lift Marigold's spirits.'

I said, 'Daisy's there?'

Netta said, 'Yes, all my girls are home for Christmas this year.'

I said that I would come over to Beeby and bring Marigold's Christmas present.

Netta said, 'We're all very fond of you, Adrian,' and put the phone down.

At about 4.30 my father rang again to say that my engagement had appeared in the *Leicester Mercury* on the family announcements page and that people had been ringing Wisteria Walk non-stop to ask about Marigold. He said, 'Your mother has took it hard, Adrian. She's gone to bed with a double dose of Prozac. She's not stuffed the turkey, nor nothing.'

I ran to the corner and bought the *Leicester Mercury*. The notice was in a box. It stood out prominently on the page. It said:

Michael and Netta Flowers
are delighted to announce the engagement
of their precious daughter Marigold
to
Adrian Mole.
We wish them peace and spiritual fulfilment
for the future.
Wedding arrangements to be announced at a later date.

The *Leicester Mercury* has a circulation of 93,156, with an estimated readership of 239,000. My blood ran cold.

I realized on the way back to the bookshop that most of the shops along the High Street were closed. I had intended to run out at lunchtime and do some Christmas shopping and now it was too late. I had a few moments of madness. One was when I ran into Habitat and asked if they sold sledgehammers. Another was barging into HMV and begging to be shown the Johnny Cash section.

Some of our customers were equally panic-stricken. By 5.30 we were the only shop open on the High Street.

A crowd of drunken builders who had been drinking all afternoon when they were meant to be shopping for their wives and girlfriends stormed in and asked for help with choosing suitable books.

Between us, Mr Carlton-Hayes and I off-loaded our entire stock of cookery books, including a signed Delia Smith and a Rick Stein complete with his dog Chalky's pawprint.

One of the builders, a plasterer, bought a book on falconry for himself and said he would be back after Christmas to look for similar titles. Before he left the shop, he noticed the plaster around the fireplace 'looked dodgy' and offered to stop by some time in the new year and give us a quote.

I locked the door and turned the closed sign to face the street. A frantic dark-haired woman ran up to the door and shouted through the glass, 'Do you sell replacement bulbs for fairy lights?'

I shook my head and mouthed, 'Sorry.' My heart went out to the poor woman.

Before I left, I selected a few books for my own family, Pandora and Nigel.

When I showed Mr Carlton-Hayes the announcement in the *Leicester Mercury* he said, 'I never believe anything I read in the papers, my dear.'

I have just rung Wisteria Walk and asked if I was still welcome tomorrow. My father answered. He lowered his voice and said, 'Things are bad here, son. Rosie's phoned to say she's not coming for Christmas. Your mother's upstairs crying and playing Leonard Cohen at volume ten.'

I could hear Leonard Cohen in the background, croaking out a song about sex and death.

My father said, 'I'd love to see you tomorrow, son. I need somebody to help me through the day.'

As I drove to Beeby on the Wold, I caught occasional glimpses of families preparing for Christmas Day. I thought about William in Nigeria and Glenn in his barracks in Aldershot, and hoped that they had checked their emails, where I had posted electronic Christmas greetings. In my heart I knew that they would have preferred a proper card.

Marigold was in her Cinderella coach bed. It is a tragedy of her life, and mine, that she is one of the ugly sisters. She gave me my Christmas present and insisted that I open it in front of her. It was the loft doll's house. She had made many additions since the last time I saw it. It had a swan on the balcony and there were two children. The boy looked like me and the girl looked like Marigold. The detail was amazing. She had made a minuscule Dualit toaster and a cafetiere.

She said, 'Do you like it?'

I said, 'I don't know what to say.'

She said, 'I've worked day and night on it. I've hardly slept. That's probably what made me ill.'

I said, 'You must rest now. Stay in bed over Christmas and I'll see you in the new year.'

Marigold said, 'But we've hardly seen each other since we got engaged.'

I held her hand and said, 'We're not really engaged, are we, Marigold?'

She said, 'No, not without a ring.'

I gave Marigold her present and asked her not to open it until the morning. I did not want to see her disappointment – it was a rare unsigned copy of *Offally Good!*, my cookery book, published as a tie-in to the TV series.

Marigold held her hand out and pulled me down towards her. I caught my shin on the side of the coach bed, the loft doll's house was knocked over and Marigold, our two children and I were knocked on to the floor.

Before I left Marigold's bedroom I said very clearly, 'So you agree, we're not engaged?'

She nodded and sank back into her pillows.

Daisy was downstairs in the drawing room, shivering next to a miserable log fire.

I said, 'Did you know that there is not a single healthy fire in the whole of Dostoevsky's oeuvre?'

She said, 'I've never read Dostoevsky, and with good luck and a fair wind I shall never have to.'

I felt strangely liberated and asked her to name her favourite books. She said, 'I spend every waking moment living at first hand. I'm the narrator and star of my own life. I'm hungry for everything. I don't want to live vicariously through books. I want to touch, taste and smell life.'

She took a glass from the mantelpiece and drank. I realized that she was very drunk. She wobbled a bit on her high heels.

She said, 'I knew Marigold would get you. She always got her own way when she was a kid. You don't love her, do you?'

What sounded like a small choir was singing 'The Holly and the Ivy' in the next room.

I answered Daisy's question by shaking my head.

She said, 'Tell her quickly and get it over with. She doesn't want a long engagement.'

I said, 'I've told her that we are not engaged.'

Daisy said, 'So you're free, are you?'

I said, 'I've just remembered who you remind me of. It's a thin Nigella Lawson.'

She said, 'I remodelled myself on Nigella last year. Had the boobs done, the hair dyed, the lips plumped up. But I'm no domestic goddess. I loathe domesticity.'

She reached out and removed my glasses. I felt as though I were standing naked in front of her.

She said, 'I like the way your hair curls on the back of your neck.'

I said, 'I meant to go to the barber's.'

She said, 'No, don't cut it.' She stroked the back of my neck and said, 'I know you are honouring a dead dog tomorrow or something, but *do* come for Boxing Day lunch. I need an ally.'

'The Holly and the Ivy' came to an end and we moved to opposite ends of the fireplace.

When I put my glasses back on, the world seemed to be suffused with colour.

Wednesday December 25th
Christmas Day

Woke with the usual adult disappointment that there was not a sack of toys at the end of my bed. The sky was grey and it was drizzling. Why can't the weather give us a break for once and snow on Christmas Day?

As I drove to Wisteria Walk, I passed a few kids trying out their new Christmas presents. A man in pyjamas and a dressing gown was supporting a kid on a bike along the pavement. A little girl in a nurse's outfit was pushing a doll's pram behind them. They didn't seem to mind the rain.

The atmosphere in my parents' living room was more Pinter than Dickens. There was a Christmas tree in the corner of the room but it was a scraggy affair and looked as though it was apologizing for its almost bare branches. My mother had done her best with three sets of Christmas lights, baubles and tinsel. I was pleased to see that the 'bell'

I had made out of an eggbox and a pipe cleaner when I was seven had been hung in a prominent position at the front of the tree. I sensed that my mother was depressed.

She said, 'My heart's broken, Adrian. I was so looking forward to Rosie coming home for Christmas.'

I asked where Rosie was. Then I remembered she wasn't coming.

'In Hull!' she shouted indignantly. 'Nobody spends Christmas in Hull!'

My father said, adding to the misery, 'It's William I miss. Remember him last Christmas, Pauline. He loved that drum kit we bought him.'

My mother said, 'Please, George, don't mention that precious little boy's name. I can't bear to be parted from him.'

'And I'll miss having a few drinks with Glenn,' said my father. 'He was somebody to go to the pub with.'

My mother said, 'And it's the anniversary of the new dog's death. Christmas Day will never be the same again. I will never forget the sight of that poor dog choking to death on a turkey bone.'

The presents were still unopened under the tree. I added mine and we sat around talking about past Christmases and toasted absent friends with Safeway's Bucks Fizz.

At 11 o'clock my father put on the Russian hat with the ear flaps that he wears in the winter and said that he had to go out and fetch something. I watched him get into his second-hand camper van and drive off.

I said to my mother, 'I'm surprised you let Dad wear that hat, Mum. He looks so *weird* in it.'

She said aggressively, 'Mozart, Van Gogh and Einstein were not conventional men.'

I went into the kitchen and stuffed the limbless and wingless turkey. There were still some ice crystals inside the bird, but quite frankly, diary, salmonella poisoning seemed quite a welcome prospect.

At 11.30 my father returned, carrying a large cardboard box on which he had stuck a polyester red-ribboned bow. The three of us stood around the tree. He passed the box over to my mother and said, 'Happy Christmas, Pauline. I hope this makes up for what Adrian did last year.'

The box was obviously heavy and my mother quickly put it down on the coffee table. She opened the cardboard lid and a strange-looking puppy peered out. It was the most peculiar dog I have ever seen. It looked like Rod Hull's Emu with a Kevin Keegan perm. It started slobbering all over my mother's face in a disgustingly unhygienic manner.

My mother and father bent over the new puppy as though they were worshipping the Messiah. I hardly got a look-in for the rest of the day. I was merely the galley slave who had killed their last dog.

My Christmas presents were the usual tat. The worst was from my father: a golf set that consisted of three golf balls, a tiny golf ball 'towel', a pewter tankard inscribed 'The 19th hole' and a pair of dimple-palmed golfing gloves.

My father said, 'I know you hate golf, but I didn't know what else to get you.'

*

My mother let me in on the secret of the 'Mole Christmas gravy'.

'I was hoping to pass the secret recipe on to Rosie, but since she's not here,' she said bitterly, 'I'll pass it on to you.'

She told me the secret in the kitchen with the door closed.

'You boil the turkey giblets in three pints of water with an onion, a carrot and a potato. Then you strain the liquid and some turkey juice from the roasting pan, and dissolve two chicken Oxos in a cup of the hot liquid. Next mix a little Bisto in an eggcup –'

'Why an eggcup?' I queried.

'Because,' she said scornfully, 'you don't want the gravy too thick, do you? Add the ingredients together, carefully simmering for a time, until *voilà*! You've got the Mole Christmas gravy.'

I was incredibly disappointed. I told her that I had expected to hear about a magic ingredient, some rare and exotic spice I'd never known of, something available only at Christmas time, bought after dark from a mysterious foreign woman.

My mother said, 'No, all the ingredients can be bought in the Co-op.'

This is another boyhood illusion shattered.

My mother urged me to ring William in Nigeria. I did so reluctantly. He told me that his stepfather, Wole, had bought him a new bike. As he chatted on about his new life, and his half-brothers and sisters, I felt a powerful longing to hold him in my arms, and sniff his skin, and hold his sticky little hands. I wondered if the stepfather had been pushing William and his bike along a dusty pavement in Lagos. Perhaps I shouldn't have given him up so easily.

I told him about the new puppy and he asked me if it had a name yet. I told him that it was a Mole tradition that dogs were not given a name.

He said, 'You won't kill the new dog, will you, Dad?'

I told him quite firmly that I had not killed the last one.

My mother took the phone from me and my father crowded next to her. I left the room and sat on the stairs. It is a horrible thing to see your old parents crying. The hall was full of packing cases and boxes. The bed I had slept in since childhood had been dismantled and was leaning against the wall.

I was reheating the Christmas gravy when Glenn rang me on my mobile to say that he was being posted to Cyprus. I asked him if I would see him before he left and he said no, he was leaving tomorrow morning at dawn. I didn't like the sound of that word 'dawn'. It was suggestive of urgency and danger and I felt my stomach churn with fear for him. I tried to sound normal and asked him if he'd received his Christmas present.

There was a slight hesitation, then he said, 'Yes, Dad, thank you. It was just what I wanted.'

He is such a kind boy. I will forgive him for telling me a lie. The sad truth is, diary, that I forgot to send him a Christmas present. I was planning to blame this unforgivable oversight on ParcelForce.

When I told my parents that Glenn was going overseas,

my mother's face drained of colour. She said, 'Not Iraq!'

I told her that Glenn was too young at seventeen to be sent to Iraq, but he was old enough to go to Cyprus. However, diary, I don't like to think about the boy being out of the country, not with the world in such turmoil.

At 5 o'clock there was a one-minute silence for the dog that I was accused of murdering at that hour exactly a year ago today.

At the end of the silence I said, yet again, 'I did not give that dog a turkey bone!'

But it was obvious that neither of my parents believed me.

My mother went outside into the garden and put a poinsettia plant on the dog's grave. When she came back in, my father gave her a piece of kitchen towel with which to wipe her eyes.

He put his arm round her and said, 'Do you want me to dig him up when we move, Pauline?'

My mother said, 'No. He was happy in the back garden, pulling the washing off the line.'

They smiled fondly at the memories, though I remember my father going berserk when the dog had pulled his best jeans off the line and dragged them through the mud.

After eating a slice of Yule log and cracking a few of the easier nuts, I went home and left them watching a video of Christmas 2001, which mainly consisted of a William Mole drum solo, but they didn't seem to mind the din.

Thursday December 26th
Boxing Day

I woke with a sense of excitement, but couldn't remember what I was looking forward to. Then I remembered. I would be seeing Daisy Flowers at Beeby on the Wold.

It annoyed me that Marigold always came out to greet me before I had a chance to park the car. I like a moment on my own to compose my thoughts before I enter another household.

She held a twig of mistletoe above our heads and kissed me on the cheek. She was wearing a full-skirted, sequined dress, more suitable for *Come Dancing* than Boxing Day lunch.

I managed to sit next to Daisy, who was elegant in black. She asked me how Christmas Day had been. I said it had been hell.

She said, 'It couldn't have been worse than here. Poppy's hair got caught up in the Magimix when Mummy was creaming garlic mash. And Daddy got drunk on his foul mulled wine and started to cry about Mummy and Roger Middleton.'

Netta Flowers handed round home-made crackers. She said, 'I can hardly bear to see them destroyed. It took me weeks of working until the early hours to make them.'

I pulled a cracker with Marigold. The novelty was a plastic ring with a gaudy pseudo-ruby stone. Marigold asked me to put the ring on the third finger of her left hand.

When I did so she shrieked, 'Look, family, look, family, I'm properly engaged.'

How we all laughed.

Netta said, 'I'm sure as soon as the jewellery shops open Adrian will be buying you something rather splendid. Perhaps a large cluster of diamonds would suit you, Mazzie.'

I realized then that Marigold had not informed her family that the engagement was off.

A strange thing happened to me. I disassociated myself from my surroundings. I seemed to hover above the table. Voices sounded as if they were coming from afar.

I can now see, sitting here in the silence of my loft apartment, that I was in a state of acute anxiety this afternoon. If it hadn't been for Daisy holding my hand under the table, I might well have broken down. I am like a man who is trapped in a grain silo – the harder he digs, trying to get out, the more the grain pours in, trapping him still further.

Friday December 27th

My parents moved to the top left-hand corner of a windswept field today. Their address is The Piggeries, The Bottom Field, Lower Lane, Mangold Parva, Leicestershire. Most of their furniture and possessions have been put into storage, though to be quite honest, diary, it would have been kinder to the furniture to have put it out of its misery by setting fire to the lot.

We battled against a north-east wind to erect the tent. It was dark long before the last peg had been battered into the muddy ground. We sat in the back of the camper van with the new puppy while my mother made tea on the tiny Calor gas stove. The wind screeched and moaned around the vehicle and rocked us as though we were in a cabin cruiser on the high seas.

I didn't like to leave them there and almost asked them to come home with me and stay until at least one of the pigsties had been converted. But then I thought about my father's noisy toilet habits and kept my mouth shut.

As I trekked across the field towards my car, parked in the dark lane, I was overcome with sadness because at least they had each other and I had no one to share my troubles with.

Saturday December 28th

Our sale started today. Mr Carlton-Hayes told me that he'd had a serious talk with Leslie over Christmas and that he intends to implement all my suggested changes.

I am to be given the title Manager and am in sole charge of ordering new books, meeting reps, organizing a readers' club, buying a coffee machine and crockery, setting up a computer and going online. These changes are to be phased in gradually, as we do not want to alienate our regular customers, who are always going on about the necessity of having an independent bookseller on the High Street.

Mr Carlton-Hayes's duties are onsite domestic valuations, banking, wages, repairs and rebinding. At busy periods we will both work on the till. We are going to open our lavatory to the public and reorganize the shelves so that we can fit in more furniture.

Mr Carlton-Hayes did not mention raising my salary, but I expect this was a simple oversight.

An elderly woman wearing a rabbit's paw brooch came in and complained that I had sold her *Trainspotting* by Irving Welsh as a Christmas present for her 76-year-old railway enthusiast husband.

She said, 'It's nothing but filth and Scottish words. My husband had to double his blood pressure tablets after reading it.'

I swapped it for *Murder on the Orient Express* by Agatha Christie.

Sunday December 29th

Brain-box Henderson phoned me this morning, interrupting the omnibus edition of *The Archers*. He had heard that I was associated with the Leicester Madrigal Society and wondered if he could join. I gave him Michael Flowers's phone number.

I asked him if he had managed to sort out the Fossington-Gore/George Foreman grill farrago. He said that he had managed to swap the grill for an electric juicer.

He wanted to talk about the situation in Iraq. He is another Doubting Thomas regarding the Weapons of Mass Destruction. I cut him off by saying that my coffee was boiling over on the stove, and anyway the swans were making such a racket outside I could hardly hear what he was saying.

An hour later Marigold rang to say that Brain-box Henderson is auditioning tomorrow night. She asked me what I was wearing to the fancy dress party on New Year's Eve.

I said, 'I will probably go as the French writer Flaubert.' She said, 'Shall I go as Coco?'

Then Gielgud honked so loudly that the rest of her words were lost. It would make a change to see Marigold dressed elegantly for a change.

Monday December 30th

I got up in darkness this morning. My car was covered in a thick layer of frost. I had to scrape my windscreen clean with my Visa card, before driving to the Piggeries to check that my parents had survived the night. I drove by Wisteria Walk and said goodbye to the empty house. There had been some happy times there – not many, but certainly some.

There was a evil wind blowing when I got to the Piggeries. Half of the tent had blown down and was flapping in the wind. I opened the door of the camper van quietly. My parents were lying separately on two shelves, one above the other. The ugly puppy woke and started yapping.

My father stirred and muttered, 'Let it out for a pee, Adrian.'

I opened the door and the puppy ran across the field towards the lane. I had no choice but to follow it. There is hardly ever any traffic, but it would be just my luck for the stupid dog to be run over by the only vehicle to use the lane that day.

I caught up with it in the boundary ditch. The water came up to its neck. I dragged it out by its collar and carried it back to the camper van, where it was soon swaddled in the best towel and given hot milk to drink. I, on the other hand, was offered no refreshment and was told to look in the tent for another towel.

My God, it is a desolate place. As I was setting off to the car, my father said, 'There's no high ground between here and the Urals, Adrian. This wind is coming straight from Russia.'

I turned back to wave and saw my mother, who was dressed in a donkey jacket, dungarees and wellington boots, applying scarlet lipstick. What a waste. The only person she'll see all day is my father.

Tuesday December 31st
New Year's Eve

I asked Mr Carlton-Hayes if I bore a resemblance to Gustave Flaubert. He screwed his eyes up and said, 'If you were stockier, had longer hair and a large moustache, perhaps there would be a fleeting likeness.'

Encouraged by this, I went to Party! Party! – the fancy dress hire shop – in my lunch break. I took a copy of *Madame Bovary* with me and showed Flaubert's portrait to a gormless assistant and said, 'I want to look like this.'

He went into the back of the shop. I was surrounded by last-minute customers jostling for a view of themselves in the full-length mirrors. There was an Elvis, a clergyman, a Nell Gwyn – complete with plastic oranges – and a tube of Colgate toothpaste with her husband, a toothbrush.

The gormless boy came back with a black wig, a curly black moustache, a floppy cravat and a velvet smoking jacket. When I finally got to the mirror I was quite pleased with what I saw.

I was the first guest to arrive at the party.

Pandora opened the door to me wearing her usual belly dancer's fancy dress costume. She said, 'You're early. We're not quite ready yet.'

I said, 'The invitation says "8 till late" and it is exactly 8 o'clock.'

She said, 'You still haven't realized that it's a social sin to turn up on time, have you?' She then gave me a flashy pink jewel and a piece of Blu-Tack and asked me to fix it into her bellybutton. After a few minutes, when I'd managed to fix it in place she turned her attention to me again and said, 'Who the fuck are you meant to be?'

I took *Madame Bovary* out of my smoking jacket pocket and showed her the title.

She said, 'You're Madame Bovary's husband?'

I said, 'Isn't it obvious? I'm Gustave Flaubert.'

She said, 'No, Adrian, it is not at all obvious.'

I was given the job of strategically placing little china bowls of expensive snack foods around.

The Lawns won an architectural award when it was built in the late 1970s. It was designed for entertaining: the downstairs rooms flowed into each other but were on several levels. The decor had undergone many changes since I first visited the house in 1982. Then it was full of books, potted plants and Indian rugs; now it was a creamy, decluttered, multi-levelled 'space'. Tania Braithwaite had certainly had the builders in since my father left her and returned to my mother.

I was mortified that it was not Coco Chanel who emerged from a taxi outside the Lawns, but Coco the Clown.

Marigold was wearing an orange fright-wig, a large checked jacket, hooped trousers, a bowler hat and flapping comedy shoes. She had completely misjudged the rules of fancy dress – that young women should dress alluringly. It was only women as old as Tania Braithwaite, who was dressed as a carrot, who could break this rule.

When I remonstrated with Marigold, saying, 'You've got a passably good figure, why hide it under a clown's costume?' she said, 'I thought it would be fun.'

I tried to explain to her that clowns were not 'fun' and in fact were deeply unfunny, even sinister. She took the false red bulbous nose off that she was wearing and blew her own.

Tania Braithwaite came out to greet Marigold and said through a slit in the carrot, 'Adrian, why is it that your women seem to spend most of their time weeping?'

I said coldly that, apart from her daughter, Pandora, all the women I had loved had been sensitive creatures who were easily moved to tears.

Then the carrot put her arm around the clown and led her off to be introduced to my family and friends.

Nigel had a toy golden Labrador at his feet and was wearing a scruffy false beard. He was David Blunkett. He said, 'I've just been introduced to your fiancée. She reckons you're getting married in the spring. I presume I'm going to be the best man?'

I said, 'She is my ex-fiancée, and anyway a best man needs to have good eyesight as he has many duties to perform.'

My mother and father turned up carrying bulging black bin liners which contained their fancy dress clothes. They hogged both bathrooms for half an hour before emerging as Dolly Parton and Saddam Hussein.

Parvez and his wife, Fatima, had come as Robin Hood and Maid Marian.

Parvez said, 'I hope you're controlling your spending, Moley.'

I didn't tell him about Barclaycard's generosity.

Fatima said, 'I've just been introduced to your fiancée. She's obviously got a sense of humour.'

I said, 'She is my ex-fiancée, Fatima.'

Fatima said, 'You'd better tell her that. She's talking about an April wedding.'

I glanced across the room at Marigold, who was talking earnestly to Brain-box Henderson, who had flattered himself by coming as Tarzan. In my opinion, he should not have worn the black shoes and grey socks.

Pandora put a CD of Motown hits on and turned the volume up. I sat with my fingers crossed, hoping that my father's bad back would prevent him from taking to the floor with the other guests.

My mother frugged over to me in what she imagined to be a playful manner and said, 'Shouldn't you be dancing with your fiancée?'

I said, 'She is my ex-fiancée. I told her in clear, un-equivocal terms on Christmas Eve. She is here as Tania Braithwaite's guest, not mine!'

Anyway, it was impossible to get near enough to dance with Marigold due to the wire hoops inside her trousers and her comedy shoes.

My mother glanced over at Marigold and said, 'Yes, it's a tragically sad choice of costume. Perhaps you should take a full-page advert in the *Leicester Mercury* to explain to half of Leicestershire that you are no longer engaged to the poor cow.'

At 11.59 p.m. Pandora gathered her guests together in the living room and turned on Radio Four so that we could hear Big Ben strike 12. But nothing was heard. Radio Four was silent.

It was my father who started the panic. He shouted, 'Iraq has sent a Weapon of Mass Destruction and flattened Big Ben.'

This was deeply ironical, since my father was at that moment dressed as the Iraqi leader.

Pandora shouted above the din that she was a minister of the crown and would be one of the first to know if our country had been attacked.

After a few moments a Radio Four announcer apologized for the non-appearance of the Big Ben bongs, but Marigold took it as a portent of doom. She said, 'A barn owl flew in front of my taxi on the way here. That always signifies death.'

I said, 'Barn owls have to cross the road somehow, Marigold.'

The partygoers sang 'Auld Lang Syne' in the traditional cross-armed manner. I held a hand with Rocky (Othello), Pandora's ex-lover, who had arrived late but seemed to be her escort for the night, and the flipper of one of Tania's neighbours, Mrs Moore, who had restricted her enjoyment of the party by coming as a penguin.

When the singing died down, I asked Rocky if he still owned his chain of gyms around Oxford.

He said that he had sold the gyms and was doing a degree course in African studies. He looked across at Pandora, who was doing her party trick – balancing a chipolata on the end of her nose – and said, 'She's asked me to be her guest at the Afro-Caribbean constituency New Year's dinner. Do you think she's just using me, Aidy?'

I said, 'I'm saying nothing, Rocky, but on the Chinese New Year she invited Wayne Wong and his family to the Palace of Westminster. The photos got as far as the *Hong Kong Times*.'

*

At 1 a.m. my mother and the carrot started reminiscing about Ivan Braithwaite, to whom they had both been married (though not at the same time, of course).

The carrot said, 'Poor Ivan, dead for two years and two months today, Pauline.'

My mother batted her huge false eyelashes and said, 'I still feel responsible for his death.'

The carrot said with a viper's tongue, 'Pauline, you mustn't blame yourself. I'm sure you didn't *make* him swim back half a mile to that small island to see if you'd left your sunglasses on a rock. And if you did, how could you have known that he'd get cramp and drown on the way back?'

A single tear fell from my mother's eye and she said, 'Yes, but five minutes after he'd left the shore I found the sunglasses in my beach bag – I'd been too hot and bothered to look for them properly!'

The carrot said coldly, 'None of this came out at the inquest.'

I thought it wise to intervene at this point and led my mother away before the novelty vodka she was drinking loosened her tongue further.

At around 2 a.m. I slid the patio doors open and went outside for a breath of fresh air. The stars blazed in the black sky and once again I felt a boyish wonder that the same moon was shining on me in Ashby de la Zouch, on Glenn in Cyprus and on William in Nigeria.

I wondered how Daisy was spending the first few hours of the new year.

2003

Wednesday January 1st 2003
New Year's Day, holiday (UK, Rep. of Ireland, USA, Canada and Australia)

I woke up this morning and was horrified to find Marigold next to me on the futon. She was still dressed in a few pieces of her clown outfit. When she turned over to face me, I saw by the morning light that she was wearing smeared full clown's make-up. I was completely naked. I pulled the duvet over my head, unwilling to face the day.

Marigold put her arms around me and said in a tiny voice, 'You're a wonderful lover, Adrian.'

I said coldly, 'Have you got a bad throat? Do you want a Strepsil?'

She said, a little more vigorously, 'Our lovemaking went on for hours.'

'Hours?' I questioned.

'Well, at least twenty minutes,' she said.

I was appalled at the thought that I could have been in any way sexually excited by a woman dressed as Coco the Clown. What does this mean? I was with my mother at the circus once when a clown sat on her knee and she screamed and pushed him off. Is there a connection? I must know.

Twenty minutes is good going for me.

*

I was desperate to go to the toilet, but I didn't want her to see me naked. I asked Marigold about her movements for the day.

She said, 'I'm all yours. I've got nothing to do and nowhere to go. I was hoping that you would take me out to lunch.'

I said, 'I'm an unconventional man, Marigold, but I draw the line at going out for New Year's Day lunch with a clown on my arm.'

Eventually my bursting bladder forced me out of bed. I stayed in the bathroom for longer than was strictly necessary. Under the shower I tried to remember how much I had drunk the night before and when I had lost consciousness. How did I get back to Rat Wharf? The last thing that I remember is drinking a glass of a purple-coloured drink which Pandora said was a tropical cocktail.

When I came out of the bathroom, Marigold was leaning over the balcony, talking to the swans. She started to tell me a fairy story about a prince who had been turned into a swan. She gestured towards Gielgud, who was pecking at the floating litter on the opposite bank.

She said, 'Perhaps he's a prince waiting for a human girl to free him from his swanhood.'

I said, 'Why don't you go down and peck him on the beak? But remember, a swan can break a girl's arm, y'know.'

I was finding her presence extremely irritating. My head was pounding and my mouth tasted so vile that I was surprised my tongue had not fled from it in disgust, to cower in a corner of the room. I couldn't wait for her to leave.

*

When she went to have a shower I wrote my New Year's Resolutions:

1. I will never see Marigold Flowers again.
2. I will stick to my usual drinks: lager and lime, red wine at £4.99 a bottle and above, and dry whites.
3. I will work out how much money I owe.
4. I will read aloud to poor blind Nigel on a regular basis.
5. I will learn how to operate my home entertainment centre.
6. I will eat five pieces of fruit and vegetables every day.
7. I will email William and Glenn on a weekly basis.
8. I will prove to Latesun Ltd that Saddam Hussein does have Weapons of Mass Destruction and get my deposit back.

Marigold was wearing my white bathrobe when she came out of the shower. She asked me if I had any clothes she could borrow to go home in. I gave her a kaftan I'd brought back from Tunisia, a pair of jogging trousers and the three-quarter-length Parka I used to wear when I had my moped. There was nothing I could do about shoes. Marigold's feet are only slightly larger than those of a Tiny Tears doll, so she wore the one-size-fits-all comedy clown shoes to walk to the car park.

It was unfortunate timing. We passed Mia Fox on the stairs and Professor Green in the car park. I felt obliged to stop and introduce Marigold to them. Perhaps I should have explained why she was so very badly dressed, but I didn't want to upset Marigold and have her crying all the way to Beeby on the Wold.

Before she got out of my car I shook her hand and said, 'Unless we run into each other, this could be the last time we meet.'

She said, 'Don't be so silly,' and ran, somewhat clumsily because of the clown shoes, indoors.

Thursday January 2nd
Holiday (Scotland)

The *Daily Telegraph* claims that Saddam Hussein has hidden 360 tons of chemical weapons, 30,000 Weapons of Mass Destruction launch mechanisms and 3,000 tons of chemicals. I have snipped out the article and sent it to Latesun Ltd with a note:

Dear Johnny Bond

Please read the enclosed article. As you see, it appeared in the *Daily Telegraph*. I'm sure you will concur with me that the *Daily Telegraph* can be trusted implicitly. I look forward to receiving your cheque for £57.10 in the near future.

Yours sincerely

A. A. Mole

Friday January 3rd

Mr Carlton-Hayes told me that his nephew is a major in the army, stationed in the Gulf. Apparently, Tony Blair sent a Christmas message to British troops in the Gulf: 'Prepare for war.'

Thank God Glenn is not eighteen until April 18th. The war with Iraq will be over by then.

I picked up a copy of *Survivalist* in WH Smith. There was an advertisement inside for a biological and chemical protection full-body suit. I may send for one. Rat Wharf is very near the epicentre of Leicester.

Saturday January 4th

A busy day in the shop, exchanging unwanted Christmas presents. I was pleased to exchange a copy of Barry Kent's *Making Love with Wendy Cope* for Simon Armitage's *All Points North*.

I told Mr Carlton-Hayes that my association with Marigold Flowers was over.

He said, 'I think that's wise, my dear. The Flowers family have a way of sucking you into their dreadful world.'

Nigel rang and said, 'You promised you would come round and read to me. Was it a blag or will you keep your promise?'

I told him that I was free tomorrow.

He said, 'You can start with the Sunday papers then. Bring an *Observer* with you.'

Sunday January 5th

Lord Jenkins of Hillhead, formally Roy Jenkins, died today, aged eighty-two. Had he been able to pronounce his Rs he would almost certainly have become prime minister.

My mother rang and invited herself and my father for Sunday lunch. I said that I could not give them lunch because I had a prior engagement, reading the Sunday papers to Nigel.

My mother said, 'Me and your dad were looking forward to being somewhere dry and warm for the day. It's been raining non-stop for two days. The tent's flooded out and it's impossible to keep anything dry. I think your father is going down with trench foot. And living in the bloody camper van is sending me stir crazy.'

Nigel was totally unappreciative, snorting impatiently when I stumbled over a few words of a 3,000-word article in the *Observer* about the inadvisability of Britain and America going to war with Iraq. He is, like Ken Blunt, anti-American and has been since he went to Disneyland, where he had to wait for two hours in the queue for the Jungle Cruise, during which time a man in a Mickey Mouse costume who was meant to be entertaining the queue called him a 'son of a bitch' when Nigel complained about the long wait.

Monday January 6th

Still raining. The swans are swimming in the car park.

Tuesday January 7th

The car park at Rat Wharf is like an ice rink. Gielgud and his wife looked like a bad-tempered Torvill and Dean this morning.

Wednesday January 8th

I visited my parents after work tonight and found them in a pitiful state. It was very hard for me to leave them shivering over their table-top Calor gas heater. As I trekked across the frozen field towards my car, I was reminded of Alexander Solzhenitsyn's *One Day in the Life of Ivan Denisovich*. I did not have rags wrapped around my feet, but the soles of my shoes were far too thin for the weather.

Thursday January 9th

When I got home from work, I rang my mother on her mobile and asked if the camper van was still iced up inside.

She sounded stranger than usual. She said, 'I'm chilled

to the marrow and your father's hands are blue. We haven't had a hot meal for days.'

I took pity on them and rang Domino's and asked them to deliver a Full House Deep Pan Pizza to The Piggeries, The Bottom Field, Lower Lane, Mangold Parva.

I then rang my parents to tell them that hot food was on the way.

My mother said, 'Thank you, Aidy. I knew you'd come and rescue us, and take us back to your place.'

I told her about the pizza and she went quiet. Then she said sort of weakly, 'Thank you.'

I hoped that she was not in the first stages of hypo-thermia.

At 8.30 Domino's rang to say that their delivery driver couldn't find a house called the Piggeries at an address called the Bottom Field, Lower Lane, Mangold Parva. I gave more precise directions. However, at 9.20 my mother rang to say that the pizza had still not been delivered.

She said, 'I can't stand another night trapped inside this van with a depressed man and a hyperactive puppy.'

I reassured her that, according to Michael Fish, the cold snap would soon be over.

Went to bed, but couldn't sleep. Got up and phoned my parents and invited them to stay in the car park at Rat Wharf. They said they might take me up on the offer.

Friday January 10th

The camper van was in the car park at Rat Wharf this morning. I entrusted my parents with a key and allowed them to use the facilities while I was out at work. However, I stressed that this was strictly a one-off act of mercy.

Mr Carlton-Hayes and I have started modernizing the shop. I put a poster in the window advertising the formation of a readers' club to meet monthly at the bookshop.

Mr Carlton-Hayes said, 'I'm looking forward to widening my social circle. I'm so terribly old that most of my friends are dead.'

I confessed to him that I was thinking of the commercial rather than the social benefits.

He said, 'I sometimes think that Leslie tires of listening to my book talk in the evenings. Leslie is more of a television person.'

I told him that I was also looking forward to discussing literature.

I went to Debenhams and bought a Kenco coffee machine, and to the deli to buy fresh-ground coffee. There was a choice of twenty-four different types of coffee bean and I could choose to have my eventual bean of choice coarse-ground, medium-ground or fine-ground.

I dithered in front of the identical-looking beans in their plastic-lidded boxes. The girl stood by with a scoop and a brown paper bag in her hands. After a few moments she began to tap her foot impatiently.

I said, 'What do you recommend?'

She said, 'I don't know nothink about 'em. I'm on work experience.'

A woman who looked like a horse who had been standing behind me gushed, 'The coarse-ground Blue Danube is absolutely delicious.'

It would have been churlish to ignore the woman's advice, so I acted on her suggestion.

Saturday January 11th

Four people have joined our readers' club. The first meeting is to be held on Wednesday January 29th.

Mr Carlton-Hayes has suggested that we should all read *Animal Farm* by George Orwell. I told Mr Carlton-Hayes that I read the book when I was fourteen and didn't need to read it again.

A couple of sofas that Mr Carlton-Hayes bought in the sale from Habitat were delivered today. The mysterious Leslie is running up two pairs of loose covers in a suitable fabric as Mr Carlton-Hayes said he did not think that lime green fitted the ambience of the shop.

When I got home I tried to watch *Brief Encounter* on the old-film channel, but for some reason known only to Zap, the god of remote controls, it wouldn't stay on channel but kept flashing to BBC 24, where dull news-readers with dull haircuts wearing dull suits sat in dull studios speaking dully about dull world events. However, I did see the *Ark Royal* leaving these shores, carrying with her 3,000 marines on their way to the Gulf to join the 150,000 American troops already stationed there.

When I saw the families of our brave boys standing on the cliffs of our Sceptred Isle, waving to their loved ones, a lump came in my throat.

Sunday January 12th

I spent a few hours on *Celebrity and Madness*, but I am beginning to think that the book will never be finished, mainly because not a single celebrity has agreed to be interviewed.

Went to Homebase, bought a hanging basket full of winter-flowering pansies and a bracket from which to hang it, got home, realized had not got any tools, went back to Homebase, bought electric screwdriver, screws, got home, realized had not got Rawlplugs, went back to Homebase, bought Rawlplugs, came home, it was dark, realized had not got torch, went back to Homebase, it was closed, will hang basket tomorrow.

Monday January 13th

Mr Carlton-Hayes has sold some Marks & Spencer shares and raised the capital to buy a computer for the shop.

I rang Brain-box Henderson at Idiotech, the company he runs which specializes in providing technological services for idiots.

According to Nigel, he works an eighteen-hour day to blot out the memory of a girl who left him standing at the altar of the Whetstone Baptist Church, together with

150 guests, a Scottish piper and a chauffeur-driven vintage car. Apparently, Henderson ended up going on honeymoon to Barbados with his mother. No wonder he looks prematurely aged.

Brain-box agreed to interface with some OEM resellers and give us a ball-park figure for sourcing and installing a wire-free, Internet-enabled network, including inventory and book-search facility.

He said that he had attended a meeting of the Madrigal Society and couldn't remember the last time he had so much fun. He went on to say that Marigold was 'a diamond of a girl' and that I was 'a lucky sod to have snapped her up'.

I told him that I was no longer engaged to Marigold and that in fact our relationship was over.

Brain-box said, 'You must be devastated to lose a girl like that.'

To head him off from talking about his own failed romance, I invited Henderson to Rat Wharf for a drink on Wednesday night. My evil plan is to inveigle him into correctly setting up my home entertainment centre and rationalizing the five remotes. To throw him off the scent, I told him I have also invited Nigel.

Ken Blunt, Gary Milksop and the two serious girls came to Rat Wharf for the first writers' group meeting of the new year. Three-quarters of the session was wasted listening to their complaints about the arrangements for the writers' group Christmas dinner.

Ken Blunt read another of his anti-American poems.

Gary Milksop droned on about his wanky novel, and

how difficult it was to bring to an end. He said, 'Each of my characters wants to carry on living.'

I wanted to say that each of his characters deserved to die, violently and painfully, but I kept quiet.

Gary read on silently, then turned to his acolytes and said angrily, 'Which of you typed this chapter? It's littered with spelling mistakes.'

The one with the fringe said nervously, 'It was me, Gary. Sorry, I was premenstrual.'

I read one of my own poems, composed during a slack period in the shop:

> 'Mr Blair,
> You have nice hair.
> You blink a lot
> To show you care.
> Dictators quail
> And tyrants wince,
> Prime Minister,
> You are a prince.'

Ken Blunt said, 'How long did you spend writing that?'
I told him, 'Less than five minutes.'
Ken said, 'Thought so.'
The silence that followed was broken by a commotion on the balcony. I got up to see Gielgud vandalizing the basket of pansies. His beak was dripping with compost. I grabbed the nearest suitable object, an egg whisk, and threw it at the rampaging swan.

One of the serious girls said that she would report me to the Royal Society for the Protection of Birds. She wouldn't have been so protective of Gielgud if he had turned around and broken her arm.

Tuesday January 14th

I was scrolling through my phone, looking for my dentist's number (pain in half-submerged wisdom tooth), when I came across Daisy's name. We had exchanged phone numbers on Boxing Day, after Daisy said that she really ought to have the number of an emergency bookseller, just in case she woke in the night and needed literature.

We were both a little drunk on her father's odious home-made red onion wine.

I said, continuing the analogy, 'My middle of the night fee is probably more than you want to give.'

She said, 'So if I rang you in the early hours and said I needed a good er . . . Kipling, would you come?'

A prude might have said we were talking dirty, a gossip that we were flirting, a pragmatist that we were networking and a literalist that we were talking about an emergency call-out service for bibliophiles.

In agony with wisdom tooth. Can't speak, can't eat, can't laugh. Can drink, but only with a straw. Drove to dentist in Ashby de la Zouch.

Stern receptionist said, 'Dentist no longer does NHS patients. Mr Marshall only sees private patients these days.'

Drove around Ashby looking for an NHS dentist. Severe pain forced me back to Marshall's surgery, where

I begged the receptionist for an urgent appointment.

Things have certainly changed since I was last there in 1987. There is a tank full of tropical fish in the ceiling above the dentist's chair.

Mr Marshall invited me to call him Marcus and, after examining my teeth, told me that a full course of treatment, including the removal of the wisdom tooth, would cost me £999 excluding VAT and the dental technician's fees and the services of an oral hygienist.

I was off my head on Nurofen Extra and had spent a sleepless pain-crazed night, so I nodded my agreement and passed over my Visa card.

I am calmer now.

Wednesday January 15th

Drinks with B-BH and N.

Mia Fox has complained yet again about the noise from my apartment. She came down tonight to ask when the party was going to finish. Brain-box Henderson was demonstrating the home cinema freeze-frame option. Unfortunately it was the brandy butter scene from *Last Tango in Paris* and Marlon Brando's bum filled half my wall. I saw the look of disgust on Ms Fox's face.

I said, 'I can't understand why I never hear your noise through my ceiling.'

Ms Fox said, 'I live simply, without any form of sound reproduction. I think, I meditate and I walk barefoot. I converse with no one. I live in silence. My apartment is a sanctuary, a retreat from the world.'

I asked her what she did for a living.

She said, 'I work in air traffic control at East Midlands Airport.'

'A stressful job,' I murmured.

'Yes,' she said, 'and I have to be on duty at 6 a.m., and your pornographic film party is keeping me awake.'

Brain-box came to defend me, saying, 'Adrian is the last person to be interested in pornography and we're certainly not having a party.'

'We're certainly not,' said Nigel, who'd been in a strange mood all evening. 'I've had more fun unblocking a drain!'

Brain-box Henderson unfroze the plasma screen and Marlon Brando's bum began to gyrate and Mia Fox left.

Brain-box showed me how to use the remote several times, but I couldn't concentrate properly. I was too aware of Mia Fox's hypersensitive nerves.

I asked Brain-box if he could modulate the sound in any way.

He looked at me as though I was mad and said, 'You can't have quiet sound nowadays, Moley. THX is here to stay.'

He offered to drive Nigel home, which saved me a job. I was glad to see the back of them.

I got undressed and lay on my futon and tried to stifle a cough. I was conscious that Mia Fox was lying above me and that a coughing fit could keep her awake and thus cause a mid-air collision.

On re-reading this entry I realize that I should have written 'Brando butter' rather than 'brandy butter'.

Tuesday January 21st

I have been very ill for the past five days. At one point (Friday 17th at 3 p.m.) it was touch and go whether I would be admitted to hospital with a severe upper respiratory infection.

Dr Ng's receptionist said Dr Ng could not come out to me because I had moved out of his practice area. She said, 'You should find yourself another primary healthcare centre.'

I asked her what a primary healthcare centre was.

She said, 'It's a doctor's surgery.'

I was in no condition to drag myself around the primary healthcare centres of Leicester and ask to be taken on to their books.

I rang NHS Direct and the nurse on the end of the line said, 'You could send for an ambulance, but why don't you have a Lemsip and tuck yourself up in bed and see what happens, dear?'

I chose the Lemsip option, but, as I said, it was touch and go.

Eventually Mr Carlton-Hayes came to my rescue by asking his next-door neighbour, Dr Sparrow, to visit me on a private basis. Sparrow was very kind, but his prescription, which was also written on a private basis, cost me £30 at the BUPA pharmacy. I asked if they accepted credit cards, and the pharmacist said, 'Yes, but we add a 5 per cent surcharge for admin costs.'

Nigel and Brain-box Henderson have both been laid low by the virus, which is suspected to have originated in Indonesia from intensive prawn breeding. Globalization is a double-edged sword.

Wednesday January 22nd

In my absence, Leslie has been helping out at the shop. I hope he/she is only a temporary helper. Why can't I frankly and fearlessly hit the nail on the head, seize the pig by its tail and simply ask Mr Carlton-Hayes if Leslie is a man or a woman?

Thursday January 23rd

I was thrilled to receive a text from Daisy today:

Dear Mr Kipling, Hear through the Leicester grapevine that you have been tossing and turning in your bed. Sounds like fun. Love French Fancy.

Dear French Fancy, Wish your buns were in my oven. Mr Kipling.

Friday January 24th

I managed to crawl into the shower today.
    Daisy texted:

Dear Kipling, My muffin is moist. French Fancy.

After hours of racking my brains, I rang my father, who is an expert on Mr Kipling's cakes. He gave me a comprehensive list of Kipling products. Throughout my childhood, there were at least three boxes of miniature cakes a week in our cupboard.

He said, 'Right, let me light a fag.' I heard him sucking on one of his filthy cigarettes, then he said, 'Have you got pen and paper?'

I told him I had.

'Right,' he said again, 'you've got your Mini Battenbergs, French Fancies, Iced Fancies, Coconut Classics, Butterfly Cakes, Toffee and Pecan Muffins, Apple and Custard Pie. Then there's your mother's favourite, Apple and Blackcurrant Pie. Then you've got Jam Tarts, Strawberry Sundaes, Cherry Bakewells, Almond Slices, Country Slices, Bakewell Slices, Angel Slices.'

I heard my mother shouting from the field, 'Caramel Shortcakes, Viennese Fingers, Flapjacks and Chocolate Slices.'

My father shouted back, 'The boy rang me, Pauline. Why do you always have to muscle in?'

My mother shouted defiantly, 'Blueberry Muffins and Apple Pies.'

I know how my father feels. My ex-wife Jo Jo always finished my sentences for me.

Dear French Fancy, I would like to batten your berg.
Kipling.

Saturday January 25th

Another text from Daisy:

Dear Mr Kipling, I'm a bit of a Bakewell tart. Do you want to eat the cherry on my muffin? Love French Fancy.

Dear FF. Yes. K.

An invitation arrived this morning. It said:

> Please join us on Sunday February 2nd 2003
> from 4 p.m. at the Hoxton Gallery, London N1,
> to preview a new exhibition of faecal paintings
> by Catherine Leidensteiner.

Somebody had scribbled in the bottom left-hand corner in thick black ink 'PTO'. I turned the card over and read, 'Please come. It should be a hoot!!! French Fancy.'
    Surely faecal paintings was a misprint and it should have read foetal paintings?
    I RSVPed by ringing the number given and leaving a message of acceptance with a robot.

Sunday January 26th

I almost won £5,000 today! My newsagent had run out of the quality Sundays so I was forced to read the scandal rags. The sex in them stuck in my throat, but in a moment of boredom I opened an envelope that had been inserted inside the colour supplement. It said, 'If you tear open this fortune bag, will you find a platinum ticket inside worth £10,000 cash?' I opened the envelope. It said, 'CONGRATULATIONS! YOU HAVE FOUND A GOLDEN TICKET!'

I was slightly disappointed, as gold is less valuable than platinum.

With this ticket you have been awarded one of the gifts listed!

£5,000 cash
32″ Sony TV/DVD/video player
Your mortgage paid for one year
Holiday to Cyprus
£250 B&Q gift vouchers
Credit card paid up to £2,500
£450 of British hotel weekend break accommodation vouchers
£125 worth of Woolworths vouchers
£300 cash payment
A Lake Windermere cruise
Six months' supply of Supreme Kutz Kat Food

Game code 29801.

To claim your gift, call the hotline and you'll be informed which gift you've won from those listed. Your game code refers to which of the gifts you can claim. At the end of the call you'll be given a personal claim number. This is very important! Write this number below and complete the rest of the details and send it to the address shown.

If you haven't got a phone, you can apply for a claim number and then play by post (see below).

To claim your gift you must include:

1. This ticket
2. Claim number
3. A 20p coin or first-class stamp

Without these items we cannot send your gift or notification.

I will cut to the chase. After a telephone call lasting six and a half minutes, during which an overexcited man repeated what I had already read, he informed me that I had won six months' supply of cat food. However, he cautioned me to remember that I might be sharing my prize with other lucky winners. I decided not to post a claims form, mainly because I haven't got a cat and never intend to get one.

Monday January 27th

I saw a scruffy man on the towpath this morning. He was wearing a dark jacket on which was pinned a post office badge. He was carrying a bundle of letters in his hand. Assuming he was a postman, I told him my name and address and asked him if he had any post for me.

Unfortunately he spoke very little English. I asked him where he came from.

'I am Albania man, David Beckham good, Manchester United good,' he said enthusiastically, sticking up his thumbs.

I stuck my thumbs up in return and carried on walking to work.

Tuesday January 28th

Gielgud barred my way on the towpath this morning. He wouldn't let me pass. I was forced to climb the chain link fence to the MFI car park and walk to work the long way.

The authorities should be informed. He is a clear and present danger.

Wednesday January 29th

Mr Carlton-Hayes and I spent most of the afternoon moving furniture around, so as to accommodate the readers' club, which holds its first meeting tonight. Four people had put their name down – a modest number, but these are early days.

Lorraine Harris turned up first. She is stunningly beautiful, black and owns her own hair salon. While I was making the coffee I told her that my ex-wife, Jo Jo, was Nigerian. Lorraine looked at me and said, 'So?' I hope she's not going to be difficult.

Melanie Oates's first words to me were, 'I'm only a housewife.' She said she had joined the group because she wanted to help her children with their 'prospects'.

Darren Birdsall had put on a suit, shirt and tie for the occasion. I was very touched. He reminded me that the last time I saw him was on Christmas Eve, when he'd been drunk and wearing his plasterer's clothes.

'So you were half plastered,' I said.

He smiled politely.

Mohammed Udeen works for the Alliance and Leicester. He said that reading was his main love after his wife and children.

We were settled in a comfortable semicircle around the fire with cups of coffee or glasses of juice when Marigold tapped on the shop door. I went to the door and told her that I was about to begin a very important meeting and couldn't talk.

She said, 'But I've come to join the readers' club. Let me in.'

I didn't want to have a scene on the doorstep, so I let her in and she went and sat down in my vacant chair.

I fetched another chair out of the back room, but it was the one with the wobbly leg and I was slightly uncomfortable for the rest of the evening.

Mr Carlton-Hayes led the discussion by talking about the nature of totalitarian governments. According to him, *Animal Farm* is about the old Soviet Union and Stalinism. When Mr Carlton-Hayes said that the carthorse, Boxer, represented the Trades Union Congress, Darren said, 'I thought Boxer was just an 'orse.'

Mr Carlton-Hayes patiently explained to Darren what a metaphor was.

Darren quickly grasped the idea and surprised us all by saying, 'So when I've plastered a wall and I'm, like, looking at it, and it's all lovely and smooth, and I think that the wall is like a deep still lake without a ripple on it, that's a metaphor, is it?'

Mr Carlton-Hayes said, 'Not exactly. That's a simile. But if you'd said that a freshly plastered wall was a newborn baby waiting to be clothed, you'd be using a metaphor.'

The 'housewife', Melanie Oates, wanted to know if *Animal Farm* was a good or a bad book.

Mr Carlton-Hayes said that books could not be judged by moral standards, and that it was up to the individual reader to make that judgement.

Lorraine said that she thought the pigs, Napoleon and Snowball, were nightmares who sold out the other animals while feathering their own nests.

Darren asked, 'Is feathering a nest a metaphor?'

And when Mohammed confirmed that it was, there was a ripple of applause from the group.

Marigold listened in silence mostly and then, after Darren said the sheep in the book were like *Sun* readers, she burst into a passionate defence of Mr Jones, the cruel, drunken farmer.

I didn't know where to put my face.

She continued, 'Farmer Jones is obviously heading for a nervous breakdown and has probably suffered from a stress-related illness for many years. And remember Mrs Jones. She deserted him at the beginning of the book. No wonder he took to drink. And I don't see why Farmer Jones shouldn't have made a profit out of the animals. I mean, they are only animals.'

There was a silence of the sort that is often described by lesser writers as stunned.

Eventually Darren said, 'I reckon it's like what's happened to the Labour Party. Four legs good, two legs better – Socialism good, New Labour better.'

Mohammed asked, 'If the sheep are Labour MPs, which animal in the book is Gordon Brown?'

At the end of the session, Mr Carlton-Hayes said, 'You didn't have much to say, Adrian.'

I said, 'I didn't want to dominate the proceedings.'

But the truth was, diary, that I remembered *Animal Farm* as being simply a book about animals on a farm.

After the meeting Darren stayed behind, talking to Mr Carlton-Hayes about other Orwell books, and I was forced to drive Marigold home because the last bus to Beeby on the Wold had left hours before.

I asked why she had come down on the side of the oppressor rather than the oppressed.

She said, 'Farmer Jones and Daddy have a lot in common.'

I said, 'I thought your father was a man of the left.'

She said, 'Not any more. In the shop today he said anyone who is a socialist over the age of thirty is a damn fool.'

When I let her out of the car I warned her that she mustn't in future rely on me for a lift home. I said, 'We're finished, Marigold. That means we don't meet socially.'

She covered her ears with her hands and said, 'I'm not hearing you.'

Michael Flowers appeared at the front door in his bedtime-kaftan, and I drove off.

Thursday January 30th

Went round to the granny annexe to read *Private Eye* to Nigel.

He said, 'You don't understand half of what you're reading, do you, Moley?'

I had to admit that I didn't.

He said, 'Pick a novel that you think you'd enjoy reading and bring it next time you come.'

When we were sharing a bottle of Japanese beer he asked me if I knew that Iain Duncan Smith's great-grandmother was Japanese.

I said, 'No, but I always thought there was something of the Orient about him.'

Nigel said, 'I wonder if he is genetically predisposed to liking sushi or is any good at origami.'

I told Nigel that he shouldn't fall into the racial-stereotype trap.

Nigel said, 'Oh, shut your gob, you repressed English wanker.'

The next readers' club book is *Jane Eyre* by Charlotte Brontë.

Friday January 31st

Glenn rang to say that he is still in Cyprus but his unit has been confined to barracks because of the fighting between soldiers and the local Cypriot youth. He said he can now receive parcels from home.

I asked him what he missed most, thinking that he would say Marmite or Cadbury's Creme Eggs, but he said, to my surprise, 'The family.'

Saturday February 1st

I have sent Glenn a parcel of 'improving books', Marmite and Cadbury's Creme Eggs.

Sunday February 2nd

I travelled to St Pancras with Midland Mainline. I think it was a mistake to ban smoking in carriage A as the riff-raff that used to congregate there are now dispersed throughout the train.

I could not afford to take a black cab to Hoxton but I did anyway. I was glad that I had decided to wear all-black, because everybody at the exhibition was similarly attired, apart from one woman, obviously an eccentric, who was wearing a red dress.

I was handed a miniature bottle of Moët & Chandon, complete with a silver drinking straw and a catalogue. On the front cover was a picture of what I took at first glance to be a disposable nappy filled with poo. I thought it must have been an optical illusion, but when I pushed through the throng of black-clad art aficionados into the main gallery I saw that the walls were hung with tastefully framed, stained, disposable nappies.

I stood in front of one entitled *Overnight Nappy*.

A woman next to me said, 'I love its *soddenness*, its *mundanity*. It's a visceral reminder of our animalism.'

The man next to her murmured, 'It's certainly different.'

She said, 'We need something over the fireplace in the sitting room. What do you think?'

He said, 'The brown bits would tone with the sofas.'

Daisy slid her arms around my waist from behind and said, 'What do you think of *Overnight Nappy*, Kipling?'

I said, without turning round, 'I know a lot about art, but I don't know what I like.'

She said, 'I hope you don't want to buy anything, because everything in the exhibition has been bought by Saatchi.'

I turned round to look at her. She was wearing a black dress that showed her beautiful arms, shoulders and breasts, *à la* Nigella. Her black hair was loose around her sultry face. She exuded a musky sexiness that almost made me swoon.

She asked, 'Do you want to meet the artist, Catherine Leidensteiner?' and indicated the woman in the red dress.

I said, 'Why not?'

Daisy skilfully wove us through the crowd. She seemed to know everybody in the room.

I said, 'You've got a lot of friends.'

She said, 'I'm in PR, sweetheart – they're not friends, they're clients.'

I was thrilled to be called 'sweetheart' by a woman who could easily be mistaken for Nigella.

Catherine Leidensteiner was surrounded by admirers.

Daisy said, 'Catherine, I would like to introduce you to my friend, Adrian Mole.'

The artist extended an elegant hand and said, 'How do you do?'

My tongue seemed to swell in my mouth and I could think of absolutely nothing to say to this woman, but Catherine said, 'I see what you mean, Daisy. That combination of soft grey eyes and long dark eyelashes is, somehow, heartbreaking.'

She said to me, 'Daisy tells me that you keep the flames of culture burning in Leicester.'

I said modestly, 'I just sell a few books,' and congratulated her on selling her pieces.

She said, 'I must admit, I'm very relieved. Have you seen the price of Pampers these days?'

How we laughed.

Daisy lived around the corner in Baldwin Street, in a one-roomed studio conversion in a building that used to make boiled sweets. Her place smelt of pineapple chunks. We were in bed together within ten minutes of stepping into her spectacularly untidy room. Our clothes made a small black mountain on the floor.

I have never seen so many shoes, bags, belts and items of jewellery in one place, outside a retail outlet.

The sex was fog khed dkybwlcu ghtr gthfdsw, as Mr Pepys might have written.

*

Daisy came with me to St Pancras, where I only just caught the last train. I hadn't had time to wash before I left her place and her smell stayed with me until I showered it off at Rat Wharf.

I wanted to tell somebody about Daisy, but it was too late to ring Nigel. I went out on to the balcony. Gielgud was there, asleep next to his wife, with his head tucked under his wing. I'm glad he was asleep. It would have been ridiculous to talk to a swan, and anyway he hates me.

Monday February 3rd

Went out on my balcony this morning. Gielgud was attacking what looked like a dead body in the reeds on the opposite bank. Fearing the worst, I rang the local police station. A recorded message told me that PC Aaron Drinkwater, our local community police officer, was away from his desk but would get back to me later if I left a message on his voicemail.

A couple of minutes later Professor Green banged on my door and told me there was a postbag full of letters in the canal.

We walked down to Packhorse Bridge and crossed to the opposite towpath. Gielgud and his gang were at a safe distance now, paddling towards the town.

We heaved the postbag out of the water. Almost the first letter I saw was addressed to me. It was from M&S, offering me a store card.

Professor Green and I tried to remember what the organization that delivers the letters is called these days.

Was it still Royal Mail, Consignia, Post Offices Ltd, Parcelforce or just the post office? Neither of us knew who to contact. Eventually I made an executive decision, dialled 999 and asked for the police. After a short delay a woman requested my name and address, and then asked what the problem was. I explained about the postbag in the canal.

The policewoman said, 'It's hardly an emergency, sir. You are asking me to divert police personnel from possible life-and-death duties.'

I said, 'I'm not asking for a team of frog persons and a police helicopter, am I?'

She said, 'Our patrol cars are engaged in fighting crime, sir.'

I told her that I had passed a patrol car in a lay-by on the A6 last week and both of the policemen inside had been eating Kentucky Fried Chicken.

She said, 'I am terminating this call now, but you might be hearing from us some time in the near future. Wasting police time is a criminal offence.'

Professor Green and I dragged the sodden postbag to the basement of the Old Battery Factory to await collection by the authorities. Although I am increasingly of the mind that there are no authorities who want to take responsibility for anything whatsoever these days.

I was late for work. Mr Carlton-Hayes was very understanding about my mailbag problem. He has been writing weekly to a double murderer in Dartmoor Prison for years, but the murderer phoned recently to complain that he hasn't received any letters for the past month. Apparently the murderer is being released on licence soon. If I was in charge of the Dartmoor and District sorting office, I would be sleeping uneasily in my bed.

At lunchtime I went to the Flower Corner and asked if they would send £50 worth of English garden flowers, via Interflora, to Daisy's office.

The florist said, 'There are no English garden flowers in February, sir. Not unless you want £50 worth of snowdrops sending.'

I asked her to suggest something appropriate.

She said, 'Are the flowers to mark a special occasion, sir?'

I found myself blushing – something I hadn't done for years. I wanted to tell this friendly stranger all about Daisy. How beautiful she was, how exciting life seemed when I was with her.

The florist took charge of me and said, 'I think £50 worth of cut hyacinths would look and smell wonderful.'

I wrote on the card:

French Fancy, Can't stop thinking about your muffin. Mr Kipling.

At 5 o'clock Daisy texted:

Kipling, Wow! Love and thanks. Am away now until 14th. Come to London on 15th. Please. French Fancy.

Tuesday February 4th

I was harassed by Gielgud on the towpath this morning. He had murder in his eyes. I took my red scarf off and flapped it in front of him, but he stood his ground. A bloke on a bike came to my rescue. I cannot stand this constant intimidation. Something will have to be done.

I was staggered when Brain-box Henderson dropped an invoice into the shop today. The ridiculous boffin is charging me £150 for 'Professional Services' while he was at my drinks party the other night!

He said, 'I've given you a 50 per cent discount because we're friends. And I've only charged you for one hour.'

I pointed out the unfairness of him charging me at all, adding that I was unable to use the home entertainment centre due to Mia Fox's extraordinary audio and neuro-hypersensitivity.

I have decided to be proactive and put my faith in English law.

Dear Mr Barwell

I am currently being harassed by swans. Is it possible to take an injunction out against them?

I would value your advice. I have tried to ring you many times, but your secretary tells me that you are hardly ever in your office.

I hope you will not charge me for this short letter. It is only an enquiry.

As you cannot fail to see, I have enclosed a stamped-addressed envelope.

Yours,

A. A. Mole

Thursday February 6th

My ex-wife, Jo Jo, phoned today. She was barely polite to me and said, 'I'm only ringing you to prove to William you are not dead.' She put the boy on the phone.

He monologued about his young life and times. The boy hardly drew breath. I don't know where he gets his verbosity from. Jo Jo and I were not given to talking much. After we were married, we hardly exchanged a word. Perhaps William has inherited the gift of the gab from my mother. He asked me when I was coming to Nigeria to see him and I said, 'Soon.'

Friday February 7th

I visited my parents after work. They were crouched over a small bonfire, cooking something in a pot which was hanging from a metal tripod. They were both swathed in layers of ragged clothes. Their faces were blackened by the smoke from the fire. It was like a scene from Antony Beevor's *Stalingrad*.

My father got up and brought a canvas fold-up stool from the tent, and I sat down and tried to warm my hands on the fire. The new puppy was cavorting in the mud with what looked like the thigh bone of a large animal in its mouth. They had made no discernible progress in knocking down the pigsties. I asked why.

'Your father can't lift the sledgehammer,' said my mother with barely concealed contempt.

My father got up and stirred the brown stuff in the cooking pot. I noticed how frail and gaunt he looks these days. I felt a pang of pity for him. At this stage of his baby-boomer life he should have been sitting in his slippers by a mock gas fire in a room with four walls, watching the *Antiques Roadshow*, instead of giving in to my mother's unreasonable desire to live in a converted pigsty.

I told them that I would ask Darren, a plasterer of my acquaintance, if he knew of a sledgehammer operative who would be willing to knock down two pigsties for a pittance.

My mother offered me a bowl of the brown stuff from the pot. I lied and said I wasn't hungry.

I stopped for a bag of chips at the Millennium Fish Bar on the way home. I asked for extra salt and vinegar and the woman behind the counter said, 'You should go easy on the salt and vinegar at your age.'

I left the shop without responding, but when I got into the car I looked at my face in the rear-view mirror. Did I look so old/ill that a chip shop assistant felt obligated to give me healthcare advice?

Saturday February 8th

Letter from Glenn today.

Dear Dad

Thanks for the parcel. You could not have sent nothing better. Me and Robbie had all the Marmite on the first day. We bought a big sliced loaf from the NAAFI and made toast. We had the Creme Eggs for our pudding. They was a bit squashed but we picked the bits of silver paper out and they was OK.

Robbie is reading *All Quiet on the Western Front*. He says it's good. He's looking forward to reading the other books you sent as well. He says he's going to read *Catch-22* next and after that *Poetry of the First World War*.

Getting by in Greek is not much help here, Dad. I tried speaking a bit of Greek, but everybody here talks better English than what I do.

There is a rumour that we are moving to Kuwait soon. I am learning to be a communications technician. It is quite interesting. I have wrote to William and told him that I will save up and check him out in Nigeria next year.

Mum has wrote to tell me that she cries about me every night as she is worried I will be sent to Iraq. Will you go and see her for me, Dad? Also she has got a parcel to send, but her post office on the estate has been closed down because the old people have had their pension books took off them. She says she can't queue up in the big post office in Leicester because of her veins.

Robbie and me are playing a darts doubles match against the SAS tomorrow night. Wish us luck, Dad. They are hard bastards. If we win they will beat us up, and if we lose they will still beat us up.

Love from your son, Glenn

I sat for a few moments despairing that such a bad grammarian could have sprung from my loins. I fought against the impulse to correct his letter in red ink and return it to him.

When I got to the shop I took down *The Times Atlas of the World* and found Kuwait. The sight of tiny Kuwait squashed between the huge expanses of Saudi Arabia and Iraq filled me with a horrible foreboding.

I rang Sharon and arranged to see her at a time when Ryan is out.

Sunday February 9th

Sharon met me at her front door with the moon-faced, hairless baby on her substantial hip. She told me that the child is 'called after Donna Karan'. I forced a sickly smile on my face and said, 'So it's a girl. Hello, Donna.'

'No, 'e's a boy. 'E's called Karan. Ka-ran,' she repeated, as though she was teaching English as a second language.

She invited me into her living room. Had the room been a person, it would have slashed its wrists. A thick layer of depression covered it. Sharon had ignored William Morris's dictum that everything in a house should be either beautiful or functional. Everything Sharon had seemed to be ugly, unnecessary or broken.

She put Karan in a car seat in front of the television to

watch British soldiers in Kuwait changing into chemical-
warfare suits. When they put the masks on, Karan began
to cry.

She took a letter out of her handbag and gave it to me
to read:

Dear Mum

I was wondering if you had thought any more about you
and Dad getting back together. I know Dad comes across bad
sometimes and that he is always moaning about things he
can't do nothing about, but he is all right deep down.

I know you think he is a snob, but it's just that he likes things
tidy and clean. Don't worry about Pandora. Dad will never get
her. She is out of his league. Me and Robbie are both in love with
Britney Spears, but we know we will never go out with her either.

I know you and Dad slept together after my passing-out
parade. I nearly passed out again when Ryan told me. It shows
there is a chance, Mum. Why don't you ask Dad to come
round and cook him a dinner or something?

I know Dad is lonely because of all those books he reads.
It's worth a try, Mum. Give all the kids a kiss and tell them I
will send them all a real Cyprus sponge each.

Love from your son, Glenn

PS It's Robbie's birthday on February 27th. Can you send him
a card? He has not got a family because he was sent into care
due to his mum knocking about with Chinese sailors and his
dad knocking her about when he found out.

I folded the letter and gave it back to her, unable to
speak. I managed to croak a few words of farewell at the

door and I think I managed to hide my emotions quite successfully, though later Sharon rang me and asked me if I felt 'OK now'.

She reminded me that I had left Glenn's parcel behind and Robbie's birthday card.

Monday February 10th

Posted two birthday cards to Robbie and Sharon's parcel to Glenn.

Darren came into the shop after his work to plaster around the fireplace. He gave me the mobile number of a bloke called Animal. 'He can't do a four-piece jigsaw,' he said, 'but he picks up a sledgehammer like it's a bag of feathers.'

The L&R writers' group met at Rat Wharf. In attendance were Gary Milksop, the two serious girls, Ken and Glenda Blunt and myself. There were complaints because I charged them fifty pence each for a cup of coffee. I pointed out that Blue Danube cost £3.20 a bag.

Milksop has written a poem about blindness. He wants me to pass it on to Nigel.

> 'Hello darkness my old friend
> I am happy to see nothing
> I am saved from the banality of seeing
> I have an inner eye
> I see into men's souls.'

One of the serious girls said, 'It's absolutely brilliant, Gary. It's incredibly profound.'

Ken Blunt said, 'You've copied the first line from a song by Simon and Garfunkel.'

Glenda said, 'Dustin Hoffman sang it in that lovely film *The Graduate*.'

She went on to talk about Dustin Hoffman's film career. I tried to control the discussion and bring it back to poetry. I talked about my own attempts at writing an opus entitled *The Restless Tadpole*, but Glenda constantly interrupted as she remembered various Hoffman performances.

The meeting eventually lost focus and broke up in confusion, with several people talking at once.

Ken said, when Glenda was in the bathroom, 'Don't worry, Adrian, I shan't be bringing the wife again.'

I read Milksop's poem down the phone to Nigel. He laughed for quite a long time before saying, 'Yeah, I keep forgetting that I can "see" more than sighted people. Aren't I a lucky boy?'

Tuesday February 11th

I was just locking the shop door and asking Mr Carlton-Hayes if I could take Saturday off, when Michael Flowers rang on my mobile.

I mimed to Mr Carlton-Hayes that it was his nemesis on the phone, and he pulled a face and mouthed, 'Oh dear.'

Flowers barked, 'I need to speak to you tonight. I'll expect you at Beeby at 7.'

I said, 'What do you need to speak to me about?'

Flowers said, 'It's a matter of great importance. I do not wish to talk about it on the telephone.'

This phrase has always puzzled me. What else is the telephone for? I told Flowers that I would be there at 7, though I resented this change of plan. I had been looking forward to a quiet night in, preparing my clothes for the weekend in London.

Poppy answered the door to me.

I said, 'What's up?'

She said, 'I don't know.'

I asked Poppy where Daisy was.

'She's touring European capitals with Jamie Oliver, promoting his new book,' she said.

I felt a sharp stab of jealousy. I had always been jealous of Oliver's success. Not only is he good-looking, but he can cook and has a beautiful wife.

I said, 'If he lays a finger on Daisy, I will rip his head off.'

Poppy looked astonished and said, 'His wife is with him, and why should you care anyway?' She led me into the sitting room.

Marigold was lying in a foetal position on the sofa. Netta was massaging her feet. Michael Flowers stood in front of the fireplace with his legs apart, tugging at his beard. Nobody invited me to sit down.

Flowers said to Marigold, 'Do you want to tell him, darling, or shall I?'

Netta said to Michael, 'You can see the state the poor child's in. You must tell him, Michael.'

I looked at Poppy, who shrugged and continued chewing her hair.

Flowers said, 'A hundred years ago I would have had you horsewhipped.'

I asked him why.

He said slowly and menacingly, while advancing on me, 'Because you promised to marry my daughter, you seduced her, you impregnated her and now I learn tonight that you have deserted her.'

Retreating slightly, because he was bearing down on me, I said to Marigold, 'Why didn't you tell me?'

She said, in a martyred voice, 'You no longer love me. Why should you care?'

Before I could say anything else, Flowers roared, 'How could you not love this adorable girl and her unborn child?'

Netta said, 'Marigold is emotionally fragile. She takes rejection very badly.'

Poppy said, 'The last time she was chucked she went off her head.'

I said that I would appreciate some time alone with Marigold. When they had left the room, I asked her how far gone she was.

'How far gone?' she repeated, as though the expression was foreign to her.

'You know what I mean, Marigold,' I said. 'How far gone is a natural question to ask in the context of an announcement that you are pregnant.'

'Oh, context,' she said dismissively.

'How pregnant are you?' I said, taking another tack.

'I don't know,' she said. 'I'm no good at maths. I must have conceived on New Year's Day.'

I did a quick calculation in my head. September. I smelt the decay of autumn. I saw the mist and the phrase 'mellow fruitfulness' came into my head. I saw myself pushing a baby buggy down a path covered in dead leaves.

I asked, 'Have you had a pregnancy test?'

She shouted, 'Yes! And it was positive! And don't ask me to get rid of it.' She started to get hysterical and screamed, 'I will not have an abortion.'

Michael and Netta Flowers burst in. Marigold threw herself into Netta's arms and Netta said, 'Tell us what you want to happen, darling. What would make you happy?'

Marigold sobbed, 'I want to keep my little baby. I want to marry Adrian and I want to live happily ever after.'

Five minutes later I left the house, having promised to marry Marigold on the first Saturday in May. Stepping over the threshold of Chez Flowers was like being beamed up into the Starship Enterprise. I entered as Adrian Mole, but emerged as a spineless manifestation of Michael Flowers's will.

On the way home I switched on Classic FM. An opera called *Nixon in China* was playing. The atonal wailing and caterwauling perfectly matched my mood.

Why, diary, am I, a sentient being, leaving the earth and everything I love to embark on an unknown journey to cold outer space with a woman I do not love, have never found sexually attractive and who sucks the oxygen out of my body, leaving me gasping with boredom?

Wednesday February 12th

I was woken to the sound of *The Nutcracker Suite* vibrating through my floorboards. It sounds like Professor Green has updated his stereo. I lay on my futon, reluctant to face the world. For a few brief minutes I gave myself up to the music. If Marigold had a daughter, would the child go to ballet lessons? I imagined a little girl with Marigold's slightly protuberant teeth and my glasses in a tutu, dancing on pointed toes.

I've always liked the name Grace. Grace Pauline sounds OK. Grace Pauline Mole.

The law has let me down.

Dear Mr Mole

Thank you for your letter of February 4th where you enquired as to the possibility of serving an injunction on a flock of swans whom you assert are causing you distress.

I have asked my legal partner, Phoebe Wetherfield, to pursue the matter on your behalf. Ms Wetherfield specializes in civil law. I have taken the liberty of arranging an appointment with her (for you) so you can discuss your problem in more depth.

Please note, Mr Mole, I do not give free advice. I charge a fee commensurate with the time taken as set by my professional body and approved by the Law Society.

I attach my invoice with the work outlined up to today's date.

Reading instruction	£50
Consulting Ms Wetherfield	£90
Writing letter	£50

£190 for a casual enquiry! I shall report him to the Law Society. He has taken advantage of me when the balance of my mind was out of kilter.

In a rage I went out on to the balcony, ripped up Barwell's letter and threw it into the canal.

Mia Fox's voice shouted, 'You disgusting litter lout, don't you care about the environment?'

Gielgud came from behind the reeds, where he's been skulking, and pecked at the scraps of soggy Conqueror. I hope they choke him.

Worries
Baby
Marriage
Daisy
Money
Glenn
William
Swans
Weapons of Mass Destruction

Thursday February 13th

Mia Fox came down today to complain about the noise my little portable radio makes! She said that she did not want to listen to *The Archers* when she was practising her meditation.

I said that I did not realize that the sound seepage was so severe, and pointed out that, out of courtesy to her, I no longer turned on my home entertainment centre when she was at home. She said that she could still hear my telephone conversations and knew when my washing machine was about to go into spin mode.

I said, 'We have been duped, Ms Fox. These apartments are meant to have cutting-edge sound insulation.'

I haven't told anybody about Grace Mole. I want to tell Daisy in person first.

Put suit in express cleaner's. Told woman stain near crotch was Bisto paste when eggcup slipped. She obviously didn't believe me.

Went to the Flower Corner and ordered one red rose to be sent to Daisy's office. Woman said, 'Do you think one rose romantic?'

I answered, 'Yes.'

She said, 'Wrong. Two dozen red roses, two dozen times more romantic.'

I said, 'Go ahead and send two dozen.'

I was just about to go to bed when Netta rang to remind me that it was Valentine's Day tomorrow. I lied and said that I had already ordered Marigold's Valentine's Day token.

Friday February 14th
Valentine's Day

Went to the Flower Corner and asked woman to send one red rose to Marigold. Rose cost £5, delivery charge was £3.50. Wrote on card, 'To Marigold from Adrian'.

The florist said, 'No love, or best wishes, or fondly yours?'

I explained the situation to her. She was remarkably patient, considering it was one of her busiest days of the year. She suggested I write, 'To Marigold from . . . ?'

The woman is a born diplomat. She should be working at the United Nations.

Mr Carlton-Hayes asked me how many Valentine's cards I got today. I told him I had received two – the usual one from my mother and one from Marigold.

I asked Mr Carlton-Hayes if he celebrated Valentine's Day.

He said, 'Of course. Leslie brought me a glass of pink champagne with my coffee this morning, and I gave Leslie a rather pretty antique wine stopper, and tonight we're dining at Alberto's in Market Bosworth.'

The shop was busy today. We sold out of our entire stock of love poetry and most of the Shakespeare sonnets.

Marigold rang as we were closing and asked me to meet her at Country Organics. When I got there she told me that she had booked a table at Healthy Options, the new restaurant in Chalk Street.

There was a candle burning on the table between us and the owner, an obese man called Warren, smarmed around, giving the 'lovely ladies' a single red rose in a cellophane sleeve.

Marigold said, quite ungraciously I thought, 'That makes two roses I've had today.'

The Valentine's Day menu stated that 'all our food is cooked with tender loving care and is as fresh as a field of newly mown grass'.

However, when the kitchen door swung open I saw a youth in chef's whites taking a bowl of steaming pasta out of a microwave. Shortly afterwards, a large lorry drew up in front of the restaurant and a delivery man brazenly trolleyed boxes of pre-prepared, chilled ready-meals through to the kitchen.

Marigold had chosen to wear a burgundy blouse printed with green leaves. 'I found it in Marks & Spencer's,' she said. 'They are rowan leaves, I think.'

I nodded and felt the urge for strong drink. I asked Marigold if she would join me in a bottle of Shiraz. She quickly covered her glass with one hand, as though I had asked her to share a bottle of Domestos, and said, 'I can't drink again until the baby is born.'

I told her that, according to family legend, my own mother drank three cans of Guinness a night and smoked thirty cigarettes a day when she was pregnant with me.

I ordered the steak and ale pie, with purée of leek and cranberries. Marigold nibbled at a disconsolate-looking Caesar salad.

Our conversation was stilted. I asked Marigold how many Valentine's cards she had received. She brought two from out of her bag. One was mine from the Flower Corner. The other had a picture of a Victorian girl on a swing and inside, using words and letters cut from a newspaper ransom-note style, a verse read:

Marigold, please be my wife,
Say you'll share my lonely life,
My sweet and lovely Marigold,
Stay with me until we're old.

She said, 'It's a beautiful poem. Thank you, darling.'

I said, 'I didn't write it. You've obviously got a secret admirer.'

She said, 'You're jealous, Adrian.'

I said, 'Not of the poem – it's typical of "poetry" written by non-poets. It is what we call, in the trade, doggerel.'

She said, 'At least I can understand it. Nobody can make head or tail of *your* poetry.'

I let it pass and urged her to hurry up and eat her salad. I couldn't wait to get out of there. The restaurant was cold and smelt damp, and I was sick of Warren asking me every two minutes, 'Everything all right, sir?'

Over heart-shaped strawberry tartlets, Marigold talked about the wedding arrangements. She said, 'I'd like you to have your stag night at least a month before we get married. I don't want you to be found naked and chained to a lamppost covered in tar and feathers on the morning of our wedding.'

I nodded meekly, all the while thinking, SAVE YOUR BREATH, MARIGOLD. THERE WILL BE NO WEDDING.

A pseudo-Gypsy violinist came into the restaurant at 9 o'clock and worked his sycophantic way around the tables. When he stopped at ours he played 'La Vie en Rose'. He ordered me to take Marigold's hand and I did, but all I could think about was Daisy.

I know I was expected to give the violinist a tip, but all I had in change was £1.53 and I thought that there was a real threat that he might curse me and throw it back in my face. So I gave him nothing.

I asked Warren to call for a taxi to take Marigold home and walked back along the towpath to Rat Wharf. Gielgud and his wife were gliding along the canal, side by side. Perhaps they had been out to a different canal for dinner.

When I got home I found a package containing a gift-wrapped box of Mr Kipling's French Fancies outside my door. There was no message and no card, but I knew who they were from.

Nigel rang to tell me that he, Parvez and Fatima are travelling down to London tomorrow in a coach organized by Parvez's local mosque. They are going to demonstrate against the war in Iraq. He asked me if I wanted a seat on the coach.

I declined, saying, 'Nigel, I trust Mr Blair. All the top-secret information passes over his desk. He said in the September dossier that we are in danger from Saddam and his Weapons of Mass Destruction. Why can't you accept Tony's word, do your patriotic duty and get behind our troops?'

Nigel said, 'Don't fucking lecture me on patriotism. It was me who stood for eighteen hours in a queue a mile long to file past the Queen Mother's coffin.'

I said I hoped that he would enjoy his outing.

He said, 'We're meeting Pandora at the VIP enclosure

in Hyde Park. Doesn't that tempt you, Moley? You know you're still mad for her!'

I said, 'If Pandora speaks out publicly against the war it will be the end of her political career.'

Saturday February 15th

I had to stand all the way on the train. Anti-war protesters had hogged all the seats. To my surprise, the vast majority of them looked like ordinary, respectable people.

Daisy met me off the train. To my alarm, she was wearing a red T-shirt which said, in large black letters, 'Stop the War!' I was anxious to get her back to Baldwin Street, but she said, 'We couldn't get to Baldwin Street if we tried. There are expected to be a million people on the streets, sweetheart.'

If I had known that Daisy wanted me to march before making love with her, I would have worn more comfortable shoes.

I kept quiet to her about my support for Mr Blair, but I could not bring myself to join in with the anti-war chanting and neither did I buy a whistle and blow it continuously.

When we joined the main march, Daisy shouted out many cruel and uncomplimentary slogans about Mr Blair and Mr Bush, and got the crowds excited. She certainly has a gift for rabble-rousing.

We couldn't get near to the stage in Hyde Park due to the massive crowds, so I was spared the embarrassment of meeting up with Pandora and my friends, and having to explain why I was there with Daisy.

When Pandora took the microphone, Daisy listened to her with rapt attention. She cheered every time Pandora made a reference to the probability that Saddam's Weapons of Mass Destruction did not exist. I wanted to stick up for Glenn and Mr Blair, but I kept quiet. I was outnumbered by over a million to one.

Later, in bed, in the untidy room in Baldwin Street, I asked Daisy if she wanted to read the manuscript of my work in progress, *Celebrity and Madness*.

She said, 'No, sweetheart. I know I may not be much of a reader, but I don't want to find out that you can't write. I don't think I could love you if you were a terrible writer.'

With pretended nonchalance, I asked her if there was anything else that precluded her loving me.

She said, 'I couldn't love anybody who was a supporter of war with Iraq.'

I said, 'Let's take a hypothetical situation, Daisy. Could you love me if I had made a sister of yours pregnant and promised to marry her on the first Saturday in May?'

Daisy got out of bed and walked about the chaotic room, searching for her cigarettes and lighter. She looks less like Nigella Lawson when she is naked. She took several deep draws on her Marlboro and said, 'Which of my sisters have you impregnated and promised to marry?'

I said, 'Marigold.'

She didn't come to the station to see me off. I stood all the way home on the train. At Kettering, Daisy sent me a text:

Fuck off for ever, you four-eyed git.

So, diary, I glimpsed paradise and then had it cruelly snatched away.

Sunday February 16th

I drove through the rain to Mangold Parva, parked my car in the lane and trekked across the fields towards the pigsties. The dog came to meet me, lolloping along on his spindly legs. He ran past me towards the lane. In the distance I could see my mother, up a ladder, bashing at something on the roof. My father was sitting in the doorway of the tent, sheltering from the rain. An excessively tall man with a mullet hairstyle came from behind the second pigsty, carrying a sledgehammer. I presumed it was Animal. It was one of those awkward social situations: I was too far away to speak to him, but neither could I ignore his presence. I raised my hand in greeting and he raised his in return.

When I got near enough to say, 'Hello, Mum,' my mother turned her head and then started screaming, 'Ivan! Ivan! Come back! Come back!'

My heart froze. Had she finally cracked under the burden of guilt she must be carrying for causing Ivan Braithwaite's death?

She screamed, 'Bring him back, Adrian! Bring Ivan back!'

I ran to her and wrapped her in my arms and said, 'Nothing can bring Ivan back, Mum.'

She pushed me away and said, 'Run after him before he gets to the lane!'

Animal put his fingers in his mouth and executed a fantastically loud whistle. The dog turned around immediately and ran back towards us.

I said, 'I think it is in extremely bad taste to call the new dog after a dead husband. Why have you broken with tradition? Mole dogs don't have names.'

My mother said, 'I'm sick of tradition. I'm reinventing myself. I'm bored with being Pauline Mole. I crave change and excitement.'

I noticed that Animal was looking down from his great height at my mother with an adoring expression on his big face. I waited to be formally introduced. My parents seemed to have forgotten their manners since they moved to a field, so I introduced myself. I asked what his real name was. He looked puzzled and said, 'Animal.'

My father hung the kettle over the tripod, and we sat around the fire and waited for the water to boil. I did not want to tell my parents in front of Animal that Marigold was pregnant and that I had promised to marry her on the first Saturday in May, but he seemed to be a permanent fixture, so when we were finally sipping our tea, I said, 'By the way, congratulations are in order. You're going to be grandparents again in September.'

My mother put her tea down and reached to embrace

me. She said, 'It's wonderful news. I heard from Nigel that Pandora spent the night at your place. You've made my dream come true.'

My father said, 'Thank God you're not marrying that mardy-arsed clown woman with the teeth and the glasses. I dread to think what any kid of hers and yours would look like.'

My father is a grand master of the faux pas. During his brief marriage to Tania Braithwaite, he sat next to a stranger at a dinner party and contributed to the conversation about childbirth by saying that, in his opinion, all male gynaecologists were sicko perverts who only chose gynaecology because they couldn't get their rocks off in any other way. The table went quiet and Tania said icily, 'George, I don't think you were introduced to Barry. He's a consultant gynaecologist.'

I said to my father, 'When you hear what I've got to tell you, you'll wish that you hadn't made that cruel comment about Marigold.'

My mother went totally Mediterranean, shouting, 'No! No! Not Marigold! Please God! Not Marigold!' She reached up to the sky, as if to pull the storm clouds down on to her head, and shouted, 'Why? Why? What have I done to deserve this?'

Animal rolled a cigarette with one huge hand and silently handed it to her.

I said, 'If it's a daughter she might be called Grace.'

But I think only Animal heard me. My parents had turned their backs on me. I heard my father say, 'We'll have to stick by him, Pauline. If he's marrying the Quorn Queen, he'll need all the help we can give.' My mother quavered, 'I know I'm a post-feminist feminist, but you could *braid* the hairs on Marigold's legs.'

Monday February 17th

My financial situation is now desperate. The bank wrote to me today to inform me that my 'credit zone' had expired. As a consequence, I am overdrawn to the extent of £5,624.03. They have asked me to rectify this oversight and have charged me £25 for their letter.

I rang Parvez tonight and asked him to draft a letter on my behalf to the bank. He told me if I was a small business I would be declared bankrupt. He demanded a meeting with me before any decisions were taken. He ordered me to destroy all my credit and store cards before I left the house in the morning. He said, 'You can't be trusted, Moley.'

Tuesday February 18th

Salvation! My application to the Bank of Scotland for a MasterCard with a £10,000 limit was successful. Ergo, my credit and store cards are still intact. Parvez is such a drama queen.

I now have a MasterCard to put next to my Visa card. They look good together in my wallet. They have also sent me, by separate post, four cheques made out to Adrian Mole. Each cheque is worth £2,500. All I have to do is sign them and pay them into my bank and the money will be available immediately. At lunchtime I paid three into my bank to clear my overdraft. The fourth I folded and put into my wallet for emergencies.

Wednesday February 19th

Met Parvez at lunchtime in the wine bar opposite the shop. He asked me if I had cut up my credit and store cards.

I said, 'No, I couldn't find the scissors.'

I told him not to bother writing to the bank, because sufficient funds had already been paid into my account. He lectured me about my lifestyle and warned me that I was heading for trouble if I continued spending at my current rate.

I told him that I was re-engaged to Marigold because she was expecting my baby in September.

Parvez said, 'I'm glad you're doing the right thing. A kid needs a father, innit?'

My mother rang and said that she and my father had been talking about my engagement to Marigold non-stop for the past three days. She said, 'We need to talk to you urgently, Adrian. Can we call round to Rat Wharf some time soon?'

Thursday February 20th

I never want to speak to either of my parents again. How dare they tell me how to live my life, who to marry and who to impregnate? I am thirty-four years old.

A thousand British paratroopers flew to Kuwait today, joining the 17,000 already there. I expect that this is only sabre-rattling on Mr Blair's part. If Saddam doesn't back down soon, over a quarter of the British Army will be deployed in Iraq.

Sharon rang to ask me if I thought there was definitely going to be a war. I reassured her that Saddam Hussein was bound to back down and admit that he had a vast stock of nuclear and biological weapons.

She asked me if there were sandflies in Kuwait and told me that when Glenn was young he was badly bitten by them on Skegness beach. I lied and told Sharon that there were very few sandflies in Kuwait.

Friday February 21st

My mother left a message on my voicemail, saying that she was sorry about her behaviour yesterday. She said, 'I shouldn't have said that Marigold is a manipulative hysteric who has worse dress sense than Princess Anne. If you want to go ahead and ruin your life, that's fine by me.' She ended by saying, 'None of your family and friends can understand it, Adrian. They all think you must have gone off your head.'

I wanted to tell my mother the truth – that I am not going to marry Marigold – but I did not want her to think that she can boss me about like she did when I was a little kid.

Mr Blair is in Rome to see the Pope, who is against the war. When asked what he would say to His Holiness, Mr Blair said, 'I obviously know the views of the Pope very well and they are very clear. Let me just make one thing also plain. We do not want war. No one wants war. The reason why last summer, instead of starting a war, we went to the UN was in order to have a peaceful solution to all this.'

I read this statement to Sharon over the phone, hoping it would comfort her, but she is determined to think the worst, that Glenn will be sent to the front line in Iraq after he turns eighteen on April 18th this year.

I'm still with Mr Blair 100 per cent. I predict one day Mr Blair will receive a sainthood from the Pope.

I hope Mrs Blair's close relationship with her life-coach guru, Carole Caplin, will not jeopardize Mr Blair's place in history.

Saturday February 22nd

Marigold came into the shop soon after we opened this morning. I was in the back, setting up the coffee machine, when I heard her voice asking Mr Carlton-Hayes if he knew of a book on wedding etiquette.

He said, 'I'm a little surprised that you should want to consult such a book. Somehow I can't see your father in a top hat and tails.'

Marigold said, 'Daddy loves the traditions of old England. His friend is going to lend us a horse and cart to take me to the church. And, after we're married, to take Adrian and me to the reception in the village hall.'

By the time I came out of the back room, Mr Carlton-Hayes knew more about the wedding than I did.

Sunday February 23rd

God knows I'm not a religious man, and I'm far from being a Seventh Day Adventist, but I do think that shops should be closed all day on Sundays.

I was made to go ring shopping today with Marigold. An observer might have thought that she was a frail, weak creature, somebody like the unnamed cardigan-wearing heroine of *Rebecca*, but they would be wrong. Marigold has the indomitable will and steely determination of the housekeeper, the mesmeric Mrs Danvers.

I was led to a tiny shop in an alley off the marketplace. Above the door it said 'Henry Worthington, maker of fine jewellery, established 1874'. We had to ring the bell to be admitted. A snooty youth in a tweed suit, with an ID badge which said 'Max Tusker, Assistant Manager', let us in, saying, 'You may have to wait a while. Everybody's buying gold because of the war.'

We sat on little velvet chairs and waited. There was a small crowd at the counter. Among them was a gangster type with his moll. He was trying on a weighty-looking gold necklace.

I whispered, 'How vulgar,' to Marigold.

Unfortunately my whisper coincided with a lull in the murmur of general conversation in the shop. The gangster turned around and glared at me and said, 'Vulgar? I don't fink so. I'm spending 15K on this bit of bling.'

I looked away and studied a silver christening beaker in a glass case next to me.

Eventually it was our turn and we were attended by Max Tusker, who seemed to have already decided that I was a cheapskate. When he asked me superciliously, 'What price range are we looking at, sir,' the alien from the Starship Enterprise said, 'Oh, I'll leave that up to my fiancée.'

Marigold sneered openly at any ring under £1,000 – including those priced at £999.99. She borrowed Max Tusker's jeweller's glass and examined each carat of every diamond ring she was shown. She wanted to know the provenance, history and quality of each gem. The only questions she didn't ask were the financial ones.

She eventually set her heart on a platinum diamond and sapphire ring of extraordinary brilliance, costing £1,399. Because Tusker had treated me with almost open contempt, I affected nonchalance on being informed of the price. When asked how 'Sir' would like to pay, I said casually, 'Oh, I'll just write a cheque.'

Marigold requested that the ring be engraved on the inside 'To my beloved Marigold, my love for you is as deep as the sea, Adrian'. Tusker quoted us £2 a letter. He asked if we wanted to choose wedding rings before the price of gold went through the roof.

I refused to wear a wedding ring when I was married to Jo Jo. I did not see that little band of gold as a symbol of everlasting love but as a golden circular trap. However, faced with Max Tusker's pushy salesmanship and Marigold's eagerness, I agreed to cast my eye over a tray of wedding rings. There were far too many. After a while they all looked the same. I should have been born in the old Soviet Union, where choice was not a problem. Marigold chose a ring for me. When it was on the appropriate finger I felt my life blood ebb away. I visualized myself in the future. Unless I did something very soon, I would be handcuffed, shackled and gagged.

I was already in a slough of despair, so when told that the three rings came to a total of £3,517 I nodded mutely and wrote out a cheque.

Later, in Starbucks, as I sipped my mocha, I composed a letter in my head:

Dear Account Manager

I wrote a cheque for £3,517 on Sunday February 23rd made out to Henry Worthington, Jewellers, while the balance of my mind was disturbed. I am taking antibiotics for a serious viral illness.

Please cancel this cheque.

Yours, etc.

I wrote 'Daisy' in the froth of my coffee. When Marigold asked, 'What have you written, darling?' I used a teaspoon to scoop a little of the chocolate and cream into my mouth.

Monday February 24th

Marigold collected the ring from Worthington's this afternoon and brought it round to show me at the shop. She was upset because the engraver had made a mistake and had written inside the ring 'To my beloved Marigold, my love for you is as deep as the sea, A. Drain'.

Mr Carlton-Hayes and I laughed out loud. Marigold started to cry and accused Max Tusker of deliberate sabotage. She asked me to accompany her to Worthington's to complain.

Tusker would not accept any personal responsibility. He blamed the mistake on my handwriting, and the engraver, who was slightly dyslexic. The ring is being re-engraved for no charge. Marigold is going to collect it on Wednesday afternoon, after she has been to buy maternity support-tights from Mothercare.

Tuesday February 25th

Skipped through *Jane Eyre* in preparation for readers' club tomorrow night. In between listened to Iraq news on radio. Mr Blair spoke like a true war leader. He said, in answer to a request from Hans Blix for more time to find the Weapons of Mass Destruction, 'This is not a road to peace but folly and weakness that will only mean the conflict is more bloody.'

Mr Blair looks at the camera lens with such a knowing expression, as if to say, I am privy to top-secret information, I know more than I can say. That is why the British people must trust Mr Blair.

Wednesday February 26th

Mr Carlton-Hayes brought his little Roberts radio into the shop today. He wanted to listen to Prime Minister's Question Time, and also to the 2 p.m. parliamentary debate, after which the Commons was to vote on whether or not this country goes to war with Iraq.

I told Mr Carlton-Hayes about my long platonic relationship with Pandora Braithwaite, who was now a junior minister in the Department of the Environment.

Mr Carlton-Hayes said, 'Ms Braithwaite has announced that she will be voting against the government, together with the usual suspects. But, my dear, there are a few Tory rebels. Ken Clarke, John Gummer and Douglas Hogg have announced that they will be walking through the 'No' lobby in defiance of their leader, Iain Duncan Smith.'

I asked Mr Carlton-Hayes from where he came by this insider knowledge.

He said, 'I shave to the *Today Programme* on Radio Four. Pandora Braithwaite was on yesterday morning, talking about her close friends Parvez and his wife, Fatima. She was enormously sympathetic to the world of Islam.'

I could have told Mr Carlton-Hayes the truth – that, to my certain knowledge, Pandora had only seen her old school friend Parvez twice in the past twenty-two years. But why destroy an old man's illusions that everything he heard on the *Today Programme* must be true?

The ring is still at the jeweller's. The dyslexic engraver has been sacked and is, according to Tusker, taking Worthington's to a tribunal. Marigold said she was feeling 'queasy' and asked if she could spend the rest of the afternoon in the shop sitting by the fire. I could hardly refuse, although she was an annoying distraction because of her frequent sighs and hardly audible moans. She stayed on for the readers' club.

The first few minutes of the meeting were taken up with an argument about Iraq between Mohammed and Marigold. Marigold's main point was that Saddam ought to be thrown out because he murdered and gassed his own people.

Mohammed said quietly, 'But Mr Blair is not proposing to change the regime in Iraq, Marigold. He is proposing that we should invade Iraq because Saddam has violated the United Nations resolution 1441 and to stop him using Weapons of Mass Destruction against his enemies.'

Lorraine Harris said, 'It's about the oil, innit? We haven't got none left. America's is running out. There might be a revolution in Saudi Arabia an' Iraq's got loads. It's done an' dusted.'

Darren Birdsall said, 'I reckon that George Bush is sort of like Mr Rochester and that Jane Eyre is a bit like Tony Blair.'

'So who's Saddam?' said Mr Carlton-Hayes.

'Saddam is the mad wife in the attic,' said Darren.

I had only skipped through the novel, so could not contest this unlikely analysis of *Jane Eyre*. But throughout the meeting I kept seeing Tony Blair in a long frock and a poke bonnet, making a deep curtsy to gruff Mr Rochester.

Melanie Oates, who still prefaced nearly every contribution with 'I'm only a housewife but . . .', said that she did not understand why Mr Rochester had gone blind at the end of the book.

Lorraine shook her head violently, making her short dreadlocks flail from side to side in her excitement to answer the question. 'That Charlotte Brontë knew what she was doing. Jane Eyre was a plain girl, yeah? An' no hero is gonna fall in love with a dog, right? So Charlotte Brontë made that geezer Rochester blind, right? So that way he can marry a mirror-buster. Am I right or am I wrong?'

Darren said admiringly, 'I reckon you're right, Lorraine.'

Mr Carlton-Hayes said, 'Lorraine, you've given me an insight into the part that beauty, or lack of it, plays in the book.'

Darren said, 'Do you reckon the fire in the attic was a metaphor for the kind of argie-bargie that had gone on in Mr Rochester's past life?'

An interesting discussion followed, but was immediately curtailed when Marigold started talking about the cost of fire insurance.

Mohammed spoke with some passion about the harsh teaching methods at Lowood School. He said it reminded him of being taught the Koran at the mosque in the evenings when he was a little boy. 'But I am grateful now,' he said quietly.

Our next book is *Madame Bovary*.

At 10 o'clock Mr Carlton-Hayes switched the little radio on and we heard that the government had, with the backing of the Conservative Party, won the debate.

Mr Carlton-Hayes said quietly, 'So, we are going to war.' He sat down in an armchair next to the dying embers in the fireplace.

Marigold asked me to take her for a drink in the wine bar across the road. We didn't stay long; the place was full of drunken teenagers. When one of them lurched into our table, knocking over Marigold's mineral water and my red wine, we left.

Lay awake, thinking about how I feel about the coming war. I have always been an admirer of Ken Clarke and Roy Hattersley. If these two stout patriots are against the war, am I in the wrong camp?

Another worry: if Saddam's Weapons of Mass Destruction can reach Cyprus, they can certainly hit Kuwait, where Glenn is stationed.

I wanted to ring Daisy and tell her how worried I was about Glenn, but she is refusing to take my calls.

Thursday February 27th

Mr Carlton-Hayes has been quiet all day. I overheard him talking to old Mr Polanski from the delicatessen this afternoon. He said, 'I have been a Labour man all my life, Andrezj, and I did not think I would live to see a Labour prime minister taking the country to war.'

Mr Polanski said sadly, 'We are old men, Hughie. We know about war.'

Friday February 28th

Iraq has agreed to destroy all of their small stock of AL Samoud 2 missiles. Perhaps this gesture will avoid war. I hope so. Glenn is eighteen on April 18th. It is possible, though highly unlikely, that he could be fighting in Iraq in forty-nine days' time.

Saturday March 1st

A statement from Barclaycard. I owe them almost £12,000. The minimum payment is £220 per month. So in effect I will be working for Barclaycard one day a week until the debt is paid some time in 2012!

Sunday March 2nd

Marigold brought her mother round to Rat Wharf this morning to show her where 'I'll be living after I'm married'.

Netta walked around like a Health and Safety Inspector. I was struck yet again by her porcine features. She was much, much prettier than a pig, but the wide nostrils, large earlobes and piggy eyes surely spoke of some ancient farmyard collision of human and beast. I shuddered when I remembered Orwell's pigs, strutting round the farmhouse on their back legs. She pronounced that my apartment was a feng shui disaster. She said, 'All your wealth is being lost down your lavatory, and the misalignment of your futon is sapping your sexual energy.'

Marigold said to me, 'Perhaps that's why you seem to have gone off sex.'

Netta turned to Marigold. 'A handful of sunflower seeds on his quinoa porridge should bring him back up to the mark.'

I slid the glass doors open and we went outside.

Netta said, 'This place is entirely unsuitable for a young baby,' and pointed out that the balcony was particularly dangerous. 'A toddler's head could easily get trapped in the rails.'

Marigold was wearing orthopaedic shoes, similar to those worn by her mother. Together with the mini backpacks they were both wearing, they looked like German tourists about to embark on a walking holiday.

Netta had brought with her two sachets of raspberry fruit tea. While they were brewing she said, 'Michael and

I thought it would be jolly to have a little drinks do next Sunday evening to celebrate the engagement and to discuss the wedding arrangements. So if you'd like to invite your best man, a couple of ushers, one bridesmaid and your parents of course.'

I said, 'Isn't it a bit early to be arranging the wedding?'

Netta said, 'Adrian, dresses have to be made, suits have to be hired, a marquee has to be ordered, the church notified, bellringers booked, the village hall cleaned and disinfected, a cake commissioned and somebody has to cross the Channel to buy champagne.'

I fell silent.

Marigold asked me who I would choose for my best man.

I said, 'I suppose it ought to be Nigel. He's my longest and best friend.'

Netta said, 'Is that the blind chap? But won't he make a mess of the best man's duties? I mean, fall over the altar and get the rings mixed up?'

'How about Parvez then?' I said.

'But isn't he a Muslim? Do you not think it might be a little insensitive to ask him to attend a Christian church at this politically sensitive time, when the two cultures are at war?'

Marigold said, 'Bruce Henderson is very nice. Wouldn't he make a good best man?'

I was stunned into saying, 'Brain-box Henderson has never been a close friend. Why can't I have a best woman? I'm sure Pandora Braithwaite would be delighted to do the honours.'

*

Marigold wanted to stay for the afternoon but I told her that I had arranged to visit Nigel and read the Sunday papers to him. This was a lie. However, I needed to talk to somebody about the quagmire I was drowning in.

Nigel was in the granny annexe with his guide dog, Graham, listening to *Gardeners' Question Time*. When I asked him why (he once said that gardens made him physically ill), he said, 'I'm not interested in fucking plants, flowers or pest control. I'm trying to work out from what they say to each other who's shagging who.'

I said, 'Who?'

He said, 'Matthew Biggs, Pippa Greenwood and Bob Flowerdew.'

We listened together as a woman in the audience from the Kidderminster Allotment Society asked the panel how to tell a male from a female holly bush.

Nigel cackled. His laughter has a manic tone to it lately.

I said, 'You ought to get out more, Nigel.'

He said, 'I know. I'm waiting for Graham to learn the Highway Code.'

I started to read an article from the *Observer* to him about America and Britain bombing Iraq in an apparent bid to soften up the county's defences ahead of war. But Nigel became so angry and so foul-mouthed and so abusive to me personally that I stopped.

I changed the subject completely and invited him to the engagement party next Sunday.

He said, 'I wouldn't miss it for the world, Moley.' And cackled again.

Sometimes I think he's seriously unhinged. I didn't feel able to talk to him about my problems.

Monday March 3rd

Bank of Scotland MasterCard statement arrived this morning. I shouldn't have bought that seven-piece real leather luggage set from Marks & Spencer last week. I regret it now; I never go anywhere. I owe MasterCard £8,201.83. The minimum payment is £164.04.

I owe:

MasterCard	Min. payment	£164.04 a month
Barclaycard	Min. payment	£220 a month
Mortgage		£723.48 a month
Total		£1,107.52 a month

This is £24.19 more than I take home each month after tax and insurance. I am drowning in a sea of debt. I will have to get a better-paid job.

Tuesday March 4th

Mr Brown has earmarked £1.75 billion to fund the war.

Wednesday March 5th

The foreign ministers of France, Russia and Germany released a joint declaration stating that they will 'not allow' a resolution authorizing military action to pass the UN Security Council.

So Mr Blair and Mr Bush stand alone against tyranny. Our Prime Minister has been making the speeches of his lifetime. His nostrils flare, his chin sets in a determined way and his eyes blaze with passion. He reminds me lately of Robert Powell in the television series I saw about Jesus when I was a boy. What an actor Mr Blair would have made. The National Theatre's loss is the British public's gain.

Thursday March 6th

Mia Fox has gone skiing in the Alps so I was able to watch the broadcast by President Bush on CNN. He said that war is very close.

Friday March 7th

The Foreign Secretary, Jack Straw, has issued an ultimatum that unless Saddam 'demonstrates full, unconditional, immediate and active cooperation by March 17th, Iraq will be invaded' by British troops.

Sharon came into the shop with Karan in his baby buggy. The kid looks more like William Hague every day. She said that she cannot sleep for thinking about Glenn.

My father rang today on the pretext that they had lost Nigel's mobile number. But it was clear to me that my mother was regretting her interference in my life and was anxious to have a reconciliation. After I had given him Nigel's number he said, 'Bring Marigold to the Piggeries for tea tomorrow and we will try to get to know her better.'

Saturday March 8th

Animal was knocking down one of the pigsties when we arrived. He was swirling the sledgehammer around his head as though he was competing in the Highland Games.

My parents made a great effort to make Marigold feel at home by giving her the best folding chair and offering her a baked potato cooked in the ashes of the bonfire that burns perpetually. They even got up and walked downwind of Marigold when they had a cigarette, in deference to her pregnancy.

My father asked when Marigold would be having a scan. Marigold said she didn't believe in scans because they 'desanctified the mystery of the womb'.

My father said, *sotto voce*, to my mother, 'The only bleedin' mystery is how she got pregnant in the first place.'

I was slightly embarrassed by Marigold's appearance. She has taken to wearing Birkenstock sandals. When I discreetly complained of this to my mother, she said, 'Adrian, Birkenstocks are so cutting edge they almost slash the feet.'

I asked her to translate.

She said, 'Birkenstocks are *très chic*.'

But they do not look *très chic* on Marigold; they look frumpy. She looks like a German *Hausfrau* in them. I suggested to her that it might help to lessen the orthopaedic nature of the sandals if she painted her toe-nails, but Marigold said, 'Only sluts paint their toenails.'

Unfortunately, she said this in front of my mother; she was not to know that underneath her big boots my mother's toenails are painted with Chanel's Scarlet Plum.

In an attempt at female bonding, my mother indicated the bare-chested Animal and asked, 'Are you a fan of the six-pack, Marigold?'

Marigold glanced at Animal and said, 'I don't care for men with muscles. I prefer slim, sensitive men with smooth bodies, long hair and delicate features.'

My mother laughed and said, 'Christ, Marigold, you've just described Kylie Minogue. What are you doing with Adrian?'

A wall of the pigsty crashed down and my parents applauded. Animal stood back and looked as happy as a toddler who had just demolished a tower of wooden bricks.

Marigold asked, 'What are you going to do with all that rubble?'

'Make a rockery,' said my father, 'with a central water feature.'

Marigold pointed out that there was no electricity with which to activate the water pump.

My mother said, 'Don't stamp on my husband's dream, he's a visionary.' She put her arm around my father's bent back and said, 'You can see that waterfall, can't you, George? You can imagine the sound of it as it trickles down the rocks into the pond below. You can see the ripples spreading out across the still, quiet surface.'

My father's eyes widened. 'Yeah,' he said, 'I can see it

all, Pauline. We're sitting by the side of the pond on that Homebase patio set, the green one with four chairs, table and parasol for £199 all told. The sun is setting and we've got a drink in our hands, and our fags are lit and there's no mossies.'

Marigold said, 'But Adrian told me that there is no water on the site either. How will you make your water feature without water?'

My mother said, 'Animal is going to dig a ditch half a mile long which will connect us to the nearest water main.'

I asked them how much Animal was charging them.

My mother said, '£3.50 an hour.'

Marigold said, 'Aren't you breaking the law? That's less than the minimum wage.'

My mother said, 'He lives in our tent and I provide him with three meals a day. Plus he's company for George.'

I said, 'But he never speaks.'

My mother bellowed back, 'No, but he listens to all those boring anecdotes of your father's that I'm sick of hearing.'

Marigold asked my parents if they were coming to Beeby on the Wold tomorrow evening to celebrate the engagement and discuss the wedding arrangements.

My mother said angrily, looking at me, 'It's the first I've heard about it.'

I told her that it had completely slipped my mind.

My father said, 'Is there a dress code, Marigold?'

Marigold said, 'No, just come as you are. Well, perhaps not exactly as you are.'

I was glad she made the slight qualification, because

my father was dressed in tattered army-surplus clothing and decrepit boots, and once again looked like a soldier retreating from Stalingrad.

Animal sat down on a lump of concrete and began playing with the dog. He looked like Lenny fondling the rabbit in Steinbeck's *Of Mice and Men*. I hope he doesn't absent-mindedly strangle it.

A wind blew up and Marigold shivered and said she wanted to go home.

My father said, 'We're thinking about wind farming. All this bleeding wind is going to waste. It's the best wind in the world; it comes all the way from the Urals.' His few remaining grey hairs were being blown about his head. He looked like he had a grey halo.

Marigold said she thought that wind farms disfigured the landscape.

I took her home.

Sunday March 9th

Watched the morning politics show to check on war news. Clare Short was on. She is threatening to resign from the Cabinet if Britain and America invade Iraq. She claims that we would be breaking international law unless there is authorization from the United Nations.

I was disappointed to see that, despite my advice, she is still wearing one of her scarves.

This evening's engagement party and the subsequent discussion about the wedding was the most difficult social occasion I've ever been involved in. At least a third of the guests had made it clear to me beforehand that they disapproved of my fiancée. Even Fatima, who is the sweetest of women, said, 'It will be a marriage made in hell, Moley. She ain't right in the head.'

My mother does not seem to have any normal clothes lately. She either looks like Bob the Builder or somebody in the Royal Enclosure at Ascot.

My father was wearing what he calls his best 'slacks', a blazer and a navy-blue baseball cap. When I asked him to remove his cap inside the house, my mother said, 'He can't because of the "I am a nutter" tattoo. That's why I'm wearing a hat, to keep him company.'

When Netta and my mother met, Netta said, 'How very brave you are, Mrs Mole. So few women would have the confidence to wear a hat in the evening.'

I could tell that my mother regretted wearing the hat. She kept blowing the black feathers away from her face all night.

My father panicked when he saw the food on the buffet table and whispered to me that there was nothing he could eat. 'It's all mucked-about-with stuff,' he said. I told him to relax and pointed out that there was bread, butter and cheese.

'Goat's cheese,' he complained. 'It smells like it's been festering in a goat's armpit.'

Michael Flowers did not make his entrance until the guests were assembled. There was Nigel, in Paul Smith and dark glasses; Parvez and Fatima in their traditional clothes; Brain-box Henderson in his Norman Wisdom suit; Marigold in a burgundy velvet leisure outfit; Poppy in a 1970s op-art retro dress and white boots; various Morris men and Morris women in their more prosaic civilian clothes; the woman vicar in a dog collar and black trouser suit; Michael Flowers's sister, a thin bitter woman with a wispy beard; and Alexandra, Marigold's old school friend, a timid woman with a square jaw who seemed to be afraid of Marigold.

Michael Flowers clapped his hands and asked for silence. He sounds more like Donald Sinden every day. He said, 'May I crave your indulgence and ask you to wait a little longer before we start the party proper. We're waiting for a very important guest, Marigold's sister Daisy. She is on a train that is crawling into Leicester station as I speak. She will jump into a taxi and be with us in approximately half an hour.'

When he said Daisy's name, my heart constricted and I almost fell down in a swoon. Every fibre, every atom, every corpuscle of my body wanted to see Daisy. But I also wanted to run screaming into the dark night so as to put a distance between me and her. I said, without realizing that I was speaking out loud, 'Why in God's name is Daisy coming?'

Margaret, the woman vicar, happened to be at my elbow and said, 'Isn't she one of the bridesmaids?'

We then had a very stilted conversation about the marriage service. Marigold joined us and said that she would like the words 'love, honour and obey' to be incorporated, and explained that she felt 'feminism had gone too far'.

I thought that the vicar looked a little alarmed at this

request and, in a subsequent conversation, found out that she was a radical and was hoping to 'make bishop' before she turned fifty.

The minutes waiting for Daisy's entrance were agonizing to me. I was embarrassed because my mother's hat was shedding feathers all over the buffet, and I was forced to excuse myself four times and go to the lavatory.

When I returned after my fourth visit, Michael Flowers said, 'Trouble with the waterworks, Adrian? Have you tried an infusion of mustard seeds? Give it a go for six weeks, but if you're still pointing Percy at the porcelain every ten minutes, I know a good urology chap.'

I excused myself, saying I had to go to the lavatory again. After I had bolted myself in, I washed my hands with lavender soap and stared at my mendacious face in the mirror above the washbasin. I then looked through the books that Michael Flowers kept on a shelf next to the lavatory. *Knots* by R. D. Laing, *Ulysses*, *The Rise and Fall of the Roman Empire*, *Mein Kampf* and *The Lord of the Rings*. None of them was worth anything. But I noticed that Flowers had annotated the margins of *Mein Kampf* with his indecipherable scribbling. There were a lot of exclamation marks.

I heard Daisy arrive. I let myself out and went to the top of the stairs and looked down. She was surrounded by people. Brain-box Henderson helped her off with the long black coat she was wearing. She looked up and saw me. She held her gaze and I held mine. It was impossible to tell from her expression if (a) she still loved me and would keep quiet about our brief affair, or (b) she loved me, but was so eaten up with jealousy and rage that she would denounce me in front of our families and friends, or (c) she no longer loved me and didn't care if I married Marigold or not.

Netta bustled over and introduced Daisy to my parents. I watched Daisy compliment my mother on her hat. I stayed watching as my mother took off the hat and invited Daisy to try it on. I heard Daisy say, 'I'll go upstairs and look at myself in the bathroom mirror.' When she was halfway up the stairs she said, 'Hello, Adrian.'

I said, 'Hello, Daisy.'

Marigold shouted from the bottom of the stairs, 'There's a perfectly good mirror in the hall.'

Daisy shouted back, over her shoulder, 'I need to do my make-up.'

When she got to the top of the stairs, she said quietly, 'I can't believe you're going through with this charade.'

I said, 'Neither can I, Daisy, but Marigold's having my baby. I've let down two children. I can't let down another.'

She slashed red lipstick across her lips, then plunged a hand inside the neckline of her black cashmere sweater and adjusted her cleavage.

I said to her, 'Aren't you cold in that skirt? It's little more than a belt.'

She said, 'Yes, I am cold. But I'm so miserable and unhappy that I don't care.'

She then advanced on me with the wand of her mascara, holding it like a small dagger. I backed out of the bathroom doorway and went downstairs.

When the company were assembled in what Michael Flowers called the 'drawing room', the gruesome proceedings began.

Michael Flowers introduced Margaret, the vicar, by saying, 'Netta and I reared the girls to make their own minds up about religion. I embraced humanism. Daisy is a hedonist as far as one can tell . . .'

There was polite laughter. I looked at Daisy. She took a deep swig of champagne, followed by an even deeper drag on the cigarette she'd just cadged off my mother.

Flowers went on, 'Poppy is a disciple of Ron Hubbard and is an active member of the Church of Scientology, but sweet, sweet Marigold has lately embraced the good old Church of England. Which is where Margaret comes in, so over to you, vicar.'

Margaret had a fresh, open face and a Shirley Williams hairstyle. She seemed a little too anxious to prove that she was one of us. She said, 'I think marriage is a little like the buffet table over there. On it there are things I enjoy eating, such as the ratatouille casserole and the baked courgettes. However, there are some things there I loathe and despise. I cannot abide strawberry cheesecake and mushrooms make me sick to my stomach.'

My father whispered, 'Ungrateful cow. I don't like the food, but I'm not complaining.'

Margaret stretched the food/marriage analogy until it broke. The company exhibited bewilderment and incomprehension.

Netta then passed around what she called preliminary sketches of the bridal gown and the bridesmaids' dresses. She coyly told me that I was not allowed to peek.

When the sketches got to Daisy, I saw her pull her mouth down in a sign of disgust and heard her say, 'Mint green? I look foul in green.'

I was put on the spot by Netta when she asked me if I had chosen my best man. Nigel and Parvez turned to me expectantly, but I did some quick thinking and said to my father, 'Dad, you have stuck by me in good times and in bad, will you help me out now please?'

My father took his baseball cap off and wiped his eyes with it, and my mother said, 'Adrian, you've made an old man very happy.'

After the ushers had been sorted out – Nigel, Parvez and Brain-box Henderson and a bearded Flowers cousin – Michael Flowers said, 'I would like to propose a toast to the happy couple. However, before I do, I want to say a few words about my own marriage. Netta and I have been married for over thirty years and we have been, I think, mostly happy, but now alas our marriage has finally come to an end. Netta has found somebody she loves more than she loves me, and so I must let her go.' His voice started to break and the partygoers' smiles froze on their faces. He turned to Netta and said, 'Go to him, go to him soon, my love.'

Netta said, 'What? Now? Don't be ridiculous, Michael, I have a party to run.'

My mother saved the day by saying loudly, 'A toast to Marigold and Adrian.'

There were a few feeble shouts of 'Hip, hip, hooray.'

I overheard Daisy saying to my mother, 'Every social occasion ever held in this house ends in tears and snot.'

Parvez and Fatima went up to Netta Flowers to say goodnight. Fatima said, 'We have to get back for the dog.'

When I was seeing them to the front door, I said, 'You haven't got a dog, Fatima.'

She said, 'I know, but it's what English people say when they want to go home, innit?'

The next time I saw Daisy she was wearing her long black coat and had her bag over her shoulder. I asked her where she was going.

She said, 'I've got to get out of here. I'm going to try to catch the last train back to London.'

I said, 'The station is on the way to Rat Wharf. I'll give you a lift.'

There were protests from various people, but I didn't care. Within minutes of leaving the front drive, we were parked in a lay-by hidden from the road and in each other's arms.

We started undressing as we were climbing the stairs at Rat Wharf. Within seconds of opening the front door, we were on the futon and I was enveloped in the musky softness of Daisy's body.

Mia Fox banged on my ceiling several times, but for once I ignored her and carried on with what I was doing. Afterwards, when we were drying each other after showering, I asked Daisy if she had changed her mind about war with Iraq and admitted that I fully supported Mr Blair.

She said slowly, 'My God. I'm glad you've told me, but it's like being told that somebody you love secretly votes Tory. You could never look at them in the same way again.' Then she said thoughtfully, 'It's going to be very difficult to fully commit myself to somebody who is in favour of invading Iraq.'

I said, 'Daisy, Mr Blair is liberating Iraq from the tyrant, Michael Flowers.'

Daisy laughed and said, 'I know my father is a megalo-maniac, but he doesn't rule Iraq.'

I apologized and said to her, 'No, but it was an interesting Freudian slip. Do you think, Daisy, that you are against the war because you are subconsciously revolting against your father?'

Daisy said, 'There's nothing *subconscious* about it. I kicked my father in the balls once. It was when he was trying to force me into a minibus he was driving to Glastonbury. It was the first time I ran away to London. I hated festivals, the mud, the veggie burgers and having to listen to Dad and Netta in the next tent, grunting like farmyard animals. So no, I'm against the Iraq war because it's illegal, immoral and stupid.'

We talked about Marigold endlessly. Daisy said, 'Marigold always spoiled everything for me. On my eleventh birthday she sneezed all over my cake and blew out the candles. Netta didn't even bother cutting it. Now it's her who's having your baby.'

I explained to Daisy that I had no memory of making love to Marigold on New Year's Eve. I told her about the purple cocktail that some unknown person had handed to me and that the next thing I remember was waking up in bed with Marigold.

I asked Daisy if she felt guilty. She flicked her wet hair over her face and started to brush it. From behind this black curtain she said, 'I don't *do* guilt. It's a totally negative emotion. It's self-indulgent and corrosive.'

When the sky began to lighten I made coffee and, although it was cold, we put our coats on and sat out on the balcony talking quietly. Gielgud and his wife were grooming each other on the far bank.

Daisy asked, 'Are you going to marry Marigold?'

I said, 'It's the baby, Daisy.'

It wasn't the answer she wanted. She got up and went inside and started to get dressed. She whirled round and said, 'I'm going to ask you two questions. The first is, do you love her?'

I answered immediately, 'No.'

The second is, 'Do you love *me*?'

This time I answered, 'Yes.'

She said, 'So tell her the wedding is off before they hire the fucking marquee!'

I didn't tell Daisy that I had already written a cheque to Celebration Marquees of Seagrave.

I asked Daisy for advice on how to tell Marigold.

She said, 'I don't care. Hire a billboard. Get the Red Arrows to write it in the sky. Announce it on the *Trisha Show* or write her a fucking letter. Now drive me to the station. I've got to be at Canary Wharf by 10.30. Chris Moyles is abseiling off the sixteenth floor to promote Radio One.'

On the station platform we clung together like long-separated identical twins, when I murmured, 'I don't know what you see in me.'

She said, 'I'm not frightened of you and your voice is incredibly sexy.'

When the train pulled out, she got up from her seat and ran to the door, pulled the window down and shouted, 'Write the fucking letter!'

Monday March 10th

Jack Straw wants Saddam Hussein to make a television broadcast admitting having Weapons of Mass Destruction. I hope Saddam complies. I could then get my deposit back and win a moral victory from Latesun Ltd. And Glenn will be safe.

I sat with a pad and pen in front of me for over an hour, trying to compose a letter breaking off my engagement to Marigold. All I managed to write was:

Dear Marigold
   This is the most difficult letter I have ever had to write . . .

Then the members of the writers' group started to turn up – Ken Blunt, followed by Gary Milksop and the two serious girls. The meeting was acrimonious. I inadvertently started a row when I said that I was glad to be able to stop thinking about the war for once and concentrate on writing.

Ken Blunt started shouting that it was a writer's duty to write about war, and that he was not interested in the type of writing that goes on for three fucking pages, wanking on about the colour of a fucking autumn leaf.

Mia Fox banged on the ceiling and I asked Ken to keep the language down. Gary Milksop whined that he resented Ken's personal attack and reminded Ken that he, Gary, had written a short story recently called 'The Autumn Leaf'.

Ken said, 'You should rewrite "The Autumn Leaf", Gaz, and change the setting to Afghanistan or somewhere with a bit of edge to it.'

Gary said that he followed the advice of successful professional writers and always wrote about what he knew. And he knew autumn leaves.

One of the serious girls said, 'And Gary has never been to Afghanistan, he is a literary writer. He's Leicester's Proust.'

Midnight
A text from Daisy:

Kipling, Have u told her yet. Love French Fancy.

Texted back:

Darling French Fancy, I am composing the letter. Love Kipling.

Tuesday March 11th

Disaster. Gielgud broke Gary Milksop's arm last night. At least, the swan was responsible for Gary slipping on the swan shit on the landing and falling down the stairs. He turned on the two weeping girls and said, 'You're both to blame! You know I can't see in the dark.' They drove him to A&E, where they waited with him for six and a half hours.

The next I heard of the incident was from Gary's

solicitor, John Henry of John Henry, Broadway and Co., who rang to find out my postcode.

Between serving customers in the shop I composed a letter.

Ms Marigold Flowers	Unit 4
Chez Flowers	The Old Battery Factory
Beeby on the Wold	Rat Wharf
Leicestershire LE19	Grand Union Canal
	Leicester LE1

Dear Marigold

This will be a very difficult letter to write, but I can no longer live a lie. The truth is, Marigold, that I am not nearly good enough for you. You outclass me in looks, intelligence and in your marvellous ability to construct doll's houses from waste materials. I am not worthy of your love, dearest. Try to forget that you ever knew me.

I will, of course, provide for the baby and be as good a father to him/her as I can in the circumstances.

I will arrange to collect the engagement ring at a future date when you have had time to come to terms with this news.

Yours, with thanks for the good times,

Adrian

I put it in an envelope, I affixed a stamp to the top right-hand corner, I wrote the address on the front, I took it to the post box, but I could not deliver the final *coup de grâce*.

I put the envelope back in my pocket and walked home to Rat Wharf, passing two post boxes on the way.

Midnight
Daisy texted:

Kipling, Have you sent the letter? French Fancy.
   I texted back a one-word reply:

No.

Wednesday March 12th

I was woken at 6.30 this morning by a violent ringing on my intercom buzzer. It was another foreign person with a Special Delivery letter from Mr John Henry's firm of solicitors.

Mr Henry has asked for an interim payment upfront of £5,000 to allow his client, Mr Gary Milksop, to employ a typist to enable him to continue working on the manuscript of his novel.

I tried to ring Gary before going to work, but all I got was his feeble voice on his answer phone saying, 'Hello, I'm not here. I've had my arm broken by a swan and I'm staying with my mother until further notice. Please leave a message after the tone and I'll get back to you as soon as I'm able to manipulate the buttons on my phone with my left hand.'

Marigold met me after work and we walked together along the towpath to Rat Wharf. She looked quite pretty and talked excitedly about our coming wedding. I still had the letter in my pocket and thought how glad I was that Marigold did not have X-ray vision like Superman.

I was sure that Marigold would be able to detect at once that Daisy had been in my apartment, but her mind has been taken over by an alien force called Wedding Plans.

All she could talk about was the minutiae of the arrangements. She asked me to look through a catering brochure with her. We ended up quarrelling about the shape of the vol-au-vents to be served at the reception. She prefers the heart-shaped ones at seventy-nine pence each plus VAT, whereas my preference is for the traditional round ones at fifty-nine pence.

The vol-au-vent row led to which of us had the most monstrous mother and only stopped when Marigold screamed, 'You couldn't find my clitoris if you were led there by Sir Ranulph Fiennes!'

After she'd slammed out, I consulted *The Joy of Sex* and discovered that I'd probably been paying too much attention to relatively unimportant bits of her genitalia while ignoring the clitoris even though it had been staring me in the face for the last few months.

After she'd gone, I felt inspired and wrote another letter.

Ms Marigold Flowers
Chez Flowers
Beeby on the Wold
Leicestershire LE19

Unit 4
The Old Battery Factory
Rat Wharf
Grand Union Canal
Leicester LE1

Dear Marigold

Can I be honest with you? I have recently discovered that I am gay. The signs have been there for some time (perhaps this explains why I did not stumble across your clitoris). I almost bought a chandelier recently. I have taken to wearing rubber gloves while doing my housework and I have noticed myself using waspish humour as a method of communication.

I have not yet taken the plunge sexually, but it can only be a matter of time before I meet a man with whom I can share a civil union.

The rings cost me rather a lot of money. Perhaps you could ask Worthington's if they will take them back. If so, please use the money to buy whatever you need for the baby.

I hope we can remain friends.

Yours,

Adrian

At midnight, Daisy rang from a restaurant to ask if I had written the letter. I told her that I had.

She said, 'So when will she get it?'

I said, prevaricating, 'I haven't posted it yet. It's raining.'

She shouted, a little drunkenly, 'I would walk through a fucking monsoon for you!'

I promised her that I would post it on my way to work.

Thursday March 13th

I dropped John Henry's swan/broken arm letter into my own solicitor David Barwell's office before work. Later that morning, Angela rang to say that Mr Barwell would not act on the letter until my account was paid in full. I still owe him £150 plus VAT. I used my MasterCard and paid up.

For the rest of the day I tried to decide which of the two end-engagement letters to send to Marigold. Which was the least cruel: the 'not worthy' or the 'I'm gay' one?

After work I hovered over the post box at the end of the High Street. I even played eenie, meanie, miney, moe. But when I got home the letters were still in my pocket.

I drove out to the Piggeries and sat for a while with Animal and my parents. There is something very comforting about a bonfire.

When I got back to Rat Wharf I wrote another letter:

Ms Marigold Flowers   Unit 4
Chez Flowers   The Old Battery Factory
Beeby on the Wold   Rat Wharf
Leicestershire LE19   Grand Union Canal
                                                    Leicester LE1

My dearest Marigold

Can I be honest with you, darling? I can no longer live a lie. For some time I have been dressing in female clothes and calling myself Brenda. I love the feel of silk, lace and winceyette on my rough male flesh.

I will entirely understand if, in the circumstances, you run from me like a startled faun, but when you do, try to remember me with compassion. None of us can help our genetic make-up.

Yours ever,

Brenda

PS What is the name of that divine blue eyeshadow you wore on Boxing Day? I must have it!

I have just looked it up. I used the expression 'run from me like a startled faun' in my 1981 diary, when I was writing to Pandora. I knew I had heard it somewhere before.

I switched my phone off so there was no, and could not be any, call from Daisy.

Friday March 14th

My mother rang me at work today to ask me if she should stop dyeing her hair red. She said, 'Do you think I should go for the older woman grey-blonde highlight look?'

I said, 'Isn't this a question you should be asking your hairdresser? I'm a bookseller, Mum.'

She said, 'I'm worried about you. I thought you looked terrible last night. You're thin, you can't be eating properly and you've got rings round your eyes. I know you're not sleeping. You're not happy, are you?'

I asked Mr Carlton-Hayes to take over at the till and went into the back room with my mobile.

My mother said again, 'You're not happy, are you, love?'

For some reason tears came into my eyes and I couldn't get my breath. I think it must have been the kindness, perhaps the motherliness, in her voice that set me off. It's a tone I haven't heard often enough in my life.

When Mr Carlton-Hayes had finished serving a customer he came through to the back room to find me. He said, 'My dear,' and handed me a clean white handkerchief that smelt of distilled fresh air. I blew my nose and tried to hand it back to him, but he said, 'No, keep it, my dear.

Leslie always sends me out with two clean handkerchiefs in the morning.'

I said he was lucky to have somebody to care for him so well.

He said, 'Not lucky, blessed.'

I tried to apologize for my uncharacteristic behaviour.

He said, 'I'm not awfully good at the heart-to-heart stuff, I'm afraid. Leslie says it's the fault of being sent away to public school. But if you find it helpful to what I believe is called "unload", I would be very happy to listen.'

I could tell that he was deeply uncomfortable and was relieved when a mad-woman bag lady came in shouting that Jane Austen was inside her head, telling her what to do.

There were twelve text messages on my phone by the time I got home to Rat Wharf. They were all from Daisy. They did not make pleasant reading.

I switched my phone off and sat down again with a pad and pen.

Ms Marigold Flowers	Unit 4
Chez Flowers	The Old Battery Factory
Beeby on the Wold	Rat Wharf
Leicestershire LE19	Grand Union Canal
	Leicester LE1

Dear Marigold

Can I be honest with you?

The man you know as Adrian Mole is an impostor. I have been on the run since I was falsely accused of violating a dolphin off the Cornish coast in 1989.

The police are closing in on me so I must go underground.
Farewell, dearest,
Malcolm Roach
(aka Adrian Mole)

I didn't think she'd believe this so I wrote another.

Ms Marigold Flowers	Unit 4
Chez Flowers	The Old Battery Factory
Beeby on the Wold	Rat Wharf
Leicestershire LE19	Grand Union Canal
	Leicester LE1

Dearest Marigold

This is a letter I hoped I would never have to write.

For some years I have been suffering from a rare medical condition which produces a murderous rage, which in turn makes me prone to sudden fits of violence. I have been secretly seeking a cure, but alas I have been told by a specialist in my condition that there is no hope for me.

The specialist has advised me not to marry. I quote: 'No woman is safe with you, Mr Mole. You must reconcile yourself to living alone.'

Naturally, I am gutted by this news and I beg you to give me time and space in which to grieve for what could have been.

God, how will I live without you, you achingly beautiful, fascinating woman?

Love, as ever,

A.

Out of all the letters I have written I think the letter immediately above will cause Marigold the least pain. Although, thinking about it, will Marigold worry that the baby will inherit the murder gene?

Saturday March 15th

We were busy in the shop this morning. There has been a rush on books about weaponry and warfare.

Michael Flowers rang. He wants to see me on an 'urgent' matter relating to the future of our country.

I left a message at Country Organics, to say that I did not have a free window.

Flowers rang again and accused me of ignoring his call. I explained that I had left a message at the shop saying that I did not have a free window.

He said, nastily, 'Since you did not leave your name and the line was bad, I assumed it was a cold call from a double-glazing salesman.'

He trapped me into meeting him at the Good Earth vegetarian café at one o'clock. He was already there eating a bowl of thick mush when I arrived at dead on one, but he looked at his watch and said impatiently, 'Glad you decided to turn up.'

He always puts me on the back foot. I started to say that I was exactly on time, when he said, 'Look, now you're finally here can I explain the purpose of this meeting?'

Once again I tried to insist that I had not been late.

But he said, 'Adrian, I'm a very busy man. Can we *please* get on?'

He started by saying that our fair country, its traditions, its heritage, was being subsumed by Europe, and that our race was being forced to kneel to the bloated bureaucrats in Brussels. He then ranted on about fish quotas, loss of sovereignty and England's humiliating failure to score any points in the Eurovision Song Contest. He predicted that England would be swept away on a tide of cappuccino and straight bananas.

I wondered why Flowers had called me to a meeting to hear his views about Europe.

He lowered his voice and looked around the café as if the mild-mannered vegetarians nibbling their greens were al Qa'eda operatives. 'I'm starting a Leicester-shire branch of the United Kingdom Independence Party,' he said, 'and I wondered if I could rely on your support?'

I said that I knew very little about the UKIP, and was there any literature?

He drew a Union-Jack bedecked pile of slithery leaflets out of his satchel and gave me one.

I put it in my pocket and said I would read it later.

Flowers barked, 'All you need to know is that UKIP is the only party with the guts to stand up against a bunch of Gauloise-smoking appeasers.'

I said that I quite liked being a European.

Flowers said, 'You like it now, Adrian. But will you like it when they ban our national anthem?'

I thought, 'Yes I would. I hate "God Save the Queen".' But I said nothing.

He stood up and said, 'I'm asking my supporters for an initial contribution of £500.'

After he'd gone, leaving me with his bill, I read through the leaflet. Apparently one of UKIP's luminaries was Jonathan Aitken; another was Geoff Boycott.

When the shop was empty of customers and we were having our tea at afternoon break, I gave the disengagement letters to Mr Carlton-Hayes to read and asked him for his advice.

To my surprise he seemed to find them quite amusing. When he'd finished reading them, he said, 'None of them are quite suitable, my dear. If I were you I would write something like:

My dear Marigold

You are a lovely woman, and I'm frightfully sorry about this, but I now realize that I do not love you enough to want to marry you. In these circumstances it would be terribly silly of us to get married.

If you *are* having our baby, I will of course support you and the child.

I'm most awfully sorry to be such a frightful cad, but I feel honour bound to tell you the horrid truth.

Please do not contact me.

Yours truly

Adrian

He tapped the letter out, using one finger on his old Remington typewriter. I thanked him, but I will not send it.

*

I showed the UKIP leaflets to Mr Carlton-Hayes and confessed to him that I was afraid of Michael Flowers.

'You have every right to be afraid of him, my dear,' he said. 'He's an English fascist. They don't goosestep down the High Street because they know we would laugh at them, but they are wearing jackboots nonetheless.'

Marigold met me at the shop and we went for a meal at the Imperial Dragon. Wayne was very cool to me, and when I asked him what was wrong, he said, 'Why didn't you invite me to your party?'

I said it was only a small gathering.

He said, 'That geek, Brain-box Henderson, was there.'

Marigold said, 'Bruce Henderson was my guest, and he is not a geek.'

Wayne said, 'You're wrong there, Marigold. He won "Geek of the year" at school.'

I didn't enjoy the meal at all and only managed to eat a king-size prawn and a mouthful of rice. Apparently Netta has started to hand-stitch and embroider Marigold's white bridal gown. The hem of the dress will be embroidered with rowan leaves. The mint green bridesmaids' dresses, satin with puffed sleeves and asymmetrical hems, have been cut out, although 'Daisy is refusing to cooperate: she won't send Mummy her measurements, she's such a bitch. She always spoils everything. We were going to Glastonbury once, in the minibus, when for no reason at all she kicked out at Daddy and ran away. Me and Poppy and Mummy and Daddy had a lovely time, despite the mud, so more fool her, I say.'

*

Wayne Wong has installed a karaoke machine, and a black bloke got up and tried to sing 'Lady in Red' to his girlfriend, who was, surprise, surprise, wearing a red dress.

Marigold sighed deeply and said, 'I wish you were romantic.'

This was unfair, because at that very moment I was thinking that Daisy's hair was like the smoke of an erupting volcano.

After a mind-numbingly boring discussion about bridesmaids' shoes, I paid the bill and took Marigold home to Beeby on the Wold.

She asked me to come in and reminded me that she would be away for the next five days, as she was an exhibitor at the Doll's House Society of Great Britain's bi-annual show, at the National Exhibition Centre in Birmingham, and would I join her for a night at the hotel she was staying in.

I reminded her about my M6 phobia, and said that, regretfully, it would not be possible. I excused myself by saying that I could feel a migraine coming on and I needed to take my medication.

She offered me a tincture of bark, but I declined.

We kissed goodbye at the front door. As I was kissing her I wondered if it would be for the last time. I fervently hoped so.

I tried to ring Daisy, but her phone was switched off. I left the following message:

Daisy

It's me, Adrian. (long pause) I don't know what to say – I haven't told Marigold yet. I need your help. I've drafted five letters, but none of them hit the right note. Please, don't give up on me, I think about you constantly. I adore you, Daze. Goodnight, sweetheart.

Sunday March 16th

Text from Daisy: 'Check your email.'

After the usual difficulty and a five-minute call to the helpline, I opened my email.

Kipling,
Draft of letter attached.

I opened the attachment: It read:

Dear Marigold

It is not your fault that you have grown up to be a manipulative, hysterical hypochondriac. You have been hopelessly indulged by your parents.

You have taken advantage of my kind gentle nature and have drained me emotionally and financially.

But hey, I'll recover. Keep the poxy ring.

Thanks for the good times, not.

Adrian

PS I think it must be obvious from the above that I will not be marrying you on 6th May 2003.

I was shocked at the harsh tone of Daisy's letter; she is obviously not a woman to cross. Am I jumping out of the frying pan and into the wok?

I needed to be with the two people who would, despite our differences, give me unconditional love, so I drove to the Piggeries.

The countryside looked fresh and green. I tried to work out why my life had become so complicated where women were concerned. I parked the car in the lane and stood for a moment watching a lamb in the field opposite. It looked as though it was drunk with joy, dancing and kicking its heels. I envied it its joyful celebration of being alive. Then I remembered that in a short while it would be dead and packaged and displayed on a meat counter somewhere. I turned away and trudged across the field.

My parents had spotted my car and were waving, with every appearance of delight. My mother came to meet me, threw down her cigarette and gave me a tight embrace. She said, 'You're a bag of bones, when did you last eat?'

I told her, truthfully, that in the last twenty-four hours I had eaten a prawn and a mouthful of rice. She led me to the open fire and said, 'I'm going to cook you a full English breakfast, with fried bread.'

My stomach was indifferent, but my heart was nourished. She took off her woollen gloves and began to fry bacon, sausages, tomatoes and fried bread over the open fire in a blackened frying pan.

The foundations had been laid for both pigsties, and Animal was laying blue bricks for the dampcourse.

While I waited for the food I gave my parents the Marigold disengagement letters to read.

My father's advice was, 'Send her the dangerous-nutter one, son.'

My mother said, 'They're all ridiculous. Why don't you tell her the truth, before Netta has made the bloody bridesmaids' dresses?'

My full English breakfast looked and smelled delicious, but I couldn't eat it all and shared it out between Animal, my father and Ivan the dog while my mother was in the camper van fetching a fresh pack of cigarettes and a notepad and pen. She then sat by the fire and drafted what she called 'an engagement curtailment letter'.

Dear Marigold

Ever since I was a little boy I have preferred to live in the world of fiction. I have found the real world to be a harsh place. I avoid confrontation and am easily manipulated by people who have a strong sense of themselves.

I am very sorry, but I cannot marry you. I do not love you. The truth is, I love your sister, Daisy. And I think she loves me.

I read the letter twice, and then said, 'How long have you known about Daisy?'

My mother said, 'Since your engagement party. Is it true?'

I said, 'Yes.'

My father said, 'You're a witch, Pauline.'

My mother said, 'I've got eyes in my head, George. I saw Adrian and Daisy looking at each other. I'm surprised they didn't burst into flames.'

It was a wonderful relief to be able to talk about Daisy. My father said, 'She's a cracker.'

And my mother advised me to snap her up quickly, before she goes off the boil.

I went home to Rat Wharf and wrote what I was determined would be the letter I would definitely send to Marigold.

Ms Marigold Flowers
The Ring Road View Hotel
Balsall Common
Warwickshire cv7

Unit 4
The Old Battery Factory
Rat Wharf
Grand Union Canal
Leicester le1

Sunday March 16th

Dear Marigold

I hope you are well. I am quite well, apart from a constant feeling of dread that I can't seem to shake off.

I have some grave news, I'm afraid. (At this point it might be wise to seek the company of one of your fellow doll's house enthusiasts.)

Marigold, I can't marry you on May 6th, or on any other date.

You are a beautiful, intelligent woman, and your skill at making miniature furniture is breathtaking. I am personally devastated by my inability to love such a prize as you, but the sad truth is that I am unworthy of you. I have many psychological flaws that prevent me from making any woman happy. As my ex-stepmother pointed out once, my women seem to spend most of their time in tears.

Believe me, you have had a lucky escape, Marigold.

I will of course support you financially and practically when the baby is born and will have him/her on alternate Sundays from 10 a.m. to 6 p.m. (If wet, 10 a.m. until 2 p.m.)

Please do not contact me. I am already in pain and to hear your voice would cause me considerable agony.

Yours, Adrian

Monday March 17th
St Patrick's Day

Called in at local post office before work. Told postmaster essential letter reaches Ring Road View Hotel tomorrow morning without fail.

He said first class was unreliable. Must pay £6.95 for Special Delivery, guaranteed before 9 a.m. next day. 'Must be an important letter,' he said.

I told him contents of letter explosive.

He said, laughing but nervous, 'Hope not real explosives.'

I told him I was talking metaphorically.

He said, 'Better not to use words like "explosive" when country is on Orange Alert and there are tanks at Heathrow.'

I texted Daisy:

FF, Letter sent to M.W is off. Love K

She texted back:

K.
UR Fab.
ILY.
FF

My mother rang me at the shop in a panic. She said, 'I know you're at work, but I need you to come to the Piggeries. Your Dad's hurt his back, trying to lift a hod of bricks.' Then, sounding surprised, she said, 'He's asking for you, Adrian.'

I explained what had happened to Mr Carlton-Hayes, who said, 'Another family crisis. You're rivalling *The Forsyte Saga*. But of course you must go.'

When I got there, my father was lying on an improvised stretcher made out of a roofing sheet. His face was grey with pain.

My mother said, 'I told him to let Animal do the heavy work, but he had to prove he's not past it, didn't he? And now he's broken his back.' She started to cry. 'He'll never walk again. He'll be in a wheelchair and I'll never be able to push him across this field.'

Animal grunted something to my mother and she grunted back. They communicate like primates. However, I understood when he started filling the kettle from the water carrier that he was asking if he should make some tea.

When I tried to lift my father's head so that he could drink from the cup, he screamed so loudly that birds flapped from the trees in alarm and I said to my mother, 'Call an ambulance' and handed her my mobile phone. There was the usual confusion about the address, but after half an hour we heard the siren and I crossed the field to meet it.

When I explained the circumstances and pointed out the Piggeries in the distance, the paramedics didn't look too pleased. The shorter one of the two asked, 'How much does your dad weigh?'

I said, 'About eleven stone.'

They looked even less pleased. As we crossed the boggy field, they muttered between themselves about health and safety.

I followed the ambulance as it made its way to the Royal Hospital. Then I waited in the A&E department for somebody in a white coat with a medical qualification to give my father a large dose of opiates and put him out of his misery. I stayed until my mother begged me to go home, saying that my constant commentary about the inefficiency and chaos in the casualty ward was driving her mad and making things worse.

Shortly after I got home, she rang to say that my father had been taken up to the David Gower ward. She said, 'He's still in pain, they can't find the key to the drug cabinet and they're short-staffed at the hospital pharmacy. So I've given him a few of my Tramadol to help him sleep.'

I told her that she couldn't possibly stay at the Piggeries on her own.

She said, 'I'm not on my own; I've got Animal with me.'

I said that she couldn't stay with Animal because he was, without wishing to be rude, an animal.

She said, '*Au contraire*, he's one of nature's gentlemen.'

George Bush has just issued an ultimatum: Saddam Hussein must leave Iraq within forty-eight hours or face invasion by a coalition of British and American troops.

Robin Cook has resigned from the government. Although you are a highly principled politician and a devotee of the racetrack, Mr Cook, posterity will find that you have backed the wrong horse here.

Tuesday March 18th

By eleven o'clock this morning there had been no word from Marigold. I rang the post office to find out if my registered letter had been safely delivered. A Customer Liaison Officer at the post office told me that there was no way of checking until the postman had returned from his round.

At 12.10 precisely I was on my knees cataloguing Fish of the British Isles. I was feeling mildly apprehensive, waiting for the telephone call from Marigold, when two dark shadows fell upon me – Netta and Michael Flowers.

Mr Carlton-Hayes hovered nearby. I got to my feet still clutching *Fish of the North Sea*. Flowers was literally chewing his beard. Netta held a faxed copy of my disengagement letter, which she thrust into my face.

She said, 'You've broken my little girl's heart.'

Flowers roared, 'You are a despicable piece of working-class shit. My wife was stitching those exquisite bridesmaids' dresses until three o'clock this morning.' He came towards me and raised his fists.

I instinctively protected myself with *Fish of the North Sea*. The edge of the book caught him in his right eye, and he reeled around, barging into the shelves, knocking books to the floor and bellowing that I had blinded him.

Mr Carlton-Hayes did his best to pull Netta away from me. A young female customer hurriedly left the shop. It was an ugly scene.

Flowers eventually stumbled out of the shop with Netta, saying that he would call the police and have me prosecuted for grievous bodily harm.

Netta said, screwing up her piggy face, 'We will be suing you for breach of promise.'

After they'd gone, we put the closed sign on the door and tidied the shop and I apologized to Mr Carlton-Hayes for bringing my personal life into the shop again.

He said, 'Don't fret, my dear. I landed Flowers a few good punches during the mêlée.'

After work I went to the Royal Hospital. When I asked about George Mole, the nurse at the desk told me that he was 'still uncomfortable'.

I asked, 'Is that hospital code for "still in agony"?'

She said, 'He's been ringing his bell all day. He seems to think he's in a hotel and he's calling down for room service. It's the drugs.'

*

My father is in a bay with three other patients. When I got to his bedside, my mother got up and said, 'Thank God you've come, I'm dying for a fag.'

She was dressed for the building site and, not for the first time in my life, I felt ashamed of her appearance. Her big reinforced toe-capped boots looked incongruous in the hospital ward.

My father was lying flat on his back staring somewhat woozily at the ceiling. I asked him how he was.

He said, dreamily, 'I think the drugs are kicking in. I haven't felt as good as this since the sixties.'

When my father closed his eyes, my mother and I went outside to the main entrance and stood in the plastic smokers' shelter where I told her that I was now formally disengaged from Marigold.

She said, 'Thank God for that,' then told me that my father would have to have an operation to remove two damaged discs.

I asked her if it would affect his mobility. She said, laughing in the face of trouble, 'I don't think so. Your dad's always been a bit spineless.'

I phoned Daisy; her voicemail message said that she was unavailable.

At 3 a.m. I was awakened by furtive scurrying sounds. I went to investigate and saw three brown shapes emerge from a floor cupboard I had left open. One of the brown shapes ran over my naked foot.

Further investigation revealed a half-eaten packet of

Walkers Beef and Onion crisps. I'm sharing my loft apartment with rats.

Wednesday March 19th

Phoned Environmental Health at Leicester City Council and left a message for the rat-catcher asking him/her to come to Rat Wharf ASAP and to bring extermination kit.

A meeting with Barwell, my solicitor, to discuss the swan-shit-on-the-stairs litigation.

Barwell told me that he'd heard at a Rotary Club dinner that Gary Milksop's solicitor had consulted a barrister, Alan Ruck-Bridges. 'He's a Rottweiler, Mr Mole. He got a judge to award a million in damages and costs to a woman who got her big toe stuck in a faulty bath tap.'

He advised me to settle out of court before my costs escalated. I agreed to think about it, but it is a sad day for British justice. The Old Bailey statue must be hanging its head in shame.

On the way out, Barwell's secretary handed me a bill for immediate payment. The subtext was that unless I paid up, I would be kept prisoner in her outer office. Barwell now employs a security guard to keep his growing list of disreputable clients in order and to confiscate their cans of lager.

I wrote a cheque for £250 and handed it over. I said, 'Do you happen to know the penalty for killing a swan?'

She said, coldly, 'No, but it should be hanging or life imprisonment.'

As I left Barwell's premises, Daisy rang. I was overjoyed to hear her voice. She said that her mother had phoned her and that Marigold had been devastated by the news and that her father had been in eye casualty at the Royal Hospital for most of Tuesday.

I asked Daisy if our relationship was still on. She said, 'I wish it weren't, Aidy, but I'm afraid I'm crazy about you.'

I said I would get on a train after work and come to Baldwin Street.

She said, 'I'm not there, darling, I'm in Paris doing the PR for a designer hotel.'

We talked briefly about the war, which is due to start tomorrow.

Daisy said, 'The French are incredulous that America and Britain are preparing to bomb Baghdad.' She asked me if I was worried about Glenn.

I said, 'Yes, of course.'

But the truth is, diary, the boy has been halfway down my list of worries lately.

Marigold rang, to tell me that she was in hospital with a suspected miscarriage. She said, 'I read your letter and I felt my womb lurch.' She had admitted herself to an accident and emergency department. She begged me not to tell her parents.

She sobbed, 'I couldn't bear it if I lost our baby, could you, Adrian?'

'No,' I said. 'I'll come immediately. Where are you?'

The phone cut off before she could answer. I dialled

1471 but was told by a robot that the number had been withheld. I waited for her to ring back, images of Marigold miscarrying the baby filling my head as I paced the floor.

After half an hour I started to ring round the hospitals in Coventry and Birmingham – but nobody by the name of Marigold Flowers or even Marigold Mole had been admitted. I rang the Ring Road View Hotel and asked if they knew which hospital Marigold had been admitted to. The receptionist did not speak very good English and could not help me.

I took my clothes off and got into bed, but I hardly slept. Gielgud sounded as through he was playing a discordant trumpet all night and the rats passed by my futon several times.

Thursday March 20th

The war with Iraq started today.

I heard on the radio that the American military has just promised that the war will begin with the unrestrained bombing of Baghdad; a massive 'Shock and Awe' assault will make the world quiver in its boots with respect.

Marigold rang early this morning to tell me that the doctors were discharging her. The baby was safe 'for now', but she must have complete rest and take things very easy. She asked me to pick her up from Birmingham City Hospital, maternity unit. She said, 'You won't forsake me, will you, darling?'

It wasn't until I got on to the M69 that I remembered that 'Do Not Forsake Me, Oh My Darling' was the theme tune from *High Noon*. For the rest of the journey I couldn't get the song out of my head.

I drove along the M6 boxed in by two huge juggernauts. I didn't trust myself to enter the fast lane, as I didn't feel that I was in full control of my emotions, or the car.

I rang Mr Carlton-Hayes at the shop and told him that I wouldn't be into work today and briefly told him why. He knows about my M6 phobia and told me to take deep breaths if I felt a panic attack coming on.

I had expected to go to the ward to pick Marigold up and help her with her luggage, etc. But to my surprise the poor girl was standing outside the main entrance to the maternity unit, alone and in a biting wind, wearing her beige anorak, on which she had pinned her NEC exhibitor's pass. Her luggage was at her feet.

I was disgusted at the hospital's lack of care, diary. It was only two days after her suspected miscarriage. I wanted to go in and lodge a formal complaint, but Marigold became agitated and said, 'I just want to leave this place, Adrian. I've been through a horrid ordeal.'

I told her that I would be making a formal complaint when we got back to Leicester, but she said, 'I'd rather forget all about it. Promise me you won't write.'

I brought the car round and she sat in the front seat with her hands clasped around her belly, protecting our child. It was enough to make the gods weep. When we reached the motorway, she said, 'I don't think I can be conscious while you're driving on the M6.' She pulled the lever and reclined the seat, took her spectacles off and handed them to me and went to sleep.

She looks quite pretty when her face is at rest.

My mobile rang. It was Daisy, from Paris. I said, loudly, that I didn't want double glazing and disconnected the phone.

She woke as we reached the end of the motorway and started talking about the wedding. I steeled myself, and said, 'Marigold, we are not getting married.' I don't know how I managed to avoid causing a serious pile-up on the slip road. It is not easy to drive when somebody is pummelling your head, arms and shoulders with her tiny fists.

When we arrived at Beeby on the Wold I took Marigold into the house. Netta and Roger Middleton were in the drawing room sitting in front of the ostentatiously small television set watching 'Shock and Awe' being carried out over Baghdad.

After a lot more shouting and angry recriminations I left, saying that I would come back tomorrow. Roger Middleton saw me to the door. I asked if he had moved in permanently.

He said, 'You've buggered up the grand plan. Netta and Michael were going to sell the house once Marigold was married. Now it's just one big cock-up.'

I said that I was sorry. I seem to do nothing but apologize lately.

*

When I got to Rat Wharf I risked Mia Fox's wrath by switching on my home entertainment centre. The sound of the bombardment reverberated around the apartment. The wine glasses tinkled on the shelf. I felt the shock waves of the bombs underneath my feet. The screen was filled with huge orange explosions contrasting with the black Baghdad sky. I was very shocked and totally awed. I had to remind myself that this was not a Hollywood blockbuster – that it was happening in real time, to real people. I thought about the little Iraqi kids, who must be terrified. What would their mums and dads be saying to them? I wondered if Mr Blair was watching with his family and speculated on what he would be saying to his own children about the bombs falling on Baghdad.

I rang Daisy. She sounded drunk and rambled on about double glazing. Then she said, 'I'm in my hotel room watching Baghdad burn. Do you still think Tony Blair is the bee's knees?'

I told her I would ring tomorrow when she was sober.

Friday March 21st

On the little radio in the shop I heard the news that eight British and four American servicemen had been killed today when a helicopter crashed over Kuwait.

A few moments later, Sharon rang me and said, 'If owt happened to our Glenn they'd tell the next of kin straight away, wouldn't they?'

I assured her that if Glenn was hurt the British army would let his next of kin know immediately.

I got involved in a row between Netta, Michael and Roger Middleton tonight, after work. It seems that none of them wants to take responsibility for looking after Marigold during her pregnancy and after the baby is born. All three are blaming me for ruining their lives. I almost weakened and said that Marigold could come and live with me in Rat Wharf but, thank God, I didn't.

I went upstairs to see Marigold. I tiptoed in so as not to disturb her. She was sitting up in bed eating a bar of organic chocolate and reading *Hello!* magazine. She was half-watching Shock and Awe on her portable television.

When I told her that I felt sorry for the little kids in Baghdad, she said, 'Don't weaken, Adrian. You can't make an omelette without breaking eggs. They will be grateful to us when they are walking to the polling stations to cast their votes.'

I asked her how she was.

She said, 'I'm feeling dreadful, but Mummy suffered with each pregnancy.'

I asked her if she had seen her own GP yet.

She said, 'There's no need.'

Netta came in and said, 'Pregnancy isn't an illness, it's a perfectly natural function. It's you men who have medicalized it.'

It was obvious that Marigold had not told her parents about her suspected miscarriage.

I stayed another hour but left shortly after Marigold

had an imaginary conversation with the baby inside her womb. I didn't so much mind her talking to the baby; it was when the baby 'talked' back.

Daisy sent me an email.

Sorry, but I can't get over this war thing. I am outraged at Britain's involvement in the whole filthy business. I joined a huge protest march yesterday and it was wonderful to be amongst so many people who felt like me. Have you changed your mind since the bombing started? Please say yes, because I do love you. Ring me tomorrow at Baldwin Street.

At ten o'clock tonight Mr Blair addressed the nation. In a voice heavy with a sense of history he appealed to the British people 'to be united in sending our armed forces our thoughts and prayers'. To the people watching in Iraq, he said, 'Our enemy is not you but your barbarous rulers.'

I was very moved by Mr Blair's sincerity. The country should rally round and support him in his hour of need.

Saturday March 22nd

I asked Mr Carlton-Hayes if I could leave the shop early and meet the rat-catcher at my apartment.

He said, 'Your home sounds marvellously Dickensian, my dear.'

I said that, on the contrary, my apartment had been shortlisted for a Best Use of Former Industrial Space

Award, and that the last thing I had expected had been to find it overrun by rats.

Mr Carlton-Hayes twitched an eyebrow and said, 'You didn't get a clue from the address?'

I tried to be polite to the bloke who turned up by calling him a Rodent Operative, but he said, in a surprisingly posh accent, 'I'm not into verbal obfuscation; I call myself a rat-catcher.'

When I asked if he wanted coffee, he enquired about the blend. I told him it was a Guatemalan 'Fair Trade' medium roast, and he gave a tiny smile that could have been approval but seemed more like amusement that I had been crass enough to choose that particular brand.

He found rat droppings under the kitchen units and behind the panel in the bath, and traces of rat urine around the futon. I urged him to exterminate the creatures and remove all trace of them. He said that he would lay some traps and come back in ten days.

While he was setting the traps we somehow got on to the subject of women, and I told him about my catastrophic relationship with Marigold. He commiserated with me and told me that he had once been one of the most successful chartered accountants in the East Midlands, until a client called Sonia had ruined his health and reputation and forced him into rat-catching.

I phoned Daisy. She answered immediately and said, 'Have you changed your mind about the war?'

I said no, and that I still supported Mr Blair.

She snarled, 'Have you not seen a photograph of

that eight-year-old kid, Ali? The one who's had both arms and both legs blown off by your fucking bombs?'

I said, 'Yes, but . . .'

She said, 'Don't ring, don't text, don't fax, don't call round, don't contact me again. I asked you to choose between me and Tony Blair, and you chose him. Goodbye.'

Sunday March 23rd

My father has had his operation. He was back on the ward complaining that the nurses won't push his bed into the lift, take him down six floors and push him to the main entrance so that he can have a cigarette.

I took him a bunch of grapes today. Tomorrow I will take him a bunch of nicotine patches.

Monday March 24th

Wrote to Geoff Hoon.

Mr Hoon MP
Ministry of Defence
The War Office
Whitehall
London SW1

Unit 4
The Old Battery Factory
Rat Wharf
Grand Union Canal
Leicester LE1

March 24th 2003

Dear Mr Hoon

Forgive me for writing to you at what must be a very busy time. I am the father of Private Glenn Bott-Mole, of the

Leicestershire Fox Regiment, which is presently stationed in Kuwait.

Glenn is a very immature seventeen-year-old and his clumsiness is a family legend. He celebrates his eighteenth birthday on April 18th this year and thus becomes eligible to be sent to the battlefront in Iraq.

I fear that Glenn will prove to be a hazard to himself and his fellow soldiers in such a life-and-death situation and I respectfully request that you contact his senior officers and advise them of the boy's unsuitability for battlefield duties.

May I add that I am fully supportive of the government's stand against barbarism.

Mr Hoon, you are widely unpopular at the moment, but I feel sure that the public will warm to you again when the Iraqi people take to the streets in their millions to cheer the arrival of the coalition troops and the liberation of their country.

Yours sincerely

A. A. Mole

Tuesday March 25th

Michael Flowers sent a work-experience boy from his shop to my shop with a note this morning.

Adrian

Netta and I are deeply disappointed in you. Your neglect of and apparent indifference to Marigold lately is tantamount to cruelty.

She is having a difficult pregnancy, caused, I am sure, by

your callous refusal to marry her and thus legitimize the baby.

We are sufficiently concerned about our daughter's health to have booked a recuperative holiday for her on the island of Capri at a charming hotel we have stayed at many times. Netta will accompany her and I am writing to ask you to contribute towards their lodging and travel expenses.

As you know, I am a poor man. My mission in life – to educate the people of Leicester in correct nutritional practices – has largely failed. There have been complaints that our unwashed organic vegetables take too long to prepare and are riddled with worm-holes!

I expect to see you soon. Your contribution to Marigold's recuperative holiday is £999.50.

Yours in peace
Michael

PS Cash would be appreciated; the bank is being difficult.

I did a long and complicated calculation and discovered that I have no money in my current account and none available on either of my credit cards. After a phone call I found out that store cards do not advance cash. However, it would be good to get Marigold out of the country and off my conscience for two weeks, so I have no choice but to break into my hitherto sacred building society deposit account.

I showed Michael Flowers's note to my father in hospital tonight. He said, 'Ditch the bitch.'

When I left he was wearing a nicotine patch on both arms.

On the way out, I asked a nurse if there was a medical reason why my father was lying flat on his back without a pillow.

She said, 'It's not medical, it's financial. If your father wants a pillow, you'll have to bring him one from home.'

Wednesday March 26th

A cruise missile hit a marketplace in Baghdad, killing many civilians. Kofi Annan said in a very small voice that 'People around the world are questioning the legitimacy of the war against Iraq.'

Wrote to the council today.

Leicester City Council
New Walk
Leicester LE1

Unit 4
The Old Battery Factory
Rat Wharf
Grand Union Canal
Leicester LE1

March 26th 2003

Dear Sir or Madam

I have tried many times to contact you by telephone. I wish to complain about the behaviour of a flock of swans, namely the creatures that inhabit the stretch of canal between Pack-horse Bridge and Dye Works Lane. I do not know which department is responsible for the behaviour of swans.

I would like to know:

a) Is culling permitted?

b) Is the Grand Union Canal Leicester City Council property? and

c) To whom do I apply to effect a council tax rebate due to
swan misbehaviour?

A swan recently broke a man's arm; will you please alert
your legal department that a claim against Leicester City
Council is imminent.

I look forward to your rapid response.

Yours faithfully

A. A. Mole

Lorraine Harris was the first of the readers' group to
arrive; she told me that she had been plaiting hair all day,
for a wedding. She said to me, 'Your hair's getting long.
Are you growing it?'

I said that I had been too busy to go to Ken at Quick
Snip.

She said she had been talking in the salon about
Madame Bovary, and that several of the women had asked
if they could get it on DVD.

The discussion about *Madame Bovary* got quite heated
at times.

Lorraine Harris said that Emma reminded her of her
best friend in Jamaica who had married a quantity sur-
veyor who was so boring that people called him Lockjaw.

Mohammed said, 'I was very disturbed by this book.
It condones adultery and the accumulation of debt. I was
also concerned about the child of the marriage. Mrs
Bovary was a very neglectful mother.'

Melanie 'I'm only a housewife' Oates said hesitantly, 'I

think *Madame Bovary* is a very good book. I couldn't put it down. I wanted her to run off with her soldier lover and I couldn't bear it when he let her down.' She looked around angrily at the men in the room. Her voice rose. 'There's not one man you can trust, not one. You're all the same.'

Mr Carlton-Hayes fiddled nervously with his pipe.

Lorraine Harris said, 'I thought Flaubert was out of order making Emma kill herself, just because she'd gone over her credit limit and bought a few bonnets and ribbons and stuff.'

Darren said, picking at the plaster on his jeans, 'Sorry, I didn't have time to change. I came straight from work. I think it's the best book I've ever read. That bit where Doctor Bovary does surgery on the village idiot's club foot was so real, I had to get up and take two extra-strong Nurofen. I really felt the pain.'

Mr Carlton-Hayes said that Flaubert was a marvellous writer and his sentences were so beautifully constructed, he used to beat out the rhythm on his writing table. Mr Carlton-Hayes demonstrated by reading a sentence aloud and beating on the side of the armchair he was sitting in.

Before Darren left I gave him a copy of *Jude the Obscure* and said, 'I think you'll like this.'

Mr Carlton-Hayes has chosen *William, the Outlaw* by Richmal Crompton for the next book. When they were buying their copies, Lorraine said, 'I ain't really into kids' books no more.'

Mr Carlton-Hayes explained that William Brown was an English comic hero and that his adventures were essential reading.

Thursday March 27th

At midday Geoff Hoon announced that British forces have evidence that Iraq is ready to use chemical weapons against Allied forces.

I have sent a text message to Johnny Bond at Latesun Ltd:

Weapons of Mass Destruction have been found. Please refund my deposit and apologize. An ex-customer.
A. A. Mole

Friday March 28th

My father seems to have recovered quite well and is alert enough to be keeping notes of everything that goes wrong with his treatment. He showed me his notebook. The last entry read, 'At four o'clock a porter came to take me down to theatre for a hysterectomy.' He had misspelled 'hysterectomy', but I let it pass. He has been fixed up to Patient Line, a new service which provides each patient with their own television, radio and telephone line at a cost of £2.50 a day. He is able to watch the war in Iraq 24/7.

Saturday March 29th

At 7 o'clock this morning the BBC reported that last night British troops raided Basra to destroy two statues of Saddam Hussein. They then withdrew to their fortified camp on the outskirts of the town.

I have no doubt the citizens of Basra will be rejoicing in the streets when they wake up and see Saddam's effigies have been toppled in the night.

At 6 o'clock this evening the Pentagon admitted that seven US Tomahawk missiles had missed their targets.

At 6.30 my mother rang from my father's bedside to say that it had just been reported that a Tomahawk missile had landed near Kuwait City. She said, 'Have you heard if our Glenn is safe?'

I said that the Commander of British Forces in the Gulf, General Mike Jackson, did not have my mobile number.

She said, 'There's no need to be sarcastic, Adrian. I'm worried sick about the boy.'

I heard my father say, in a masterful voice, 'Give me the phone, Pauline.' To me, he said, 'This is bad news for fans of hi-tech weapons. Tomahawk missiles are meant to be capable of finding a target 690 miles from the launch site, weaving in and around buildings, navigating their way in the dark and hitting something the size of a post-office letter box more accurately than the bleeding post office. And the bloody things cost $600,000 each. I'm gutted, Adrian, the technology has let us down. David only had a bleedin' sling but he managed to hit Goliath smack between the eyes.'

I asked him how long he had been a fan of hi-tech weaponry.

He said he had always liked guns, tanks and other

weapons but it was only lately that he had dared to admit his interest. He added, almost whispering, 'Your mother's never known the real George Mole.'

I asked to speak to my mother again, and said, 'Is it tonight we have to change the clocks?'

She said that it was.

I asked if it was forwards or backwards; I can never remember which.

She said, 'It's easy: spring forward, fall back.'

I said, 'But do the clocks go backwards or forwards?'

She said again, 'Spring forward, fall back.'

I broke off the call, saying I had left something in the oven. I can't talk to her when she is in one of her moods.

Sunday March 30th

Mothering Sunday. British Summer Time begins

The Americans are on their way to liberate Baghdad.

Marigold rang in tears to ask why I had not sent her a Mother's Day card.

Sharon rang in tears to say that she had received a Mother's Day card from Glenn. 'There was sand inside the envelope,' she wept.

My mother rang in tears to ask me why I had not sent her a Mother's Day card.

I went to the Piggeries this afternoon and took a card bought in the BP garage which showed a mutton-dressed-as-lamb type of mother sipping champagne in a nightclub. I also bought her two bags of logs and a packet of firelighters. There is no point in buying her flowers; there is no ledge in the camper van on which to put a vase.

However, one of the pigsties now has four walls and will soon have a roof. When the sun came out, briefly, my mother took her plaid shirt off and sunbathed for a while in her T-shirt and dungarees. I noticed that she has developed very impressive muscles in her upper arms.

When I went into the camper van, I saw that Animal had also given my mother a card. I felt a twinge of jealousy. For how long will the brute be sleeping in their tent?

Monday March 31st

Gordon Brown has now set aside £3 billion, and said, 'The armed forces need to be properly equipped.' Surprising, since I have studied his body language on television and he doesn't seem too keen on the war.

Tuesday April 1st
April Fool's Day

Glenn rang me on my mobile to wish me a happy birthday for tomorrow.

I asked him where he was and he said, 'Outside your front door, I'm on my mobile.'

I ran to the door and yanked it open. But there was nobody there. The idiot boy said, 'And Happy April Fool's Day, Dad!'

I failed to see the joke and again asked him where he was.

He said, 'I can't tell you exactly where, that's classified information. But I'm still in that country that begins with K and there's still a lot of sand about.'

It was on the tip of my tongue to tell him how much I loved him and worried about him, but I couldn't quite manage to get the words out. I asked him what it was like out there.

He said, 'It ain't 'alf 'ot, Dad,' without any sense of irony.

I ran home at lunchtime to meet the rat-catcher. He filled a small sack with dead rats from under the kitchen units. He said, 'There is forensic evidence pointing to new nest-building behind the bath. I'm surprised you haven't heard them moving about.'

I said, 'Well, they're not assembling scaffolding or using a concrete mixer, are they?'

He said, 'Why are you being so defensive, Mr Mole? There is no shame sharing your house with rats. Perhaps you are hard of hearing.'

I told him that I was not yet thirty-five and that the reason I had not heard nest-building activity was that I automatically switched on Radio Four as soon as I entered the bathroom.

We talked about *The Archers* and agreed that political correctness was in danger of crowding out the agricultural storylines.

I said, 'The next character they introduce will be a

native American woman called Running Deer, who pitches her tepee in the car park of the Bull.'

He laughed so hard he almost dropped his bag of rats.

He remembered our last conversation about women and asked about the Marigold situation. I said, 'I still have dealings with her, because I am the father of her unborn child. So I'll never be entirely free of her, will I?'

He said that he had fathered two children, a boy and a girl, but was prevented from seeing them by a court order.

I asked him why. He said, shiftily, 'I've got a bit of a temper.'

Watched *Midlands Today*.

The first item was about a pensioner from Nottingham who had beaten off a mugger with a cucumber.

The second item was about the rescue of a dog called Butch, who had been stuck down a drain for three days in a village called Humberstone. His rescue involved the police, the fire service, an RSPCA emergency vehicle and a WRVS mobile canteen. Personally, I would have left the dog down the drain to starve until it had lost enough weight to enable it to climb out by itself.

The third item showed Pandora Braithwaite standing on Westminster Green, opposite the Houses of Parliament, announcing that she has resigned from her job as a junior minister in the Department of the Environment. She looked sad and angry and beautiful. She said that she would 'continue to work tirelessly for my constituents in Ashby de la Zouch, but I cannot support the invasion of Iraq'.

Wednesday April 2nd

My birthday.

I am thirty-five today. I am officially middle-aged. It is all downhill from now. A pathetic slide towards gum disease, wheelchair ramps and death.

I do not feel able to celebrate, not with Glenn at war.

After work, I drove to the Piggeries to take my mother to the hospital. Animal has made amazing progress. The roof timbers are in place, and he's completed digging the trench that will eventually bring fresh water.

I opened the present that Marigold had sent round to the shop at my father's bedside. It was a birthday cake that would not have been out of place on a bird table.

Call me old school, but I think it should be compulsory for a birthday cake to have jam, icing and candles. People who make birthday cakes with wholegrain flour and decorate them with sunflower seeds should be given a community service order and be compelled to go to punitive cake-making classes. I'm serious about this, diary. Am I becoming more right wing now that I'm middle-aged?

My father had sent one of the nurses out to buy me more golf guff! A diamond-patterned jumper and a golf-ball warmer. When I asked him why, he said, 'You're being stubborn. You haven't given it a chance. You're thirty-five now, son, and you've never played a round of golf.'

He made it sound as if I had never tried to tie my own

shoelaces. Anyway, I don't see why he is so supportive of golf, he was thrown out of the Fair Green Golf Club for wearing cut-off jeans on the green during a heat wave in 1993.

My mother gave me a lump of wood with a depression in the middle. I asked her what it was and she said, 'It's a receptacle. Animal carved it out of an old timber from the original pigsty.'

I said, 'What's it for?'

She said, 'It's for putting things in: apples, cufflinks, car keys, whatever.'

After I had taken my mother home, I called round to see Nigel. Nigel's mother was in the granny annexe pressing his shirts. The poor woman could hardly reach the ironing board, even though it was on its lowest setting. She was only four foot ten when I was a teenager, and she has shrunk over the years. Apparently, she has to sit on three cushions to reach the steering wheel in the car.

Nigel had bought me a new polyphonic ring-tone for my mobile phone. He made me audition the various sounds. There was Eskimo Nose-Singing, a dog barking, a lion roaring, a sheep bleating, a whale singing, a baby crying, the brakes of a London bus, a thrush singing, Bach's suites, 'Hungarian Rhapsody', *Carmen, Jesus Christ Superstar*, 'Jerusalem', a Zulu chant and a Dalek shouting, 'Ring! Ring!'

After long deliberation I chose the Zulu chant.

Got home and switched on my television, listening on the headphones because Mia Fox was at home. The Allied bombers are making one thousand sorties a day. Shock and Awe does not appear to have worked so far. The people of Baghdad have not taken to the streets. Not even to flee them.

I want Daisy so badly my toes curl whenever I think of her.

Thursday April 3rd

Gielgud and his wife, whom from now on I will call Margot, after Margot Fonteyn, the ballet dancer, are building a monolithic nest directly opposite my balcony. They are using a mixture of natural and manmade materials. Reeds, twigs, grass, bits of old rope, a pair of nylon knickers left on the towpath and what appears to be a torn up copy of the *Spectator*, all held together with mud.

When I got home from work both my credit card bills had arrived. I was shocked: my MasterCard is £200 over the agreed limit of £10,000. They are demanding the £200 immediately and a further £190 within twenty-eight days. Barclaycard wrote to ask if I wanted to join their wine club, and asked for a minimum payment of £222, also to be paid within twenty-eight days. I ticked the box to order a selection of twelve bottles of New World wines.

Friday April 4th

A letter from Robbie, written in a good clear hand.

Dear Mr Mole

Thank you very much for the birthday card and also the books. I would be very grateful if you could see your way to sending some more. I have enclosed a cheque to cover the cost of the books and postage. Glenn got me a cake, made by the lads in the field kitchen. I don't know how they managed it, because things are a bit tricky here.

At the time of writing I am trying to open a tin of pineapple with Jerome K. Jerome. I have read bits to Glenn, but he only laughs at the stuff about the dog, Montmorency.

Yours sincerely

Robbie

Saturday April 5th

I pointed out to Mr Carlton-Hayes today that we are not maximizing the rooms behind and above the shop.

He said, 'But I have no desire to expand the business that dramatically. Think of the extra staff that we would have to employ, and the commensurate paperwork. I'm too old to burden myself with such worries.'

I reminded him that he was paying thousands in business rates for what was almost empty space.

I watched from the balcony tonight as Gielgud and Margot put the finishing touches to their nest. They don't know how lucky they are. It costs them nothing and they don't have to go to IKEA.

Sunday April 6th

I replied to Robbie's letter today.

Dear Robbie

I'm so pleased you are enjoying *Three Men in a Boat*. It is one of my own favourites.

I would be happy to send you some more books.

Do you trust me to choose them for you, or do you have favourite authors?

Give Glenn my love and tell him to wear his helmet at all times, and please do the same yourself.

Best wishes, keep safe.

Mr Mole

Monday April 7th

Today we closed the shop and went to do a valuation at a large Victorian villa in Leicester's red-light district. I was reluctant to take my car, so we took a taxi. As we lurched over the speed bumps and negotiated the chicanes of the mean streets, I pointed out the sights: the crack delivery boys in their hooded tops speeding along the pavements on their BMXs, the teenage prostitutes shivering in their cropped tops and hot pants, their arms clasped around their bodies.

Mr Carlton-Hayes said, 'Poor creatures.' He could have been an etymologist reluctantly pinning specimens to a board.

We were met on the doorstep of number eleven, Crimea Road, by Lawrence Mortimer, son and executor of Mrs Emily Mortimer, who had died in the house some five weeks previously. Mortimer threw the cigarette he had been smoking on to the pavement and said brusquely, 'It's a mess in there. My mother stopped doing any housework years ago.'

We followed him into the large hallway. Every visible wall was lined with bookshelves. Books were stacked on the floor, on furniture, on chairs, on the kitchen table and next to the draining board. The stairs were a rat run of books. They were in the bath and filled every bedroom.

Lawrence Mortimer said, 'As you can tell, my mother went doolally years ago. Me and my wife tried to get her certified in 1999, but her doctor said collecting books wasn't a reason for having her put away.'

'Indeed not,' said Mr Carlton-Hayes, 'or I should have been confined to a padded cell many years ago.'

I could hardly breathe for excitement; one of the bedrooms I wandered into was filled entirely with children's books in plastic covers. I prayed that Mr Carlton-Hayes would not display his own excitement.

'I need 'em moving quick,' said Mortimer. 'There's some good furniture and carpets under these bleedin' books.'

We climbed up into the attic rooms: they were chock-a-block with crime-fiction paperbacks. Lawrence Mortimer kicked at a pile of Ed McBains and said, 'I've got plans for this house. I reckon I can get at least four asylum-seekers to a room.'

To my astonishment, Mr Carlton-Hayes said, 'Oh,

I'm sure you could squeeze at least six to a room, Mr Mortimer. These asylum-seeker chappies are usually on the thin side.'

His irony was lost on Mortimer, who cocked his head and resurveyed the room as if trying to visualize six bed spaces on the attic floor.

I asked Mortimer if he was a reader. 'Not for pleasure,' he said.

'So you don't want to go through and select a few favourites?' I asked.

'No,' he said. 'I just want rid.'

It was the first time I had been to a valuation where the owner of the books had offered to pay the bookseller to take the books away.

In the taxi going back to the shop, Mr Carlton-Hayes said, 'He's such an unpleasant fellow that I don't feel the least bit guilty. We're saving those books from the skip.'

We allowed Mortimer to pay us £50 to take all the books away. The taxi driver congratulated us on our obvious good spirits; we could not stop smiling. The Mortimer collection was the bookseller's equivalent of finding gold in the Klondike. One thing haunts me though: Lawrence Mortimer told me that his mother had died in bed with a book in her hand. When I asked the title of the book he said, 'I dunno, it was just a book. What's it to you?'

When I replied, 'The unexamined life is not worth living,' he said, defensively, 'I saw her at Christmas and Easter. I'm a busy man.'

Tuesday April 8th

Mr Carlton-Hayes has enlisted the help of an ex-bookseller friend of his called Bernard Hopkins to help catalogue the Mortimer collection. According to Mr Carlton-Hayes, Hopkins is an alcoholic who drank a thriving business away; he is perfectly competent and congenial providing he can down a bottle of Absolut Vodka a day. It's when he can't get it or afford it that problems arise.

I received the following letter from the council today re: Swan Harassment.

> Neighbourhood Conflict Co-ordinator
> Leicester City Council
> New Walk
> Leicester LE1
>
> April 4th 2003

Dear Mr Mole

Your letter regarding the nuisance you have experienced from your neighbour, Mr Swan, has been passed to this department, the Neighbourhood Conflict Unit.

We offer a reconciliation and conflict-resolution service.

You and Mr Swan would be brought face to face to talk about your differences. You would meet on neutral territory, and our Conflict Resolution Facilitator would be present.

If you wish to avail yourself of this service, please telephone, write or contact me by email on nuisanceneighbour.gov.uk.

I do not have Mr Swan's address. If you send it to me, I will contact him immediately.

Yours sincerely

Trixie Meadows

Neighbourhood Conflict Co-ordinator

Wednesday April 9th

US Marines toppled Saddam's statue today. I watched it on television with the sound turned down.

Mia Fox complained the other night about the *Archers* sound seepage. She said, 'I do not want my thoughts interrupted by ludicrous storylines. I don't believe for a minute that Lynda Snell would give Robert two llamas for his birthday.'

Thursday April 10th

Michael Flowers sent the work-experience boy round with another note.

Adrian

You cannot possibly know, since you have not enquired, but Marigold has been barely able to walk, due to extreme fatigue. However, she has bravely said that she will make a huge effort to go to Capri on April 16th, as she does not want to let Netta down.

I have paid for their Italian sojourn in full. I am asking you to pay your share, today, as promised.

M. Flowers

Mr Carlton-Hayes is baffled as to why I am paying for Marigold's holiday. I reminded him that Marigold is having my baby.

At lunchtime, I went round to my building society and withdrew £1,000 of my precious life savings.

Friday April 11th

The United States published a pack of fifty-five playing cards today, identifying its most wanted suspects. Saddam is the Ace of Spades.

Posted Glenn's birthday card and present at the post office round the corner from Rat Wharf. The postmaster was telling an old lady that his post office was being closed down and that she would have to go to another post office in future.

I waited impatiently while she said, 'But I can't manage the bus. The steps are too high.'

After a lot more tedious lamentation from her about the good old days, I gave him my parcel. He read the BFPO address and said, 'Kuwait? You must be worried about your son, sir.'

I said that I was hoping that the war would be over soon. He told me that his son had joined the army but had left after three days, after he was called a Paki bastard on the parade ground.

I said he should have reported it to an officer.

He said, 'It was an officer who insulted my son.'

I apologized on behalf of the British Army, signed his petition and said that I hoped the government would reprieve his post office.

Mia Fox knocked on my door five minutes after I got home from work. She said, 'I heard you put your key in the door and switch your kettle on. They tried to deliver your wine this afternoon. I took it in for you.'
I went upstairs to collect the wine and was disturbed to see that if she stood on the far right of her balcony she could see my glass-bricked bathroom. I must get those curtains made.

In bed I was tormented by a vision of the old lady in the post office trying and failing to step on to a bus. I am obviously suffering from some sort of anxiety condition.
I must make an effort to register with a doctor.

Saturday April 12th

A terrible thing happened this morning. While I was out in the back making coffee, a young man was knocked down and killed by a delivery van outside the shop. It could easily have been me – obliterated by a collision of time, space and bad luck. How fragile our lives are. How easily they are taken away.
In the afternoon, weeping girls started laying cellophane-wrapped flowers on the pavement where he died.

I read some of the tribute cards on my way home. Even the uneducated turn to poetry when they have to express extreme emotion. One read:

> Maz, you were a
> lovely lad.
> Always nicc and
> never Sad.

And another.

> God said, 'Maz, it's time to go,'
> So you went
> We'll miss you so

A yob in a hooded top laid a bunch of orange carnations on Maz's shrine and asked if I was Maz's brother, Anthony. I said I was not. The yob said, 'Right, only Anthony works in a library and wears glasses. I fought you must be 'im, like.'

Sunday April 13th

Why, oh, why do none of the clocks in the city show the correct time?

Why, oh, why do the doors in public buildings squeak so horribly?

Nigel rang to tell me that he is suffering from post-blindness depression.

In an attempt to counsel him, I asked him what was the worst thing about being blind.

Nigel snapped, 'I can't fucking see!'

To give him a change of scene, I asked him if he would like to go with me to visit my father in hospital.

Nigel said, grudgingly, 'If that's all that's on offer.'

My father didn't look well today; the post-operative wound in his back has become infected and he is running a high temperature.

A defeated-looking cleaner called Edna was mopping rancid water from a bucket around his bed.

When I asked my father how he felt, Edna answered, ''E 'ad a bad night and I 'ad to force 'im to eat 'is breakfast, didn't I, George?'

My father nodded weakly.

Edna said, 'When I've finished cleanin' the ward, I'll come back an' freshen you up.'

When she had moved further up the ward, my father said, 'Edna is the salt of the earth, she's keeping me alive. All the bleeding nurses in here are too posh to wash. I told one yesterday that my bum was sore and she said, 'I've got a first-class degree, Mr Mole. I'll contact the bed-care-management team when I've got a minute.'

To lighten the conversation I told them about Maz.

Nigel said, 'He should have looked before crossing the road.'

I said that this was undoubtedly true but that he could at least show some compassion.

Monday April 14th

Maz's shrine has grown to a size that is surely dispro-
portionate to the youth's age and popularity.

According to the headline in this evening's local paper:

Maz Died a Hero's Death

Young hero dies on Gran mercy mission. Martin Forster
(Maz) died while on a mercy mission to buy new batteries
for his grandmother's hearing aid, the grieving family
revealed today.

The shrine is proving to be a bit of a nuisance. It is
blocking the entrance to the bookshop and the books
from the Mortimer estate are due to be delivered this
morning.

I asked the policewoman who was on duty by the
shrine if the flowers could be moved along the pavement a little. She accused me of having no respect for the
dead.

When she went off duty I pushed the shrine a few feet
along, nearer to Habitat's window. I'm sure Maz won't
mind.

There was a new poem pinned to a ragged teddy bear.

God was short of an angel, so he took Maz from this earth.
God, he said, 'I want a lad who has been good and kind
　　since birth.'
So when you look at a starry sky

And think of Maz, and cry,
Weep not, but see that shooting star, it's our angel going by.
Night, night, son
Love from Mam, Dad and your devoted pets, Rex,
    Whiskey and Soda

I wept over this grossly mawkish poem.

I have cancelled tonight's writers' group due to rat activity, Gary Milksop's litigation against me and general despondency about life.

Ken Blunt said on the phone that he was sick of the way the writers' group was being run and offered to take over the chairman's role.

My life is very slowly falling apart. I have signed another of the Barclaycard loan cheques and paid it into my account. I think, but I'm not sure, that I am now hopelessly in debt.

Tuesday April 15th

Before leaving for work I rang the War Office and left a message on their voicemail, asking if Mr Hoon had received my letter regarding Private Glenn Bott-Mole.

CCTV footage of me moving the flower shrine was shown on *Midlands Today*, at 6 p.m., and the *Ashby Bugle* ran the headline, 'Callous Shopkeeper Disturbs Shrine'.

The article stated:

Ex-celebrity chef, Adrian Mole, thirty-five, was accused by a grieving family today of being heartless and despicable. 'We are gutted and devastated,' they said. Nathan Silver, a professor of anthropology from Loughborough University, said, 'Disturbing a sacred shrine that honours the dead is taboo in every culture worldwide.'

Marigold rang and shrieked, 'Mummy said you're on the front page of the paper for vandalizing a grave. Everyone hates you.'

I told her that it was page five, and that it was not a grave but a shrine, and I said I would entirely understand if she wanted nothing more to do with me.

She said, 'No, you're still the father of my child. It's important that we keep in touch.'

Michael Flowers came on the phone and asked me to drive Marigold and Netta to Birmingham Airport. 'Their flight leaves at 6.10 tomorrow morning. So you'll need to be at Beeby on the Wold by 4 a.m., at the latest.'

I heard myself agreeing to this.

Wednesday April 16th

I rose at 3 a.m., showered, dressed, beat Gielgud away from the driver's door of my car and drove to Beeby on the Wold.

There was a small mountain of luggage on the

doorstep, which I loaded into the boot. Then Marigold emerged from the house, helped by Michael Flowers, who was still in his plaid dressing-gown.

Marigold was wearing a smock-type thing, what looked like maternity trousers and the Birkenstocks. Netta was similarly attired. During the journey to Birmingham Airport, Netta and Marigold talked between themselves about how unfair it was that women have to carry a baby inside them for nine months. They then discussed what the baby would be called and decided between them that Rowan would suit both sexes. I was not consulted.

Netta had requested that a wheelchair be available to take Marigold to the aircraft. While this was being arranged, the check-in clerk asked me, for insurance purposes, what was wrong with Marigold. I answered, truthfully, that I didn't know.

As I watched the plane hurtle down the runway and throw itself into the sky, I felt my spirits rise, and on the return journey my rear-view mirror told me that I looked ten years younger. For the first time in my life, I forgot to be frightened and drove at 70 miles an hour down the fast lane of the M6.

Later in the morning I was introduced to Bernard Hopkins. He is tall and stooped and has an egg-shaped head flanked by tufts of lifeless black hair. The capillaries carrying the blood around his face appeared to be making their way to the surface and some were in danger of bursting. He seemed exasperated by life. He appeared to be slightly drunk and was smoking a cigarette. Mr Carlton-Hayes normally bans smoking in the front of the shop, but Hopkins seems to have carte blanche to do anything he likes. He is possibly the rudest man I have ever met. On being introduced to me he said, 'You've got the look of a nancy boy about you. Are you a poof?'

Mr Carlton-Hayes, surely the most gentlemanly of gentlemen, watches Hopkins with obvious delight, as a besotted parent might watch a precocious toddler – whereas I long to take Hopkins's baggy corduroy trousers down and give him a few hard smacks on the back of his legs.

Still, he knows his stuff and he loves books. He almost fainted with pleasure when he found a three-volume set of the Andrews & Blake 1807 first American edition of Boswell's *Life of Samuel Johnson*. He showed them to me and said, 'Take a gander at these, cocker. You don't get many of these to the kilo.' He drew his hands across the volumes muttering, 'Original full-gilt-stamped diamond patterned Moroccan, complete with portrait and folding facsimiles.'

It was like an incantation. I hope to be fluent in bookselling jargon one day. I asked him how much the set was worth.

He said, 'A kosher punter might spring a monkey, cocker.'

I've no idea what Bernard is talking about half the time.

He asked me to join him for a drink at lunchtime, so we went to the Dog and Duck around the corner. He was horrified when I ordered a still Malvern water.

He said, 'Why come into a pub, cocker? Why not stay at work and stick your head under the cold tap in the bog?'

I found myself telling Bernard about my spiralling debts.

He said that he had been pursued by creditors since he was a young man at Oxford.

Thursday April 17th

Hopkins is supposed to be cataloguing the Mortimer collection, which is now stacked in the back room, but he keeps wandering into the front of the shop.

A pretty medical student came in today looking for a cheap copy of *Gray's Anatomy*. I was showing her the three copies we had in stock when Bernard Hopkins shoved his nose in and started questioning the competency of women doctors.

'It was a bint doctor killed my old mother,' he said. 'The bint was too bloody busy with her lipstick and sanitary towels to give my poor old mum the expert medical attention she deserved.'

The medical student was clearly taken aback by this assault on her sex and left the shop empty-handed.

When I remonstrated with Hopkins, he said in a choked-up voice, 'My mother was a saint. I lived with her until she was ninety-six, and do you know, Adrian, she washed my handkerchiefs by hand, rinsed them in rosewater and ironed them so that they came to a point. Every morning she would take one from the drawer and put it into the breast pocket of my jacket before I went to work.'

He took a scruffy tissue from his trouser pocket and wiped his eyes before continuing, 'She was still beautiful at ninety-six. She didn't have a single wrinkle on her lovely face, and her hair was jet black. *Jet black* at ninety-six.'

I said, 'Bernard, you seem to have idealized your mother. It's obvious that behind your back she dyed her hair.'

He flew into a rage, and when Mr Carlton-Hayes came out of the back office to find out what all the shouting was about, Bernard accused me of calling his mother a harlot.

I told Mr Carlton-Hayes that I had only suggested that Bernard's mother dyed her hair.

Mr Carlton-Hayes said, 'Oh, the famous black hair.' He raised one eyebrow but said no more.

What is it with old men and handkerchiefs?

Friday April 18th
Good Friday (Bank Holiday UK, Canada and Australia)

Glenn is eighteen today. I hope to God that he is not sent to Iraq. My nerves won't stand the daily agony of wondering where he is and what he's doing.

So far the Iraqis have not thrown rose petals in front of the coalition forces' tanks. On the contrary, there has been widespread looting, pillaging and armed resistance. Mr Blair's liberation is their invasion.

Saturday April 19th
Easter Saturday

The bad publicity about the shrine has affected trade in the shop. My mother thinks that I should associate myself with a charity. Ivan has recently been diagnosed with epilepsy. She suggested that I hold a charity auction in aid of Canine Epilepsy Research.

She said, 'If you want to win the hearts and minds of the British people, you need to be photographed with a dog.'

I went round to see Nigel and asked him if I could be photographed with his blind dog, Graham.

Nigel snapped, 'Graham is not a blind dog. A blind dog would be no fucking use to me, would it? Graham is a guide dog, and no, you're not exploiting him for the sake of your poxy public image.'

I didn't mind too much; Graham is not a very attractive dog. He's the only Golden Labrador I've ever seen with a squint and stumpy legs.

Nigel said that Graham is the only creature he has ever truly loved.

Sunday April 20th
Easter Sunday

My home entertainment centre blew up this morning, preventing me following the progress of the war. I am hungry for every scrap of information and every picture of the war. Last night I thought I saw Glenn riding on an armoured vehicle, but I may have been mistaken. I phoned Brain-box Henderson and asked him if he gave advice over the telephone. He offered to call round. I said, 'Brain-box, I can't afford you. Just give me some cheap advice over the phone.'

He said, 'I'm at a bit of a loose end, Moley. I'll come round and do an onsite appraisal, FOC. Perhaps we can have a spot of lunch later? My golf club do a decent roast and four veg.'

The prospect of spending most of the day with Brain-box Henderson filled me with dread, but I had worked out what FOC meant, and if he could reconnect me to the outside world free of charge, I judged it to be a price worth paying.

Brain-box turned up at 11.30, dressed for the golf course in a sweater similar to the one my father had given me for my birthday. I made some fresh coffee and talked to him while he disentangled the cables and rewired the plugs. He said, 'You're running too many plugs from the one socket and it's overheated.'

I laughed mirthlessly, and said, 'You've just described my life, perfectly.'

Brain-box, ignoring my philosophizing, said, 'All you need is a good multi-socket extension; I've got one in the car.'

When he had got everything working, we watched CNN for a while. I felt my chest constrict and my palms sweat when footage was shown of British soldiers patrolling the streets of Basra.

I asked Brain-box if he had any children. He automatically made the usual male joke, and said, 'None that I know of.' Then his face twitched a bit and he said, 'I'd love to have a kid, but the girl I wanted to have them with left me standing at the altar. I'm not like you, Moley; I'm not very good with women.'

I said, 'Brain-box, I'm disastrous with women. My romantic life is a shambles.'

Brain-box said, 'But you're marrying one of the loveliest women I've ever met.'

I said, 'Haven't you heard? The wedding is off.'

He said, 'I'd heard it was rocky, but I didn't know it was officially off. Does that mean that Marigold's free?'

I said, making a small joke, 'She's not free, Brain-box. She's cost me a fortune.'

Brain-box said quietly, 'Money's no problem; I've got nobody to spend it on but myself.'

We called in at the Piggeries on the way to the Fair Green Golf Club to pick up my father's clubs. My mother and Animal were in the tent with all the flaps down when we arrived. When she eventually stumbled outside, I asked her what she'd been doing.

She said, 'Animal was helping me de-flea the dog. I'm glad to see you wearing your dad's birthday present, but isn't your hair a bit long for a golfing jumper?'

The roof is on the first pigsty. My mother is certainly getting her money's worth out of Animal.

The Fair Green Golf Club is sandwiched between the heavy haulage distribution centre near junction 20 of the

M1 and the new, windowless business park. Brain-box was a little scornful about my father's golf clubs – he said that they were almost museum pieces – but I dragged them around the eighteen-hole course and they served me well enough. I didn't disgrace myself; I was only sixty over par, which is not bad for a total beginner.

As we sat down to a tepid and soggy very late lunch, Brain-box said, 'It's nice to have friendly company for a change. You're the next best thing to a woman, Moley.'

I looked around the dining room in the club house and said, 'I've just realized what's wrong: there are no women in here.'

'No,' said Brain-box. 'They're not allowed in at the weekend.'

I told him that if he wanted to meet women he should hang around wine bars or the patisserie counter in Sainsbury's.

He said, 'I do all my shopping online. And anyway, I've met the girl I want to marry.' He blushed, hacked at a piece of dried-up Yorkshire pudding and said, 'It's Marigold.'

'My Marigold!' I said.

'She's not your Marigold now, is she?' he said.

I said, 'No, but she's having my baby.'

He said, 'It wouldn't bother me, you're fairly intelligent and not bad-looking. I'd give your kid everything it needed, and I know I can make Marigold happy.'

I said that I would do everything in my power to help him win Marigold's affection. Brain-box took my hand and shook it, then held it for an uncomfortably long time.

Brain-box dropped me off at the hospital on his way home. My father was thrilled to wake up and see me sitting next to his bed wearing the golfing sweater and holding his bag of clubs. He said that sixty over par was astounding for a novice. 'I'm proud of you, son.'

Monday April 21st
Easter Monday (Bank Holiday UK)

Is the war in Iraq over? Jay Garner, the retired former US General, arrived in Baghdad to take up the post of Iraq's post-war civil administrator. Thank God. This means Glenn will soon be home.

Sharon rang to say that she is using a pair of old sheets to make a banner to drape across the front of her house saying, 'Welcome home, hero'. She asked me for some money so that she could buy the red, white and blue paint for the lettering. I could hardly refuse and said that I would drop off £20 on my way home from work tomorrow.

Tuesday April 22nd

The pretty woman medical student came in and bought a copy of *Gray's Anatomy* this morning. I apologized for Bernard Hopkins's sexist remarks.

She said, 'It didn't matter, he's obviously clinically mad.'

I explained that Bernard's eccentricity was considered normal in the antiquarian and second-hand book trade.

I was buying mangoes at the market at lunchtime when I bumped into Michael Flowers. He told me that he had heard from Netta in Capri. The hotel was marvellous and Marigold had recovered her spirits. Mother and daughter had been undergoing various therapies.

Wednesday April 23rd

The phone call I have been dreading. Glenn rang to say he was now stationed just outside Basra, in southern Iraq. He told me that he'd been frightened for his life earlier that day when an angry mob had surrounded him. He'd been out on patrol and he'd given a little kid a boiled sweet from his army rations. The kid was laughing and sucking the sweet one minute; the next he was choking to death because the sweet had got stuck in his windpipe.

Glenn remembered the time his brother, William, had a similar accident with a Nuttall's Mintoe and I saved his life by holding him upside-down by the ankles, so he did the same to the Iraqi kid.

'I had to shake him about a bit, Dad,' said Glenn, 'an' it probably didn't look too good from his family's point of view. I tried to explain, but I can't speak Iraqi and nobody seemed to understand what "boiled sweet" meant, so I weren't too popular.'

So much for winning Iraqi 'hearts and minds'.

Thursday April 24th

Bernard Hopkins has sorted the crap from Mrs Mortimer's collection and I have arranged to hold a book sale in aid of Canine Epilepsy Research. Pandora is coming to draw the raffle; she needs to placate the dog-lovers of her constituency after she made some wild and reckless statements about dog shit in public places. Mr Carlton-Hayes and Bernard Hopkins have kindly volunteered to help out on the day.

Friday April 25th

Tariq Aziz, the former Iraqi Deputy Prime Minister, surrendered to US forces in Baghdad, but eight British soldiers have been blown up in a grenade attack by what have been called 'small pockets of resistance'. How is it possible that my son has gone to war? Since the day the boy came to live with me I have made myself responsible for his wellbeing. I made sure he ate a reasonable diet, that he wore his vest in the winter, that he took his hayfever pills when the Met Office warned of a high pollen count. I used to lie awake worrying when he started going to the town on Friday nights and didn't come home on the last bus. Whenever he left the house I'd remind him to use pedestrian crossings and avoid eye contact with drunken strangers. And now the boy is in Iraq without my protection and there is nothing I can do.

Saturday April 26th

I have cut a piece out of the *Guardian* and sent it to Mr Blair. It may help him to defend himself against his critics when they ask where the Weapons of Mass Destruction are. According to Dr Popper, the eminent philosopher, 'No number of sightings of white swans can prove the theory that all swans are white. The sighting of just one black one may disprove it.'

I can imagine Mr Blair using this quote during one of his many television appearances. He is on the television almost as often as Michael Fish, the weather bloke.

I have ordered a state-of-the-art Smeg Home Refrigeration Unit on Brain-box Henderson's advice. It is computerized and informs you when the food inside is about to reach its use-by date. I am sick of opening my ordinary fridge and finding that the food has gone off.

Sunday April 27th

I had intended holding the charity book sale on the pavement outside the shop using several trestle tables and the hand-held microphone from Glenn's old toy karaoke set. But the weather conspired against me and after I had chased the Canine Epilepsy Research posters down the High Street, where they had been blown by the wind, I admitted defeat and lugged the tables and books back inside the shop.

This change of venue proved to be very inconvenient; it seemed that every epileptic dog in the East Midlands had turned up with its owner, and several vicious fights took place, which Bernard Hopkins broke up. The *Midlands Today* camera crew did not materialize as promised.

But when Pandora arrived to make a passionate, hypocritical speech about the importance of dogs in British society and the government's support of canine research, she had a documentary film crew with her. She is the subject of a television series called *The Public Life of Pandora Braithwaite*, which will be screened to coincide with the publication of her autobiography some time in July.

I congratulated her on how young she looked in her red leather Prada jacket, designer jeans and high-heeled boots. She whispered, 'It's the Botox, everybody in the Party's having it.'

I asked if Mr Blair had undergone the non-surgical procedure.

She said, 'Not yet, but haven't you noticed how young and well Gordon is looking lately?'

The *Ashby Bugle* sent a reporter and a photographer, but they did not want to photograph me or write down anything I had to say; instead, they took a photograph of Pandora surrounded by epileptic dogs. As far as I was concerned it was a public-relations failure, although the sale made £369.71. Less £3.19, which was the cost of the bleach and disinfectant I had to buy to clean up after the dogs.

I asked Pandora if she wanted to go to Wong's for a meal, but she said she had a meeting with the elders at the mosque and was going back to London immediately afterwards, which was just as well because my mother rang to say that my father had been discharged and could I pick him up from the ward and take him back to the Piggeries.

I'm not a medical expert, but in my opinion my father was not ready to be discharged. He could hardly stand unaided. After waiting an hour for a porter to bring a wheelchair I lost my patience and borrowed a wheelchair from an obliging hospital visitor.

There was a strong wind blowing outside, so I took my coat off and wrapped it around my father and pushed him to the car. When he was seated inside and had lit a cigarette, I pushed the wheelchair back to the ward.

It is pathetic how institutionalized he has become. On the journey to the Piggeries he looked at his watch and said, 'Five o'clock: the supper trolley will be coming round now.'

Ivan went crazy when he saw my father being helped across the field and came running towards us, barking with joy. My mother had made up a bed in the camper van with clean sheets and pillowcases, and my father climbed on to the ledge and went to sleep.

Monday April 28th

Nigel rang to say he had heard that I had been golfing with my 'new best friend', Geeky Henderson. He said, 'What next, Moley? A Saga cruise? An allotment? Membership of the National Trust?'

I asked him if the Guide Dogs for the Blind had agreed

to let Graham stay permanently. He said that Graham had indicated that he was happy to stay.

I said, 'Nigel, I know Graham is clever, but even he can't talk.'

Nigel said, 'That's what you think,' and put the phone down.

Tuesday April 29th

Marigold is too ill to travel and is being forced to stay for another two weeks in Capri.

The work-experience lad brought another note from Flowers.

Dear Adrian

Alas, poor Marigold has been taken ill, having overexerted herself while sightseeing.

She and her mother have been forced to stay on at the Hotel Splendid. I'm sure you are as concerned as I am, and agree that the poor girl must stay until she feels able to travel home to England.

I think £1,000 from you will cover this.

Peace

M. F.

I immediately rang Brain-box and gave him an update on the Marigold situation. He said he was only round the corner, setting up a laptop in the office of Fanny's, the lap-dancing club, and would meet me at the shop as soon as he had finished.

I have to admit that Brain-box is a marvel with technology. Within half an hour he had booked a flight to Naples, a ferry to Capri and himself into the Hotel Splendid. He said, 'I have never done anything like this in my life before.'

I suggested to him that he should run across the road to Next and ask an assistant to rig him out with clothing suitable for Capri in April.

Brain-Box did as I suggested: he was Trilby to my Svengali.

When I told my mother about Marigold, she said, 'When I was pregnant with you I worked an eight-hour day in a pie factory, dug an allotment at the weekend, did all the laundry by tramping on it in the bath, wallpapered a terrace house, ran a mobile hairdresser's after work and went dancing on Fridays. I smoked thirty fags a day and drank a brandy and ginger before going to bed, every night.'

Wednesday April 30th

With hindsight it was probably a mistake to invite Bernard Hopkins to the readers' club meeting where we were to discuss *William, the Outlaw* by Richmal Crompton. He was obviously drunk and occasionally offensive, although Mr Carlton-Hayes did not rebuke him once.

Lorraine started the discussion by saying, 'This book cracked me up, man. That William, I tell you, he's a proper nutter.'

Darren said, 'Once I realized it weren't a cowboy story, I really got into it. I used to belong to a gang, but when we broke into an old lady's house to get our footballs back that she'd collected over the months, we ended up in court. I got probation, but the leader of the gang, Dougie Willis, was put away.'

Mr Carlton-Hayes chuckled. 'Yes, it's remarkable how lenient the authorities were with William's propensity for arson, burglary and fraud.'

Mohammed said, 'What I want to know is, why the author, Mrs Crompton, allowed William Brown to behave so badly? The boy grew up in a respectable, middle-class home, with good parents, a servant and a gardener and with all the advantages of his class. Mrs Crompton does not explain why William chose to be an outlaw of society.'

Lorraine said, 'I blame that Mr Brown. He was always bigging it up with his briefcase and his trilby hat. He was always on his boy's back. It's no wonder William went a bit wild.'

Melanie said peevishly, 'Pardon me for saying, Mr Carlton-Hayes, but I don't see why you asked us to read a kiddies' book. And another thing, all the books we've read so far have been old-fashioned. Don't get me wrong, I like old-fashioned books. I adored that Jane Austen thing on the telly, but when are we going to read something modern?'

Mr Carlton-Hayes flushed a little. Melanie had inad-

vertently touched a nerve: the most recent novel he had
read was *Couples*, published in 1968, and Bernard Hopkins goes about saying that nobody has written anything
decent since Nabokov, so it was up to me to come up
with a contemporary novel. I suggested *White Teeth* by
Zadie Smith.

I asked Bernard Hopkins if he had enjoyed the evening.

He said, 'Not my cup of Darjeeling, cocker. I've been
more intellectually challenged at a kiddies' swimming
gala.'

When I got home I found an email from Brain-box:

Have just arrived at Hotel Splendid. Marigold and her
mother are out on a sightseeing trip to the rim of
Vesuvius. They are calling in at Pompeii and are due
back tomorrow. Wish me luck. Yours, Bruce.

Thursday May 1st

I phoned International Directories, and after being put
through to the Hotel Splendid in Grimsby and the Hotel
Splendid in Barcelona, I was connected to the Hotel
Splendid in Capri.

I asked to speak to Mr Henderson. An Italian bloke
said in perfect English, 'Mr Henderson is not in the hotel,
sir. He has gone on a trip to see the Blue Grotto, sir.'

George Bush has just declared 'an end to major military
combat in Iraq', so the war is officially over.

Glenn rang tonight. I asked him when he was coming

home. He said, 'Not for six months. I'm on peace-keeping duties, Dad.'

I asked him what it was like out there, and he said, 'Not good.'

I asked him if there was anything he wanted.

He said, 'Some body-armour would be appreciated. Me and Robbie are sharing ours.'

I asked him if he was joking.

He said, 'No,' then added, 'I've got to go, I'll try and ring you later, Dad.'

Friday May 2nd

I phoned the Hotel Splendid early this morning and asked to speak to the two English ladies, Marigold and her mother, Netta Flowers. The Italian on the reception desk said, 'There are many English ladies staying in the hotel. What do they look like?'

I said, 'They are both very badly dressed.'

He said, 'All the English ladies are badly dressed, signor.'

I told him that Marigold had thin hair and wore glasses and Netta, her mother, looked a little like a tall, blonde, pinker, piggier Mussolini.

He said, 'Yes, I know the ladies. They are having breakfast on the terrace.'

While I waited for Marigold to come to the phone I heard seagulls, laughter and the tinkle of expensive china. Eventually the receptionist said, 'She is 'ere.'

Marigold's frail voice trickled down the phone. I asked her how it was that she was fit enough to go on a strenuous trip to the rim of a volcano but was not able to get on a plane and fly back to England.

Marigold said, 'I dragged myself to the top of Vesuvius because of the health-giving properties of breathing volcanic fumes. Mummy thinks the baby is depleting my mineral reserves.'

I told Marigold that Brain-box Henderson was at the hotel with the cash to pay for their extended holiday.

Marigold said, 'Bruce is here?'

She did not sound displeased.

I then heard Brain-box's high-pitched laugh and Marigold squealed, 'Bruce, I can't believe you're here.'

Then the phone went dead.

Saturday May 3rd

Another letter from the City Council.

Neighbourhood Conflict Co-ordinator
Leicester City Council
New Walk
Leicester LE1

May 1st 2003

Dear Mr Mole

Just to keep you informed, I have written to Mr Swan, c/o The Swans' Nest, Rat Wharf, Leicester, to inform him that a

complaint has been lodged against him at the Neighbourhood
Conflict Unit.

Meanwhile, Mr Mole, I suggest you keep a record of Mr
Swan's antisocial behaviour.

Yours sincerely

Trixie Meadows

Neighbourhood Conflict Co-ordinator

I phoned immediately to put the record straight regarding
'Mr Swan', but a computer told me that Trixie Meadows
was not at her work station.

Sunday May 4th

I am reading *Lolita* by Vladimir Nabokov. His main
character is called Humbert Humbert, which shows a
lack of imagination on Nabokov's part. Surely he could
have thought up a different surname.

Monday May 5th
Bank Holiday

Went to Sainsbury's. Felt a sense of despair as I stood in
front of the Mr Kipling shelves. I know I will never live
with the woman I love. I must try to reconcile myself to
being unhappy; it ought to be easy. After all, I am not an
American who expects to be happy as a constitutional
right. I filled my shopping basket with a selection of Mr
Kipling's finest confections.

In the short queue at the check-out a tanned woman in a track suit whispered to her partner, 'What an appalling diet. People like him are a drain on the National Health Service.'

I heard her because every sense and organ in my body is on red alert. My nerve endings are so sensitive that mere existence is painful. Perhaps I am coming down with the flu.

Tuesday May 6th

Credit card bills were waiting for me when I got home from work; I was too depressed to open them. I put them in the kitchen-gadget drawer. The one I never use.

Wednesday May 7th

When I got home from work I found a note slipped under my door. It said: Please call PC Aaron Drinkwater.

I rang the number on the note and was put through to PC Drinkwater's voicemail. A lugubrious voice said, 'This office is only manned between the hours of 9 a.m. and 5 p.m. on Wednesdays, Thursdays and Fridays and from 1 p.m. to 3 p.m. on Mondays and Tuesdays. The office is closed at the weekend and on bank holidays. If you need to speak to me, please leave a short message with your name and number, and I'll do my best to get back to you, although due to operational duties this may sometimes be subject to delay.'

Thursday May 8th

I have left seven messages on PC Drinkwater's voicemail. The last one was slightly abusive. I accused him of shirking his duty to the community and said, 'I expect you're sitting with your feet on your desk, reading the paper and having a laugh at my expense.'

I now regret my loss of temper, and am waiting for the sound of a truncheon hammering on my door.

Friday May 9th

Brain-box rang: there was pure happiness in his voice. He said that he was interacting wonderfully with Marigold and her mother and that the dynamic between the three of them was wholly positive. Marigold was looking enchantingly beautiful, and last night they had danced on the terrace to 'Love is a Many Splendored Thing', sung by Antonio, one of 'their' waiters.

Sunday May 11th

Went to the Piggeries in the afternoon. The windows were being installed in number-one pigsty, by Malcolm and Stan, from a firm called Keencraft. Animal was fitting the front door.

*

My mother was attempting to lay bricks in pigsty number two. She said, 'It's so frustrating, Adrian. Every time I lay a brick the mortar squeezes out. It's like biting into a vanilla slice, but without the pleasure.'

I pointed out that she was using too much mortar.

She said irritably, 'All right, clever clogs. Show me how it should be done.'

After a few attempts, I admitted to her that bricklaying was harder than it looks.

My father was sitting on the steps of the camper van looking miserable. I asked him why he was so depressed.

He said, 'A bloke from the sustainable-energy unit came out in the week to check us out for a wind farm, and what day did he choose, Adrian? A day when there was not a bleedin' breath of wind. Not a breeze. Not a stir in the air. It was as still as a dead cat's dick. Any other day, it's blowing a bleedin' gale. But oh, no, he has to call the day that the wind round here packed its bags and went to bleedin' Ibiza.'

Monday May 12th

The writers' group meeting was held at Rat Wharf. I'm sick of looking for a quiet pub in the city centre where it is possible to discuss literary matters. City-centre landlords seem to have got rid of all the furniture and gone in for what is now called vertical drinking. The pubs have been taken over by drunken young people who stand around sucking beer from a bottle through black drinking straws.

Ken reiterated that he was very dissatisfied with the way the group was being run. He laughed sardonically and said, 'It's not even a group, it's just you and me, now.'

I listened to his latest polemic about the Iraq war.

> 'Donald Rumsfeld,
> There are things you say you know you know
> There are things you say you know you don't know
> What you don't know is that you'll never know
> How much you don't know.'

After he had gone, I thought back to the glory days of the Leicestershire and Rutland Creative Writing Group, when the members would sit enraptured for hours, listening to my novel, *Lo, the Flat Hills of My Homeland*.

We had started out with sixteen members, but these rapidly dwindled, and now there was just me and Ken.

Tuesday May 13th

Bernard Hopkins and Mr Carlton-Hayes had a heated discussion about the Iraqi war today while they were cataloguing the crime-fiction books from the Mortimer collection. I heard Bernard Hopkins say, 'They found a mass grave today, Hughie. Fifteen thousand Shiites packed together like commuters on a Thameslink train, except the poor sods are dead.' His voice broke with emotion, or drink. It's always hard to tell with Hopkins.

Mr Carlton-Hayes raised his voice slightly and

said, 'Bernard, my dear, I have never disputed that Saddam Hussein is a thoroughly unpleasant chap, but I still consider that we invaded a sovereign country illegally.'

I thought about Glenn and hoped that by now he had been allocated his own body armour.

Wednesday May 14th

Brain-box Henderson called into the shop today. Love, his Next wardrobe and the Italian sun have transformed him. He went to Capri a geeky computer boff and arrived back in Leicester a tanned Lothario. His half-bald head looked like a shiny conker and the clumps and tufts that used to give him the appearance of a mad professor had gone. When I complimented him, he flushed and said, 'An Italian barber.'

I asked him how things stood between him and Marigold.

He stammered, 'She's an amazing girl. She made a tiny sunbed out of a matchbox, a few dead matches and a scrap of cloth. We talked for hours, Adrian. One night I didn't go to bed until one o'clock in the morning.'

I asked him what had kept him up so daringly late.

He said, 'We were talking about you. Marigold is very bitter. She says she can't understand how she fell in love with you in the first place. She said you prefer characters in books to people in real life.'

I said, 'So what is your precise relationship with Marigold now?'

He said, 'I want to marry her.'

I asked him if he had told Marigold this.

He said, 'Yes, after a firework display over the Bay of Naples.' His face went a bit gormless as he remembered the scene.

Somewhat impatiently, diary, I asked him how Marigold had responded.

He said, 'She didn't say yes, but she didn't say no, either.'

Friday May 16th

Using my binoculars, I ascertained that Gielgud's wife has laid seven eggs. My worst fears have been realized. When the eggs are hatched, the canal will be overrun with swans.

Saturday May 17th

Listened to *I'm Sorry I Haven't a Clue* in the bath. I have heard this amusing programme many times, but I still do not understand the rules of Mornington Crescent. Strange, since I must be one of the most intelligent men in the East Midlands.

Sunday May 18th

I wrote to Radio Four.

I'm Sorry I Haven't a Clue
Production Office
Radio Four
The BBC
Broadcasting House
London W1A

Unit 4
The Old Battery Factory
Rat Wharf
Grand Union Canal
Leicester LE1

May 18th 2003

Dear Sir or Madam

I write as a long-time listener to your amusing programme *I'm Sorry I Haven't a Clue.*

I must have missed the broadcast when Mr Humphrey Lyttleton explained the rules of Mornington Crescent to the panelists.

I wonder if you would furnish me with them.

Yours faithfully

A. A. Mole

Monday May 19th

I decided to write again to the City Council Neighbourhood Conflict Officer, Trixie Meadows.

Leicester City Council
New Walk
Leicester LE1

Unit 4
The Old Battery Factory
Rat Wharf
Grand Union Canal
Leicester LE1

May 19th 2003

Dear Trixie Meadows

There is no Mr Swan. The swan in question cannot be dignified by the prefix 'Mr'. He is a mute, a creature not a man. He cannot be talked to or reasoned with, because he is in fact a wild *animal*.

He is dangerous and completely unreasonable. He is constantly defecating on the towpath, the car park and occasionally in the entrance of the Old Battery Factory, where I live. He is making my and my neighbours' lives a misery. Unless the authorities move swiftly to alleviate this grave situation, I fear that a violent act will ensue.

Yours,

A. A. Mole

Tuesday May 20th

PC Aaron Drinkwater battered on my door early this morning, waking me from a deep sleep. Throughout the ensuing interview I was at a great disadvantage, as I needed to urinate urgently. I was inhibited by the glass-bricked bathroom.

PC Drinkwater gave me a formal caution and told me that the Crown Prosecution Service had been sent a transcript of my conversation with a 999 operative, who claimed that I had been abusive and had wasted police time on February 3rd 2003.

I explained about the postbag, but he cut me off impatiently and said, 'We've also had a complaint that you've been throwing rubbish into the canal.'

I denied this vehemently. He then drew a small plastic bag from his trouser pocket. It contained a few scraps of the letter I had torn up and thrown over my balcony months ago. Bearing in mind the advances made in forensic science, DNA and nanotechnology, but mainly because one of the scraps of paper bore my name, I admitted the offence. The policeman leaned against my kitchen counter and gave me a mini-lecture on the environment and ended by saying 'one of those beautiful swans could have choked to death'.

So, I do not have a natural ally in PC Drinkwater.

Wednesday May 21st

Letter from Glenn.

Dear Dad

I am sorry to bother you, but I have got a bit of a problem, which I hope you can help me with. Is there a book in your shop that tells people how to stop being scared? I am scared every time I go on patrol in Basra. Sometimes it is so bad that I am shaking. I don't think anybody has noticed yet, so I'm not in trouble or anything. It's just that I am worried that if trouble starts I will let the rest of the lads down.

Dad, I feel like running away when the crowds start throwing stones and petrol bombs.

If there is a book, it could teach me not to be so scared of having my balls shot off, like one of the Yanks did last week.

Also, Dad, when we are at the checkpoints, the people can't tell what we are shouting at them, and we can't tell what they are saying to us. So everybody gets mad with each other. So if there is a book, could you please send it to me.

Loads of love

From your son, Glenn

PS Don't tell Mum I am scared. Tell her I am having a good laugh and getting a suntan.

Thursday May 22nd

I showed Mr Carlton-Hayes the letter I had received from Glenn and confessed that I was worried sick about his inability to communicate with the Iraqi people. I said, 'Glenn has problems communicating in English; his inability to understand and speak Arabic could kill him.'

Bernard Hopkins said, 'Don't worry, cocker, the bloody towel-heads understand the barrel of a gun.'

Mr Carlton-Hayes sent him into the back room to catalogue a crate of Penguin Classic paperbacks bought at auction.

Mr Carlton-Hayes said that during the Second World War he had been given flashcards with German phrases on one side and English on the other.

Knowing he had trained as an Egyptologist and was an Arabic speaker, I asked him if he could do the same for Glenn.

We worked on the cards together, and after some thought came up with:

1. Please get out of the car
2. Please put your hands in the air
3. Please open the boot
4. Please do not throw stones
5. Please do not hurt me. I am only eighteen years old
6. I am a liberator, not an invader
7. Thanks for your co-operation

There was a lot of argument about number six, but Mr Carlton-Hayes and I agreed to differ.

Friday May 23rd

Dear Glenn

Please find enclosed a copy of *How to Master Your Fear*. I found this useful when I developed a phobia of driving on the M6.

Try to take deep breaths when you leave your barracks: mind over matter can always help.

Try to think about a happy time. Do you remember that Sunday afternoon at Rampart Terrace when you were thirteen and you beat me at Monopoly? Me, you and William toasted some bread on the coal fire with my Grandma's old toasting fork. We drank tomato soup out of those special tomato-shaped mugs we bought from the 'Everything for a Pound' shop. You were wearing your first pair of genuine Reeboks and you said 'Dad, I'm happy.'

As you see, I have also enclosed some flashcards that me and my boss, Mr Carlton-Hayes, have made up for you.

Mr Carlton-Hayes has sent you an anthology of poetry written by a soldier in the First World War. He's put a note inside the book.

I think about you all the time, son. Be assured you are in Iraq fighting for a good cause.

Much love from
Dad

My dear Glenn,

I hope you don't mind me writing to you, but your Father showed me your letter. I served in the Second World War as an infantry man. I spent most of my war service in a state of terror. It is entirely normal to feel as you do. I hope Siegfried Sassoon's poetry will reassure you. Some of it is savage stuff, but it is a truthful account of war, as you will know when you read it.

I send you my very warmest wishes,
Hugh Carlton-Hayes

Saturday May 24th

An adolescent boy wearing a hooded top, with the hood up and half-obscuring his face, came into the shop and mooched around the shelves. When I asked if he needed help, he said, 'Have you got a book called the Bible?'

Unfortunately, Bernard Hopkins heard this exchange and said with false puzzlement, 'The Bible? Tell me, young cocker, who's it written by?'

The youth blushed. 'I dunno,' he said. 'Weren't it God?'

This made me, Hopkins and Mr Carlton-Hayes laugh quite a lot.

The youth is doing a humanities project on the subject of fathers and sons. He has chosen God and Jesus.

I asked the youth why he had not availed himself of the school library. He said he had been banned from the library for eating a satsuma in there and spitting a pip and 'accidentally' hitting a boff girl called Louise Moore.

Warming to his theme of why he had been forced into a bookshop, he told us that his mum refused to get connected to the Internet, so he couldn't download from websites and copy stuff for his project like other kids. He made it sound as though his mother made him walk barefoot to school.

Bernard Hopkins took over the sale and sold the youth an *Illustrated Children's Bible* for seventy-five pence, wherein Jesus had blond hair and blue eyes and looked a bit like a long-haired David Beckham. It was only slightly mildewed.

Sunday May 25th

Brain-box Henderson rang me this morning and asked if he and Marigold could visit this afternoon. I made throat-cutting gestures down the phone, but agreed to see them.

Brain-box's tan has faded a little and some of his geekiness has come back, but I have never seen him so happy. Marigold is transformed; pregnancy seems to suit her. They can hardly keep their hands off each other. It was sickening, diary.

They want to get married and had come to ask me for my blessing, and to talk about the unborn child.

Brain-box said, 'I'm keen to adopt the baby, Adrian. Shall I get my solicitor to draw up some papers?'

I said, 'I'm too poor for the law. Can't we discuss this after the baby is born?'

Marigold said, 'I knew he'd be difficult, Bruce.'

Brain-box said to Marigold in a surprisingly authoritative manner, 'Don't *start*, Marigold.' He then covered her face in tiny kisses.

I had to turn away.

He then said to me, 'I'm quite prepared to help you out financially, Adrian. I know you are strapped for cash.'

I thought about 'Grace' in her tutu and said, 'I don't want to sell my parental rights.'

A child began to scream outside, then there was the sound of a man's voice, loud and angry. We all went out on to the balcony. A middle-aged man and a young boy were in a canoe being attacked by Gielgud. He was flapping his wings and pecking at the man's paddle.

Brain-box said, 'He's a vicious creature.'

I said to Brain-box, 'He's only protecting his eggs.'

The man and the child paddled off and Gielgud returned to the nest.

Marigold said she felt unwell and Brain-box put his arm protectively round her and took her home.

As they were leaving, I casually asked Marigold how Poppy and Daisy were.

She said, 'Poppy's on holiday in Albania, but Daisy's had to move back to Beeby on the Wold.' She laughed and then said with some satisfaction, 'She got thrown out of her flat for trashing the place when she was drunk.'

I asked if Daisy had lost her job.

Marigold said, 'Not yet, she's commuting.'

I have to see her, diary.

Monday May 26th
Spring Bank Holiday

I tried ringing Daisy's mobile, but the line has been disconnected. I drove to Beeby on the Wold and parked my car in the pub car park, and walked across the fields to where I could see the back of the house.

There was nobody in sight, but it calmed me to know that Daisy could be somewhere near. I sat with my back against a tree for over an hour. I had nothing to read and nothing to do except watch the clouds move across the sky, listen to the birds singing and follow various insects as they stumbled through the grass. As I walked back to the car I made a vow to myself that I would win Daisy back, marry her, and have children with her.

Tuesday May 27th

A letter from Trixie Meadows.

> Neighbourhood Conflict Co-ordinator
> Leicester City Council
> New Walk
> Leicester LE1
>
> May 27th 2003

Dear Mr Mole

I found the tone of your letter most offensive. Mr Swan is obviously in need of help, not condemnation.

You say he is mute. Is he in touch with the Speech Therapy Department at the Leicester Royal Hospital, and is he aware that Social Services can help with his incontinence?

Perhaps Mr Swan's problems are the cause of his antisocial behaviour. I still feel that reconciliation and negotiation is the path we should take towards a satisfactory outcome.

Calling Mr Swan 'a creature, a wild animal' and threatening violence can only be counterproductive.

Yours sincerely

Trixie Meadows

Neighbourhood Conflict Co-ordinator

11.35 p.m.
Daisy, Daisy, Daisy.

Wednesday May 28th

Bernard Hopkins opened the discussion on Zadie Smith's
White Teeth by drawling, 'It wasn't bad for a bint, but
Salman does it better.'

I said to Hopkins, 'You use Mr Rushdie's first name
with familiarity. Do you know him?'

Hopkins tapped the side of his nose and said, 'I had
him as a houseguest when he was on the run from
al-Qa'eda.'

Mohammed said heatedly, 'You are confusing the fun-
damentalists with a terrorist organization.'

Hopkins said, 'They're all the same to me, cocker.'

Mohammed snapped, 'But they are not all the same.
They are as far apart as the Reverend Ian Paisley and the
gay Bishop of Boston. Both men would call themselves
Christians.'

Lorraine Harris said, 'This is a wicked book. I know
people like the people in the book. I was laughing so
much I made the bed shake.'

Darren confessed he hadn't read it. He was still
immersed in *Jude the Obscure*. He then went on to confide
to the group that his constant reading was 'causing a few
problems with the wife'. He said he had bought a bookcase
for the living room, which had meant moving the furniture around, and his wife had 'gone mardy' because

the television set was now too far away from the socket.

Mr Carlton-Hayes nodded sympathetically though it was inconceivable to me that he could have experienced such domestic dramas.

I suggested that Darren take a present home to his non-reader wife: *Not a Penny More, Not a Penny Less* by Lord Archer.

I was asked to name the next book. I suggested *Stupid White Men* by Michael Moore. Bernard Hopkins blustered and swore and said, 'If I'd written a book called *Stupid Black Men*, I'd have been had up by the race relations industry.'

Mohammed said quietly, 'May I suggest it would be helpful to all of us if we read the Koran?'

Mr Carlton-Hayes said, 'An excellent suggestion.'

On my way home I called in at all the fashionable pubs and wine bars, but Daisy was not in any of them.

I read the first few pages of the Koran in bed tonight. It brought me closer to Glenn somehow.

Friday May 30th

The manager of Habitat rang to say that Bernard Hopkins was asleep on 'an item of garden furniture'. I went round to collect him. Before I woke him up I bought myself a new Anglepoise lamp. It's time I got down to it and did some serious writing. If I can't have Daisy, I can at least write a book about her.

Saturday May 31st

Daisy! At my front door! No make-up, hair a mess, but still beautiful, in combats and a top that showed her midriff. She said, 'You have to read this.'

She came inside and handed me a pink silk-covered diary with a lock. On the front it said 'The Secret Journal of Marigold Flowers'.

Daisy said, 'Turn to May 25th.'

I did as she asked and read in Marigold's backward-sloping hand:

Bruce and I went to see Adrian today to talk about the wedding and what will happen when the baby is born. I wanted to tell Bruce in the car on the way to Rat Wharf that I'm not having a baby. That I've been telling lies to everybody, but I couldn't bring myself to do it. I am frightened of losing Bruce.

I said to Daisy, 'Did she confess to you, Daisy?'

Daisy said, 'No, I was up in her bedroom and I picked the lock. I saw her in the bathroom last night. Her belly is completely flat. I thought you ought to know, seeing as you are the father of the phantom kid.'

I said, 'Is nothing true any more? Is there honey still for tea? Are there Weapons of Mass Destruction? Am I actually standing here and are you flesh and blood, or are we holograms, Daisy?'

She said, 'We're flesh and blood. And after you've made me a cup of coffee, we'll prove it.'

Sunday June 1st

I got no sleep last night; I stayed up talking to Daisy. We drank three bottles of wine and ate two bags of Doritos and a large bowl of salsa. Pudding was a ripe mango which we devoured in the bath naked.

Daisy managed to get the CD-player going and we danced to *Motown's Greatest Hits*. I have never danced naked before. It was OK once I got used to my genitalia swinging about. Mia Fox thumped on my door with her fists, but Daisy shouted, 'Get a life, you poor sad cow!'

Later, as Daisy slept beside me, I thought about the many times I had forgone pleasure for the convenience of other people. Whereas Daisy took her fair share of whatever was going.

Tuesday June 3rd

Daisy returned to Beeby this morning to replace Marigold's book of revelations and collect her suitcase. She met me at the shop after work and I took her to catch the London train; she is going on a book tour to promote Edwina Currie's diary.

As her carriage disappeared into the tunnel beyond the station, I felt the possibility of a new assertiveness fall away and resolved to buy Mia Fox a bunch of flowers by way of apology.

I need Daisy to light my life. Without her I will never metamorphose from caterpillar to moth.

I noticed that Donald Rumsfeld was now saying that the Weapons of Mass Destruction may never be found. This came as a considerable shock.

However, Mr Blair said he has 'no doubt at all'.

Wednesday June 4th

Met a postman in the car park this morning, I told him that I was surprised to see him so early. He asked me in broken English for my name and address, then handed me my post.

There was a letter from the Automobile Association, informing me that they now provided gas and would I like to switch from my present provider. There were also two credit card bills demanding payment and threatening that unless I paid the overdue amounts immediately, I would have to pay the balance in full. There were veiled threats that if I failed to make immediate payments my credit rating would be affected.

Diary, I had no choice but to withdraw the last £3,000 from my building society deposit account. I live in a capitalist system, but I have no capital.

Where has all the money gone? I've nothing to show for it apart from the futon and a few pots and pans.

Thursday June 5th

An appalling statistic – 63 per cent of Britons believe that Mr Blair misled them about Iraq's Weapons of Mass Destruction; 27 per cent believe he deliberately lied.

I don't know what I think any more.

Friday June 6th

I worked late at the shop tonight. When I left at 10 p.m. the High Street was full of young drunks of both sexes carousing from one bar to another. I walked in the middle of the road to avoid them and was almost knocked over by a taxi full of teenage slappers. One of them screamed out of the window 'Gerrout the road, Granddad.'

It is no wonder that middle-aged people lock themselves into their houses at night.

Saturday June 7th

I went to see Nigel after work to read to him as promised. He has chosen *Crime and Punishment* by Dostoevsky. The Russian names are impossible to pronounce and each time I stumble over one, Nigel sighs and mutters something to Graham.

I told him that it is now possible to train Shetland ponies as guide horses for the blind. Apparently, they have better memories than Labradors.

Graham got to his feet, looked at me, and growled.

Nigel said, 'Good dog, Graham. Good dog.'

I told Nigel about Marigold's phantom pregnancy and that I was now having a secret affair with Daisy, Marigold's sister.

Nigel said, 'Dostoevsky would have a job keeping up with you, Moley. Your life is stranger than fiction.'

I made Nigel promise that he wouldn't tell anybody about Marigold's phantom baby. I said, 'I haven't had a chance to confront her about it yet. Marigold's away with Brain-box at an IT fair.'

Nigel rang a number on his mobile and said, 'Pandora, have you heard the latest in Moley's psycho-drama . . .'

I left in disgust.

Sunday June 8th

Went round to Sharon's after ascertaining that Ryan would be out. When I asked where he was, Sharon said, 'He goes to a pole-dancing club called Honeyz every Sunday dinner.'

I said, 'Don't you mind, Sharon?'

She replied, 'No, it saves me cooking.'

Karan was there, crawling on the sticky carpet. I asked her where the other children were.

She said, 'They're out with their dads. It's access day.'

We talked about our boy, Glenn.

Sharon said, 'I can't bear to think of 'im out there, Aidy. 'E 'ates loud explosions. Remember 'im on Guy

Fawkes night? 'E used to cover 'is ears up when the bangers went off.'

I said, 'We did have some good times. Not many, but a few.'

She said, 'I often think about that time we were going out with each other, I've never had a better bloke than you. You never shouted at me, or slapped me about.'

I asked her if Ryan slapped her about.

She said, avoiding my eyes, ''E's a bit heavy-handed with me sometimes, but 'e never touches the kids.'

Later, she cheered up a little and told me that she has been offered a job by the New Deal as an Obesity Co-ordinator. However, it is conditional – she has to lose three and half stone first.

I encouraged her to go on a diet, and said, 'Glenn will be back in five months. Make him proud of you, Sharon. Lose weight, get a job and kick Ryan out.'

11.30 p.m.
Daisy back, with mangoes.

Monday June 9th

I had forgotten completely about the writers' group. Ken Blunt turned up at seven-thirty. I introduced him to Daisy, who was wearing only a bath towel. The futon showed the evidence of our recent lovemaking, and Daisy's Vivienne Westwood bra and knickers were lying in the middle of the floor. Given these circumstances, I had no option but to confess to Ken that Daisy and I were having an affair.

Ken said, 'I've got a woman in Nottingham I see now and then.'

I said, 'I'm surprised, Ken, I thought you were happily married.'

'That's why I'm happily married,' Ken said. 'What Glenda don't know won't hurt her.'

The three of us sat out on the balcony. Daisy asked, 'Do swans stick to the same partner?'

Due to my extensive knowledge of swans, I was able to tell her that swans stay together until one of them dies.

We drank two bottles of wine between us and talked about love. Ken grew a little maudlin and said that he had often thought about telling his wife about the woman in Nottingham. 'I'm sure Glenda would understand.' He was slurring his words slightly.

Daisy advised him to keep his mouth shut. When I asked her what she would do if she found out that I was cheating on her, she said, with a flash of her mother's Mexican eyes, 'I would cut your balls off.'

Ken and I shifted uncomfortably in our chairs.

All in all it was a very pleasant evening.

When Ken had gone, Daisy said, 'It was lovely to have somebody here who knows about us. It makes it more real somehow.'

I asked her what she loved about me, and she said, 'Your kind face, your gentle voice and the way your hair curls on the back of your neck.'

I was slightly disappointed; I had expected her to mention my intelligence, general knowledge and wit.

Tuesday June 10th

I'm not sure if Daisy is living with me or not. She seems to be living out of a flight attendant's suitcase. She is in Newcastle today, promoting a new uplift bra against a background of the Millennium Bridge in full tilt.

Mr A. Mole
Unit 4
The Old Battery Factory
Rat Wharf
Grand Union Canal
Leicester LEI

I'm Sorry I Haven't a Clue
The BBC
Broadcasting House
London WIA

June 7th 2003

Dear Mr Mole

Thank you for your kind comments about *I'm Sorry I Haven't a Clue*. The rules of Mornington Crescent were formulated long before I came to work on the programme as a Production Assistant. I have been too embarrassed, and rather afraid to ask the chairman of the show, Mr Humphrey Lyttleton, who can be rather abrasive at times.

I do hope you understand my dilemma.

Yours sincerely

Jessica Victoria Stafford

Wednesday June 11th

I was late getting to work. Bernard Hopkins said loudly within Mr Carlton-Hayes's hearing, 'Late again, cocker?

No probs. I don't mind in the least doing your work for you.'

I seethed all morning. I now strongly suspect that Bernard Hopkins is after my job.

Thursday June 12th

The computerized Smeg fridge I ordered months ago has finally arrived from Italy. It is truly state of the art. It indicates when food needs replacing and is past its use-by date.

Friday June 13th

At 4 a.m. the fridge woke me up to tell me that I had run out of milk.

I picked Daisy up from East Midlands Airport tonight. She had flown in from Dublin, where she has been promoting stag and hen weekends for a travel company.

We went late-night shopping at Asda and bought mangoes, champagne, bread, cheese and Flash bathroom cleaner.

Saturday June 14th

Daisy and I discussed this morning how to tell Marigold that we know about the phantom baby.

We agreed that we would have to go to Beeby on the Wold and give her an opportunity to tell the truth. However, as we were dressing, my phone rang and Brain-box said, 'Adrian, I've got some bad news for you. I'm afraid that Marigold lost the baby while we were away.'

He sounded very sad; I hadn't the heart to tell him the truth. Instead I said, 'I'm sure you will give her lots of babies in the years to come, Brain-box.'

Later Daisy and I went to the Flower Corner and sent Marigold a bouquet. Daisy said to the woman, 'No triangular flat arrangements, please.'

On the card I wrote:

Dear Marigold, It was not to be. How sad. Love Adrian

Sunday June 15th
Father's Day

It is certainly Father's Day for Gielgud today; seven cygnets passed my balcony this morning.

I said to Daisy, 'They looked as ugly as sin.'

She said, 'I was ugly when I was a kid. It didn't help that Netta insisted on knitting our school uniforms, including the fucking motto, "Can't pay, won't pay." I was always being thrown off the bus.'

I asked her what kind of school it was.

She said it was a private school run by anarchists.

*

I'm taking her to the Piggeries this afternoon to meet my parents in her new role as my lover.

Glenn texted from Iraq to say:

Happy Fathers Day, No cards in shops, no shops

There was nothing from William.

I let Daisy take the wheel of my car, and she drove us to the Piggeries. She is a fast but careful driver. She said, 'I used to hate the countryside and used to feel nervous unless I had a pavement under my feet. But I quite like this.'

By 'this', she meant the gentle slopes of southern Leicestershire and the tunnels of trees that we passed through.

When we got out of the car, I saw my mother and Animal stop their work on the pigsties and my father emerge from the camper van and look towards us. Ivan ran straight to Daisy and jumped up, smearing mud all over her combats. But she didn't seem to mind.

Daisy struggled a bit in her heels, then kicked off her shoes and broke into a run to embrace my mother.

My mother took Daisy to see the renovated pigsties and I gave my father his Father's Day present, *Golfing for Cats* by Alan Coren. I thought it might appeal to him. The front cover is illustrated by a cat, a golf club and a swastika.

I said, 'It's full of very funny pieces. It'll make you laugh.'

He said, 'How many times do I have to tell you, Adrian, I don't need to read another book. Once you've read *Jonathan Livingstone Seagull*, every book ever published is redundant.'

His voice choked up, as it always does when talking about Jonathan. 'That seagull pushed himself to the limit, Adrian. And it killed him.'

We cut the little Mr Kipling Father's Day cake we bought on the way. I invited Animal to come and join us, but my mother said, 'He's a bit fragile today, Adrian. He doesn't know who his dad is.'

When we were about to leave, my mother muttered to me, 'She's a star, Adrian. Try and hang on to her. Talk to her, tell her she's beautiful and buy her flowers.'

Monday June 16th

Took Daisy to catch the London train. She is organizing a charity dinner for the RNIB.

Glenn phoned!

He sounded unlike himself. I asked him what the banging noises in the background were.

He said, flatly, 'Fireworks, Dad.' He asked me if I'd ever seen a dead body. I said that I hadn't. He said, 'I have.'

There was a longish silence. I wanted to say many things to him: that I loved him and was sorry I'd let him down when he was a little kid. Instead, I told him that

I'd sent him and Robbie more books via the BFPO, and that they should reach him soon.

He said, 'To tell you the truth, Dad, we ain't got a lot of time for reading, but I wondered if you'd do me a favour? Can you go to the Army Surplus and buy me and Robbie two pairs of Altama American Combat Boots instead? You'll be able to recognize them – the soles look like blocks of Cadbury's Dairy Milk. I'm size nine and Robbie's size ten. Only, when we walk across armoured vehicles, the British boots melt in the heat and fall apart.'

I said that I would attempt to buy them tomorrow.

He said Robbie's learned one of the poems off by heart. I asked him which one.

He said, 'I'll put him on.' Then I heard Glenn shouting, 'Robbie, Robbie, come and say that poem to my dad.'

But Robbie shouted, 'No, No.'

Glenn came back on the phone and said, 'He's too shy.'

Before he rang off he thanked me for the flashcards and said they should be really useful. He said he would write to Mr Carlton-Hayes when he had the chance.

Tuesday June 17th

Bought boots, with Visa card, at a total cost of £125. I stuffed them full of non-meltable kiddie sweets from Woolworths' pick-'n'-mix.

I haven't told Daisy that I'm heavily in debt. She thinks nothing of spending £500 on a handbag.

Tuesday June 17th

The AA have come to my rescue on many occasions: there was the time I ran out of petrol on Bodmin Moor, the chaos caused when I locked the keys in the car in Old Compton Street and held up the Gay Pride march, and the numerous call-outs I have made because I had allowed my spark plugs to get damp. But the AA has surpassed itself today: they have written and offered me their special AA Visa card. 'Apply and take advantage of our 0% interest on balance transfers for six months.'

This offer is like finding a clearing in a jungle; my plan is to pay £1,000 off each of my credit cards using the AA's money. This will solve my short-term financial problems; I do not have a long-term plan.

William rang me on my mobile from Nigeria. I was conscious of every minute that passed as he rambled on about what sounded like an unremarkable game of football. At the end of the conversation, he said, 'The reason I am ringing you, Dad, is because I want to swap my Christian name.'

I asked him what he wanted to be called.

He said, 'Wole. It's more African.'

I said, 'That's your stepfather's name. Won't it be confusing?'

He said, 'No. We don't look the same. He's taller than me.'

I said it was OK by me and put the phone down.

William will soon tire of his new name, Wole Mole.

Wednesday June 18th

More *Crime and Punishment* tonight.

Nigel's guide dog, Graham, is getting above himself.

I was washing up the few plates and glasses for Nigel, when I felt Graham's nose against my leg. I looked down and saw that the dog had got a tea towel in its mouth. I found this annoying, because I had intended to let the crockery and glassware dry on the draining board. Because of the dog's interference, I had to dry the pots and put them away.

Thursday June 19th

Our new computer is finally installed. Its grey slitheriness looks out of place on Mr Carlton-Hayes's cherrywood desk.

Brain-box Henderson gave us all an hour's lesson on how to operate the Sage stock control and invoicing system and the ABE book-search facility.

After ten minutes, Bernard Hopkins wandered off and took a book from the shelves and sat down to read.

When the hour was up I was none the wiser as to how the computer's systems worked, because Henderson spouted a lot of incomprehensible gobbledegook. But Mr Carlton-Hayes asked him intelligent questions and seemed to understand his answers.

When Henderson had gone, Mr Carlton-Hayes called Bernard Hopkins over to the computer and said, 'Look,

Bernard, every published book in the world is at our fingertips.'

The three of us watched in wonder as the world's literature scrolled across the screen. I felt a mixture of pride at mankind's achievement and regret that a slower and more gentle time had passed.

Friday June 20th

Mr Carlton-Hayes showed me a letter he had received at the shop this morning.

Dear Mr Carlton-Hayes
Thank you very much for sending the poetry book and for helping my dad write those cards. They have come in useful.
Best wishes,
Glenn Bott-Mole

Dear Mr Carlton-Hayes
This is Robbie muscling in on Glenn's letter. I have thoroughly enjoyed, if that's the word, the volume of Siegfried Sassoon's war poetry. He knew what he was on about, that's for sure.
I have learned 'Survivors' off by heart.
Thanking you once again.
Robbie

PS By the way, I am Glenn's best friend.

Mr Carlton-Hayes said, 'I shall send the lad *Memoirs of a Fox-hunting Man.'*

If only he had been referring to Glenn.

Saturday June 21st

Mr Carlton-Hayes asked me when I was going to take my annual two weeks' holiday. I told him that I couldn't afford to go away.

Hopkins said, 'I don't believe in holidays. Why go somewhere else for a drink?'

My AA Visa card arrived in the post this morning. I saluted it.

Sunday June 22nd

After a lot of thought, I have decided to give Tim Henman some advice on how to win the men's singles title. I have sent him an email c/o The All England Lawn Tennis and Croquet Club.

Dear Tim Henman

I hope you will not take offence at what I have to say, but as a keen student of human nature I think I may be able to help you realize your ambition to win Wimbledon.

a) Do not let your parents attend any matches. In fact, if they try to get on to the Centre Court, have them thrown out by security staff. If my parents were watching me doing my work, I would also go to pieces.

b) Wife, Lucy, ditto.

c) Try to attract more glamorous fans. Your present followers are the type of women that trainspotters marry.

d) Ask Vinnie Jones to show you a more threatening clenched-fist, forearm-lifting gesture.

e) Forbid your fans from shouting out, 'Come on, Tim!' It makes you sound as though you are coming fourth in the egg and spoon race at junior school.

I think you will find that if you implement my suggestions, you will win the nation's heart and almost certainly be made BBC sports personality of the year.

Yours,

A. A. Mole

My father was readmitted to the Royal Hospital this afternoon, after telling my mother that he was dying. The wound in his back is infected again. I went to see him, and took a pillow with me, just in case.

Monday June 23rd

Daisy rang from her hotel room in Bristol. She said that the author she is on tour with drank too much wine before their reading in Waterstone's and ended up haranguing the audience during the question and answer session because a young man asked, 'Where do you get your ideas from?'

The author had shouted, 'From the Tesco's Ideas Counter, pillock!'

I asked who the author was.

She said, 'Marshall Snelgrove. You won't have heard of him, he writes sci-fi. His galaxy is set in a kangaroo's pouch.'

I asked her what she was wearing.

She said, 'Your favourite, nothing.'

Tuesday June 24th

Pandora rang to ask about Glenn. I told her he was in Basra and was scared and unhappy. She said, 'I'm furious with you for letting him go to that obscene war.'

She asked me if I thought Glenn would talk to her, in confidence, for an article she was writing for the *Observer*. I said, 'There is no such thing as "in confidence" any more.' And refused on Glenn's behalf.

She said, 'OK. My autobiography, *Out of the Box*, is published in a couple of weeks. Will your shop host the regional launch?'

I said I would talk to Mr Carlton-Hayes tomorrow and ring her back.

Wednesday June 25th

Readers' club.

Mr Carlton-Hayes started by saying, 'I ought to open this meeting by admitting that I am not an advocate of organized religion but, having said that, I was profoundly moved by the Koran. And as a bookseller, I am always terribly excited by the notion that a book can be central to the lives of a billion people throughout the world.'

He then invited Mohammed to say what the Koran meant to him.

Mohammed said quietly, 'The Koran as I interpret it helps me to live my life. I follow its rules, I take comfort from its teachings, and I use it for guidance when I am uncertain and need to hear God's word.'

Darren interrupted and said, 'I was proper surprised to read about Adam, Abraham, Moses and Jesus. It weren't all that different from the Bible.'

Lorraine said, 'Yeah, and Pharaoh, who's a right evil bastard.'

Melanie Oates said, 'What I liked about it was the language. I was reading it in a deckchair in the garden, and it was like I was hypnotized. A bit scary really – I should have been watching the children in the paddling pool.'

Mohammed said, excitedly, 'Melanie, you have hit the spot. The Koran helps us to meditate, it should be read sitting cross-legged on the floor, then its power is revealed.'

I said, 'The carpet is a bit dirty, but if nobody minds?'

I heard Mr Carlton-Hayes's knees crack as he sat down and crossed his legs in front of him. The rest of us joined him, forming a circle, and Mohammed began to chant. As he read, his body swayed in a slight oval pattern, and took on a rhythm of sixty beats per minute.

'In the name of Allah, the Beneficent, the Merciful,
All praise is due to Allah, the Lord of the Worlds.
The Beneficent, the Merciful,
Master of the Day of Judgement.
Thee do we serve and Thee do we beseech for help.
Keep us on the right path.
The path of those upon whom Thou has bestowed
    favours. Not of those upon whom Thy wrath is brought
    down, nor of those who go astray.'

Melanie said, 'It's very rhythmic. Do you think Flaubert
ever read the Koran?'

Mr Carlton-Hayes said, 'Almost certainly. It is one of
the greatest books in the civilized world.'

We stayed sitting on the floor, and Mohammed
explained that his personal interpretation was not
shared by anybody else, including his sons. 'Each Muslim
interprets the Koran in their own way,' he said.

Melanie sighed and said, 'I'm a bit disappointed to
hear that. I was hoping to find some definite rules on
how to live my life.'

At the end of the meeting we spontaneously applauded
Mohammed, and I think he was quietly pleased.

Thursday June 26th

I went to see my father after work. My mother was
already at his bedside, dressed in her builder's overalls
and steel-toe-capped boots. I was there when his consult-

ant came to give him the results of the blood and urine tests they had done earlier in the week.

The consultant was pink and podgy and called Mr Fortune. He said to my father, 'George, it's as we feared, you've got a super bug.'

My father said, 'Super.'

I don't think he fully realizes the seriousness of his condition. He obviously thinks that a super bug is a more superior type of bug.

Mr Fortune said to me and my mother, 'MRSA is a bit of a bugger to treat. He's on a very powerful anti-biotic mix already, and we don't have much more up our sleeve.'

My mother said, 'I'm relying on you to get him back on his feet, Mr Fortune. He's needed back at the pigsty.'

Mr Fortune looked my mother up and down and I felt an explanation was needed.

I said, 'My mother is converting a pigsty into a dream home.'

Mr Fortune said, 'Splendid. I live in a converted cow-shed myself.'

As I walked to my car, I passed Animal. He was teaching Ivan to sit up and beg.

Friday June 27th

Went to the bank today and withdrew £2,000 in cash courtesy of the AA card. Then paid it back over the counter. £1,000 went to Visa and the other £1,000 to MasterCard.

The bank clerk, a middle-aged woman with nine chins, said, 'Pardon my presumption, but you are paying over the odds for your cash. Would you like to see our accounts manager?'

I said, 'The AA loan is interest free.'

She said, wobbling her chins, 'Not for cash it isn't.'

So my attempt to give myself a breathing space has failed. I am in an iron lung of debt.

Daisy came for the weekend. I picked her up from the station. She brought two large suitcases with her, full of shoes and clothes.

Saturday June 28th

Had a mango session last night so had to clean the bathroom floor before I went to work. I left Daisy in bed reading an article in the *Independent* about Ali, the little boy who had both arms and both legs blown off by an American bomb. Apparently he was here having major surgery. I wanted to say something, but we have agreed not to talk about Iraq, Weapons of Mass Destruction or Marigold.

When I came back from work, Daisy had filled the remaining wardrobe space with her stuff. She has got twenty-seven pairs of shoes. Some of them she can't walk in at all and has never worn.

She had moved my furniture around and tidied my bookshelves. She had obviously been out shopping: there were white flowers on the worktop and the fridge was full of the food we both like. Our underwear was conjoined in the washing machine.

She said, 'I don't know what happened to me, I came over all Snow White.'

I said, 'Don't do it again, Daisy. Domesticity is the death of romance.'

I opened my emails.

Hi, Moley

Great news! Marigold has made me the happiest man in the world and agreed to fit me up with a ball and chain. Yes, she has said she will be Mrs Bruce Henderson.

We are not hanging about, we are tying the knot on Saturday July 19th at the Heritage Hotel, Little Smeton. I wonder, Moley, would you do me the great honour of being my Best Man?

Marigold is in agreement with this, though she thinks it would be good if you had a haircut before the 19th.

Poppy has agreed to be Matron of Honour, and I'm sure Daisy will agree to be a bridesmaid; it's just a matter of tracking her down.

Marigold is being a real trouper about losing the baby. She hasn't mentioned it once.

Yours, Bruce

Please reply ASAP

Later, when we were lying in bed, Daisy asked me if there was anything I didn't like about her.

I said, 'Your swearing,' and asked if there was anything she didn't like about me.

She said, 'You read too many fucking books.'

Sunday June 29th

I took Daisy to visit my father today. He is on his fourth course of antibiotics but is showing no improvement. Daisy told me, as we were walking down the corridor towards the David Gower ward, that about 5,000 patients a year die in British hospitals of MRSA. I can't imagine a world without my dad in it.

We passed Edna, who was rubbing a filthy rag over the door to the entrance of the ward.

Edna said, 'I've just fed your dad his dinner. He didn't eat much.'

My mother was happy to see us and told us that she had received an invitation to the wedding. She said, 'Your dad won't be well enough to go. Would you mind if Animal was my escort for the day?'

I said, 'Yes, Mum, I would.'

Monday June 30th

My patriotic support of Henman is over. An interviewer asked what he did in the locker room during the breaks for rain. Did he read books?

Tim, one of England's heroes and role models replied: 'NO, I NEVER READ BOOKS. BOOKS ARE BORING.'

I thought about Arthur Ashe, John McEnroe, Boris Becker and Bjorn Borg, who were all booklovers, and wondered if there was a connection between literature and winning the men's singles final at Wimbledon.

Tuesday July 1st

All three of my credit-card bills arrived this morning. I put them, unopened, in the gadget drawer.

Wednesday July 2nd

Jo Jo rang from Nigeria. She said, 'Your son waited all day yesterday for his birthday present to come from England. My heart bled for him. When I put him to bed, he said, "Mamma, perhaps the airplane bringing the parcel from Dad has crashed."

'I told him that he was almost certainly correct. Every half an hour he checked for emails, and whenever the telephone rang he ran to answer it. Glenn remembered to send a card, as did his friend, Robbie, whom William has never met. I hope you are ashamed of yourself.'

Diary, I am. How could I have forgotten William's birthday? Why didn't my mother remind me?

Thursday July 3rd

Letter from Robbie.

Dear Mr Mole

Thank you very much for the boots. They fit spot on.

Glenn was lucky the other day, wasn't he? I think he took it hard, but he hasn't told me much. I expect he told you a bit more. He is always bragging that he can talk to you about anything.

Some of the Iraqi people are OK, but we have to wear our helmets all the time now. Sometimes it's stones, sometimes it's bullets. We have stopped giving the little kids sweets.

I wouldn't mind a bit of English rain right now; it is ninety-five in the shade.

Well, I have come to the end of the page, so I will say goodbye.

Best wishes,

Robbie

I immediately rang Sharon and asked her if she had heard from Glenn. She said that Glenn had rung her in the middle of the night, but the line was so bad she couldn't make out what he was saying.

All the MOD lines were busy.

10 p.m.

Henman was knocked out of the men's singles quarter-final today by Sebastien Grosjean in four sets. The last took only thirty-two minutes. Naturally, Henman's wife and parents were there watching the match. When will he learn?

Friday July 4th
Independence Day (USA)

Went to see my father in hospital. Edna was telling him that asylum-seekers have been stealing the Queen's swans and cooking them. Apparently over one hundred swans have disappeared from the River Lea in the East End of London.

In Edna's opinion, the asylum-seekers should be sent back to face whatever murderous regime they had fled from.

I could see that my father wanted to agree with Edna, but he kept his mouth shut.

To cheer him up, I bought him the latest *Jane's Missiles and Rockets* (An Enthusiast's Guide).

No nurses were available, so me and Edna gave my father a stripwash and changed his pyjamas.

On the way back from the hospital I listened to Peter Allen and Jane Garvey on Five Live. They were discussing the Asylum-seekers Eat Swans story.

Mrs Garvey was of the opinion that this was an urban myth, similar to the one about the dead granny transported on the roof of a car in a roll of carpet.

A listener from Wolverhampton rang the programme convinced otherwise. He shouted that swan-eating asylum-seekers could expect a £5,000 fine or six months in prison.

Which, if true, seems to me to be unnecessarily harsh. Surely swans are vermin.

Saturday July 5th

Letter from Glenn.

Dear Dad

Sorry I haven't wrote, but there is not much time, and when we are not on patrol we are eating and doing our washing and trying to get some kip. The Yanks are lucky, they have got air conditioning, but we have not got it, I don't know why.

Me and Robbie got the boots this morning, they are great, thanks a lot, and the pick and mix went down well with the lads, thanks a lot again.

Dad, I don't know what I'm doing here. Half the people are glad Saddam has gone, and half the people are trying to kill us. Trouble is; we can't tell which is which no more.

One of the cooks here, Tommy Cumberbush, has read that cookery book you wrote years ago. When Robbie told him you were my dad, Tommy asked me for my autograph.

I can't wait to go on leave, Dad; I'm fed up with people trying to blow me up.

Road blocks are the worst. Me and Robbie tried using the flashcards, but an Iraqi translator attached to our squad said that the Arabic was dead old-fashioned and didn't mean what the English words meant on the other side of the card. So it's back to doing Charades, that game you used to make us play at Christmas. But I was no good at Charades. Nobody could guess when I did *The Good, the Bad and the Ugly*. Remember?

I was in an armoured vehicle the other day when we was caught in a blue on blue and our sergeant got his fingers blown off.

Dad, if anything happens to me, promise you will look after Mum. That bastard Ryan will do a runner one day, like all the others.

Give my love to Granddad. I hope he gets well soon.

Love

Your son, Glenn

PS Sorry this is such a moaning letter, but I'm a bit fed up today.

Sunday July 6th

Daisy entertained my father at his bedside today by telling him about the Summer of Love video she has been promoting in London all week. She said, 'Do you remember Acid Bungalow, George? Their big hit was "I am a Greenhouse".'

My father smiled and said, 'I went to see them at a Rock Festival on the recreation ground, next to the football club. I was eighteen and had a twenty-nine-inch waist, and my hair was longer than Adrian's is now. A girl with bells on her skirt put a flower behind my ear and said, "This is the dawning of the age of Aquarius." I didn't know what she was talking about.'

My mother said, 'I remember Acid Bungalow. I used to love Terry, the lead guitarist, the one with the long red hair.'

Daisy said, 'Poor Terry. When we went to Broadcasting House he thought he was in the Priory for rehab. I felt more like his nurse than his PR person'.

My mother said, 'I do envy you, Daisy. It must be fantastic mixing with celebrities on a daily basis.'

Daisy sighed and said, 'Most celebrities are totally talentless tossers. I'm sick of pandering to their ludicrous demands, feeding their horrible little dogs on Raspberry Ruffles and Badoit water.' She dropped her voice and said, 'When I was promoting a book by a certain round-the-world yachtsman, he confessed to me one night in the hotel bar that he'd spent the whole of the voyage moored up in a harbour in Malta.'

Monday July 7th

'A Bad Day at Black Rock'.

Barclays Bank

Dear Mr Mole
Unpaid Direct Debits
I am writing to advise you that you have insufficient funds to meet the direct debit payments listed below.

Insurance	£40.00
Debenhams	£200.00
Mortgage Co.	£723.48

We have debited your account at £35.00 per item for costs incurred, as detailed in our terms and conditions. Please ensure that you have sufficient funds to meet future direct debit payments.

Yours sincerely

Jason Latch

Personal Account Manager

Barclays Bank

Dear Mr Mole

Returned Cheque

I am writing to advise you that we have returned your cheque Number 001876 for the sum of £58.00 in favour of the Imperial Dragon marked 'Unpaid, please refer to drawer', due to insufficient funds in your account.

We have debited your account £25.00, as detailed in our terms and conditions.

Yours sincerely

Jason Latch

Personal Account Manager

£130 for two letters. I was tempted to write Jason Latch an offensive letter, but I cannot afford to pay for his reply.

Tuesday July 8th

Another letter from the bank.

Barclays Bank

Dear Mr Mole

I write to advise you that your personal account is over-drawn in excess of your approved overdraft limit by £1,282.76.

Please telephone your personal account manager to confirm that you will be paying sufficient funds into your account to bring you within the terms of your approved overdraft limit.

Meanwhile, do not write any further cheques on this account.

Yours sincerely

Jason Latch

Personal Account Manager

Phoned Parvez in a panic, but he was at the mosque. Fatima joked that Parvez was praying that Barclays would give me an extension on my overdraft. She said, 'What's happened to you, Moley? You're spending like you was Michael Jackson or somethink.'

I told her I was trying to fill an emotional void. I blamed my parents because they had brought me up to hide my emotions. I recounted the time I came down-stairs to find my goldfish, Cagney and Lacey, floating on top of their bowl. I had sobbed over their bloated bodies, but my parents were indifferent to my grief, and my father had said, 'Flush 'em down the lav for Christ's sake, they're stinkin' the bleedin' place out.'

My mother had, it's true, passed me a piece of toilet paper to dry my eyes but had then gone on to blame me for the fishes' death, saying, 'I told you when you won a prize at the Hook-a-Duck to choose a fluffy toy, but you had to choose the fish, didn't you?'

My father sneered, 'Everyone knows a fairground fish is already on its last legs.'

Fatima said, 'So you're blamin' dead fish for the fact that you bought a talking fridge?'

I sensed that I was not receiving a sympathetic hearing and said I would ring Parvez when he got back from the mosque.

Phoned Parvez again. Fatima said, ''E's took the kids to the fair, an' I told 'im to keep away from the Hook-a-Duck.'

I phoned him on his mobile but couldn't hear a word he was saying for the screaming. He was on the Wheel of Death with his kids.

Wednesday July 9th

When I arrived at work this morning there were thirty-eight cardboard boxes stacked on the shop floor. They were from Gorgon Press, Pandora's publisher.

Bernard Hopkins had been told to order 350 copies of *Out of the Box* using the online ordering service.

Mr Carlton-Hayes cast a practised eye over the boxes and said, 'I think Bernard may have slipped up.'

He estimated that we now had 750 copies in stock. He

asked me how many copies I thought we could sell. I told him that Pandora had kept me in the dark over the contents of her autobiography. He handed me a copy. A moody photograph of her lovely face was on the front; her name was written in what looked like red lipstick across her forehead; the tip of her tongue was poking out between her full moist lips.

The publishers had slipped a publicity brochure inside the book with some early reviews. A quick professional glance ascertained that they were what is known in the trade as 'mixed'.

'A searing indictment of the moral vacuity of the Blair government and an unusually frank account of Dr Braithwaite's political and sexual credo' *Spectator*

'A naughty, racy, pacy glimpse behind the scenes at Westminister' *Sun*

'Braithwaite is astonishingly frank about her public and private life. "When I was a junior minister at the Department of Ag. and Fish, I asked if I could go out with a trawler fishing for cod. The conditions were appalling. I lost a Cartier watch overboard; it was sucked from my wrist by a huge wave. The trawlermen were amazingly kind to me and the skipper used to join me in my bunk to petition me about quotas."

'"I regret nothing in my life. I have been privileged to be part of the working of one of the world's great democracies. As I said to Bill Clinton, 'My sex life is full of light and shade – we all need Monicas and Hilarys in our lives.'

'"Bill laughed his easy laugh and said, 'Pan, if you'd kept your pretty legs together oftener, youda made a great Labour leader.'"'

I turned to the index and was both alarmed and pleased to see that 'Mole, Adrian' was given three entries.

Page 17: 'My first boyfriend was a shy, spotty boy called Adrian Mole. I loved him with a passion that blinded me to his unprepossessing appearance. There was something primeval about my love for him. I wanted to protect him from the world.'

Page 38: 'My political awakening coincided with the faint stirrings of sexuality. My childhood sweetheart led a protest against the school-uniform regulations that only allowed the wearing of black socks. Adrian courageously wore red socks to school one day. It was my first organized protest. At the time I interpreted his choice of colour as symbolizing revolution and dissent. However, Adrian has since told me he only wore red socks because his black ones were in the wash.'

Page 219. 'A Mole in MI6 took me out to dinner one night and told me that the September dossier in which Mr Blair informed the country that Weapons of Mass Destruction could be deployed in forty-five minutes and hit Cyprus was "missing the caveats and conditionals of the latest reports".'

I turned to the index again. Under 'lovers', it listed 112 entries – 112! I can count the women I have had carnal knowledge of on the fingers of one hand!

Mr Carlton-Hayes was reading the invoice from Gorgon Press Ltd. He said, 'My dear, I rather think that our computer has made the most monumental mistake. It has ordered 750 copies on a no sale, no return basis. But we can't possibly sell so many copies.'

I told Mr Carlton-Hayes that I would do some local publicity in advance of Pandora's book-signing event on Saturday.

Thursday July 10th

Letter from Mortgage Co.

Dear Mr Mole

We have noted with concern that three direct debit payments have not been received. If this is an oversight, please make an immediate payment of £2,100.00 direct to one of our branches.

We enclose a new Direct Debit Mandate.

If you are in financial difficulty and require assistance, please telephone the above number to speak to one of our Mortgage Debt Advisers.

May we respectfully remind you that if payment is not received, the ownership of your property could be at risk.

Yours sincerely

Jeremy Yarnold

Manager, Mortgage Arrears

After two glasses of red wine, I went to the gadget drawer and opened and read all the letters inside. It was worse than I thought.

I couldn't sleep, so I listened to the World Service on the radio. A woman doctor was giving a live interview from Baghdad. Her maternity hospital has no water or electricity and the drugs and anaesthetics had run out last week.

She said, 'Thieves and looters come in here with guns and take our equipment. Things were bad before the invasion because of the sanctions but now things are worse.'

A woman was screaming in the background.

I got up and drank the rest of the wine. I crave the comfort of sleep.

Friday July 11th

I was on Radio Leicester this morning talking about *Out of the Box*.

The interviewer was a genial, literary man called John Florence. He asked me a lot of penetrating and uncomfortable questions about Pandora.

He said, 'Do you agree with me, Adrian, that Pandora Braithwaite is a bit of an enigma. On the one hand she's intellectually brilliant. I think she astonished us all in Leicester when she stood up at the Labour Party Conference last year and welcomed the Chinese Trade Delegation in fluent Mandarin, in a speech lasting over half an hour. But, on the other hand, she sometimes, how can

I put this delicately ... well, not to put too fine a point on it, she's notched up a few blokes on her belt, hasn't she?'

I said, carefully, aware of the listening multitudes, 'Pandora is a modern woman. She is not constrained by historical vetoes on female sexual behaviour.'

Florence said, 'Did you support her recent resignation from the government or do you think that she was simply drawing attention to herself?'

I said, 'My son Glenn is in Basra; I'm a little concerned myself that the Weapons of Mass Destruction have not yet been found, though, of course, I am very relieved that they have not been used against our troops.'

Florence said, 'When I last interviewed you, Adrian, you were working on a serial killer comedy called *The White Van*. Did anything come of it?'

I said, 'No, I wrote it for a specific ensemble of actors, and none of them was available.'

Florence said, 'So, listeners, Pandora Braithwaite, MP, will be signing copies of her autobiography, *Out of the Box*, at Carlton-Hayes bookshop in the High Street at one o'clock tomorrow. And please get there early, because Adrian tells me they are anticipating a huge crowd.'

He then pressed a button and the traffic woman came on to inform the listeners that traffic on the London Road was at a standstill because of a broken water-main at Saxby Street.

Parvez @ Wong's. 7 p.m.
It was supposed to be a meeting about my finances – though Parvez persisted in calling it 'a debt crisis meeting'.

I handed him two sheets of paper. On one was written my monthly income and expenditure, and on the other a list of the amounts of money I owe, and to whom.

Income

Income, Wages	£1,083.33 a month

Money Owed to Me
Latesun Ltd	£57.10

Monthly Expenditure

Mortgage on Rat Wharf		723.48
Household Insurance		40.00
Management Charge, Rat Wharf		83.33
Ground Rent		20.83
Car Loan		225.00
Car Running Costs		100.00
Barclaycard		300.00
Bank of Scotland MasterCard		280.00
AA Visa Card	(Unknown, waiting for first bill)	
Debenhams		200.00
Bills/Utilities	Elec.	60.00
	Water	15.00
	Council tax	79.12
	ntl	60.00
	Broadband	35.00
	Mobile	55.00
	Wong's	200.00
	Food	200.00
Total		£2,676.76

Debts

Mortgage	£181,902.00
Barclaycard	12,168.00
MasterCard	10,027.00
AA Visa Card	(Unknown, waiting for first bill)
Debenhams Store Card	9,011.00
Habitat Store Card	627.00
Solicitors	150.00
Bank Overdraft	4,208.00
Total	£218,093.00

Parvez gave a quick accountant's glance and said, 'You're in shit street, Moley.'

'You earn £1,083.33 a month and you pay out £ 2,676.76! And you owe on top of that over £200,000 in loans, mortgage and credit cards, and you ain't keeping the payments up, so you got phenomenal interest accruing.'

I said, 'But put it in perspective, Parvez. With a telescope the human eye can see 7 zillion trillion stars.'

I wrote the number out in full for him on the paper tablecloth:

7,000,000,000,000,000,000,000

Parvez said, 'And your point is?'

I said, '7 zillion trillion is four times every grain of sand in the world. Doesn't it make you feel insignificant, put things into perspective?'

Parvez lifted the lid of the bamboo steamer basket and pronged a pancake out with a chopstick.

'So,' I said, 'in the scheme of things, an earthly debt of about £200,000 is nothing, *nothing*!'

Parvez spread Hoi Sin sauce over his pancake. 'Barclays an' the rest of 'em ain't gonna automatically think about the sky at night, are they, man?' He tried to pick up strips of cucumber with his chopsticks, failed and used his fingers. 'They're gonna want their money!'

He added slivers of spring onion, a clump of crispy duck, rolled the pancake up and chomped on it with his big teeth. A diamond glinted on a front molar – testimony to the time Parvez was a stranger to the mosque. 'Barclays's computer ain't got a heart or soul, Moley; it ain't got no knowledge of the stars. It's a machine, innit?'

I started, 'In the scheme of things . . .'

Parvez interrupted, 'In the bleedin' scheme of things, you've gotta stop spending more than you earn, and you can't afford to live at Rat Wharf, so the first thing you gotta do is put it on the market.'

Wayne Wong, who was attempting to balance our table by placing a squashed cigarette packet under a recalcitrant leg, said, 'I was serving a couple last night, an' the main topic of conversation was Adrian Mole and how he's bought a talking fridge.'

I asked who the couple were.

'A black woman with red hair and a white geezer with a square head and a tattoo of a rose on his neck,' said Wayne.

Lorraine Harris and Darren Birdsall, *tête-à-tête*!

Wayne said, 'And your last cheque bounced, Moley, so it's cash from now on.'

*

I have to see Parvez again in his office on Wednesday evening after work.

Saturday July 12th

Daisy couldn't decide what to wear this morning and ended up with her entire wardrobe discarded on the floor.

I asked her what was wrong.

'It's that bitch, Pandora Braithwaite,' she said tearfully. 'She's so elegant and beautiful and thin.'

I told Daisy that, to my sure knowledge, Pandora wore a padded bra and paid a personal consultant at Selfridges to choose her clothes. 'And,' I said, 'she's only thin because she's had at least half of her body liposuctioned away.'

The last bit was not true but I needed us to get out of the apartment and down to the bookshop. There was a lot to do before Pandora's book signing at 1 p.m.

Daisy was not entirely eclipsed by Pandora's appearance, but it was a near thing.

After I had introduced the two most important women in my life, they looked each other up and down forensically. It was like introducing Maigret to Inspector Morse. Every detail of dress and nuance of expression was noted.

Then Daisy said, 'Is that suit Yves St Laurent?'

Pandora said, 'Yes, I must be bloody crazy wearing white linen in a dusty old bookshop.'

Daisy bridled a bit and said, 'There is no dust! I've been cleaning since nine this morning. That's why I'm in jeans and this old Gucci jacket.'

Pandora looked at Daisy's black leather jacket and said,

'Yes, I almost bought that jacket but . . .' The implied insult was left hanging in the air.

Daisy showed her nervousness by taking a lipstick out of her jacket pocket and daubing her lips.

Pandora lit a cigarette and said, 'Adrian tells me you're in PR. Do you know Max Clifford?'

Daisy said, 'Of course. Max is the master, he taught me everything I know. I'm afraid I haven't believed anything a politician tells me since.'

Pandora said, 'Quite right, we're all liars, but most of us mean well.'

Daisy said, 'I love your shoes. I've got them in pink.'

And I relaxed. I think I am beginning to understand women.

I had taken the precaution of ringing the police station earlier in the week to ask if they could provide a constable to help with crowd control. The policeman they sent was Aaron Drinkwater and he didn't look too happy when he turned up at 12.45 to find only three people queuing at the table stacked with 750 hardback copies of *Out of the Box*. He came into the back room and said to Pandora, 'We had to call the riot squad out last week when Nicholas Parsons opened the new Kwik Save in Peatling Parva.'

At 1 p.m. Pandora was escorted to the signing table by Mr Carlton-Hayes, who made a gracious short speech of welcome.

The three people in the queue had been joined by a fourth. But this person was under the impression that Pandora was a bookshop assistant and asked her to help him find a copy of Ann Widdecombe's *The Clematis Tree*.

*

At 1.15 there was nobody waiting to have their book signed.

Aaron Drinkwater said sarcastically, 'I don't think you're in any danger of being trampled underfoot by the mob, Ms Braithwaite. So I'll leave you to it.'

Mr Carlton-Hayes said, 'Perhaps the rain has kept people away.'

Pandora, seated behind a phalanx of unsold books, said, 'It hasn't rained for three days.'

I said, 'Everybody in Leicester is on holiday for the first two weeks of July.'

But one glance out of the window showed this to be a wild exaggeration. There were throngs of potential book-buyers passing by – some even stopped to look at the *Out of the Box* window display before carrying on to buy other things in other shops.

At 1.30 Tania Braithwaite came in and bought five copies but this was obviously an act of parental love.

At 2 p.m. with only ten copies sold, I bought one for my mother and Mr Carlton-Hayes bought one for Leslie. Pandora swept out of the shop with her head held high.

Daisy said, 'As soon as she turns the corner, she'll burst into tears. Shall I go after her?'

I advised Daisy to leave well alone.

Brain-box rang tonight and asked me if I had arranged his stag night yet. I was greatly alarmed and said that I hadn't realized that the best man's duties extended to the stag night. Brain-box said that he would email me the contact numbers of his friends. He said that only one date was convenient, Tuesday 15th. Daisy said that she would ring Stagrutters.co.uk and find out what was available on Tuesday night.

After she got off the phone she said I could choose between a pub crawl in Dublin, a guided tour of sex clubs in Amsterdam, paint-balling in private woodland or go-karting in Norwich.

I said, 'Daze, isn't there anything more cerebral?'

She said, 'No, Kipling, it has to be a rite of passage. Men are scared of women. The stag night is a reassertion of their masculinity.'

She said she had been asked to Marigold's hen night and had been told to dress up as a French waitress. 'It's so typically English,' said half-Mexican Daisy. 'They think that only filthy foreigners can be sexy.'

I asked Daisy if she would use her contacts and book twelve men on the Dublin pub crawl.

Sunday July 13th

Daisy was up at 5 a.m., washing, ironing and packing her little trolley suitcase. I took her to catch the 7.19 train to London. On the way I asked her where she got her energy from. She said, 'Drugs.'

I hope she was joking.

Thereafter, the usual Sunday routine: the Piggeries, the hospital, writing letters. When Daisy is away the colour drains out of my life.

Monday July 14th

I read that today is Swan Upping Day, when the swans on the Thames are counted. Perhaps it was my imagination but Gielgud looked even more arrogant than usual.

It seems that the Queen has the ownership of all unmarked mute swans and is responsible for their welfare and, I presume, their behaviour.

Ken came to Rat Wharf for the writers' group meeting. It was a pleasant evening, and he suggested that we walk along the towpath to the Navigation Inn for a drink.

He said, 'They've still got chairs and tables in there. And if you ask for a straw with your beer you get chucked in the canal.'

The trouble started as soon as we set foot on the towpath. Gielgud and his wife had been putting the cygnets to bed or something. When they heard us discussing the state of the English novel, they flew on to the towpath with beating wings, hissing beaks and maddened eyes. My glasses were knocked off my face and Ken trod on them in the confusion.

Nobody's arm was broken, but it was a near thing.

We carried on to the Navigation Inn because, as I said to Ken, 'I will not be kept from my cultural activities by a couple of paranoid swans.'

Ken said, 'I don't know how much longer we can call ourselves the Leicestershire and Rutland Creative Writing Group. Can two people be called a group? And neither of us lives in Rutland.'

I said, 'I know I haven't been much good as a chairman lately.'

Ken said, 'We've had some successes. Gladys Fording-bridge has come second in a national poetry competition.'

He took a half page he had torn from the *Ashby Bugle* and showed it to me. Gladys was on her sofa surrounded by cats and holding a framed certificate. Her winning poem was printed alongside.

> *Gladys Fordingbridge: An Iraqi Child Questions*
> *a Weapons Inspector – Hans Blix*
> Has Saddam got a pussy?
> Has Saddam got a cat?
> Why yes, he is wearing one
> Under his hat.
>
> Why is he wearing a cat on his head?
> Because he is bald.
> He would rather be dead
> Than admit that his regime of fear and despair
> Has led to the loss of his raven black hair.
>
> Is that why Saddam's
> Got a cat on his cranium?
> Hush, child!
> Now tell me,
> Where is the uranium?

I said, 'It's nonsense.'

Ken said, 'To be fair, it won the nonsense category.'

I said, 'But Saddam isn't going bald, is he?'

Ken said, 'Don't get so agitated, Adrian. Nonsense is nonsense. The owl and the pussycat didn't go to sea in a beautiful fucking pea-green boat, did they? Anyway, she won two hundred and fifty quid – that's a lot of cat food.'

I said, 'I'm very pleased for Gladys,' and I hope I sounded sincere, but the truth is, diary, I could hardly breathe. Jealousy gripped my heart and lungs, and I felt as though I was walking through custard.

Ken seemed to be known in the Navigation. Several old raddled-looking men nodded when we went in. The landlady was behind the bar. She had a tattoo of a snake curled around a sword on one bicep and a Virgin Mary and Jesus on the other.

When she'd served our drinks and we were sitting side by side on a banquette, Ken pulled a piece of folded-up paper out of his wallet and gave it to me to read.

A bomb was dropped on a house in Iraq
A family were sleeping.
But thank God no civilians were hurt or killed, or burned
    alive or torn apart by the bomblets from the mother
    bomb.
Nobody's legs were torn from their sockets,
Nobody was blinded,
Nobody's child bled to death,
Nobody's husband suffocated in the rubble.
Nobody's baby choked on its own vomit,
Nobody's wife died in a huddle in the corner of a room.

Nobody's mother screamed in terror and pain.
It was not a bomb, it was ordnance,
It was not a war, it was a conflict,
Nobody was hurt, nobody was killed,
There was only collateral damage.

I said he needed to improve the punctuation and pointed out that he had used the word 'torn' twice. I also suggested he finish the poem with a few lines of explanation. But Ken said the reader would work it out.

We worked on the poem together, the raddled old men occasionally shouting comments across the pub floor. The sight of pens and paper seemed to excite them.

One shouted in a reedy voice, 'What's that you're writing, Ken, your will?'

Ken said, 'No, it's a poem, Jack.'

Jack laughed and piped, 'Eh up, watch out, lads. Watch your arses: we've gorra Oscar Wilde 'ere.'

Ken's face darkened. He said, 'Ask my missus if I'm a puff, an' if you don't believe her, ask my girlfriend.'

Everyone laughed, but I wondered how long it would be before somebody told Ken's wife, Glenda, that Ken had been in the Navigation bragging about his girlfriend. Leicester is a one-street village when it comes to gossip.

Nobody Hurt by Ken Blunt
A bomb was dropped on a house in Iraq.
A family were sleeping.
But, thank Christ, no civilians were hurt or killed.
Or burned alive, or torn apart by the bomblets from the
    mother bomb.

Nobody's legs were blown from their sockets,
Nobody was blinded,
Nobody's child bled to death,
Nobody's husband suffocated in the rubble.
Nobody's baby choked on its own vomit,
Nobody's wife died in a huddle in the corner of a room.
Nobody's old mother screamed in terror and pain.
It was not a bomb, it was ordnance.
It was not a war, it was a conflict.
Nobody was hurt, nobody was killed,
There was only collateral damage.

For the rest of the evening we talked about women. Ken told me that the woman in Nottingham was not just a 'fancy woman'. He said that he had been in love with her for four years. He said, 'I've got a bad heart. What if I drop down dead at work, who would tell her? She wouldn't come to my funeral, would she?'

I offered to be the intermediary between Ken and the woman in Nottingham and if necessary accompany her to Ken's funeral.

Ken cheered up and said, 'If there's anything I can do for you in the same line, let me know.'

I told him that my troubles were financial and spiritual, but I thanked him anyway.

Tuesday July 15th

I decided to write to the Keeper of the Swans.

To the Keeper of the Swans   Unit 4
Windsor Castle   The Old Battery Factory
Windsor SL4   Rat Wharf
                                          Grand Union Canal
                                            Leicester LE1

                                              July 15th 2003

Dear Keeper of the Swans

I am writing to you regarding a gang of swans that habitually congregate on the towpath below my loft apartment. I know that the collective noun for swans is FLOCK, however, their conduct and behaviour is delinquent and to describe them as a gang seems more appropriate. This gang of swans, led by a large cob I call Gielgud, constantly intimidate passers-by and visitors to my apartment.

I am as fond of wildlife as the next man, indeed I once worked for the Department of the Environment as a Senior Newt Development Officer, but I'm of the opinion that when it comes to the crunch, human beings must take precedence.

I am therefore making a formal request that the swans be moved to another site, although in Gielgud's case I think culling may be a more suitable option, as he is quite clearly a psychopath.

I fear that Gielgud will never understand that since Mr Prescott's liberalization of the brownfield sites, many more canalside developments will be built and that swans and humans must learn to coexist peacefully.

I welcome an early reply to my letter. The situation is desperate, and I am here under siege. I'm sure you know that a swan can break a man's arm.

Yours faithfully

A. A. Mole

PS I'm sure you will agree with me that should a human fatality occur, Her Majesty the Queen could end up in court. She is, after all, the owner of all the swans in England, and as such bears a heavy responsibility for their conduct.

The stag party boarded the plane to Dublin at 5 p.m. Brain-box quickly got drunk on two glasses of complimentary Pomagne. He took a pair of gargantuan plastic breasts out of his overnight bag and walked up and down the aisle displaying them to the other, mostly irritated, passengers. The stewardess asked him several times to sit down, and when he refused she threatened to ask the Captain to turn the plane round and return to East Midlands Airport.

As the best man, I had to take charge of the situation, and led Brain-box back to his own seat.

Michael Flowers said to me, 'Bruce is such fun. He and Marigold share a sense of humour.'

I said, 'I can't see what is funny about a grown man sporting plastic breasts.'

Flowers said, 'It's a lusty English tradition.'

*

Michael Flowers led the party around Dublin. Craig Thomas and I took it in turns to guide Nigel, Brain-box was supported by his other friends from the Lawnmower Racing Club that he belongs to.

The club secretary, a fat bloke called Brian, said, 'People call us Grass-Heads.'

Nigel muttered under his breath, 'And some people call you dickheads.'

It is surprising what you find out about people on such occasions. I didn't know that Brain-box raced lawn-mowers for a hobby.

The Shelbourne Hotel wouldn't let us in, but Nigel threatened to call Radio Eire and report that they were refusing to serve a drink to a blind man, so they let him in and he stayed there for the rest of the evening. I was glad to be rid of him.

Had I been on my own, I would have enjoyed following in the footsteps of James Joyce, but as it was, I followed behind Brain-box, who was now wearing a large plastic arse and telling indifferent Dubliners that he was marrying the most beautiful girl in the world on Saturday.

We ended up in the bar of the Bridge Hotel overlooking the Liffey. Michael Flowers got into a row with the barman when he tried to buy a round of drinks using punts he has had since 1989.

Fergal, the barman, said reasonably enough, 'We only take euros at this bar, sir.'

Flowers started to denounce the European Union, shouting that the Irish had sacrificed their glorious past and were now on their knees, genuflecting not to the Pope but to the bureaucrats in Brussels.

Fergal said, 'I wouldn't know about that, sir.'

Fortunately, at that moment, Brain-box collapsed on the table, spilling Guinness and scattering salted peanuts on his way. With Craig Thomas's help, I carried him up to his room, undressed him and put him to bed. I was interested to see that he was wearing red silk boxer shorts on which was embroidered 'Caution: Contains Weapon of Mass Destruction'.

Craig Thomas said, 'Brain-box is hung like a donkey. Don't you remember him in the showers at school?'

I said that fortunately time had eroded the memory.

Wednesday July 16th

Nigel, whom I was supposed to be sharing a room with, stumbled in at breakfast after I had spent a virtually sleepless night waiting for him to return. He said, 'I met a delicious beast called John Harvey.'

I said, 'What does he look like?'

'I d'no,' said Nigel, 'but he felt good.'

Brain-box and the lawnmower racers were very quiet on the plane home, and Michael Flowers was nursing a spectacular black eye.

I was back at work by eleven. Mr Carlton-Hayes said that the imam from the mosque in Pandora's constituency had been in and bought ten copies of *Out of the Box* as a gesture of solidarity.

*

Went to Parvez's house straight after work.

Parvez said, 'I've spoken to the Inland Revenue this morning, Moley, and it ain't good news, man.'

I felt an artery constrict in my neck as I waited for what he was going to say next.

'When you was cheffing for Peter Savage at Hoi Polloi, how much tax did you pay?'

I told him that my wages were paid somewhat erratically. Peter Savage, a habitual drunk and cocaine sniffer, used to snatch a fistful of banknotes from the till at the end of the week and hand them over to me, often without counting them.

'And you didn't pay no tax?' checked Parvez.

'No,' I admitted.

'And Savage didn't pay no tax on your behalf?' Parvez asked.

'Savage was incapable of speech most of the time,' I said.

''Cos they ain't got records, the Inland Revenue estimated your earnings at £1,000 a week,' Parvez said.

'Never!' I shouted, 'I earned a pittance. I lived above the restaurant. I had a deep-freeze cabinet as a bedside table.'

Parvez said, 'Yeah, but Hoi Polloi was a celebrity hangout and you was a top London chef, Moley.'

'I defrosted offal!' I protested.

'Well, you're under investigation by the Special Tax Squad, so you'd better find some sort of records,' Parvez said. 'Ain't you got a diary for them years?'

I explained to Parvez that my diary had been destroyed when the house burned down in 1998.

Fatima came in with two cups of coffee and told Parvez

she had been reading through the Koran and couldn't find the bit that said that women couldn't work part-time as school dinner ladies.

I drank my coffee and quickly left before Fatima started canvassing my opinion.

When I was driving home I realized that I hadn't faced the full horror of my tax situation. I rang Parvez on my mobile and asked how much I owed.

But Parvez said, 'I can't talk now, I'm in the middle of a domestic. Come and see me tomorrow night.'

Thursday July 17th

Some of the things Ken said on Monday night are bothering me, diary.

Mr Bush proclaims that America is fighting for democracy and the rule of law, yet 608 prisoners at Guantanamo Bay are there without trial. The false claim that Saddam Hussein tried to buy uranium from Niger. The fact that Hans Blix, the weapons inspector, is certain that Weapons of Mass Destruction do not exist. And what Glenn tells me about the anarchy on the streets of Basra.

I am low physically and mentally. Parvez is to blame, though it is not his fault. I have brought disaster on my own head. I can hardly bear to hold the pen and write these words down, but I must face the unpalatable truth. Apart from my mortgage, I *repeat*, apart from my mortgage, I owe **£119,791**!

I knew something was wrong when Fatima opened the

door to me. She could not look me in the eye. She led me up the stairs to Parvez's office in silence. Parvez stood up behind his desk when I came into the room and shook my hand. It was not his usual informal greeting of a cuff on the shoulder.

I sat down and Parvez said, 'Moley, you're up shit street without a paddle. The tax man says you owe £72,800 for unpaid tax between the years 1996 and 1999.' He let this sink in and then added, 'Plus interest.'

Eventually, when I could control my voice, I asked Parvez what would happen to me if I could not pay the Inland Revenue.

He said, 'You have to pay them, Moley. As Shakespeare said, "There is only two certainties in this life, death and taxes."'

I got up and looked out of the window at Fatima's pretty, gauzy clothes blowing on the washing line. 'I'll have to kill myself,' I said.

'You can't afford to kill yourself,' Parvez said. 'And, anyway, you owe me three hundred quid for professional services.'

I told him that I still had some credit available on my AA card.

But Parvez said, 'Moley, you're digging yourself deeper into the shit.'

I asked him what I should do.

He said, 'You could start by living in the world me and Fatima live in. I don't earn much so we live in a small house, and we ain't got a talking fridge. Ours just sits under the worktop and keeps its gob shut. You can't afford a lifestyle, Moley, only a life.'

He called downstairs and asked Fatima to make some coffee. After she had placed the tray on Parvez's desk, she put her arms around me and said that she was very sorry. It was like she was talking to somebody who had been recently bereaved.

As I was leaving, Parvez said, 'You'll have to sell Rat Wharf, Moley.'

Fatima said, 'My uncle is on the council, and he is gutted because the planning committee voted to give permission for a casino to be built just down the towpath from Rat Wharf.'

Parvez said, 'And there's loads of lap-dancing clubs opening round there. One of my clients is making the poles. He can't get 'em out fast enough. It's going to be Leicester's vice quarter, innit?'

When I got back to Rat Wharf, I crept out on to the balcony, trying to avoid disturbing the swans. But as soon as I sat down, Gielgud noticed me and literally flew on to the balcony and forced me back inside.

I watched from behind the window as the sun went down behind the dye works. Someone is gutting the building and turning it into thirty-six studio flats. They have taken out the lovely arched windows and thrown them into a skip.

Friday July 18th

Parvez pulled a few strings and made me an emergency appointment for me to see a debt counsellor called Eunice

Hall at the Citizens' Advice Bureau after work. I have jumped a very long queue. I had to take as much financial paperwork with me as possible – bills, unpaid invoices, bank statements, direct debits, receipts, wage slips. I also took my credit, store and debit cards.

Eunice Hall wears grey shoes that match her hair. I trusted her immediately and confessed everything. It was a relief to speak to a stranger – somebody who had no preconceptions about me.

She let me go on about my worries for about twenty minutes. She looked at her watch several times, but I couldn't stop talking.

Eventually, she said, rather brusquely, 'Mr Mole, I am not qualified to give you an opinion on whether or not Mr Blair misled us about the Weapons of Mass Destruction. I'm a debt counsellor.' Then she asked for my financial records and read them in silence.

I handed her a note, written by Parvez, in which he explained my tax situation.

She said, 'Your accountant said you paid no tax during 1996, 97, 98 and 99.'

'Apparently not,' I said, and attempted to explain my circumstances, my job as an offal chef, my divorce from a Nigerian princess, my TV series as a celebrity chef, my inheritance of a house, my single parenthood, my house fire, which destroyed everything, including valuable unpublished manuscripts.

Mrs Hall asked, 'What kind of manuscripts?'

I explained that I was an unpublished novelist but, as soon as I spoke, I realized, with some sadness, that I

was now more a purveyor of literature than a writer
of it.

I told her about my years of living on a sink council
estate on income support with my two sons.

At the end of my account, she said, 'So you went from
riches to rags in five years at the expense of the tax-payer.'

I defended myself by telling her that I had been forced
to pay for private medical and dental treatment recently,
due to a lack of NHS provision in my area, so saving the
country money.

Mrs Hall said, 'You seem to live in a fantasy world, Mr
Mole.'

I said I didn't know what she meant.

She said, 'You have come to me for help because you
are in very serious debt. The first thing I have to do is to
make you face up to your responsibilities, and part of
that is for you to live in the *real* world. Not a fictional
world of African princesses, TV stardom, inheritances
and conflagrations in which you lose valuable manuscripts. You need more help than I can give you, Mr
Mole.'

I begged her not to abandon me, and she said, 'Very
well, but you must tell me the absolute truth from now
on.'

She looked deep into my eyes, much like the hypno-
tist Paul McKenna, and I wondered if I would wake
up in three minutes and be told by Mrs Hall that I
had been performing humiliating tasks while under
her spell.

I told her that I would do whatever was needed to get
out of debt.

Mrs Hall said, 'Your first priority is move to accommodation more in keeping with your income.'

When I got home I rang Mark B'astard's office and left a message asking him to call round as soon as possible and give me a valuation on Rat Wharf.

The sound of Zulu chanting woke me up. It was Daisy on the phone, telling me that she was at Beeby on the Wold and had just tried her bridesmaid's dress on. She said, 'It's not mint green, it's the colour of swan shit.'

I said, 'Don't let it get you down. You'll only have to wear the thing once.'

She said, 'It's not only the fucking frock. I've had my name down for a Gucci bag for eleven weeks. The shop rang yesterday to say that I'd come to the top of the list. So I went in and blew almost a month's salary on this bag, this collection of leather and gilt. But, Kipling, I'm looking at it now and I don't feel good.'

I said, 'Daisy, it sounds to me as if you're suffering from buyer's remorse. You need to stay away from Bond Street.'

There was a long silence, then she said, 'I've got my name down for silver Birkenstocks. I may cancel.'

Saturday July 19th

The wedding took place in the large conservatory of the Heritage Hotel. As we waited for the bride and bridesmaids to arrive, the sun beat down through the double glazing and Brain-box and I sweated inside our morning suits.

Margaret, the vicar, took her place behind the improvised, flower-banked altar. Then 'The Arrival of the Queen of Sheba' was played on the hotel's CD player. We turned around and watched as Marigold, attended by Daisy, Poppy and a lumpy cousin of Brain-Box's, progressed past the guests and took their places.

Marigold was wearing a strapless cream dress in oyster silk. Her face was covered in a veil. Daisy was right about the colour of her bridesmaid's dress, and I did not think that puffed sleeves and an asymmetrical hem flattered her.

It was the first time I had seen Michael Flowers in a suit, and with his beard trimmed. His injured eye still bore the signs of when he was smacked in the face by Fergal and called a 'Proddy Gobshite'. Netta was wearing a mother-of-the-bride outfit in apricot and a large picture hat.

My mother had broken an unwritten rule and was wearing white. Animal's mullet had been chopped off, and he was dressed in an immaculate three piece suit, white shirt, and a grey silk tie covered in a yellow elephant design. He looked like a dumber and taller Robert Redford.

When Marigold lifted her veil, she wasn't wearing glasses and an expert had painted her face. The lines of discontent around her mouth had been artfully concealed.

It is true, diary, that every bride looks beautiful until they ruin their hair and make-up at the disco.

*

I was nervous about making my speech, but when I came to deliver it, the words flowed easily, and it was only when my mother hissed, 'Enough already!' that I realized that I had been speaking for over twenty minutes.

When I proposed a toast to the bridesmaids, Daisy looked directly at me and gestured sexily with her tongue. I don't know what came over me, diary, a sudden mad compulsion to cleanse myself in public. I had an urgent need to tell the truth. Something took the brakes off the usual social constraints and I heard myself saying, 'While I'm on my feet and you're listening, I would like to announce that Daisy and I are in love, and have been for some time.'

Foolishly (I see now), I had expected a round of applause, cheers and even a few American-style yee-haws, but there was none of this. I sat down to silence, which was broken only by the scraping of Daisy's chair as she ran from the room.

Sunday July 20th

Nobody knows where Daisy is. Her suitcase had been taken from Beeby on the Wold.

I was accused of many things yesterday. Many angry voices were raised against me, the most angry being Marigold's, who accused me of sabotaging her wedding.

I did my fair share of grovelling and apologizing to Brain-box, Netta Flowers and my mother, for 'showing her up'. And this morning I sent an email to the hotel manager apologizing for failing to stop the fight in the car park

between my mother and Netta Flowers, during which a
trolley full of clean, pressed laundry was overturned.

But even as I flagellated myself I heard a tiny voice
inside my head, protesting, 'But I only told the truth.'

Monday July 21st

Mark B'astard came round to give me a valuation early
this morning. He told me that clients were queuing
outside his office each morning waving their cheque
books at him in their eagerness to buy a place in Rat
Wharf.

He particularly liked the Smeg fridge, and it was bad
luck that it started whining on about the stale-egg situation while he was there. He reckoned that given a lick
of paint and the removal of the rat traps, the apartment
could fetch £220,000.

He went out on to the balcony and said, 'Nobody can
afford to live in London now, and Leicester is only a
seventy-minute commute.' He asked me why I was selling up.

I said I had flown too close to the sun.

He looked puzzled, but he could not have been as puzzled as me. Why did I say it? What is happening to me?

I was reading aloud to Nigel tonight when he suddenly
burst out, 'Jesus Christ! No more *Crime and Punishment*!'

I was hurt, diary, but I managed to keep my voice light
and melodious, and said, 'Would you like me to read you
something a little less intellectual?'

Nigel said, 'No, it's not the book I have a problem with. It's your reading of the thing. Try to put a bit of Dostoevsky's tormented soul into it, will you? As it is, you sound like metrosexual man.'

'Metrosexual?' I said.

'Yeah,' he said contemptuously. 'A straight guy who's into skincare and interior design.'

I carried on reading, with a rougher edge to my voice, but when the hero, Rodion Romanovitch Raskolnikov, or Rodya for short, was trying to decide whether or not to kill the old woman, Nigel said, 'You're making him sound as if he's trying to decide between curtains or blinds!'

Graham, the guide dog, got up, saw me to the front door and let me out.

I said goodnight, and heard the cur drop the latch behind me.

Tuesday July 22nd

Robbie is dead.

A home reserve officer from his regiment, Captain Hayman, knocked on my door last night. My first reaction on being told that Robbie was dead, killed by shrapnel from a rocket-propelled grenade, was relief that it wasn't Glenn.

I made Captain Hayman a cup of coffee. He was dressed in a smart uniform, brown suit, beige shirt and displayed a row of ribbons across his chest.

I asked him why I had been formally notified.

He said, 'Robert put you down as his next of kin.'

I said, 'But I'm not related to him. He's my son's best friend.' I asked him if Glenn was OK.

He said, 'I'm sorry, I don't know the details of the incident.'

I asked him to phone and find out. I wanted to cry, but I couldn't in front of this good man who had been deputed to break the news of death.

I asked if Glenn would be given compassionate leave.

Captain Hayman said, 'No, friends don't count as far as the army is concerned.'

He told me that the army would arrange Robbie's funeral and asked me to choose the hymns and readings. He said that Robbie's body would be sent back to England in a batch of five within the next few days, and told me that he would contact me about the funeral arrangements later in the week.

Half an hour later, the phone call I was dreading. It was Glenn.

He accused me of being responsible for Robbie's death. He said, 'You told me that I was fighting for democracy, but Robbie's dead, Dad. Robbie's dead!'

He said, 'You're my dad, you shouldn't have let me go to Iraq, you should have stopped me.'

I let him shout and swear at me and didn't try to defend myself, because he was correct in everything he said.

When I told him to try and get some sleep, he said, 'After what I seen today, I'll never sleep again.'

*

When I rang to tell Mr Carlton-Hayes about Robbie, he said, 'The bastards, they send children to fight their filthy wars.'

I told him that I was feeling very low and wouldn't be in today.

Wednesday July 23rd

I am morally, spiritually and financially bankrupt.
Stayed in bed all day.

Thursday July 24th

Stayed in bed all day, switched my phone off.

Friday July 25th

Stayed in bed all morning. The fridge told me that the contents of the salad drawer had passed their use-by date. I ignored its nagging for as long as I could, then got out of bed, pulled the salad drawer out and threw the lettuce to Gielgud, who was guiding his sons and daughters down the canal.

At 6.30 I heard Mr Carlton-Hayes calling from the tow-path. I put my bathrobe on and went out on to the balcony. He was shaking his walking stick at Gielgud.

I shouted down that I would let him in and told him to press the buzzer for unit 4; it was very strange to see him in these surroundings.

He went straight to my bookshelves and examined the contents. He took down a volume and murmured, 'Thoreau's *Walden: Or Life in the Woods*, is it a favourite of yours?'

I told him that I had read Thoreau's rural experiment when I was nineteen and had concluded that the simple life was for simpletons.

Mr Carlton-Hayes placed the book on my coffee table and said, 'Perhaps you should read it again.' He was like an old-fashioned family doctor leaving a prescription.

I couldn't make him tea or coffee because there was no milk, tea or coffee. So I opened a bottle of wine and we sat on the balcony and watched the young swans.

He asked me why I hadn't phoned him.

I told him that I had been paralysed with shame and couldn't bring myself to communicate with anybody. I said, 'I believed them, when they told me our country needed to go to war, and I even encouraged my son to go to fight.'

I told him the truth about everything else that had gone wrong with my life and ended by confessing that for almost a year I had been living wildly beyond my means, spending money I hadn't got and that I was now being forced to sell my apartment.

Mr Carlton-Hayes poured me another glass of wine and said, 'Like Icarus, you flew too close to the sun, and your wings have melted, but I won't let you fall into the sea, as he did, my dear. I cannot run the bookshop without you. Bernard is a hopeless drunk and I do hope he moves on soon. He's getting rather tiresome.'

I told him that I had been having an affair with Marigold's sister, Daisy.

He took his pipe out, packed it with aromatic tobacco and set light to the bowl. He said, 'Love makes fools of us all. Leslie and I left our partners for each other thirty-odd years ago. It caused the most dreadful scandal at the time, but hardly a day goes by when I don't look at Leslie and think that I did the right thing.'

He told me that he had often talked to Leslie about me, and that Leslie had said that it would be good if the three of us met up some time. He made me promise that I would do my best to come into work tomorrow. He said that we were doing very good business lately, thanks to the recent innovations, and that he wanted to talk to me about my salary.

Saturday July 26th

I hardly slept last night. I kept doing mental calculations and trying to work out when I would be clear of debt. I concluded that I will still be paying off my credit card bills when I am a pensioner. There is no possible way I can afford to pay the capital, and the interest will mount and mount and mount with every breath I take.

At 3.30 a.m. I got up and walked about, but the consumer durables I had so recklessly spent somebody else's money on seemed to mock me in the pre-dawn light. As I passed the fridge, I heard it sneer, 'Loser'.

I went into work and was given an affectionate, almost loving, welcome from Mr Carlton-Hayes. He told me, blushing and stammering, that he had talked to Leslie last night and they had agreed that the shop could afford to pay me an extra £200 a month. I blushed and stammered my thanks. Then we turned away from each other and busied ourselves in different parts of the shop.

2004

Saturday July 21st 2004

Today is the first anniversary of Robbie's death. My mother brought a letter round to us this morning, dated yesterday.

Adrian Mole
1 The Old Pigsty
The Piggeries
Bottom Field
Lower Lane
Mangold Parva
Leicestershire

Dear Mr Mole

As you must have read recently in the press or surmised from the Butler report, Mr Tony Blair has conceded that there were no Weapons of Mass Destruction within reach of Cyprus that could be deployed within forty-five minutes.

I hope that you will now desist from writing to me and asking for the return of your deposit of £57.10.

You may be interested to note that, at the time of writing, sixty British and over a thousand American troops have been killed during the war. It is estimated that between ten and twenty thousand Iraqi people have died. Nobody knows for sure, because no official body has kept count.

Yours sincerely

Johnny Bond

Latesun Travel Ltd

Daisy said, 'Write to Johnny Bond and admit that he was right.'

At four o'clock this afternoon, Daisy and I pushed Gracie into Mangold Parva to buy a *Leicester Mercury*. I hardly miss the car, but Daisy complains that it is hard going walking down country lanes in high-heeled shoes.

On the way back to the Piggeries, we passed my mother and Animal, who were foraging in the hedgerows and feeding the occasional ripe berry to my father in his wheelchair.

My poor father is now Sir Clifford Chatterley to my mother's Connie and Animal's Mellors. But this ménage à trois seems to suit the baby boomers well enough.

My mother picked Gracie out of her pram and said to the fat little baby, 'Oo, I could eat you alive.'

Animal broke off a piece of cow parsley and Gracie took it in her fat little fist.

When we got home we opencd the *Mercury* at the 'In memoriam' page and read the notices about Robbie. There were only two: one from me and one dictated by Glenn from Bosnia.

Stainforth, Private Robert Patrick, died on July 21st 2003, in Iraq, while serving on active duty. He was sent

there because vainglorious, arrogant men wanted war
and he died a terrible death. He was eighteen years old.

> *To Private Robbie Stainforth*
> The old men safe behind their desks,
> Who dropped the bombs on you
> Will suffer in the dead of night
> For in their hearts, they knew
> They sent the young to fight and die on Iraqi soil
> To feed the cuckoo in the West
> With what it most needs:
> Oil.
>
> A. A. Mole

Stainforth, Robert (Robbie) Robbie, you were the best
mate ever. This is the poem you learned off by heart.

Glenn Bott-Mole

Survivors
No doubt they'll soon get well; the shock and strain
Have caused their stammering, disconnected talk
Of course they're 'longing to go out again,' –
These boys with old, scared faces, learning to walk.
They'll soon forget their haunted nights; their cowed
Subjection to the ghosts of friends who died, –
Their dreams that drip with murder, and they'll be proud
Of glorious war that shatter'd all their pride . . .
Men who went out to battle, grim and glad;
Children, with eyes that hate you, broken and mad.

Siegfried Sassoon, October 1917

Sunday July 22nd

'Happy people don't keep a diary.' I said this to Daisy this morning in bed.

She said, a little alarmed, 'So why are you starting one again?'

I said, 'I'm thinking of writing an autobiography.'

She said, 'Kipling, I think you're fantastically interesting, but I'm not sure other people will. I mean, you live in a pigsty with your wife and baby, bike to work, bike back, play with Gracie, work on the garden, go to bed, read, make love and sleep. What's to write about?'